RELICS

RELICS

TIM LEBBON

TITAN BOOKS

RELICS
Print edition ISBN: 9781785650307
Electronic edition ISBN: 9781785650338

Published by Titan Books
A division of Titan Publishing Group Ltd
144 Southwark St, London SE1 0UP

First edition: March 2017
2 4 6 8 10 9 7 5 3 1

Copyright © 2017 by Tim Lebbon. All Rights Reserved.
Visit our website: www.titanbooks.com

A CIP catalogue record for this title is available from the British Library.

Printed and bound in the United States

For my wife Tracey, with love.
Thanks for putting up with this old relic for so long.

PROLOGUE

The door handle creaks and she opens her eyes. The man who enters does not like her, and he has promised to make her life hell. But hell is relative, and at least his return will hold back the nightmarish memories, if only for a while.

He closes the door behind him and, instead of taking the seat across the table from her, he sits in a chair in the corner of the room. The metal legs scrape against the floor, a loud, jarring noise, and Angela jumps.

"Still twitchy," he says.

She does not reply.

Detective Inspector Volk has a big coffee mug in one hand, its outside stained with drips that might be two or three days old. Something dry and crispy is stuck to the mug's base—a crushed cookie, perhaps—and Volk's shirt is speckled with whatever he had for dinner the previous day. He holds a pastry in his other hand. His hair is unkempt and in need of a trim. He's stubbled and scruffy, but she can smell the minty waft of shower gel, his nails are trimmed and clean, and his athletic form is difficult to hide. It's only the *image* of distraction he wants to project.

In reality he's a man very much in charge.

"Cake for breakfast," he says, taking a bite of the pastry.

It snows crumbs down his front. "God bless America. Hungry?"

"I've eaten," Angela says.

He nods, and chews.

"We know everything that's happened," he says, slurping coffee, staring at her through the steam. "They've put it together back home. Forensics are still collating their reports, but we've got enough to tie you to four of the murders, at least." She can smell that it's real coffee, not that instant shit they've been giving her. There's probably a grinder in Detective Hey's office.

"Then you don't need anymore from me," she says, glancing down at her hands. They're crossed on the table in front of her. The back of her left hand is bruised and scratched, and she has a flash-memory of how that happened. A chill runs through her. She shudders, and from the corner of her eye she sees Volk stiffen.

He doesn't miss anything.

"'Anymore'? You haven't given us anything."

"Shouldn't you be recording this?" she asks.

Volk shrugs. "I'm on my break."

"Then you shouldn't be talking to me. I'm under arrest. Any questioning should be recorded, otherwise whatever case you think you can put together will be flawed. You know that."

"And I know *you* know that, too. The longer you're here, the more I'm finding out about you, Angela. You're a brilliant woman. A first class degree in criminology. Studying for your doctorate in subcultural theory. I've got some theories for you, we should chat some time."

If it's an invitation, she disappoints him by remaining silent.

"You volunteer at a local school back in the UK, helping kids with their reading. You grow rare orchids. Spend quite a lot on them, evidently. You're fit and healthy. You look after yourself, run quite a bit, gym. Probably work out at home, too. You care about yourself and your body."

"Takes one to know one."

Another slurp of coffee. She can feel Volk staring at her, but she keeps her gaze fixed on her hands.

All the things they've touched, she thinks. *All the things they've done.* She blinks and wonders whether those awful red memories will be forever imprinted on the insides of her eyelids.

"This isn't you, Angela," he says. For a moment she almost falls for the softness of his voice, the concern she hears there, and opens up. The moment surprises her because she thought she was more guarded than that, but perhaps everything she's been through has damaged her more than she believes. Maybe she's changed forever.

Of course I have. Everything *has changed forever, and that's why I'm sitting here in this run-down precinct, saying nothing. Because the change has to stop somewhere.*

"I'm ready when you want to continue the interview," she says.

Volk sighs and stands suddenly, sending the chair skidding against the wall. She jumps again at the sound of metal on the concrete floor. That high, painful *screeeeee!* that bites into her ears and claws down her spine.

"I don't understand," he says. "Angela, this isn't you, and I don't believe it's your boyfriend, either. Wherever he is."

"Vince is dead," she murmurs. She's told them that a dozen times.

"Perhaps, but that doesn't change the facts. The worst

you've ever done is get a parking ticket. And while Vince certainly isn't whiter than white, he's no killer. You're not murderers!"

"Evidence would suggest otherwise," she whispers.

"Really?" He sits opposite her now, but doesn't turn on the recorder. This is still just him and her.

She looks up and meets his gaze.

"Really?" he asks again. For the first time she thinks she sees the real Volk. He's haunted and damaged, and she wants to ask what he's seen, what he knows. He's from London, after all. Then he looks over her shoulder and continues. "Last time I saw that many bodies was the day those bastards bombed the Underground. I was a beat bobby then, one of the first on the scene at Tavistock Square, where the bus was blown up." He shakes his head and looks like he's going to say more, but instead he glances at Angela and then looks down into his coffee mug, pausing for a second before taking another drink.

"I'm not a terrorist," she says. It seems important to emphasise that. However many murders she's taking the blame for, she needs them to know that there are reasons.

But I can't tell them anything, she thinks. It all has to be silence.

Volk chuckles. It surprises her.

"You're being deported back to the UK like one."

"Well, I'm not."

"Honestly, with some of those you killed you did us a favor. Scum. We're well rid of them. Best way to cleanse the world of some of these people, that's what I say."

Angela isn't drawn in. She looks down at her hands again. *The things they've touched.*

"Detective Hey will be back in a minute, and the recording

will start again. He's a nice enough bloke, very accommodating, but so… American." Volk smiles. "No offense."

"None taken."

"So tell me now, just for my sake." He pauses and leans in. "Come on, Angela. There's no way you and Vince killed all those people. I know that and so do you."

She sighs heavily. Maybe Volk thinks it's her resistance breaking, but it is nothing of the sort. This is fear.

"So tell me the truth," he says. "Are you afraid I won't believe you?"

"No," she says, and closes her eyes again. "I'm afraid you will."

FIVE DAYS EARLIER...

1

Angela definitely wasn't a morning person. Sunlight filtered through the gap between the curtains, traffic noise rumbled outside, the noisy dog from the next street barked to be let in, and barked, and barked, but she dozed in and out, relishing the comfortable warmth of her bed. She stretched, ankles clicking, body tensing, and relaxing again brought a satisfied sigh to her lips.

She was aware of the noises from upstairs. She knew that Vince was lying there awake, listening, but she wanted these last few moments before confronting the new day.

Sometimes the best dreams came in the final seconds of sleep.

"Less than five minutes this morning," Vince said. "Hang on."

Now that he'd brought her attention to it, Angela couldn't help listening to the sound that came from the apartment above. The creaking bed had fallen silent, and she smiled as she realised she was holding her breath until…

"Yeah, there you go," Vince said. "He's finishing her off with his fingers."

"Jesus, you're such a romantic," she mumbled into her pillow.

"You know it."

She tried to stretch down into the bed, but now that they'd both acknowledged the sounds, they seemed so much more obvious. Virtually every morning the couple upstairs started the day with a screw. Sometimes it went on for quite a while. Other times, like today, it was a quickie followed by a few more minutes groaning and creaking. She and Vince had always made a joke of it. It didn't bother her much, and Vince freely admitted that it turned him on. Sometimes, that didn't bother her either.

But when he rolled against her back and she felt his interest, she offered a tired shrug.

"Wasn't last night enough?"

"Never enough," he said, nuzzling her neck. "Come on, let's make a noise."

"Make me tea."

"Tea? You've got me here, naked, and you want tea?"

"One sugar."

"You sure?"

She rolled onto her back and stretched again, then turned to face him.

"Mmm. Second thoughts… no, two sugars this morning."

"Tease."

"Need to refuel after last's night's exertions."

Vince made a mock-annoyed face, then rolled from bed and padded out into the hallway.

"You'll regret it later!" he shouted back to her. "Stuck here on your own, thoughts drifting, thinking about what you missed."

"Yeah, right, I'll regret it."

He reached the kitchen and started whistling, so he missed the single cry from upstairs.

"Keep it down, girl," Angela muttered, though really it was kind of sweet.

Over the three years she'd been living here, she had barely swapped thirty words with the couple living above her. They seemed nice enough. He was a tall, bald guy, quiet but always offering a nod and a smile. She was short and round, always dressed in black, and her hair changed colour and style pretty much every week. Angela had no idea what they did, where they worked, or where they went when they weren't at home. That was just the London way. In a city of eight million people, everyone kept to themselves.

The sound of the couple upstairs, getting up and walking around, made her realise that her own lie-in was over.

She sat up on the edge of the bed and stretched again. Yawned. Reached for the curtains and drew them open. That was one advantage of having such a small place—you could do pretty much anything from sitting down. Her apartment had a small living room made smaller by stuffed bookcases, a bedroom, a kitchen/diner and a bathroom. Vince moving in the year before hadn't made it feel as crowded as she'd feared, but simply more cozy. It was their home now, not just hers.

She liked the idea of that. He contributed to the mortgage, they split the bills, and anything left went into a joint bank account. Her parents had always told her that was the only way to be together.

While Angela was sitting on the edge of the bed thinking about visiting the toilet, Vince came in with two cups of tea. He often made a quip about Americans preferring coffee, but today he let it go. He handed hers over and sat carefully on the bed, leaning back against the headboard.

"What's today?" she asked.

"Today is a trip to Chelsea to visit a couple of new places, back to the office for a lunch meeting, then Clerkenwell to meet a client." He glanced in her direction. "You? Planning your commute already?"

"Bathroom, kitchen, living room. Work. Lunch at Merton's with Lucy. Home. Bathroom, kitchen, living room."

"Watch out for the hallway, traffic's heaviest there around nine in the morning."

"You're just jealous."

"Fucking right I'm jealous! I've got to head out with the unwashed masses while you get to sit here working in your underwear."

"I never work in my underwear."

"Naked, then?"

"One thing, always on your mind." She took a sip of tea. Vince made good tea, always better than her, and she wasn't sure how. He said it was because Americans couldn't make good tea. She said that was racism, and had come to the conclusion that it was better simply because someone else had made it.

"*All* your things on my mind," he said, reaching for her. She squirmed aside and stood, wincing a little as her knees clicked.

"Keeping fit isn't good for you, you know," he observed.

"Says the man who does obstacle courses where they electrocute you."

"Good for the libido."

She rolled her eyes, left the bedroom and walked along the hallway. He'd already got eggs from the fridge and cut a couple of thick slices of bread. She smiled. She really did love the randy bastard.

In fact, she'd known for a while that he was the one.

Vince knew as well. They'd never actually talked about it, because the idea that they'd be together forever just seemed so natural that it didn't need discussing. They'd fallen in love and made a future together without even trying.

Sometimes she had to pinch herself.

Angela had escaped the fate of many of her friends and avoided living eighty percent of her life online. She had a Facebook page which she checked a couple of times each day, and though she maintained a Twitter account, she'd never quite got the hang of it. Social media was great for keeping in touch with family and friends back home in Boston, but she refused to let it become an obsession. She enjoyed living in the real world.

Her phone stayed with her virtually everywhere, true, although she hadn't enabled it to download her emails. She used it to phone and text, and that was more than enough for her. She and Vince usually swapped a few random texts throughout the day. It was a nice way of keeping in touch.

How's things?

Cool, lunching, cinema tonight?

Sounds good. Lucy got laid last night.

Who's the lucky guy?

Her husband. Pick up a takeaway?

Indian or Chinese?

You decide.

After which I want to go down on you for about three hours.

Nothing too spicy, then.

Jokey, light, aimless chatter that they'd both forget, but which gave them a feeling of still being with each other.

Angela smiled every time her phone pinged, and laughed when Vince forwarded a comedy selfie or took a photo of a passing stranger and made a comment.

How does she get those trousers on?

Check out the beard!

Obama in high heels.

Aside from these irregular messages, she lived most of the day on her own. Immersed in research, or perhaps staring thoughtfully from the window, musing over a problem in her thesis or just… thinking.

She knew that she was lucky. Twelve grand a year to sit and write, and think, and be her own boss. With Vince earning decent money it meant that she had the opportunity to indulge her passion and chase her ambitions. When she was younger she'd dreamed of becoming a police officer, but the more she progressed into her doctorate, the more she regarded teaching and lecturing as her future. Part of that was because she saw benefits in imparting her knowledge, but more than that she loved reading, interviewing, and analyzing cases. Investigating and absorbing theories established by other people.

This encouraged her to develop her own ideas, and lecturing would give her ample opportunity to continue her research, publish papers, and perhaps even write books. Most people would kill to be in her position. For that matter, in the pages of the books and the files of printed materials that constantly covered the dining table, there were people who *had* killed. The very idea made her eager to get started.

"Delightful."

That was the word Vince used to describe her fascination with criminology. *You're delightful,* he'd say when she relayed the story of a particular murder, or read the description of a gang attack, or a riot that had resulted in death and destruction. He didn't mean it in a purely ironic way, either. He loved her complexity, and loved even more the way he couldn't quite understand these aspects of her character.

His idea of a relaxing night in was feet up watching a movie.

Hers was sitting in the bath with a glass of Pinot and a book about subcultures, deviancy, and messiah complexes. So many people spent their lives trying to discover what made a mind work. Her interest lay in what made a mind tick in all the wrong ways. Evil people fascinated her.

Some days she spent the whole morning just getting ready to work. Pacing the apartment, making endless cups of tea, changing into comfortable clothing, slipping along to the corner shop to buy a pack of biscuits, reading, swapping texts with Vince or Lucy or her mom or dad in Boston, tending her orchids.

Leaning on the kitchen sink and staring out over their small garden and the backs of the terraced houses in the next street, she'd agonise over the wasted time but also knew that it was simply her way of working. She'd eat lunch and have a productive afternoon, so embroiled in whatever task she'd set herself—to write a thousand words, or research and make notes on a particular chapter—that she'd barely notice the time flashing past.

Other days, like today, her passion was aflame, and she was into it from the first moment. She drifted away from the world and even turned her phone off, because the ping of a text would bring her back to safe, boring reality.

All morning she sat at the dining table, laptop open and research materials spread across the surface. Her current chapter played social class against environment and desire in juvenile delinquency, discussing whether gang culture and criminal intent arose more from the simple need and desire for money, or was rooted in the social structure. In effect, nature versus nurture. There were good arguments for both, and Angela was forming the data that would lead her to her own conclusion.

As yet she didn't know what that conclusion might be, and that was the most exciting aspect to what she did. She was constructing theories and personal opinions as she went. Expanding her mind. So many people of her age had already stagnated, but she was still growing.

She broke off only to make tea or visit the bathroom. Now and then she changed albums on her phone to add background noise. She barely even noticed the music, but she had never enjoyed working in complete silence.

By the time she surfaced and glanced at the clock it was almost 1:00 P.M., and she'd be late meeting Lucy for lunch.

"Shit!" She stood and snatched up her phone, turning it on and leaving it to power up while she slipped on her boots and a light overshirt. Opening the back door she breathed in the daylight. It was warm, but not too hot. The row of gardens backing onto each other were relatively quiet, only the soft grizzling of a distant baby disturbing the peace. Beyond the terraces, traffic rumbled along streets, but this enclosed space felt private and isolated, an island in the middle of the city.

Something bothered her, though...

It took her a while to figure out what it was.

No pings, she thought, and she went back inside to check her phone.

Vince always messaged her before lunch. Every day, like clockwork. He knew he wouldn't always get a reply, but that never stopped him.

Today there was nothing.

"Huh," she said. Oh well. Perhaps he had a busy day. She sent him a quick text.

All good? Been working hard today. Fancy a drink at The Bear later?

She put the phone in her pocket, pulled the door shut behind her. Stepping past the tiny front garden she turned and walked briskly along the street, passing neighbours whose names she didn't know, offering smiles and sometimes receiving one in return. There was a dead pigeon on the road, a fresh kill flattened by vehicles, soft feathers stuck to bloody marks along the middle of the road.

A crow pecked at the mess.

"Sorry," she said quickly as she arrived at Merton's. Lucy had taken an outside pavement table so she could smoke, and she smiled up at her friend. Shorter than Angela, slinky and athletic and—Vince assured her—extremely hot, Lucy had been her friend since travelling to Tufts University on a lecturing exchange five years before. Angela had been in the second year of her degree, and the two of them had hit it off and remained in touch ever since. They'd ended up living and working close enough in London to be able to see each other frequently. It almost made Angela believe in Fate.

"Your gangs get you?" Lucy asked.

"Totally in their grasp."

"Weirdo. Punishment will be severe."

"Lunch on me," Angela said.

"Good enough. I've already ordered… hope you don't mind? Got to get back on time today."

"No problem." Angela sat, and moments later two cappuccinos were placed before them. They drifted into the sort of casual, unimportant chat that easily filled an hour but would mostly be forgotten come evening. It was the comfortable talk of friends who knew each other very well.

Angela welcomed it. Sometimes her research drew a dark, heavy veil across her mind, especially after an immersive morning such as this one. Reading account after account of youth gangs and extremes of juvenile crime—at times it got to her. She did her best to keep it from Vince, though she wasn't really sure why. He supported her in everything she did, was there for her if she needed him, but for some reason, when her work depressed or disturbed her she didn't want him to know. She didn't want her research to come between them.

Somehow Lucy always made that dark veil disappear.

Yet all through lunch Angela glanced at her phone. The screen remained locked. No messages came in, and that was odd. She wanted to send Vince another text, but she couldn't do it while she was sitting here with Lucy. Though her friend always seemed to have her own phone surgically attached to her hand, Angela always berated her about it.

If she broke her own rule, Lucy would never let her forget it.

"So I'm thinking France this year instead, but Max is a pain in the ass and says he doesn't want to go anywhere they eat molluscs that don't come from the sea. What's that about? What a tit. Still, I've always fancied Brittany, what do you think?"

"It's lovely there," Angela said, nodding. She'd finished her food and was halfway through a second cup of coffee, content to listen, throwing in an occasional comment. Lucy seemed to be having an argument with her husband while he wasn't even there, and it was diverting, amusing, almost sweet. They were the most loving of couples, destined by cruel fate to never have children but still as open and giving as anyone Angela knew.

"Yeah, right, that's just what I said to him, you can't judge a country by what the people there eat, and if you don't want to eat something you don't have to, right? So anyway, I'm just going to book it without telling him, maybe go out for a meal next weekend and spring it on him, see if—"

Angela's phone pinged, and she snatched it from the tabletop, knocking her cup and spilling coffee onto the wooden surface.

"Woah, you on a promise?" Lucy asked.

The text was from her phone provider, offering her a new phone. Something inside her sank.

"What?" Lucy noticed her expression.

"Haven't heard from Vince today, that's all."

"And?"

Angela shrugged. *And?* Maybe he was just super-busy, or stuck somewhere with no reception.

"You look worried."

"Yeah," Angela admitted. Voicing her concern made it real.

"Maybe he's got no signal, or his battery's dead."

"Right, that's what I've been thinking." She tapped her phone, willing the screen to light up. Her research gave her insights into darker, grimmer aspects of modern life, and her imagination sometimes went into overdrive. Vince not texting her didn't mean he was lying dead in an alley somewhere.

It really didn't.

"What is it he does again?" Lucy had asked maybe a dozen times before. Angela always gave the same answer, and wondered why she never seemed to remember.

Maybe it's just too boring, she mused. "He works for a property firm, assessing the rentability of private and commercial properties around the city."

"Right," Lucy said. "Yeah." She looked at her own screen as she replied, thumb stroking, light reflected in her eyes.

Angela checked her messages one more time and scanned for missed calls. Made sure the volume was up, even though she'd just heard it.

"So are you guys *always* in touch?" Lucy asked, smiling coyly.

"Most of the time. Just texts through the day, usually. You know."

"Young love."

"I'm older than you!"

"Yeah, but me and Max have been together over ten years. You're still in that can't-be-without-you, get-home-and-shag-on-the-floor-before-the-front-door's-closed part of your relationship."

"Hey, now," Angela said, and she felt some of the tension lifting. "We've never done it with the front door open."

A raised eyebrow.

"Honest!"

Lucy tilted her head.

"Okay. Maybe on the floor behind the front door. Sure."

"Lucky bitch. I usually have to get Max drunk. If it's a choice of me or *Match of the Day...*" Lucy used her hands as imaginary scales, laughing. She glanced at her watch, then waved at the waiter. "I've gotta dash! Why not just give him a ring?"

"Maybe," Angela said. "I told you, I've got the bill. I'm going to stay and do a bit of reading."

"The hard life of a mature student."

"Damn right. I see a chocolate cake in my future."

"Fat and ugly."

"Takes one to know one."

Angela stood and hugged her friend. Lucy pulled back to look at her.

"You're *really* worried," she said.

"I can't help it," Angela said, trying to laugh away her concern. But the laugh caught in her throat.

"Want me to do anything? Drive you to his office or something?"

Angela knew that Lucy had to get back to work. She smiled and shook her head, pecked her friend on the cheek. "Chocolate cake," she said again, smiling.

"Lucky bitch." Lucy dashed away, pausing along the sidewalk and turning, hand at her ear. "Call me?"*If you need help*, she meant. *If you want to talk.*

Angela smiled and waved her friend away. She was glad to have her, and watching Lucy leave somehow made her calmer. She knew that good people had her back. After she paid the bill and said she'd be staying for a while, she took out her book, stretched her legs, leaned back, and opened to her current page.

Then she picked up the phone and dialed Vince's number. It rang, and rang, and eventually went to voicemail.

"Hey, it's me," she said. "Just wondering how your day's going, haven't heard from you today." A police car flew past at the end of the road, siren screaming. The familiar London concerto. "I'm having coffee in the metropolis, just ate lunch with Lucy, she sends her love. Call me or text, yeah? See you later. Love you." She disconnected and placed the phone on the table so she could see the screen.

Even though she started reading, nothing registered because she expected Vince to call back at any moment. She rarely rang him during the workday unless it was something important, and she knew he'd sense her disquiet.

But what was there to be worried about?

She was just troubling herself over nothing. He had a busy day, that was all, and maybe he was stuck in some high-powered meeting with a property developer or planning officer, or whoever else he had to deal with. In truth, even she wasn't sure what he did all day. He didn't talk about work that much, and when he did it was with a distracted air. He didn't like bringing work home, he said, because home was for the two of them.

She tried reading for half an hour, then ordered a cup of tea and some cake.

Her phone was silent.

Angela watched pedestrians passing by. She loved people-watching, and enjoyed trying to tell their stories from what they wore, how they walked, whether they smiled or frowned, whether they saw themselves as a part of the world or apart from it. This man walked quickly, half-smiling, perhaps on his way to an illicit lunchtime meeting. That woman's distracted air might be concern for a sick relative. He wore clothes too large for him, perhaps from a charity shop. She was trying to cover a tattoo on her forearm.

Sometimes she and Vince would make up a story about someone sitting at the next table or working in a nearby shop, but their combined tales would always expand into the ridiculous. Alone, Angela tried to discern the truth, because separating truth from fantasy was an integral part of her work.

"Damn it, Vince." She texted him again—terser this time,

shorter, demanding a response. When she looked up she locked eyes with someone across the street. The woman held her gaze for just a little too long before looking away and disappearing behind a parked van.

She had yellow eyes.

Angela caught her breath. *That was weird.* People in London kept to themselves, and the woman's brief stare made her uncomfortable. *Yellow eyes? Really?* She waited for her to appear around the other side of the van, but when the vehicle pulled away to reveal no one there, Angela frowned.

"Ducked into a shop," she muttered, but the awkwardness of that swapped glance stirred her from her seat, and she decided to walk home.

It was almost three in the afternoon. Maybe when she arrived home Vince would already be there.

Angela sat in the back garden for the remainder of that afternoon. She'd tried briefly to work on her thesis, but failed, and she shoved aside the guilt as she closed her books and poured a glass of wine. At least she'd made some progress that morning.

Something was wrong.

Vince often told her that he wished he was like her—calm, laid-back, not rattled by anything. She wasn't a worrier. She let life roll by and rode the waves. But now something had changed, and she wished she could place what it was.

Maybe his battery's just run down, Lucy had suggested. Angela tried to grab onto that idea, because it made some sense. Her texts would still show up on her phone as "sent." But Vince always, *always* charged his phone before going to bed, and she'd seen him check it before he left that morning.

London sounds rolled across the garden. There were more than twenty gardens set in two rows, backing onto each other with no pathway in between. The two long terraces were enclosed at both ends, blocked by two more houses, and as far as she knew there was no access to the large garden area other than through the buildings. Most people grew large shrubs or small trees around their plot's perimeter, forming a sort of urban forest landscape, and the sounds that did intrude from beyond were distant and faint. A siren, perhaps, or sometimes the drone of a plane passing high overhead.

From the buildings came the cries of babies, chattering of children, the buzz of television sets, occasional raised voices, music, and during the weekend the sounds of clinking glasses and laughter. Considering they were packed so close together, she hardly ever saw any neighbours, and the couple upstairs never seemed to take advantage of the garden they shared. The plot was large enough for some patio furniture, a barbecue, and a few plant pots.

She and Vince had made love out there once, lit only by starlight, the danger of being seen a delicious thrill. They had argued out there, too. Raised voices, then an uncomfortable silence. Sometimes they sat together and read, a bottle of wine on the table between them.

She wished for any of those things now.

Angela caught her breath, remembering something.

She stood quickly, went inside, and started searching through her handbag for her notebook. She'd written down his workplace number a while ago, though she'd never before had cause to call his firm. He was always available on his mobile, and he'd told her it was best not to call him at the office.

Screw that.

"For fuck's sake, Vince," she said as she rooted through her handbag. This was *stupid*! When he came home he'd take the piss at how touchy she was, and ask her why.

The phone pinged and her heart leapt.

Heard from Vince?

Lucy had texted. It was almost 5 P.M.

Pulling out the notebook, she scanned through it, found the number of his firm, and dialed. A woman answered.

"Anders and Milligan."

"Hi, is Vince there please?"

"No, I'm afraid he hasn't been in the office this afternoon. Who's calling?"

"Angela."

"Angela who?"

"His girlfriend. So have you seen him today?"

"Oh, hi! Yes, I saw him this morning, he had a quick meeting in the office then said he… er."

"He what?"

"He said he had the afternoon off."

"Right," Angela said, frowning. "Anything else?"

"I'm sorry, I don't know where he is. I'm sorry."

"Could you tell him I'm looking for him, if he does come back to the office?"

"Sure."

"Thanks." Angela hung up. *She thinks he's fucking someone else*, she thought. Whoever the woman on the other end of the phone had been, she'd immediately been thrown when Angela said who she was.

But no. She didn't believe it for a moment.

She paced the apartment for a few minutes, wondering what to do and who to call, and the third time along the hallway she saw that the postman had been there. She ignored the mail and strolled into their living room, looking at the three rare orchids she was growing and tending right now, trying to take comfort from their beauty and unique perfection. One of the plants had cost her almost fifty pounds. She'd thought Vince would object, but he seemed to accept her strange little hobby.

"There's money in rare things," he'd said, smiling strangely.

The post already came!

The idea hit her like a flash, driving all other thoughts aside. She ducked back into the hallway and snatched the single folded sheet of paper out of the cage behind the letterbox. Opening it up, she saw what might have been Vince's spidery, hasty scrawl.

Sorry. Love you. Goodbye.

2

Angela was done with just waiting for him to call. He *wouldn't* call. He wouldn't text. The brief, strange note felt so final, and she found herself shivering with a cold that was more than skin deep.

Nothing had gone wrong. Everything had felt so right. They'd made love the previous evening, and it was as good as ever—passionate, close, as if they were made for each other. Their conversations involved casual, easy plans for the future. She'd only known him for a couple of years, true, and Angela would be the first to admit that it wasn't long enough to really get to know someone. But sometimes it felt like they'd been together forever.

He finished her sentences.

She knew what he was thinking.

Vince couldn't have left her. Not like this.

She rushed around the apartment, trying to look with different eyes. He had never been one for physical possessions, but there were things here she knew he would never abandon—the Robin Hood book his late mother had bought him when he was eleven, with her written birthday greeting on the inner flap. The classic car mug his father had passed down to him.

Her.

Pulling on her boots and grabbing a light jacket, she punched in Lucy's number and pressed the phone between ear and shoulder.

"Heard from him?" her friend asked as soon as she picked up.

"No, nothing." For some reason she didn't mention the note. It would feel too much like an admission that he'd gone for good.

"Oh, well, I'll bet he's... gone for a drink after work, or something."

"He never does that," Angela said. "You don't believe that."

"I don't know him as well as you."

"I'm going out to wander around."

"Wander around London? Yeah, you'll find him in no time. Listen, Angie, it's probably best you stay home, and wait for him to contact you."

He has, she thought, but she still didn't say anything. The note was folded in the back pocket of her jeans, and she heard it crinkle as she bent to lace her boots.

"Just the places we go together, you know. Local. Maybe his friends' places. I just need to get out, been cooped up here all day."

"Want me to come?" Lucy asked.

"No, no, I'm fine. Fresh air will do me good."

"In London? Call me when you find it, and I'll come and get some."

"Call you later?" It was a plea more than a question.

"Sure. Take care."

"I'm only going for a fucking walk." She laughed, but worried that she'd sounded too harsh.

"Max says hi."

"Hi back. See you soon."

They disconnected and Angela stood frozen in the living room. The box set of the sixth season of *Game of Thrones* was open on the floor beside the Xbox. They were only halfway through.

"No way he'd leave it like that," she whispered.

Slamming the front door behind her, she struck up a brisk pace. The warm summer evening smelled of exhaust fumes and fast food.

She went to The Bear. It was an old pub on a street corner less than ten minutes from where they lived. Nothing distinguished it from a hundred other pubs all across London. It had leaded windows, an L-shaped bar, a pool table, a selection of board games stacked beside the unlit fire, and an old man called Clarence who seemed to be a permanent fixture at the corner table.

Every single time Angela and Vince had been there, so had Clarence. He told them that he'd seen the pub through a score of landlords, two fires, one murder, and World War II, and neither of them had any reason to doubt him. He seemed out of time, and his constantly half-full glass of Guinness only added to the illusion.

Clarence raised an eyebrow as she entered, his eyes flickering slightly as he looked for Vince. Then he went back to staring across the room.

Angela approached the bar and ordered a glass of Pinot from the barman, Mike. As he poured, she glanced around at the mid-evening drinkers. You could almost tell the time of day by the clientele. The early drinkers on the way home from work had mostly gone, apart from some strangers in the corner with loosened ties and liquid smiles. The late night boozers on their way into town had yet to arrive. Now was locals' time, and she knew at least half of the patrons by sight. She and Vince had chatted with a few of them, but she was here on her own. Apart from some nods and smiles, nobody approached. No one said a word.

Mike handed over her wine and took her money, friendly but silent. Then he moved along the bar to serve someone else.

She hadn't really expected Vince to be here. That would have been too easy, and this didn't feel like an easy situation. It was starting to feel surreal and… frightening. She was dislocated. She considered asking around, yet approaching their casual drinking friends and asking them if they'd seen or heard from Vince felt like weakness. She had no desire to look like a failure.

Why would it feel like failing? she wondered, and it took her a few moments and long sip of wine to pin it down.

"He hasn't left me," she muttered into her glass. She looked furtively over the rim. No one had heard, but she was worried they'd see her talking to herself.

She checked her phone. It was somewhere to retreat, even though she didn't like using the screen as a hiding place. There was one message from Lucy. *Take care.* But nothing else.

He'd gone to the trouble of delivering that note to her, why not a text? Perhaps he'd lost his phone. Maybe he'd thrown it away. She clicked on the news app, focused on London, and before she even realised it she was scanning for news of street muggings, accidents, murders.

But he left that note!

She tucked two fingers into her back pocket and felt the folded reality of it. He'd touched that piece of paper, taken time to write those final words to her. Goodbye had been his intention.

"No Vince tonight?" a voice asked. Nathan was a young kid approaching twenty, good company and wise beyond his years. He was usually on their quiz team when they came on a Sunday evening. Vince called him their Font of Sport.

"Working late," Angela said, lifting the empty glass to her lips to hide the lie.

"Get you one?" Nathan asked.

"Nah, I'm off—just popped in for a quickie."

"Quizzing on Sunday?"

"Yeah," Angela said, and a flush went through her, a sudden realisation that not only had Vince gone, but there would be a future without him. She was living minute by minute as she waited for contact from him, but barren days and weeks stretched ahead, and she had no fucking idea what she was going to do.

Nathan nodded, and moved on to join his friends. Angela watched him go. Then she walked from the pub, eyes down so that she didn't see anyone else. She wanted to leave. There were other places to look, and it was already edging toward nine o'clock.

Cars grumbled along the road, horns sounding at junctions. A dog or something else howled at the setting sun. A siren sounded in the distance. London never slept, but it was slipping from day to night.

She went to their favorite Indian restaurant, the Spice Garden, and looked in through the front window past the display menu. It was buzzing. There were a few people eating alone, but none of them were Vince.

Walking north toward Clapham Common Tube, she passed a couple more pubs they sometimes frequented, shielding her face against the windows and seeing so many people inside, none of whom she knew.

Night fell as she walked. Checking her phone every few minutes, she had three texts but none from the man she loved. Lucy checking in again, her mother asking what she wanted for her birthday, her childhood friend Andy sending a pic of his new daughter from back in the States. She replied to none of them. She didn't feel that she could, because injecting false bonhomie was beyond her now.

Close to the Tube station she paused, bought a coffee from one of those all-night coffee shops that seemed to lose its identity come darkness, and leaned outside against a wall. She had to take stock. Was she panicking, just walking all over London looking for one person in millions? Was she stupid?

There was no way she could call the police. In reality he was only a few hours late, and maybe he was already home and wondering where she was. Yet she couldn't bring herself to text him to find out.

The note might have been a trick. A random coincidence. Someone playing with her. Maybe it was Vince messing with her, some strange, contrived scheme to get her out of the house while he drew together intricate plans for a surprise birthday party. She was thirty-five in two weeks, perhaps now was the only time he'd been able to bring all her family and friends together for a surprise bash.

But on a Thursday?

She shook her head and took a swig of coffee. It was

scorching hot and tasted of nothing. She burned her top lip and cursed, licking it slowly and waiting for the pain to fade. Then Angela closed her eyes and wished she could make everything go back to normal. But as time ticked on, so normality moved further and further away.

She was surprised when her watch beeped midnight. Evening had turned to night, and things had changed, though it had been so gradual that, at first, she barely noticed. The safe, chatty noise of people had faded, replaced with sirens and swearing, the angry growl of engines, the staggering waltz of drunks looking for pubs that might still be open.

A gang of teenagers laughed their way out of the Tube station, and although they seemed good-natured, Angela felt threatened. They didn't even look at her. But she was on her own, and it was very rare that she'd be out on her own at this time of night. Out without Vince by her side.

She realised just how used she'd become to being half of a couple.

A sudden panic washed over her. Unsettled, disturbed, she walked back and forth in front of the Tube entrance, wondering what to do. Part of her wanted to go further afield, deeper into the chaos that London became at night, but the city was vast, and larger still after the sun went down. Another part of her wanted the safety of home. At least there it would smell of him, familiar things around her would form a cocoon of safety, and if and when he did come home she'd be there for him. Whatever his problem might be, he'd need her there to help him through it.

If it was their relationship, they needed to talk.

She rang Lucy. Her friend picked up on the second ring.
"What?"

"Nothing," Angela said, looking around at the cruising taxis and police cars, hurrying people, prowling dogs, and shifting shadows that constituted nothing. She felt eyes upon her, but then this was London, and there were windows and watchers everywhere. She searched the shadows and saw no one. Still, that feeling of being watched persisted.

"You home yet?"

"No. No, I'm going home now. There's no sign of him. What do I do, Lucy?"

"I don't know, babe. Get home. Get some sleep. Want me to come over?"

"No," Angela said. Bless her friend, but no. Something moved along the street, a shape ducking into a doorway. She paused, watched, waiting for it to emerge.

"I'll come by in the morning, yeah? On the way to work?"

"Would you?" She turned away from the dark doorway. It was a hundred yards away and none of her business.

"Sure. I'll bring croissants. Where are you?"

"Clapham Common."

"What? Well get a cab home, and text me when you're in."

"Okay, yeah. Okay."

"It'll all be fine," Lucy said, and Angela broke the connection.

Moments later a man approached. He was young, smiling, vaguely threatening.

"Want to buy something?" he asked.

"Like what?"

"Something precious. Something rare."

"Are you offering me drugs?" She injected as much

confidence and disapproval as she could into her voice. The man's smile slipped, he looked her up and down, then he moved on.

Angela hailed a cab. Time to go home and leave the night to itself.

She saw a fox.

The taxi rolled from the main road and twisted through a network of residential streets, a route she could only assume was a quicker way home. The fox was trotting along the pavement, purpose in its gait, sleek and low to the ground. It appeared healthier and larger than the usual urban foxes. It glanced at the cab as it passed and paused, head down as it watched the vehicle move away. It was hunched in the penumbra between streetlights. Even when she could no longer see it, Angela felt its attention upon her. Her neck tingled.

She'd seen city foxes before. They were shy but confident animals. Vince always said they knew which time was theirs. Turning to look through the rear window, she wondered where that one lived during the day.

A few minutes later, as the cab turned into her street and threw headlights across parked cars and curtained windows, a shadow shimmered in the front garden. She leaned forward in the cab, holding her breath so that she didn't steam the dividing window between passenger compartment and the driver.

This was no fox.

"Vince!" she whispered. The shadow moved again, seeming to flow against the night, leaping through the headlight beams and curling around the base of a streetlight.

The taxi stopped and the shadow moved a little more, before it too came to an angled rest beside a neighbour's car.

Nothing there. Nothing.

She blinked, no longer seeing things, and handed the driver a twenty.

Minutes later she opened the front door and closed it behind her, leaning back against it and breathing in relief. She smelled the familiar scents of home, looking along the hallway and waiting for Vince to step out from the kitchen. She expected it so much that she almost saw movement, but it was tiredness playing with her vision.

It was only as she turned to draw the security chain over the door that she saw the paper in the mail cage.

She pulled it out quickly, unfolded it.

Be safe. Don't look for me.

Crying at last, Angela sank down against the wall, and knew that now she would only look harder.

3

For a while after waking he tried to keep his dream alive. In his twenties he'd spent a long time trying to perfect lucid dreaming, reading books, watching instructional programs, and enrolling in a course at the local adult education center that turned out to be more about the instructor's bank account than anything else.

Nothing had worked. His goal of dreaming himself afloat on a drifting island, with countless naked beauties surrounding him, had never come to pass.

Now, his senses were firing and telling him the truth, but he struggled to allow the lie to persist. The lie that he was safe, secure, and at home with the woman he loved. He didn't reach out a hand, in case she wasn't there. He didn't open his eyes, in case he wouldn't see her hair swept across the pillows. Not yet.

He listened intently for the sound of lovemaking from the floor above. Maybe he'd slept through it, but he hoped not. He wanted to hear the groaning and creaks because they'd encase him in familiarity.

The stench of blood and sweat touched his nostrils. The taste of uncleaned teeth filled his mouth. His head throbbed dreadfully, the pain pulsing in time with his heart. He could feel the cold floor through the thin, dirty blanket on which he'd been sleeping, and his left arm was numb where he'd been resting his head on the bicep.

Vince opened his eyes, and he was still there.

He groaned, rolled onto his back, and sat up.

The room was large but virtually bare. There was a bucket in one corner that he'd already used too much, its stink filling the stale air. The walls were rough concrete, dripping with condensation and decorated with the memory of tiles. The only remnants were straight lines of pointing and dabs of mortar. The ceiling was low and gray, strung with wires spanning both diagonals, a couple of bare bulbs on each length. The weak lights were permanently on.

There was a single metal door in the opposite wall. He knew that it was locked. He couldn't remember being brought down here, but he could feel the weight of rock beyond the room, the pressures of the deep underground pressing down upon him.

They'd taken him down. Of *course* they had. He tried not to think of the room as a dungeon.

He felt like shit. Dried blood coated his hands and bare arms, and he could feel the crisp of it on his face, too. He wasn't sure that all of it was his own. There were several cuts on his left arm and a deeper wound across the inside of his left elbow, but he didn't think that could explain so much blood.

He frowned, trying to remember what might.

Something rattled against the other side of the door, tumblers turned, and it swung inward. Vince squinted against the stark light that flooded in from outside, then a shadow passed through the doorway and it closed again.

The woman stood there. She'd visited him twice before,

but this time she carried a tray holding food, and across her arm were slung several damp towels. She had barely said a word to him during the other two visits, and he hadn't felt much like talking.

Now, things were different. His head still throbbed from the blow he'd taken, but vague memories were beginning to surface. A story was forming, and perhaps she could fill in the missing chapters.

She walked across the subterranean room toward him. Her step was so light that he could not hear it, and she moved with a fluid, casual grace. She almost flowed. She was extremely short, her athletic frame obvious even beneath the loose trousers and long-sleeved shirt. Dark hair tied in a ponytail, cute, pointed ears, piercing green eyes, her expression was so calm that it was almost a blank. She was beautiful and made his heart ache with a shameful desire. He could read nothing in her face, and knew she probably wanted it that way.

As she knelt beside him he heard the soft click of her knees. Good. The sound was the first thing that made her real.

"It's not much, I'm afraid," she said, placing the tray beside him. Her voice was music. On the tray were a bowl of porridge, several slices of buttered toast, and a cup of steaming tea. Vince's stomach rumbled and he reached for the toast, biting into it.

It was the best he'd ever tasted.

"Good," the woman said. "Nice to see you have your appetite back. Here, let me see that arm." She reached for his left arm, lifted it, and studied the deep cut briefly before starting to wipe at it with a wet towel. It stung, but Vince was happy to let her tend him. There was a power about her, even though she was so gentle that she barely seemed to touch him. He suspected the towel was soaked in more than water.

"Who are you?" he asked.

"Mainly scratches, although the wound on your elbow should have been stitched. Too late, though. You'll carry a nice scar, but then don't we all?" She appeared to sniff his arm. "No infection. You're lucky. I know someone who could help you if there was, but everyone's lying low right now. Too much risk being out on the streets, even at night."

She dropped the towel and picked up another, turning her attention to his face. She watched him chewing the toast and he tried to hold her gaze, but had to turn away. *She's so beautiful!* As he took another bite of toast she started wiping his face.

"Sorry I haven't done this before, but I thought it was best to let you rest. I'll try to get some fresh clothes for you soon. Best that you stay here for now. Stay hidden."

"*What* are you?" Vince asked. The question didn't throw her at all. A chill stroked his spine, his balls tingled.

"You killed two of them, and they'll want revenge for that. They'll want to make us suffer, but we can't forget that you helped us—and we never will." She stared into his eyes. "*I* never will."

Behind the pulsing pain in his head flashes of memory formed, and even when he closed his eyes they were still there. He wished they'd go away. Violence, blood, and death danced before him, flooded red with every beat of his heart.

"Angela is looking for you."

"Angela!"

"We're trying to warn her off."

"I've got to go to her." Vince struggled to rise, but dizziness took him, and the woman's gentle grip eased him back down. Though small as a child, she was incredibly strong. Her hands seemed to press against him, kneading his shoulders, and he smelled her breath, her scent. It was mysterious and thrilling, fragrant and unknown. Her warmth reached him, and his skin tingled all over. He felt himself growing instantly hard. His breath came faster.

She smiled gently, then let go of him with a single shake of her head.

Vince sat against the cool wall and she pressed the hot mug of tea into his hands.

"Drink. You have to stay here. I'm looking after you, but you must stay hidden away, and you can't go to Angela."

"Why?"

"Because they're watching her, waiting for you." She looked him over, glanced at the tray she'd brought, then stood and backed away. "I'll come back later to collect that."

As she turned and opened the door, Vince placed the mug on the floor beside him, pushed himself up, and staggered across the room.

The woman turned in the doorway and he saw past her into the corridor beyond. The carpeted, smooth-walled corridor, its lights glaring and wide, panoramic windows offering a high view all across the city. A million lights burned. Traffic moved in distant streets, and aircraft lights flashed on other tall buildings. He'd thought they were way down low, but the opposite was true.

Seeing his surprise, the woman smiled for the first time.

"Hiding in plain sight," she said. "How do you think we've survived for so long?" She pulled the door toward her, and moments before she closed and locked it she whispered through the crack, "I'll be back later." The words hung in the air like a promise.

Alone once again, Vince sat back against the wall and closed his eyes, willing the pulsing pain in his head to settle.

Angela, he thought, *I'm so sorry.* The idea of never seeing her again was dreadful, so he tried to think of other things.

By the time he ate his porridge it was almost cold.

4

Angela thought she spent the night trying to sleep, lying awake in bed, glancing at her phone every few minutes even though she'd heard no pings. Struggling not to panic, and waiting for dawn to burn away the night that felt so deep. But then the sounds of enthusiastic screwing stirred her from a troubled slumber, and she realised that she'd drifted off after all.

She felt guilty about that.

She was also unusually annoyed at the couple upstairs, and padding through the apartment toward the bathroom, she hoped they'd finish quickly. They were being much more vocal than usual. Maybe they'd had nice dreams.

As she sat on the toilet, the front doorbell chimed. Startled, tugging up her pajama bottoms, it was only while she hurried along the hallway that she remembered about Lucy.

Her friend stood on the doorstep. In one hand she held two huge takeaway coffees in a cardboard tray, clutching a bag of croissants in the other. She smiled, then looked past Angela into the shadowy hallway and lifted an eyebrow.

Angela shook her head and started to cry. It surprised her as much as Lucy.

"Oh, come on babe!" Lucy said, shoving her back from

the door and closing it behind her. She hugged Angela, arms pressing close as she balanced their breakfast. "Come on. It's a lovely day, let's go through to the garden and..."

From behind and above, Angela heard her neighbours reaching a crescendo.

"You're kidding me," Lucy said.

"I've told you about them, right?"

"Yeah, but I didn't know you were living underneath Sharon Stone and Michael Douglas."

Angela laughed through her tears. "Thanks for coming."

Lucy glanced at the ceiling. "That's what she said." Then she gestured. "Come on. Garden. I'm famished." She was dressed smartly for work, and she held that healthy glow that Angela was so used to. She'd probably already run five miles that morning.

They sat in the garden eating croissants, drinking coffee, and talking over what to do. Lucy was a strong, calming influence, as she always had been, and Angela loved her for that. It was strange having breakfast with her friend instead of her lover, and she couldn't shake the idea that every hour that passed took her further from ever seeing Vince again. She thrummed with the need to do something.

She didn't show Lucy the notes, or tell her about them. She wasn't sure why.

After a few minutes Lucy said cautiously, "You know the police won't be interested."

"Yeah, I know that. They'll just say he's left me."

Lucy remained silent.

"He hasn't left me. No way."

"I don't know," Lucy said, sipping the last of her coffee.

"Well I do!"

"How?"

"Because we're in love!" Angela shouted. A few gardens away, beyond fences and shrubs left to grow high, a little dog started yapping. Elsewhere a door closed. She was airing her grief in public, but right then she didn't care.

"Okay, sweetie," Lucy said. She stood and hugged her friend tight. "I should be getting to work, but I can swing a sickie if you like?"

"I'm fine," she said. "I'll go to his office, talk with them, see if he said anything yesterday."

"You'll tell them he's missing?"

"Well, if he's just left me like you think, he might even be there."

Lucy sighed, then gathered the empty cups and bag from the patio table. Angela watched her, a sinking feeling in the pit of her stomach. By not showing her friend the notes, was she hiding from them herself?

Because she knew Vince wouldn't be at work. Behind the notes was a hint of danger, a shred of fear. She was the only one who could tease it out.

Angela had driven past Vince's office a dozen times before, picking him up or dropping him off when for some reason it wasn't convenient for him to take the Tube. It was housed in a nondescript building a ten-minute walk from Oxford Circus station, and as she dodged flocks of tourists and countless Londoners keeping to themselves, she had time to think about what she was going to say.

It was a warm, sunny day in the city. Pollution hung heavy in the air with nowhere to go and nothing to move it, and she wasn't surprised to see the first of the face masks out, similar to the type surgeons wore. They'd become more and more prevalent, and it was another reason she'd started to think about moving out of London. She could never have kids while living in the city.

There had been other boyfriends back in Boston, and an engagement while she was in her twenties, but Vince was the first man with whom she could seriously see herself being a parent. They had chatted a few times about moving out of the city, though he'd never seemed keen. He liked his job, but she thought it was something more.

She'd started to wonder if he'd ever wanted kids. It had become a deep-set worry, an ache in their relationship that had the potential to turn into a canker, and it was the one thing she'd been afraid to broach. Her own thoughts of children had never been overly powerful, not until she'd fallen in love with Vince. Then the clock's ticking sometimes became a roar.

She reached Anders and Milligan and stood outside for a moment, across the road and shielded by a bus stop. The office was on the second floor of an old building, above a ground and first-story clothes shop. The entrance door was up two steps and there was a small nameplate screwed to the wall beside a bell and speaker, but nothing else to give away the company's location. She'd asked about this the first time she'd seen it, and Vince had replied that it wasn't a business that took casual callers.

As the city bustled around her she stared. Blinds were drawn against the glaring morning sun, but she could still see a large plant pot behind one window, and movement behind another. She shifted left a little, but couldn't make out anything more.

He might be in there now, she thought. *Maybe he's a mess. Upset at what he's done to me, supported by his colleagues.*

"There, now, Vince, it'll all be okay, plenty more fish in the sea, and you did the kindest thing."

"No," she muttered. A young man standing beside her glanced in her direction, but he looked away again, unconcerned. London was full of crazies. He probably thought she was just one more.

Angela left the bus stop and crossed the road, dodging taxis, cyclists, and a buzzing clot of mopeds. She pressed the bell before she had a chance to think about it anymore, standing back and waiting for the response.

An electronic crackle, and then a woman's voice.

"Hello, can I help you?"

"Hi, I'm Angela Gough, Vince's girlfriend. Any chance I can come in?"

"Oh, hi. Sure. Vince isn't here, though."

She sounds fine, Angela thought. *Not on the defensive. Open and cheery.*

"I know," she replied. "That's what I want to ask about."

The speaker turned off, the door buzzed, and she entered a blissfully cool corridor.

She climbed four flights of stairs, and the bright young woman behind the reception desk stood to welcome her in.

"I'm Baria," she said, extending her hand. "Nice to meet you at last. Vince is always talking about you."

"He is?" Angela shook the woman's hand, thrown by the welcome.

"Sure." Baria glanced aside at a man sitting on a sofa, drinking coffee, as if looking for support. He said nothing. He eyed Angela from face to toes and up again, slowly, and she turned her back on him.

"Has he been in yet today?" Angela asked.

"No, I think he was working out today. Hang on."

The receptionist's voice lost its shiny edge. She could tell something was wrong, and may have been turning over company policy in her mind as she skirted back around the reception counter, accessed her computer, and scanned a diary grid.

"Only he left his phone at home, and I know he'll need it," Angela said, as chirpy as she could muster. "The way it's grafted to his hand, it's amazing he *can* forget it. You know?"

"Huh, yeah," Baria said without taking her eyes from the screen. She tapped a couple more keys, then stood straight again. She looked at Angela, smile back on her face.

"So if I know where his appointments are, I can take it along to him," Angela said. "I need to be able to contact him. I'm sure you do, too."

"He isn't working for us today," Baria said. "Not yesterday afternoon, either."

Angela wondered what the hell she was talking about, and tried to keep the surprise from her face. She sighed and smiled, glancing around as she gathered her thoughts.

The reception area was light and airy, with several doors leading off, all closed. Baria's desk was low and wide, uncluttered apart from the computer, phone, and a couple of other gadgets Angela couldn't place. Three tasteful paintings adorned one wall, hanging between doors and displaying scenes from old London—grander buildings, fewer pedestrians, carriages, smokestacks in the distance.

The man on the sofa stared at a magazine, but she could tell his attention was on their exchange.

"He was going to Clerkenwell for work yesterday afternoon," Angela offered. She couldn't compute what was happening here, and rather than try to fake her way forward, thought maybe honesty would be the best route. Even on the defensive, Baria seemed nice.

"Not for us," Baria said, frowning now. She glanced at the man, then walked toward one of the closed doors. "Follow me, we'll pop into his office and check out his paper diary." She nodded her head slightly for Angela to follow.

They stepped into a small meeting room, six low chairs set around a circular table scattered with building and property magazines. Casual, informal, intricately designed, and definitely not Vince's office. Baria pushed the door closed.

"You know he's freelance, right?" Baria asked, her voice low. She leaned on the back of a chair.

Angela considered lying, but only briefly. With every second that passed, her life became a more complex place. She felt like a stranger in her own skin, discovering truths that everyone but her knew.

She shook her head.

"He works for us two, three days each week," Baria continued. Her fingers tapped the chair, and she looked just over Angela's shoulder. "He's a nice guy. You're all he talks about." It was almost as if she was speaking to herself.

"Look, I'm worried," Angela said. "Things are really good between us, just… the best ever. But I haven't heard from him since yesterday, and I'm worried that something's happened to him. He's not responding to calls or texts, and that's not like him at all."

"So he *does* have his phone," Baria said.

"Of course. Like I said, grafted to his hand."

The other woman nodded cautiously, and wouldn't quite catch her eye.

"What?" Angela asked.

Baria stared at her then, an internal dialogue almost visible on her face.

"I'm getting a coffee for the gentleman out there," she said. "Vince's contact file is open on my computer." She opened the door and left before Angela could respond, crossing the reception area with a smile and a nod to the man, disappearing through another door into a small kitchen.

Angela stood at the open doorway. The man read his magazine, blinking quickly. He wore a good suit, a nice tie, but there was a spot of brown sauce on his shirt, and one of his suit buttons hung on by a thread. She was good at noticing such details. It was how her mind worked, and that ability fed into her interests and studies. But right then the thought of the law, and her criminology degree and thesis, seemed petty and far away.

She moved to the desk and sat quickly behind it, scanning the screen. Out of the corner of her eye she caught the man's surprised gaze on her, but ignored it.

She froze. Breath held.

Then she picked up a pen and Post-it note, and wrote furiously.

She scribbled down the address and left the reception area without looking at the waiting man. It was only as she pulled the door shut behind her that she thought to whisper, "Thanks." She didn't know whether or not Baria heard her.

She didn't really care.

Walking along Old Brompton Road from South Kensington station, she went further and further away from what she thought was real. Vince's second address couldn't be anywhere like this, could it? They sometimes came here together for meals, and occasionally to visit her folks when they flew over and stayed in one of the boutique hotels.

They often gazed into real estate agents' windows, marvelling at the multi-million-pound prices of apartments not much bigger than their own.

She'd always thought that the people who lived in places like this had two perfect kids, four-wheel drives, and six-figure salaries. Not couples like her and Vince.

Or just Vince.

She turned over the possibilities.

He's got a second place somewhere with another woman, another lover. Those days when he's not working for Anders and Milligan he spends there, with her, having another life during the day.

But he always came back to her at night, and there was something comfortable about that, something committed.

Or maybe I'm the lover! He's unhappily married, and when he's with me his wife thinks he's away working.

The Tube journey had been short but hot, but at least at the end of it she hoped she'd find something definitive, good or bad. Good might be that he'd been working hard to pay for this second place, in the hope that maybe she'd live with him there, when the time came to reveal it. That seemed unlikely, but she clung to the idea, nevertheless.

Bad... she could think of plenty of bad. The two notes she kept crumpled in her pocket evidenced that.

She passed shops, restaurants, and pubs, listening to the stew of languages that defined London's diverse population. People stood chatting outside some establishments, and restaurant pavement tables were taken up with diners just finishing a late lunch. Many of them were drinking. Angela always wondered at that, but here she guessed that many of the drinkers didn't work at all. She spied expensive jewelry, designer clothes, and half-empty bottles of wine that probably cost more than her entire wardrobe.

She reached Cranley Mews and turned left. Any one of the cars parked along the road could have paid for her three years of study. Mercedes, BMWs, Porsches, Bentleys, a couple of Rolls Royces, and two Lamborghinis and a Ferrari with personalised plates that could only belong to the same family. She felt intensely out of place. The street seemed quieter, too, as if the hustle of London couldn't reach this far, and she looked around for security cameras.

This might be the most foolish thing she'd ever done, yet she couldn't deny the tingle of excitement that heightened her senses. Years of study, and she couldn't actually think of a time when she'd used some of the tricks or talents she had read about. Until now. She'd bought a box of paperclips and a nail file from a newsagent at South Kensington station, and she was ready to go.

She reached the address written on the Post-it note and walked straight to the front door. It was a two-story building and there were two doors, each with a bell and speaker. Apartment B—Vince's upstairs apartment—had no name next to its bell.

The door lock was a traditional type. If it had been an electronic lock, she'd have been out of luck. As it was, she had to be quick, because any stranger seen hanging around in an upmarket area like this was likely to draw attention.

She slipped the nail file into the bottom of the keyhole and turned gently left and right. Holding it to the left, she kept slight tension on it as she slipped a straightened paperclip into the top of the hole. Breathing slowly, trying to calm her sprinting heart, she raked the paperclip back and forth a few times, feeling the pins move up and down. Then she pushed it all the way in and gingerly felt around until the first pin clicked up.

A car passed along the street behind her. Someone shouted a name, perhaps calling to a child. A dog barked, and an ambulance dopplered its way along Old Brompton Road. She resisted the inclination to look around and make sure no one was watching her. As it was now, she was someone fumbling with a key. If she glanced around, she'd start to look suspicious.

The remaining pins clicked up into place and she turned the nail file, gasping in delight when the lock clicked and the door opened inward. She tucked the makeshift tools into her pocket and entered, turning to close the door and only then glancing quickly out into the street.

An old woman walked a small dog along the opposite pavement. A postman pushed a cart, sweating in the mid-morning heat. The siren had receded into the distance, and there was no indication that anyone had seen her.

She clicked the door closed and rested her forehead against it. Taking in a deep breath, her relief at not being seen was overshadowed by a sudden nervous anticipation.

She didn't know what she was about to find.

The staircase was wide and clean, the walls bare. At the top there was another heavy door that led into the apartment, but this one wasn't locked. She turned the handle and entered, and Vince's private life opened up before her.

At first what she saw pleased her. The large, open-plan space wasn't lived in. The sitting area at the front consisted of three modern-looking sofas forming a U-shape, its open edge facing the two large windows that let in radiant sunlight. One expanse of wall was bare brick, while the others were plastered and painted the lightest shade of gray. A few pictures hung here and there, none of them particularly inspiring.

They were the sorts of prints selected for their blandness, designed to go unseen.

The combined kitchen and dining area was part of the open-plan space, set at the rear and lit by three ornamental light-wells, each reaching up through the roof and drawing in an impressive amount of sunlight. The kitchen was expensive and stark, surfaces gleaming, with no clutter. It looked clean and unused.

There was a large flat-screen television affixed to one wall, and she could see that its trailing plug hung loose, not connected anywhere. Timber fans hung heavy from the ceiling, and a circular staircase led to a mezzanine level. Up there, past the glass balustrading, she could see a couple of modern chairs and a spread of book shelving, all but empty. She was willing to bet that the few volumes she could make out weren't the sort of books Vince might read.

He might never have been up there to see the titles.

The whole place felt like that. Unlived-in, untouched, and unloved. Her brief flush of relief at not seeing things of comfort and homeliness soon gave way to an edge of disquiet. Beyond the fact that the cost of this place must be way beyond what she believed he earned, why would Vince even *have* a place like this?

Was it just a fuck pad?

She tried to imagine the love of her life screwing a woman on one of the sofas, on the lush rug beneath the TV, bent over the modern dining table, and none of it made sense. The idea seemed so unlikely that it didn't even upset her.

"This isn't somewhere to fuck someone," she whispered. Her words echoed in the lifeless space. There was nothing there to dampen them. No books, no jackets hung over the backs of chairs, no clutter of existence. This was a plain, lifeless space.

She moved through the room quickly, smelling dust and must and nothing of Vince. In the far corner a door opened into a small hallway. There were two more doors, both closed, and she chose the left one first.

It opened into a large double bedroom, and the rush of sensory input froze her in place.

Vince's clothes lay scattered across the bed, some jeans and a couple of tee shirts also on the floor. She recognised them all. The smell of his favorite deodorant wafted through the open door, a George R. R. Martin book lay propped open on the bed, an empty shortbread packet had spilled crumbs across the carpet, and on the bedside table were several cola cans. She told him that shit was bad for him, but he still enjoyed a can now and then. It appeared that here in his secret bolthole, he indulged his habit more often.

Angela felt angry, and scared. Nothing here made sense. The bed was neatly made, its surface dimpled and creased from someone sitting up against the headboard. Vince *never* made the bed. He said it was a waste of time.

She moved into the room and saw the photo frame above the bed. It contained six pictures, all of places they had been together. Polperro in Cornwall, Chester, a couple of pictures of the Welsh mountains, Brighton Pier. She recognised the snaps from their own electronic album, but quickly noticed that the pictures were all scenery. None of them contained him… or her.

Though the photos warmed her a little, she was more troubled than ever, and as she turned around something caught her eye. The wardrobe door was ajar and stuff was piled inside. She opened the door and it spilled out.

Boots. A rucksack. Waterproof trousers and jacket. Base layers. A coiled rope, a couple of sheathed knives, a heavy torch. A bound cloth roll hit the floor and unwound a little, and she finished the job with her foot. It was a tool roll, containing all manner of implements she couldn't identify, some of them pointed and sharp, others blunt-edged and hammer-like.

Just what the fuck?

She'd read about places like this. Safe-houses, crash pads, they were places where criminals came to hide away from the world. Acquiring property also allowed a criminal organisation to launder and invest its ill-gotten gains. She reckoned this place must be worth two million.

Moving quickly, she stalked back through the hallway to the other door. This must be the bathroom. Flinging the door open, the first things she saw were the packages in the dry bathtub. Wrapped in cloth, carefully tied, three of them were set carefully in the bottom, like presents ready to be handed out.

Checking the rest of the bathroom, she found nothing else unusual. She moved closer to the bath and looked down at the packages.

Something weird, she thought, hairs on her neck tingling.

Lifting one shape out, she was surprised at how light it felt. The string around it was knotted tight, so she darted back into the bedroom to fetch one of the sheathed knives, then returned to the bathroom, kneeling on the floor.

One stroke and the string parted.

She started unwrapping the package, and it was Lucy's voice that spoke to her.

Just what the hell are you doing? the voice said. *This has nothing to do with you.*

"It *is* to do with me," she said aloud. "It is!" Louder, and she found that speaking made her feel less afraid. Less secretive. This *was* to do with her, because Vince was hers and this place was his, and she had to know the truth. If he was into something criminal and perhaps dangerous, she needed to know. With what she knew already, there was no way she could just go back.

She closed her eyes and couldn't help the flood of terrible images that came at her.

I'll open this and it'll be full of drugs. Vince has gone. I can't reach him, and maybe he's dead at the bottom of some canal or in a sewer, throat sliced and balls cut off and stuffed into his mouth. She knew how some of these gangs worked. She'd been studying them long enough.

She *thought* the notes in her back pocket were in his handwriting, but maybe she'd just *wished* that on them. Maybe they were the only warnings she'd get from whoever had done something terrible.

Opening the package, she sat back on the floor, looking down at the contents. It was a strange moment. To begin with she felt nothing, as if her mind was insulating her against the reaction that must surely come. Reaching out, considering that it might be some sort of joke, at the same time part of her knew it was not. Everything was too serious for this to be a prank.

The head was the size of a large potato. The skin was parchment dry, hair fine and knotted, teeth bared where the lips had drawn back over time. The incisors were much too long and still sharp.

One eye, closed, in the middle of the forehead.

One eye, Angela thought. She shook her head, trying to work out exactly what she was looking at. Alongside the head was a small business card. Its surface was dusted with—

—old skin, real *skin, falling from this thing with one eye in the middle of its forehead, and creatures with one eye are called...* were *called—*

—and Angela was all too familiar with the name and place printed there.

Courtesy of
FREDERICK MELOY
The Slaughterhouse

Frederick Meloy, also known as Fat Frederick, was one of the most dangerous crime lords in London. He ran a place called The Slaughterhouse Bar. She'd probed about him once for a research paper, and she'd been quickly warned off by someone from SOCA, the Serious Organised Crime Agency. He relished the title Fat Frederick, but there were rumors about what he'd done to someone who once shortened his name to Fat Freddie. That story came back to her now and made her skin crawl.

She picked up the card and stared at the name.

"Slaughterhouse, Freddie?" she said aloud. "Talk about hiding in plain sight."

The relic on the floor stared at her with its single dusty eye. She reached out to touch it, then drew her hand back. She was afraid it might blink.

Instead, she took three quick pictures with her phone.

In a daze, Angela wandered back into the sterile apartment, the business card clutched in one hand. She approached the window and gazed out between the blinds.

"Cyclops," she whispered.

Down in the street, a man and woman stood together on the opposite pavement, staring up.

5

The food made Vince feel a little better, for a time. Yet however much he fought to stay awake, however scared he was for Angela, he still drifted in and out of consciousness. He tried pacing the room's diagonals and counting scratches on the walls, but in the end there was always troubled, restless sleep.

He had no way to judge how long each period of wakefulness or unconsciousness lasted, because he had no watch or phone, nor any view of the outside. The door had no keyhole. The walls were solid. His knowledge of what he'd seen past the strange woman's shoulder—the whole of strange, exotic, terrible London laid out around them, lights twinkling in the night—did nothing to take away the sense of solidity that surrounded him.

If they decided to never open the door again, he would be trapped here forever.

He had never suffered from claustrophobia, but the more he thought about that fact, the more the walls closed in. He tried not to panic. His head pulsed with each heartbeat, and he wondered whether his skull had been fractured. His vision blurred with every white-hot, clanging ring of pain. It was as if the wound was being dealt afresh every time.

Between moments of pacing and wincing and panicking, he would lean against a wall and slide to the floor, and before he came to rest he was—

—somewhere darker, damper, and deeper, cheek pressed against smooth cracked tiles, unidentifiable sounds echoing in an empty chamber, and then something slammed against his head and he groaned, slipping down toward the ground. On a wall a dozen steps from him, across a debris-strewn floor, he could see a faded poster advertising something he'd never heard of, the smiling woman so time-worn that she might have been a ghost.

His head rang. Vision swam red.

He knew that if he didn't move, the next impact might crack his skull and spill him across the ground. He let himself fall and then rolled, looking up and back at the two people who were attacking him. He knew their faces, and hated them. Both of them. The man was huge and brutal, grimacing in delight as he stepped forward to beat and pummel and kill. The woman was slim and severe, her silver hair in pigtails, age indecipherable. Blades glimmered in both of her hands, yet she seemed content to let her gorilla finish the job with brute force.

Beyond them, between the beast's legs and past the woman's hips, Vince saw a shape huddled against the wall. A shape he was protecting, because if he didn't then they would kill it. Butcher it.

The blades weren't for him.

Even though the memory suddenly slowed to a crawl, the big man was always in the way as Vince tried to make out who or what the shape was. Weak light shone from the blades and confused his vision. The memory paused, but the more he tried to see, the less clear everything became.

Then the big man surged at him again, and—

"How are you feeling?" The voice jarred Vince awake.

I never remember more than that, he thought. Maybe because it was too traumatic, and the recollection of having his skull battered was too much. Perhaps he was protecting himself.

"No," he whispered, "it was something else." He thought of that huddled figure, and how something about it—the size, the shape, the buried knowledge he must have— seemed so strange.

"Vince?" The woman was kneeling beside him, the door closed behind her. He hadn't heard her enter. He looked up at her and smiled, and everything about his troubled memories seemed to vanish into her aura. She smelled of sunlight and summer showers.

"I feel like shit," he said.

She smiled and handed him a drink. "This should help." It looked like water in a glass, but when he sipped it tasted of something he could not quite define.

"What is it?"

"It's good for you." She sat cross-legged on the floor, not quite close enough to touch. She was assessing him, one corner of her mouth still turned up in half a smile.

His heart ached with desire. It wasn't only a base sexual urge, but a soulful yearning, physical and warm and all-encompassing. He thought of Angela but did not feel guilty, because his carnal thoughts toward this woman felt so pure and innocent.

"Who are you?" he whispered, and her smile lit up his life.

"My name is Lilou. I have other names, but you…" She shrugged. "You wouldn't understand them."

"Try me."

She laughed, then, this strange woman whose name was Lilou. The sound filled the room and pushed away some of the darkness, but there were also shadows to her laughter, and shades giving her expression darker contours. Vince had always thought that sad smiles were the most affecting.

"You're not quite human," he said, never able to hold her gaze but hating to look away. He'd glance aside and feel an instant sinking sensation in his stomach, as if he'd forever lost something precious. Finding it again took only a flicker of his eyes.

"Your world has opened up," Lilou said, touching his face and urging him to look at her. "Your memories and understanding are struggling to catch up, but you'll be there soon." She smiled and was beauty personified—deep eyes filled with promise, sensual lips slightly parted, hinting at more. The sweep of her cheek, the fall of her hair. He had seen women and felt lust at first sight many times, but never like this. Never love. Where her finger still touched his face his skin burned, and he lifted his hand to press hers to his cheek. Still in pain, confused, scared at what was happening... for a moment everything was swept away.

He throbbed with passion for her. Though it was wrong it felt so right. He imagined her stripping him and washing him, bathing his wounds. He imagined her slipping out of her own clothes in this grim cell that might have been a forest glade, the sounds of a breeze in the trees and a flowing stream mimicking her cry as she lowered herself gently down onto him.

Vince sighed heavily and kissed her hand, tracing the lines on her palm with the tip of his tongue. She tasted of every good thing. He reached for Lilou with his free hand, fingertips brushing against her breast, holding, squeezing softly. She gasped. He moved closer, inhaling her scent and feeling an unbearable pressure in his groin. He pressed his mouth to the side of her neck and tasted her again, and with his other hand he worked at his belt, desperate to release himself, yearning for her touch and—

She pulled away, her smile suddenly cast in stone.

"I'm sorry," she said. The cell turned hard and grimy once more. Vince blinked and thought of Angela.

"What is it?" he asked, panting.

"I can't trust normal people anymore. *We* can't. It's not good. But you've done so much to help us and… we have no choice."

"We?"

She looked at him again.

"You're so beautiful," he whispered. Lilou sighed and turned away.

"There's someone you should meet. His name's Mallian. I could take you to him, but you have to promise me something, and it's very important."

Vince looked around his cell, because that's what it was— there was no denying. His bucket still sat in the corner, still stinking. The dirty blanket he'd slept on was screwed up in another corner. There was no reason he could possibly want to stay here.

Yet the idea of leaving scared him.

"I can't promise something before you tell me what it is."

"Yes you can," Lilou said. "It's important. For you and for Angela."

"Is she…?"

"She's still safe, although she's persistent."

"She is that," Vince said, but Lilou's dourness persisted.

"Promise that you won't try to see who you're talking to."

Vince frowned, not understanding.

"You want me to keep my eyes closed?" he asked. "Why? What, is he disfigured, or something?"

"Just promise."

After a pause Vince said, "I promise."

Lilou reached out and in a rapid, fleeting movement nicked the back of his hand with her thumbnail. It didn't hurt. A tear of blood formed and ran across his hand, dripping onto his thigh.

"By blood you've promised," she said.

Vince dabbed at the small cut and wiped the blood away. Another bubble formed. Lilou watched, then sighed.

"But you're not ready yet," she said, standing and walking toward the door.

"Wait!" Vince tried to push himself upright but the pain pulsed in again, and he swayed against the wall. "Come on, you can't keep me locked in here. It's not fair!"

"Fair?" Lilou asked. She stood with her hand on the door handle, one eyebrow cocked.

"I don't understand," he said. "None of this. What just happened between us, or this Mallian person, why I'm not ready to see him… I just…"

"That's why you need to stay here. Until you *do* understand." She nodded at the drink he'd left on the floor. "Drink that, sleep, and I'll come back soon."

He wanted to say more. Plead, beg, *demand* that he be let out, because Angela was out there somewhere, and he was certain that she was in danger.

Lilou left and the door clicked shut behind her.

Vince looked down at the little cut she'd given him, and only then did it begin to hurt.

6

By the time she left Vince's second home the couple in the street had gone. Yet all the way back to South Kensington station Angela felt watched. It might have been guilt, or the way the couple had turned away when they'd seen her looking from the window. Or perhaps it was that single closed eye, watching her.

She hadn't been able to touch the relic, and neither had she opened the other two parcels sitting wrapped in the dry bath. That had surprised her. Curiosity had always been her driving force, and ever since she could remember she had always asked *why?*

The fear of what she might find had overridden who she was.

That, and the need to escape.

The second home that Vince had kept from her had become suddenly dangerous.

Back on the streets she felt a little safer, but busy though the roads and pavements were, the sense of being watched made her feel vulnerable and alone. She walked quickly along Old Brompton Road, then a couple of hundred yards from the station she started shaking. It came over her quickly, a violent shiver that surprised her so much that she stopped dead on the pavement, terrified that she was going to puke.

Someone nudged past her with a bad-tempered mutter, and two young Japanese men paused to watch before quickly moving on. Staring at the ground ten feet ahead of her, she watched from the corner of her eye as one of them snapped her on his phone.

Those pictures on my phone, she thought, and the shivers came again.

"You okay?" a voice asked. Angela squeezed her eyes closed, established that she wasn't going to vomit, then looked up. The shakes settled. A middle-aged man stood before her, carrying a knapsack. Graying goatee, glasses, bald head, he looked in good shape, and smile lines wrinkled his face. He moved uncertainly from foot to foot, one hand held out but not touching her. Maybe he was offering her something to grab if she fell.

"Haven't had my morning coffee," she said, trying on a smile.

The man grinned and nodded sideways. They were standing directly outside a small Costa coffee shop, and suddenly that seemed like the best idea in the world.

"There are worse vices," he said, shrugging his bag higher onto his shoulders. "Take it easy." The man walked past her and she turned to watch him go, suddenly wishing that he'd stay to have coffee with her. He seemed carefree and nice.

She wasn't carefree. Not anymore. Maybe yesterday morning she had been, but everything had changed so quickly, so drastically that she could barely remember. She'd worried about this and that—her thesis, Vince's attitude toward kids—but they were negligible compared to what troubled her now.

First world problems, Lucy would have said, and although dismissive, it was often how she'd begin to talk Angela down from whatever might be troubling her.

"Coffee," Angela said, and she could already feel the caffeine rush.

She entered Costa and ordered a large cappuccino with an extra shot, then added a flapjack for good measure. She waited at the counter, but the Spanish barista waved cheerily and said that she'd bring the order over.

Angela nodded her thanks, walked toward the back of the café, and sat on a tall chair beside a high circular table. She eased back and stared past the line of customers, through the window. It was warm and bustling outside, and there was something calming about watching the world go by, instead of being a part of it.

The safe, ignorant world.

She took out her phone and placed it on the table. She'd taken three pictures before the sight of the thing, and the suspicion of being watched, had driven her from the apartment. Being alone in there with it had made her feel...

"Stupid," she said. Not the feeling, but the fear.

The barista appeared beside her and placed a giant mug and plated flapjack on the table. Angela thanked her.

Glancing to her side, she saw the couple from outside the apartment, sitting in low leather chairs to her right, just an arm's length away.

Her heart jumped and she knocked the table, spilling a splash of coffee into the mug's big saucer.

They seemed oblivious to her. The woman was black, smartly dressed, her long hair plaited and hanging over her shoulder. She rested both hands on either side of her expresso. She was beautiful in a fierce way, no frown lines but with a severe expression that made her eyes sharp as stakes. Even though she was looking at the man, Angela could feel the weight of her stare.

The man was of average height and build, wiry, and she identified him as a runner. She could always tell—the way he sat, the potential energy in his frame. She noticed the oversized GPS watch on his wrist. It was a similar model to the one she used, and she could see numbers ticking over on the stopwatch function. She wondered what he was timing, or perhaps it was counting down.

She was certain it was them. She'd only glimpsed them briefly before ducking behind the curtains. After waiting for a few seconds she'd looked again and they were walking back toward the main street, casual and chatting and perhaps never having stared up at Vince's apartment at all. Even now she wasn't sure they were anything to do with her. Perhaps they were property hunting, or killing time.

The woman said something. The man laughed. The woman's stony expression cracked a little, life touched her eyes, and then she stood and took the three steps to Angela's table.

"What—?" Angela said, wincing back on her chair.

"Quiet," the woman said. Without looking at her, she casually moved Angela's plate aside, picked up the phone, stroked the screen, and tapped several times.

"What the hell do you think you're doing?" Angela asked. She kept her voice low, not wanting to cause a scene. *But maybe I should*, she thought. The café was noisy, busy, and one shout would undoubtedly draw attention.

"Just a sec," the woman said. She glanced at Angela for the first time, as if finally noticing her, and instantly it was clear how serious she was.

Angela looked at the seated man. He was no longer smiling. He stared right at her, unblinking, coffee mug half-raised in one hand. He seemed ready to move at the slightest provocation. Coiled. Tense.

"No cloud," the woman said, dropping Angela's phone on the table.

It took a few seconds, then she realised what the woman meant. She'd been looking at her phone's setting to make sure she didn't save photos to the cloud.

Angela touched the phone screen, but already knew that the photographs of the relic would be gone.

She met the woman's gaze, this time vowing to not look away.

They stared. The café's beat went on around them. A child laughed, a man coughed, someone behind the counter dropped a cup and clapped when it bounced. Then the woman's expression cracked into a carved smile that was even more threatening, and she sat in the other tall chair tucked under Angela's table.

"I didn't tell you to join me," Angela said.

"I didn't ask." The woman turned back to the man and held out her hand. He put his own mug down, picked up her espresso cup, and handed it across. He stretched, pulled a phone from his pocket, and stared at the screen.

Maybe they'd decided that she didn't pose a threat.

"Where's Vince?" Angela asked, trying to take control.

"You tell me."

"I don't know."

"Come on," the woman said, scoffing. She lifted the espresso cup, already drained, and licked around its inside.

"Why are you looking for him?" Angela asked.

"Why are you?"

"He's my boyfriend," she replied. "He didn't come home yesterday."

"Tell us where he's gone."

"Didn't you hear me?" Angela asked, louder than she'd intended. From the corner of her eye she saw the man looking their way.

"Keep your voice down," the woman said.

"Why? Don't want to attract attention? You're rimming your cup, for fuck's sake." But she spoke quietly, just loud enough for the woman to hear, because she thought she could find out more here. She *had* to.

About Vince, his apartment, and that thing she'd seen inside.

"My name's Claudette," the woman said, offering her hand. Angela did not shake it. She looked at the man instead, and caught him watching her. He looked away. "That's Harry."

"Harry and Claudette," Angela said. "Sounds like a cop show."

"Claudette and Harry," Claudette said, "and we're not police."

"Oh, I think I know that."

"You don't know *what* you know, and that's part of the problem." Claudette picked up the flapjack and took a delicate bite from one corner. She raised her eyebrows, nodded, then offered it across to Harry. He shook his head.

"I'm leaving," Angela said. As she made to slip from the high chair, Claudette stopped chewing, and Harry tensed in his seat.

Angela smiled. "What?"

"We need to know where Vince is. He's a friend. Well, an acquaintance, I'll be honest, but we have the same boss. And that boss is very concerned about your boyfriend's disappearance."

"He's not the only one," Angela said.

"So if you know where he is, you need to tell us so that—"

"So that Fat Frederick can... what, punish him?"

"Fat Freddie's not my concern."

"You know what he does to people who call him Fat Freddie, right?"

Claudette shrugged. "You sound like you know what you're talking about, though."

"No," Angela said. "Not at all. Not really. Just... stuff, and none of it to do with where Vince might be."

"Take this." Claudette put a business card on the table. A phone number, and nothing else. "Keep it."

"Oh, very swish," Angela said. "So what the fuck was that thing in the apartment? The cyclops thing with one eye."

Claudette blinked rapidly several times, as if wiping her memory and resetting the conversation. Angela looked across at Harry. He was leaning toward them, blocking the way for a couple of women and their baby strollers. He didn't seem to care. She wasn't even certain he'd noticed.

"Just some old thing," Claudette said. "Fools pay money for old things."

"This is all about money?"

"Isn't everything?"

No, Angela thought. *Not at all*. But she said no more. These people were giving nothing away, yet beneath the melodrama their threat was obvious. They weren't putting it on.

"Call us when he gets in touch with you," Claudette said. She slipped from the tall stool. Harry stood and walked toward the front door, the two women with their strollers following him. He didn't even look back.

Claudette touched the business card with her fingertip, turned, and left the café. Outside, she and Harry swapped a few words in front of the large window before going their separate ways.

Angela let out the breath she hadn't been aware of holding.

"What the fuck was that?" she whispered, but she knew what the fuck it was. A further glimpse into a world that she hadn't known Vince inhabited, but which she knew more than most. A dark, dangerous world.

Frederick Meloy, also known as Fat Frederick, was the last person Angela wanted to see, and The Slaughterhouse was the first place she had to go. Claudette had said that she and Vince had the same boss, and Angela could only assume that it was him. His welcome card had been tucked into the package in Vince's secret apartment. That weird, haunting package…

She checked her phone again, and the pictures were definitely gone. By deleting them, Claudette only confirmed that they meant something important, yet in the blazing July sunshine, in the frantic bustle of the city, Angela couldn't help but doubt what she had seen. That wasn't like her. She was confident in her intellect, comfortable with translating what her senses told her. Perhaps it was the logic of everything she knew, doing its best to shed any memory of what had been in that apartment.

She'd decided to walk back into central London. The Tube was quicker, but she needed time to think, and being confined down there in the sweat and heat didn't appeal to her right then. Sometimes riding on the Underground felt like being buried.

Passing the Natural History Museum and the bustling crowds of visitors, she thought of all the amazing exhibits in there, pulled from the ground, separated by tens of millions of years of evolution, and tens of thousands of miles. She'd visited several times—on her own, with friends, and once with Vince on a long, touristy day spent seeing the sights of London because, he'd insisted, they just should. They'd taken pictures of each other outside famous buildings and sat on a river cruise, being told things they already knew about places they rarely saw, but which people flew thousands of miles to see.

After the museum they'd done the London Eye, Buckingham Palace, and Hyde Park, ending the day in a good boozer and getting a taxi home, drunk and happy. She'd lived in the city for almost ten years, three in her own apartment, but that was the first time she'd purposely seen it as a tourist. The glamour, glitz, and surface sheen of that day had done little to change her view of what London was, the type of place it could be, or some of the people who made it their home. She regarded it as one of the world's great cities and her home, but it had its dark underside.

Fat Frederick was one of the most dangerous people in the city. She'd come across his name a few times while researching earlier, disparate aspects of her thesis, and a Google search had brought up surprisingly few hits. Mention on an American message board, the content deleted. A couple of YouTube posts, videos also removed "due to copyright infringement." A few references on other obscure sites that seemed to have no real link with the man, his reputation, or even the city over which he cast his shadow.

She'd skimmed over these searches the first time, then returned to them a day later and started probing deeper.

One was the caption to a photograph on a dying man's charity website. He was raising money for cancer research, and there were all manner of features, interviews, and events. On the gallery page, one photo showed a group of people standing outside a posh-looking hotel—its name had been out of shot—chatting and laughing as they waited for a car. They had been to a charity ball, and the caption confirmed that more than one thousand pounds had been raised. Angela hadn't recognised any of them, and the "Frederick Meloy" listed in the caption had given her no clues. None of the people looked particularly fat. Maybe it was simply a coincidence.

Another hit appeared on a website listing live sex shows in London. A link took her through to The Slaughterhouse, a club in one of the more upmarket streets at the northern edge of Soho.

That was when SOCA had paid her a visit, and warned her off.

She'd been insistent, of course. The idea had already been planted that Fat Frederick might provide an ideal chapter of her thesis. With the man and woman from SOCA sitting on the sofa telling her why she shouldn't be doing this, the motivation had taken root and started to grow. They'd known that, too. As the man gave his reasons—being very level-headed and honest with her, insisting that she was putting herself *and* her loved ones at risk—Angela had seen the dawning realisation in the woman's eyes.

Five minutes after they left, the woman returned. Angela let her in again, but she only stood in the small hallway. She told Angela that she wouldn't plead with her, but insisted on telling her some stories that might help her make up her mind.

"Officially we can't tell you about these things, because none of them are proven," the woman said. "Even by mentioning them, I'm perpetuating the myth that Meloy has been striving to build about himself, but where I work we don't always do things the official way. So there are two stories I want to tell you. I didn't actually tell you these, and if you claim I did, or spread them, or mention them to anyone else, I'll deny all knowledge. Even whisper them to someone else, and you'll be putting yourself in more danger than you're already in."

"Already in?" Angela had said.

"We've no concrete information," the woman replied hastily, "but you've done a Google search on his name, and probed deeper." She shrugged. "He has his ways and means."

"So… the stories."

"Yeah. There was a guy, couple of years back, went to Meloy with a plan to rob a security van. Meloy isn't usually into stuff so crass. He makes his money through a complex network of protection rackets, drug trafficking, and… well, other stuff. Let's call the guy John Smith. So, Smithy's plan was good. Watertight. And it came at a time when Meloy needed an injection of cash for some other project."

"What project?" Angela had asked.

"Don't know. Wouldn't tell you if I did. Anyway, Fat Frederick got his people to go over the plans in detail, digging for loopholes, and reporting back to him that it looked good. He gave it the go-ahead, then stepped back and had nothing more to do with it. He trusts his lieutenants, and they're loyal to him. So the job happened. I can't tell you details, of course, not even where this heist took place, but they got away with it. The truck and its drivers vanished and have never been seen again. Neither has the half a million quid inside."

"Let me guess. Neither has John Smith?"

"Oh, no, he was seen again. They found his foot in a kebab shop in Croydon, his left hand in a dog's mouth in Ealing, and his head stuck on the bonnet ornament of a Mercedes out in Hillingdon. No one knows why. Some slight, perhaps. Or just Meloy cleaning up."

"So Smithy's not the one who called him Fat Freddie?" Angela had asked.

"No, Smithy's murder was planned. It was a stripper who called him Fat Freddie in one of his clubs. Probably not The Slaughterhouse, that's his main base and it's doubtful he'd... corrupt it. Although you just can't tell. Maybe it *was* there. It was an impulsive murder, and done by his own hand. That's unusual. She called him Fat Freddie, he had two guys hold her down while he went to work on her with a smashed vodka bottle. It's said he sliced off the rest of her clothes, then stripped her of some of her skin. Kept going 'til she died. It took maybe two, three hours."

"It's said," Angela replied. "Rumor? Image? If you know all this, why can't he be arrested?"

The woman had blinked, that was all. For a long moment Angela had waited for her to say something else, but then she'd rested a hand on Angela's shoulder.

"We won't warn you off him again. Still, do yourself a favor."

Angela had never seen the man and woman again, but she *had* done herself a favor, deleting her search history and trying to do the same with his name. Nevertheless, it was difficult to delete such imagery, such stories, from her mind.

Now she had heard his name again, and this time Vince was the direct link.

She wondered whether it had been Claudette and Harry

holding that stripper down while Frederick Meloy skinned her with a shattered vodka bottle.

"Watch out, love!"

"Sorry," she muttered as the man pushed past, a little girl clinging onto his left hand. She'd walked right into him. On a busy pavement it was unavoidable sometimes, but he'd made a point of commenting. Angela turned back and the kid was watching her. The guy seemed already to have forgotten the incident, thoughts of a day with his daughter, museums and ice cream on his mind.

Really noticing where she was, the smells, sights, and sounds flooded in. A car horn blared and several more answered in an angry exchange. Someone shouted in a language she didn't recognise. Brash pop music blasted from an open shop doorway, while three boys jigged and danced on the pavement, their baseball caps laid out for tips. Exhaust fumes mixed with the smell of fast food, the city heat cooking the atmosphere into a stew that was almost chewable. A gaggle of foreign students on the trip of a lifetime huddled along the curb like meerkats, waiting to cross.

And someone else was watching her. The sense of being observed was one that she'd felt several times before, and one she just didn't like. Memories flooded in. Once it had been a man staring at her through a pub window, his features distorted by stained and warped glass. Another time, lying in bed, the sense had come on strong and sudden, a startling paranoia that made her sit up and gasp. Vince had been sitting on the side of the bed, smiling down at her. Watching her sleep.

"For how long?" she'd asked.

"Ten minutes." He'd shrugged.

It had disturbed her far more than she'd ever let on.

Now, here in one of the busiest sections of London, that feeling had struck her again. Her skin crawled. The nape of her neck bristled. Her scalp tightened, and she ran her hand through shoulder-length hair as a pretext to turn a half circle, while a drip of sweat ran down her back. Piccadilly Circus was always buzzing, a hub of London tours and the focal point of numerous streets. It was like the city's heart from which many routes came and went and where, sometimes, people stopped to take stock or consult a map for their next destination.

She scanned the crowd for anyone recognisable, expecting to see Claudette or Harry. No one. She moved to the curbside so she could see the other side of the road. As she stepped out a cyclist whizzed by.

"Get the fuck outta the way!" he shouted.

She jumped back and bumped into someone.

Spun around, couldn't see who it had been.

People pressed in all around her.

She ducked into a Japanese restaurant and moved to the back, passing chatting diners and busy waitresses, accepting a menu from one and sitting at a table at the rear. She faced the front. The sense of being watched slowly faded, but still her heart hammered and a slick sweat broke out all across her body. She ordered a beer and sat back in the chair.

Her phone buzzed, causing her to jump.

Lucy.

"Oh, Lucy, I don't think I can..." she whispered, placing the phone on the plastic tablecloth, leaving it unanswered. She started to shake again. *What the fuck is happening? Am I really on the way to see Fat Frederick Meloy, the man who peeled a stripper with a smashed vodka bottle?*

"Yes," she muttered. Someone placed a beer bottle and

glass in front of her. She nodded her thanks and took a swig straight from the bottle, looking up at a display of Japanese art shelved all around the restaurant. *Dragons' heads*, she thought, and the image of that shrivelled, dusty thing in the package in Vince's bathroom jumped to mind once more. She remembered it as clearly as the photos no longer on her phone.

Fools pay money for old things, Claudette had said. But what Angela had seen in the apartment was more than old. It was real.

She shook her head. Couldn't accept that, no matter *how* it had looked, it could have been genuine. A prop of some kind, from a film or a stage show. Or something like one of these dragon heads, made for a horror-themed pub but never used. It was easy to fool people if they were in the right state of mind. Was *she* in the right state of mind? Of course. Her world unsettled, discovering Vince's secret second apartment and finding those mysterious packages in there… her love's involvement with one of London's worst.

Of *course* she was in a susceptible state of mind.

"Fuck it." Angela drained the bottle and slammed it down on the table. Whether the alcohol rush had emboldened her, or something had settled in her mind and shifted gears, she grabbed hold of the newfound determination. In one back pocket she carried the two notes Vince had sent her, telling her to be safe and not to look for him. In the other, Claudette's card and phone number.

It was time to ignore them both.

7

This is really fucking stupid.

She was standing fifty yards from the entrance to The Slaughterhouse. It was nestled between a TV production company and a shop selling old vinyl albums. Behind her a bustling market sold fruit and vegetables, and further along the street, past the doorway, the road opened up and became home to a couple of pavement cafés.

They were buzzing. The tables were full, and the street was alive with people going to and from work, wandering aimlessly. A few were tourists, probably come to visit the famous Soho for the first time. The district had a reputation to uphold, and there were still a couple of streets given over to strip clubs and porn shops, neon sad and wan in the daylight, but those who came expecting something sordid and dangerous usually went away disappointed.

Usually.

"Fucking idiot," Angela muttered. She was eating a tray of Chinese food she'd bought from a street vendor. She wasn't hungry, but simply standing there staring was probably a bad idea. Even though she was. The food was going cold, limp, and sad in a sea of grease.

Maybe Fat Frederick thought it was some sort of joke

calling his establishment The Slaughterhouse. After what she'd heard about him, Angela didn't find the joke very funny, and being here wasn't remotely sensible. She should dump the cooling food and walk in the opposite direction, jump on a bus at Oxford Circus and go home. Call Lucy. Share some wine with her while she decided just what the hell to do, who she could tell about what she knew.

But what *did* she know? Her boyfriend had vanished, told her not to look for him. She'd discovered that he had a secret home. She also suspected that he was mixed up in the London underworld. No one in their right mind would tell her to keep looking for him.

The Slaughterhouse wasn't an imposing place. A door, a small sign, a bell. She suspected the doorway opened onto a staircase leading down to a basement club. Anyone using it must first come looking for it, because there were no signs outside inviting casual strollers to come in and have a drink, watch a stripper. Get slaughtered.

Angela took out her phone—no new messages—and sent Lucy a quick text.

Found some stuff out. Will call later, but now I'm at a place called The Slaughterhouse in Soho. A club. You know, just in case.

She paused, deleted the last sentence, sent the message, and dumped the uneaten Chinese food in a bin overflowing with fast food containers. Glancing around as she crossed the street, she approached the doorway. No one seemed to be watching her, and that sense of being observed was absent. There was no sign of Claudette and Harry.

Climbing two steps and reaching for the bell, she noticed that the dark blue door was actually open several inches. She shoved it open some more. Inside was a brightly lit hallway and, as she had surmised, a staircase leading down, also well lit. There was another door beside the head of the staircase, leading through the wall and presumably into the neighbouring record shop.

It was closed and locked shut with a padlock.

"Hello?" she said, wincing at how weak she sounded. The sound of gentle jazz floated up from below, accompanied by bar smells that couldn't be mistaken—alcohol, stale sweat, and beneath them all the memory of cleaning products.

Everything told her to turn around and go home. Instead, Angela took one more deep breath from the street outside, then started down the staircase. All the way down she imagined what she might see when she turned the corner at the bottom. She had an image of what these underground boozing joints might look like, the hard, lonely clientele they attracted, the grim histories ground into stark concrete walls and ceiling like yellowed cigarette smoke.

Nothing could have prepared her for the reality.

The Slaughterhouse was a modern, bright bar, suffering not at all from the fact that it was subterranean. Much larger than she'd anticipated, it must have taken up basement space beneath the production company *and* the record shop, as well as stretching back some way. It was well lit, modern, and about a third filled with chatty, cheerful people. They sat at tables in couples and small groups, drinking and laughing, passing the time of day with light chatter. A few solo drinkers sat on stools at the long bar that took up one entire side wall. None of them fit the profile of the lonely drunk. They worked on tablets or phones, and one or two were reading magazines or books.

A few glanced over at Angela, then looked away again

just as quickly. One guy appraised her a little longer than was comfortable, but she was used to that. She ignored him and strolled confidently across to the bar.

"Getcha?" the barmaid said. She sounded Australian, all athleticism and healthy tan even beneath artificial lights.

"Er… a small Merlot, please."

"Where ya from?"

"Boston."

"Long way to come for a drink." She grinned and turned to the counter behind the bar, reaching for an opened bottle of red.

Angela hoped that ordering a drink would give her time to look around, take things in, and decide whether she was even at the right place.

A small stage toward the back of the room was empty apart from a chair, a guitar stand, and a microphone. Hardly the stage for a stripper. Furniture was new and unobtrusive, a mixture of tables and chairs, and a few more comfortable leather sofas and lower tables scattered around the edges. No dance floor.

"This *is* The Slaughterhouse, right?" Angela asked the barmaid when she brought her drink.

"Yep. Check out the prints? Settle up when you're done." She flashed a healthy smile and walked along the bar to serve someone else.

There were maybe a dozen framed pictures around the room, on the walls. Like the rest of the bar they were subtle, though when Angela looked closer she could hardly call them tasteful. They looked like artfully shot close-ups of raw meat, done in such a way that the stark red flesh, pink bone, and marbled fat looked like the contours and shades of fantastic landscapes. One showed a mountain range of ribs, another a red wasteland, a lonely bone tree in the middle distance.

They were really quite remarkable.

"Help you?"

Angela turned on her stool. A huge black man stood behind the bar, his expression nowhere near as welcoming as the barmaid's.

"I'm looking for... the owner," Angela said, realizing that she really didn't have a clue what Fat Frederick even looked like. Was he really fat? White or black? Tall or short? This man was more than six feet tall, extremely heavily built, and of an indefinable age. He didn't smile, nor did he frown. His face was a blank as he looked her up and down. Then he nodded toward a vacant corner sofa and started pouring himself a drink.

"Over there?" Angela asked. She picked up her drink and walked across, weaving between tables and catching a few people's eyes. A couple of them smiled, and she smiled back, wondering just what the fuck she was getting herself into. She slipped her phone from her pocket.

No service.

Perfect.

As she turned to sit on the low L-shaped sofa, the big man was already behind her, placing a glass of white wine on the table as he dropped down into the sofa's other arm.

"Like the place?" he asked.

"Yes, it's..." She really didn't know what to say. *Charming? Interesting?* Chrome and glass and raw meat on the walls. Laughing drinkers. A chirpy barmaid. Owned by a man who skinned strippers and stuck a dead man's head on a hood ornament.

"So?" the man said.

"I'm looking for Mr. Meloy," she said softly. It was easy

to speak above the low music, but conversation rose and fell in volume. The man seemed to have no trouble hearing her, though. He nodded, but offered no response. Still looking her up and down, assessing, but not in a sexual way.

"I'm worried about my boyfriend, Vince," she continued. "He's gone missing and I think Mr. Meloy..."

The man pulled out his phone and took a photo of Angela. He didn't hide what he was doing. Then he started swiping the phone screen. He raised an eyebrow and glanced up when she stopped speaking.

"Go on."

"Are you Mr. Meloy?"

The man smiled. He was scaring her, but Angela also was quite certain that this wasn't the man she sought. He had "henchman" written all over him. She checked his hands, forearms, and neck for tattoos, knowing that sometimes gang members carried art like a stamp of ownership. His skin was bare—as far as she could see, at least. She looked around the bar again instead, feeling his attention still upon her. It was maybe fifteen paces to the foot of the staircase. If she had to run—

"And?" the man said. Sharper this time, as if annoyed that she'd look away from him.

"I really need to speak to him." Her mouth felt suddenly dry. She needed a drink, but not wine. The bar suddenly felt false, the whole thing a stage with a show put on just to fool her. The laughter was hollow, the people didn't know each other, and no one was looking at her anymore because they'd been *instructed* not to look.

She shivered and went to stand.

She had to leave.

"Hang on," the man said. His phone rang and he answered calmly. "Yeah."

Angela took a sip of wine and swilled it around her mouth. It tasted good, but it was also early. It could be day or night down here and nothing would change, and that idea seemed to distance her even more from the world above.

Only Lucy knew where she was.

"Yeah," the man said again, nodding, staring at Angela as he listened. "That's the one. Okay, thought so. Thanks." He disconnected, placed the phone on the table, and drank his glass of wine in one gulp. "Come on," he said, standing to leave.

"Where?"

"You asked to see Fat Frederick, yes?"

Angela could only nod, hearing the gangster's name spoken aloud in her presence by someone who undoubtedly worked for him. In that moment, Vince's link to Frederick Meloy was confirmed. Her heart sank. Maybe this was all too much for her, maybe she should just—

"Word of advice, though. Never shorten his name," he said without any trace of irony. "Follow me." The man walked back toward the bar. He was huge but graceful, and carried himself well. Angela wondered how many people he might have killed.

"I think I should—" she began, standing, edging toward the exit.

The man stopped. "You've asked to see him now." His voice was low and quiet, but just for a second the chatter across the bar seemed to subside.

Angela suddenly craved daylight.

* * *

The sound of thunder was growing. It shook the ground and pressurised the air, driving a scream ahead of it, through the darkness. Rats squealed. His ears popped. The unmistakable smell of the Underground wafted over him— heat, electrics, the dust of ages and long-lost shadows.

Vince kicked out with his right foot and then his left, driving his feet up, back and up again, and he felt them connect with the man's stomach and chest. The man's *Ooph!* rivaled the growing storm's voice, and he staggered back, arms pinwheeling, toward greater darkness.

The silver-haired woman with pigtails.

A blade held low in each hand.

A shadow moving, squirming against a wall, shifting slowly as if sleepy or faint. It had a face that he knew.

Thunder became a roar, and the illuminated snake of a Tube train burst from the shadows a hundred meters away. It wasn't slowing. Light spilled and danced along the unused and abandoned platform, and shadows danced with it.

Vince looked at the woman he was fighting for, blinked slowly, and as he opened his eyes—

—a face appeared above him.

"Vince," Lilou said, and yes, it was Lilou from his memory, as well.

"I saved you," he said, surfacing from the waking dream.

"Yes. You're remembering?"

"Some. The Underground platform." He frowned and held up his hands.

"All the blood has gone now," Lilou said.

"No, it hasn't." He tried to sit up. His head pulsed, and he closed his eyes as pain followed. He felt her hands on his face.

"You're really not well enough to move," she said. "You

took a bad knock to the head."

"I should be in hospital."

"They'd find you and kill you."

"How long have I been here?" Vince asked. Life before seemed so very far away, almost like someone else's memory. All but Angela. Angela was fresh, and he felt a deep, hollow yearning for her, as if he already knew he would never see her again.

"She's looking for you," Lilou said. "We've tried to warn her off. A friend is following her, one of the few who can do so during the day without drawing attention, but she can't intervene. She's too weak, too unsure."

"Who?"

"Like I said, a friend."

"So where is Angela? How much does she know? What's she doing?" *She'll never understand*, he thought, and he tried to imagine the sweet woman he loved hearing even a portion of the wider, more terrible truth. She was intelligent and open-minded, but how would she take the fact that he was a murderer?

"She's visiting Fat Frederick," Lilou breathed, and Vince sat up straight, ignoring the pounding headache and grasping her arms.

"You can't let her!" he shouted. Tears blurred his vision at the agony, but he welcomed them. He *deserved* them.

"There's not much we can do to stop her," Lilou said. "We'll warn her again, but… she's not the only one looking for you."

"No," Vince said. "Of course not."

He had to go to her. That was obvious, his only course of action, and he could see that Lilou knew it, as well. She looked worried and sad. Even that expression made her beautiful.

"I have to go to her," he said.

"I know you want to."

"But you won't let me."

"It's not only me who won't let you—and it's not only yourself you'll be putting in danger. The things you know, the places you've seen… we're running out of places to hide."

"I'd never tell."

"And you're not fit. You might collapse in the street, draw attention to yourself. You think they won't torture you for information?"

"I know they will," he said, thinking of the big man and silver-haired woman, and what he had seen them doing. Brutality was their nature, and there were more where they had come from. "So you're looking after me," he said, lying down again. "Some milk would be nice. And something to eat."

"Of course," Lilou said, standing and backing to the door. "Of course."

Vince closed his eyes and smiled. When he heard the door click shut he opened his eyes again.

He might not have long.

Angela had giggled as the two of them had taken turns trying to pick the lock on their back door. It was for a research paper she was writing, and she'd insisted that practical knowledge would give her writing an edge. He'd agreed. Already he'd been keeping secrets from her, and it was a talent he'd used more than once between then and now.

He whipped off his belt and broke off the pin. Its end was naturally bent, but he was worried it might be too thick. The wider buckle part would be enough to put pressure on the barrel.

He listened carefully at the door for a few moments before getting to work.

* * *

It was daylight. For some reason that surprised him.

Vince paused for a moment with the door open a crack, looking through the window across the wide corridor and out over London, the city he'd once loved but was quickly growing to hate. From this height he could see far. If he had a powerful telescope, and knew where to look, he could zoom in on such dark secrets.

Somewhere north and east, Angela was trying to meet with Fat Frederick. She must have been investigating his disappearance, putting her research to good use and perhaps indulging her ambition of becoming a detective. Perhaps she'd found his place in South Kensington.

Those things in the bath, wrapped and ready for delivery.

"I'm so sorry," he whispered before he caught himself, squeezing his mouth closed and waiting for someone to arrive.

But he was alone, it was quiet, and he ventured out into the corridor. He'd thought that Lilou had walked to the left—he couldn't say why, perhaps a subconscious memory of hearing her footsteps through the thick walls—so he went right. Around a corner in the corridor he passed several closed doors. This was a functional place, not given to aesthetics, and he could not discern its purpose.

It didn't matter.

Walking, moving, felt good. Going forward toward Angela felt better. Any trouble she might be in was down to him, and all those secrets he had kept from her.

He wished he could have prevented himself from ever knowing them. Memories accompanied the pain when he blinked, the things he'd seen, the brutal murder he had perpetrated. It made no difference that the man had been trying to murder him.

The corridor ended at a fire door, and he rested his hand

on the handle for a few seconds, wondering whether it was alarmed. *"Hiding in plain sight,"* Lilou had said when he'd first seen past her to the illuminated London nightscape. In which case he might already be home free.

He opened the fire door and started down the deep staircase. Three floors and six flights below he nudged open a door and slipped into a carpeted corridor, decorated with tasteful prints and potted plants. He heard phones ringing and people talking, and smelled coffee and air conditioning. The quiet, busy hubbub of a large office.

Walking along the corridor toward a bank of elevators, Vince tried to look as if he belonged.

8

"My friend tells me you're looking for Vince. My friend's name is Cliff. He looks like one, don't you think? A cliff?"

Fat Frederick sat behind a large oak desk, sipping tea from a delicate bone china cup and looking like a million dollars. Angela really hadn't known what to expect. A fat, greasy-looking character, perhaps, with big rings on his fingers, jowls powdered with cocaine, and an ill-fitting suit because *no* decent suit could ever work for him. Bad skin, thin hair, a face etched with all the cruelties he had perpetrated or authorised. A man of the shadows, dwelling in them and relishing their dark touch.

"Er... he's big, yes," Angela said, glancing at the man who'd brought her here. Standing in the doorway, he raised an eyebrow and smiled, and it lit his face. It was the first real expression he'd shown.

"Anything else?" Cliff asked.

"No, we're good here," Fat Frederick said. "I'll call if I need you."

Cliff nodded and closed the door gently behind him.

"Good guy. Lost three aunties and seven cousins in the Haiti earthquake. Remember that?"

Angela nodded.

"Tragic." The man took another sip of tea, then waved at a chair on her side of the desk. "Please."

Fat Frederick must have been over six feet tall and maybe two hundred pounds, most of it lean muscle. He looked fit and healthy, and could have been ten years either side of thirty-five. His right ankle rested casually on his left knee, and he leaned back in his chair, shirt pulled across his tight stomach and broad chest.

He tapped his stomach, and Angela realised how much she'd been staring.

"What's in a name?" he said, chuckling. "Actually, I did used to be a fat bastard. Ten years ago I was... what, maybe five stone heavier? Then I discovered running. Really caught the bug. I did it at home to begin with, on a treadmill, because I didn't want to be seen. Then I started going out at night with a head torch. When I got a bit fitter, I'd go out during the day. I like the parks, and sometimes I'll drive out to the South Downs or somewhere else in the country. Places where no one knows me. It's a real stress relief, running, you know?" Fat Frederick stared at her contemplatively. "You look fit."

"I run, too."

"Job like mine, it pays to be fit." If he was inviting her to ask about his job—being a gangster, robbing security vans, skinning strippers—she left him disappointed.

Fat Frederick stood and stretched. He wore a wedding ring, seemed very laid back, casual, almost dismissive. "Drink?"

"Some water, please," Angela said. He went to a drinks table and poured two glasses, and she couldn't help staring. She'd spent so long reading about people like him, even considered coming to visit, hoping that an informal, anonymous interview would give her studies depth and weight. The SOCA couple had warned her off. Now she was here of her own accord, and although frightened and concerned for Vince, she was also excited.

She looked around the room, taking everything in. It was small and nondescript, containing the desk, a couple of cabinets, a compact leather sofa, and three chairs in front of the desk. One wall was taken up with a large picture of a forest scene, misty and lit from within by a silvery light. It might have been a photograph blown up, or an intricate painting. On another wall were images of old London, the sort that could be bought in any tacky tourist shop.

Hardly the refuge of a gangster. But then perhaps, even after all her study and research, her preconceptions were still gleaned from TV and the movies.

He placed a glass on the desk in front of her and sat back down. She almost found herself liking him, but she remembered what the SOCA woman had told her. Remembered it well.

There was a small button on the side of his desktop. A slight bulge on the belt at his hip. A fan of fine, spidery scars traced his left jawline, and the knuckles of his right hand were knotted and rough. She could never forget who and what he was.

"I'm glad you're looking for Vince," Fat Frederick said, "because I am, too." At that Angela's blood ran cold. It must have shown on her face, the fear, because he waved a hand and shook his head.

"We're friends. Have been for a few years. Vince is very good at what he does—"

"Which is what?" Angela snapped. The man blinked in surprise, and she felt a pulse of confidence. He wasn't used to people interrupting him.

Fat Frederick picked up a pen and opened a moleskin pad on his desk.

"What's your full name?"

"Why?"

"Because I'm asking." It was spoken lightly, but she had no choice but to answer.

"Angela Gough."

"Where are you from?"

"Boston, originally. London's my home now."

"Address?"

She paused, then told him. He could find out anyway. If Vince was in that deep with him, he probably already knew.

"Passport number?"

"Why would you want that?"

He shrugged, looking down at the pad. "Curiosity."

"I don't know," she said. "Who remembers their passport number?"

"Right. No worries. Cliff will see you out. Come back in an hour."

"Where's Vince? I'm looking for him. I need to find him, and I'm worried, and I know… I know your… reputation…"

His expression remained calm, casual. "Like I told you, I don't know where he is. I need to find him, too. That's why I want you to come back in an hour. We can talk about him some more, and I might even show you something."

A smashed bottle? A dumpster?

"I'm sure you'll have enough time in an hour to tell some friends where you are, yes?" Fat Frederick said.

"You don't mean him harm?" she asked, and it almost sounded like pleading.

"Why would I harm him? Vince is one of my very best

men." Fat Frederick, nothing like his name, stood and raised his hand toward the door. "An hour. There's a good coffee shop called You For Coffee, two streets over. You can wait there, if you like."

Angela stood and left, closing the door behind her.

Out in the hallway she started shaking, and when Cliff opened the door at the end of the short corridor, she had to hold onto the wall as she walked toward it. Inside The Slaughterhouse Bar once again, the tide of voices washed over her, the scent of smoke and alcohol, the laughter and good cheer. A young man was sitting on the stage, guitar propped on his knee. While he tuned and fussed with a music stand, a few jokey comments were fired his way. He responded with a smile.

None of this did anything to drown her fear.

"See you soon," Cliff said as she headed for the exit. She felt his eyes on her back.

"Vince is one of my very best men."

She tried to imagine the man she loved doing bad things, and once her mind started down that route there was no turning it back. As she negotiated her way through streets thronged with pedestrians on their way home from work or to the pub, she saw Vince punching someone in the face, pressing a sawed-off shotgun against a car window, holding down a woman while Fat Frederick slashed across her stomach with a smashed bottle. She imagined him touching her hand as they watched a DVD together, kissing her naked hip just where she liked it, singing in the shower.

The man she loved, doing things she could not understand.

"...one of my very best men."

Her phone buzzed in her pocket, startling her. Lucy. She answered and was assaulted with a verbal barrage.

"What the fuck are you doing at a place like that in fucking Soho you bloody idiot?"

"Hi, Lucy."

"Just *what the fucking fuck?*"

"The fuck is that I've found out a bit about Vince."

"You've found him?"

"Well, not yet, no." She glanced around, just one of dozens of people talking on their phones as they walked the busy streets. She didn't feel watched, but maybe the sensation was simply becoming familiar.

"Someone just phoned me," Lucy said. "Asking about you. A guy, didn't recognise him. I told him to jog on."

"That was quick," Angela said. That was what this hour was all about. They were researching her, and already they'd found out who her best friend was and her phone number. By the end of the hour they'd know the colour of her underwear and her first pet's name. "Yeah, he's going to help me look for Vince," she said.

"Yeah, right. Then why ask me about you?"

Angela bit her lip and edged into a doorway, watching the street pass her by.

"What's going on?" Lucy pressed. "What have you found out?"

"Not sure yet. There's a trail, I'm just not sure I'm following it properly. But I've discovered that Vince was... freelance, I guess." Freelance. Scouting and buying commercial property as a cover—and in the meantime he was one of a London gangster's best men, and he had an apartment where he kept weird old dusty things wrapped up in his bath.

Blinking, she saw that single dead eye staring at her, as if willing her to believe.

"This isn't a college project, you know," Lucy said.

"I know that."

"You sound weird."

"I'm fine, really. Can I come by tonight? I'll tell you more then, honest."

"Sure. Max is out playing squash. I'll buy wine. Good?"

"Yeah," Angela said, and it did sound good. All but the bit where she'd have to tell Lucy about what was going on. She wasn't sure that sounded good at all.

They said goodbye, and just as she started along the street her phone rang again. It was her mother.

"Mom?" Angela was instantly worried. She didn't like this feeling, that someone was trawling through her life and taking what they wanted—names, loves, details. It was intrusive. Abusive.

"Angela, hello sweetheart. Where are you? It sounds noisy."

"I'm in town. It's chaotic, as usual. You and Dad okay?"

"Fine, yes, he's out playing golf. I just had someone on the phone asking about you. Where you went to school, that sort of thing."

"That's fine, it's someone from the university magazine who's interviewing me." The lie came quick and easy.

"Oh, well. Fame at last! Everything else okay?"

"Yeah. Mom, I've got to dash or I'll miss my train and... Vince and I are out for a meal tonight."

"Somewhere nice?"

"Chinese."

"Lovely. Call me at the weekend?"

"Bye, Mom. Love you." Angela had the terrible thought that she might never speak to her mother again. It was a chilling, painful idea, and its gravity forced the world away from her, leaving her ensconced in her own bubble of wretchedness.

Vince, you bastard, she thought, but loving him wasn't a choice, and though she was scared about where he'd gone and what she might yet discover, her depth of feeling about him had not changed. Not yet.

She was taking action, and now wasn't the time to pause.

She found a coffee shop, and just as she ordered and sat down her phone rang yet again.

"We're ready for you now," Cliff said.

"I've just ordered coffee."

He remained on the line for a moment, saying nothing. She could hear faint jazz and the mumble of voices in the background. Then he disconnected.

Angela sighed and stirred her coffee, watching the chocolate sprinkles form a spiral in the frothy surface. She was in a spiral, too, and she'd put herself there. Maybe there was still time to climb out, but Fat Frederick knew a lot about her already, and he would probably make it his mission to find out more. A man like him put value on information, and she could understand that. As well as money, people like him dealt in knowledge. A skeleton in a closet could be worth more than a bucket of gold. A past misdemeanor might inspire devotion, the threat of a dark secret being revealed better currency than cash. Merely by going to see him, she had taken a step into his world.

Time to take another.

He had some coffee ready this time, and a couple of plates of biscuits and cakes. Fat Frederick was sitting on the small sofa when Cliff took her into the office, and as the door clicked closed behind the big man, he was already pouring.

"Milk, sugar?"

"Just white."

"You'll get a caffeine buzz."

"I didn't get a chance to drink the one I bought."

"Yes, sorry, it wasn't quite an hour, was it?"

"I guess you found out what you needed to know about me pretty quick."

"You're easy." Fat Frederick stirred her coffee and offered it up to her.

"Finding such personal information that fast isn't usually easy," she said. She'd researched several prominent and notorious gangland characters, and sometimes gleaning even the simplest piece of information became a drawn-out process.

"It is when you know what you're doing," he replied, shooting her a look. "You more than anyone should know that."

She wasn't surprised. He probably already knew her from a while ago, from that time she'd almost approached him for her studies. She wondered if he knew who had scared her off.

Pulling around one of the chairs, she sat opposite him. There was no way she wanted to sit next to him.

She eyed the biscuits, realizing how hungry she was. She couldn't even recall whether she'd eaten yet today, but it didn't feel as if she had. Hadn't felt like breakfast, and the rest of the day had been just too strange, staggered with surprise revelations and weirdness.

"Help yourself," Meloy said. Angela did, and he ate a couple of biscuits, too. She had the ridiculous impression that it was so she didn't have to eat on her own.

"So what does Vince do for you?" she asked.

"You know a bit about me," he said. "You hinted that you know of my reputation. Fact is, I'm a businessman who's found success where others have failed, and a lot of people don't like me for that. I run several bars and clubs across London, and my clientele are very loyal. I serve good booze at decent prices—real ale from local breweries, fine wines, good liquors, not knock-off stuff from Eastern Europe. I pay my staff well and look after them."

"So you're saying things I've heard aren't true?"

"Not saying that." He sipped his coffee. "Just that sometimes, stories are blown out of proportion. Chinese whispers. I have a disagreement with an associate about a business deal, four weeks and ten retellings later, he's at the bottom of the Thames wearing concrete boots."

Angela actually laughed. She couldn't help it.

"Concrete boots?"

"Just a saying. You know what I mean."

Don't let yourself get lulled by this, she thought, and she ate a Hobnob to pause the conversation. One of the many reasons she loved the UK was because of their wonderful cookies.

"So what does Vince do for you?" she asked again. She wasn't certain she wanted to know, but that was why she was here, why Fat Frederick had agreed to see her and researched her so that he knew she had no ulterior motive. She'd asked for this, and now it was time to see it through.

"He helps me in pursuit of my passion," Fat Frederick said. "I'm in business to make money, mostly so that I can pursue the one true thing that really sets me on fire. That passion costs lots of money, and Vince is very good at helping me spend it accordingly, on the right things and at the right times. I think you already know what that might be."

He leaned forward across the low table, staring at her.

"I saw something," she said, thinking of the one-eyed husk, the relic. "It was just a… thing. A model. An antique?"

"I'll tell you something," Fat Frederick said, leaning back on the sofa, hands on his knees. "But first, I need to see your phone on the table."

"What?"

"Phone. Table. Turned off. Cliff has already scanned you for bugs."

"He has?" Angela asked, surprised—but she took out her phone, glanced at the screen, and turned it off. No big deal. No service.

"I'm a collector," Fat Frederick said. "I always have been, ever since I was thirteen. You ask the police, or people seen as my contemporaries, and they'll tell you that was the time I started to go off the rails. Burglary, intimidation, violence. Some of it's true, but few know the reasons. I didn't need money for drugs or booze or women, or the power it brings. I needed cash to feed my new addiction. Relics. Not antiques, but the remnants of old, dead things. Parts of creatures and things that should have never existed."

Angela couldn't help smiling. Then she frowned.

That thing, staring at me with its single eye.

"Which one did you see?" he asked.

"How do you know I didn't unwrap all three?"

"Few people would."

"One eye," she whispered.

"The infant cyclops. Not as rare as you might think. They were pretty common maybe eleven thousand years back, when the Time was coming to an end. South and east England mainly, but there was a tribe in the Welsh mountains, and I've heard of some dwarf specimens in

Cornwall and northern France." He leaned forward again, gripped by the subject, enthusing.

"If an infant died, they'd wrap its body in clay and bury it, and the clay would harden into a kind of solid earthen coffin. Lots of the graves were plundered at the end of the Time, the bodies thrown aside and broken down by the elements, though a few remained whole. That head you saw, that sort of thing is relatively common. But a whole cyclops, infant or adult, that'd be quite something. Don't you think?"

"Hang on," Angela said. She was shaking her head, frowning at Fat Frederick, and she had all but forgotten the deeds he was known for, the things he had done. He was just a man telling her an outrageous story, and there was something about him—such belief, such persuasiveness—that shook her to the core. *He's not lying*, she thought. *At least, he believes that he isn't.*

"Hang on," she said again.

"Yeah," he said. "I know."

"Cyclops? The Time?"

"The era when all these weird, wonderful creatures still existed," he said, eyes wide with a childlike wonder. She couldn't help but like him, then, however threatening he was. He seemed like an innocent.

"But cyclops are make-believe," she said.

He raised an eyebrow. "You think that?"

That dusty old thing, the single eye watching me, staring *at me...*

"You should have opened the other packages."

"And what would I have seen?"

"A dragon's tooth, packed and ready to ship to Sweden, and a scrap of centaur's pelt. I'm a collector, but I trade in some of the more common relics. Good money."

"Dragon. Centaur."

"You're not believing me."

"Well…"

Fat Frederick laughed and waved a hand. "No worries. Really. But Vince is the best relic hunter I know. He's always insisted on working freelance, but I've been his main employer for over five years. Good guy. I'd even call us friends. He knows who to deal with, what's on the market, what it's worth, and how to negotiate. He also sometimes goes on expeditions to find them himself. Sponsored by me, of course."

"Expeditions," Angela said. She had a sudden memory— Vince returning home one evening with dust in his ear and the creases of his neck, and grazes on his knuckles. She'd noticed as soon as he walked in the door. He'd mentioned having to force his way into a property that had been sealed up for a long time, ready for it to be cleaned out for a new resident. She'd even believed him. "Of course."

"That's why I want him back. So if you know anything about where he is…" Fat Frederick trailed off.

"You think I'd have come to see you if I knew where he was?" Angela asked, aghast. "Really? Down here to see… *you*? With your weird stories and lies?"

He actually seemed offended.

Angela stood to leave. This was bullshit. She'd seen something weird in that apartment, but her mind was clouded with worry and confusion, every step shifting her further into a world she did not know. A world where Vince lied to her daily, and where shady couples followed and accosted her in coffee shops. Were they his? It seemed likely, but right then she didn't care.

She should have never come here. Turning her back on

Fat Frederick, she grabbed the door handle, suddenly certain that it would be locked. But it turned and she started opening the door.

"I'll show you," he said. "I have other things here. Amazing things. Those items in Vince's apartment were merely to trade, but I told you… I'm a collector. There are relics I'd never sell because they're too…"

"Where are they?" she asked.

"Too unbelievable," he continued, "and they're deeper." He nodded vaguely past her at the door.

A flutter of fear grabbed her, causing her heart to dance and perspiration to break out across her neck.

"I want him back," Fat Frederick said. "Vince has something. A gift, a second sense for these things. He and I have talked about it, and even he's not sure where that comes from. All I know is, without him I might never find anything else, ever again. And there are still wonders out there to be had."

Angela shook her head, but curiosity had her, now. Beneath all the fear of this man, she'd found something that seemed to be the beating heart of him. She'd come here unknown and uninvited, and here he was, laid bare, his desires and passions presented for her examination. Maybe the route to finding Vince was in indulging him.

"Come on," he said. "People know where you are, and I promise you, you're safe."

"Safe," she repeated.

"Perfectly." He stood and gestured to the door, inviting her to go first.

9

Cliff was standing just along the corridor that led back toward the bar, leaning against the wall and swiping his phone screen. From the bar came the strumming of a guitar and a soft singing voice. When Fat Frederick walked in the opposite direction, away from him, Angela saw Cliff take a couple of steps their way.

"Boss?"

"No worries," Frederick said over his shoulder. "Just watch the place for a bit."

"Sure." He eyed Angela, expression hardened by suspicion.

They passed through a door and Frederick closed and locked it behind them. He seemed to be doing his best to stay in front of her, keeping space between them, acting as unthreateningly as possible... and there was something else. He had an eagerness about him, like a kid looking forward to showing an adult something he'd made, or an amazing secret he had hidden away. He reached a metal spiral staircase, peered down, descended, then waited for Angela at the bottom, watching her step carefully down.

"How far?" she asked.

"It's the old basement of a building in the next street. Part of it's blocked off, belongs to my club now. All to do with something that happened in the war or…" He shrugged. "Something. Doesn't matter. Just along here, then through another door. There's an air lock, though, so we'll be in there quite close together. You okay with that?"

"Air lock?"

"They're delicate."

They?

Even if Angela wanted to turn and go back, she wasn't sure he'd let her, and she didn't want to get into a situation where there was that tension between them. For now she felt at ease, or as much as she could in the company of a man like Fat Frederick.

As he'd said, people knew where she was.

Lucy, and that's all. What if they kill her, too?

She froze, staring ahead at Frederick and trying to convince herself of his honesty.

"Don't you want to see?" he asked over his shoulder. And yes, she did want to see. Very much.

They stood in the air lock together, side by side with shoulders touching. It was uncomfortable, but the hissing of the air exchange kept silence at bay. A small buzz signaled the end of the procedure. Frederick flipped the handle and pushed the opposite door open.

"After you," he said.

"It's dark."

He leaned past her and waved a hand, and a series of lights flickered on. A narrow, low-ceilinged room was revealed, barely larger than a wide corridor and perhaps thirty feet long. Along one wall was a low table, four feet wide and propped on fine metal legs. On the table at regular intervals were glass display cases, maybe eight in total. Lighting was arranged above and around them in a very precise manner.

"The first one, there," Frederick said, mouth so close to her ear that she could feel the warmth of his breath. "My first find when I was thirteen years old. Come on, I'll show you."

Don't be scared. She wasn't sure whether he said those words or she imagined them, but as she walked toward the first case and saw what it contained, fear solidified around her nonetheless.

Fear, and wonder.

"It doesn't look much, I know," Frederick said, "but it's what set me on this course in life."

"It's..." Angela knew what it looked like, and the answer could so easily have been mundane. Yet here, now, she suspected it was far from that.

"The tip of a unicorn's horn," Frederick said. He reached out his hand, which hovered over the glass display case, not quite touching it. The object inside was perhaps eight inches long, vaguely pointed at one end and broken and rough at the other, ridged and cracked along its length. Its inside looked like quartz, dark and endlessly deep. "Beautiful," he whispered.

"It could be anything," Angela said.

"But it isn't. I found it when I was thirteen, almost fourteen, buried in a pile of crap at the back of an abandoned second-hand shop in Islington. I'd broken in with a couple of mates. Can't even remember their names, now, but I do remember how scared they got, and quickly. Both older than me. They had reputations even back then." He looked over her shoulder, as if into a distance. "I saw one of them—Jimmy, that's it—once I saw Jimmy beating up a kid who wouldn't hand over his bag of library books. Not as if Jimmy could even read. Beat the kid to a pulp, left him in the gutter, didn't even take the books in the end.

"So Jimmy and my other mate, once we were in the shop and rooting around, they got really scared. Picked up on the atmosphere of the place. Tasted the... strength, the age. The strangeness." He turned quickly to Angela and leaned in close. "Can't you taste it now?"

Between breaths, between blinks, she realised that the atmosphere around her was touched by more than shadows and depth. There was something more down here. It was like a terrible, unknowable *awareness*, a palpable pressure similar to knowing when someone was looking at her but much, much heavier. The whole moment felt like a powerful dream that she would never be able to disassociate from reality. She had never felt less in control of her life.

Her heart started racing, and sweat prickled her skin.

"It's not something to fear," he said, as if reading her thoughts. "I knew it back then, and that's why it was me who found this. Not Jimmy. Not that other idiot. They ran, and I never spoke to either of them again. Just me, rooting through that shop for six, eight hours, still in there when the sun came up, and then I found this. I didn't know what it was back then, just knew it was what I'd been looking for. When I touched it... He shivered. "You want to touch it?"

"No!" she said, backing away. "No, it's... not mine." Strangely that was the reason, but it covered other, deeper fears. *If it makes me feel like this, just being close, what will happen if I touch it?*

She wondered whether she was being hypnotised. She thought of how Frederick had been talking to her, the drink she'd accepted from him and sipped, the biscuits, and instantly disregarded the idea that any of them had been drugged. Though dreamlike, this was also far too real. She could smell the clinical sterility of this place, and the faint ozone smell of so many bulbs. The taste was of conditioned air and shadows, and her voice carried a strange, fragmented echo, passing down the wide corridor of display cases and fleeing back to her like a startled pet.

Her senses and awareness were all hers.

"It took me a while to discover what it was. I carried it with me, and a few days later a tramp stopped me and told me I had a unicorn's horn in my pocket. Simple as that, and I believed him. Simple as that. Old guy called Dean. I've seen him once or twice since then. He's a relic hunter, too, and has been for a while. But he's mad."

"Madder than you?" Angela asked, because nothing about this seemed even remotely sane. He didn't answer, but gripped her arm and urged her toward the next case. Even though his touch made her skin crawl, she let him, because there was no reason to fight. *I agreed to come down here*, she thought again. *Everything that happens from here is of my own design.*

In the next case lay a cast of a set of footprints, cracked and uneven but fixed together with pins.

"Jesus's footprints?" she asked.

"Don't be daft," Frederick said. "These are the prints of a woman from Atlantis. See the webbing between the toes?"

"That could be anything."

"It's what I say," he replied without a hint of defensiveness. "Here. Look at this." He moved along to the next exhibit and left Angela staring at the print casts for a moment longer. There *were* what looked like webbed areas between the toes. The feet were longer and thinner than usual, and the toes longer, as well. She tried to imagine who had made the footprints and when, and experienced a frisson of wonder. There was nothing to prove how these marks had been made, yet the idea was amazing.

"Angela," he urged. She went to him. He was already looking down into the next case. "I acquired this in my twenties, just after my mother died. Can you tell me what it is?"

"What, so now it's a quiz?"

He smiled. He was enjoying this, and she could see that it really was his passion. This was the real Frederick Meloy, literally and metaphorically buried deep beneath the front he needed to project up above.

It didn't make her fear him any less.

She looked down into the case. At first she didn't think there was anything in there, and she felt like one of those people in an aquarium, staring into an empty tank in the hope of seeing something amazing.

"There's nothing," she said.

"Look closer."

She did as he said, bending down close to the display case, holding her breath so as not to obscure the glass. She saw her own reflection and the haze of Meloy's face behind her, then she shifted her focus and looked deeper.

Something moved. It was like haze above a hot road on a summer's day, except more graceful, slower, even more fluid.

"What is it?" she asked, trying to keep the sense of wonder from her voice. She didn't want him to think she was enjoying this. She needed to maintain her projection of doubt.

"A witch's flying ointment," he said. "At least, the essence of some. A dreg. I'm not sure it would even be effective anymore, but—"

"Flying ointment?" Angela stood back from the case, and away from Frederick, pressing her back to the opposite wall. It felt cold and solid, the weight of the world behind it. "A unicorn horn? A woman from Atlantis? What fucking bullshit!"

Meloy blinked at her as if slapped.

He skinned someone alive for calling him Fat Freddie, she thought, and her legs were suddenly weak with terror, her bones fluid and ready to spill her to the floor. Just what the hell was she doing? Down in a basement, locked in with a murderer who was plainly mad, allowing herself to be fooled and led.

But he looked like a little boy right then, not a gang leader and murderer. He looked like someone who had just been told that everything he believed was a lie.

"You're just having trouble believing," he said.

"Damn right I am!" she replied in spite of herself. "I don't believe in the supernatural."

"It's only supernatural if nature doesn't allow it," he said. He looked away from her, along the long room and toward another door at the far end.

"I'm leaving," Angela said. "All this, whatever it is, has nothing to do with Vince. It won't help me find him, and I should have never..."

Fat Frederick turned back to her, and his expression had changed. Not hardened, exactly, but settled. He looked calmer and more at peace with how things were. It didn't matter to him whether or not she believed, but there was something that *did* matter.

"It's too late," he said. "I've shown you now. You've seen things that are dangerous, and rare, and which people would kill for." He blinked slowly and let the ghost of a smile soften his eyes. "Which people *have* killed for. If you breathe a word of this to anyone, you'll meet me, Cliff, and a vodka bottle."

"You *wanted* to show me!" Angela said. Fear blurred her vision.

Fat Frederick only shrugged.

"Let me go."

"Don't you want to see the rest?"

"No," she said, and she really didn't. This was weird, and combined with Vince's disappearance it was just too much. Her whole world had been thrown aslant. "You know I won't tell anyone. You're already having me followed, and until I find Vince—"

"I'm not having you followed."

"Harry and Claudette." She sounded much brasher, braver than she felt. Sweat tickled her sides, her armpits. Fear pulsed behind her eyes.

"Not mine," Fat Frederick said, but he knew who she was talking about, and she saw something flicker behind his eyes. She didn't quite know what it was. Each question inspired three more.

"I need to go. To find Vince." She craved Lucy's company, her garden, a glass of wine, a silent and friendly nod of greeting from her neighbours. She wanted normality, yet she was afraid that after today, that might be more difficult to find than ever before.

"Let me show you my angel," he said, and he walked toward the end of the room.

She could offer no argument. There was no sense that it could end at this point, either. Him bringing her down here had started something, and behind that door at the end of this strange basement, she might find its end.

So she followed the big man past display cases that she struggled not to look at, but had to.

One of them contained a smooth dome that might have been an egg, or a skull. Another was bare, apart from a small metal cup at its center, the surface of its dark contents reflecting the low lighting with an oily sheen. Angela thought one long case contained a snake of some kind, but as she passed it she saw the powdery, old shapes of suckers.

"This is the one relic I can never sell," Fat Frederick said, standing beside the door set in the basement's end wall. He smiled. "My precious." A coded electronic lock was fixed there. He reached for it, then glanced back.

His face was soft again, all pretense gone, all the self-awareness giving way to an expression of sheer delight. This was his reason for living and his drive, and he was about to share something very special with her.

Angela didn't want it at all, but Fat Frederick rapidly tapped in a code, the door whispered open, and she smelled the thing that lay beyond. Choice had long since been taken from her.

"Come on," he said. "I like to keep the door closed, even when I'm inside."

"Why?" Angela asked.

"Makes it feel more alive."

They entered the room, and for a few seconds Meloy obscured her view of what that small space contained. Then he reached back past her to press a button that brought the door closed again.

And she saw his angel.

It lay on a waist-high platform in the center of the small room. There was just enough space all around for one person to walk. Lights were fixed in the ceiling and hung from the plain white walls, casting a soft glow across that strange, impossible form.

Any doubts that Angela had retained—at the flying ointment, the unicorn horn, footprints and tentacle and oily blood—instantly vanished. The creature that lay before her was so alien, unreal, and unbelievable that she had no option other than to believe.

"Isn't it beautiful?" Frederick breathed.

Angela stayed close to him. His presence was a comfort. Whatever else he was, Frederick Meloy was still human.

"It looks…" Angela began, then she frowned. She couldn't say it aloud.

Alive.

The angel was the size of a young teenager, laid stretched out on its side with left arm extended, left leg bent at the knee and protruding slightly as if in mid-step. Its head rested on its upper arm. It was naked, with no sign of sexual organs. Its face was strange, eyes open, and as Angela tipped her head to one side its expression manifested. It was in pain.

"It looks alive," she said, so softly, afraid to wake this sleeping thing.

"I know," Frederick said.

"But it's… dead."

"Of course," he said. "All these things are dead. They have been for thousands of years."

"It looks so soft. So recent."

"There's no decay. Nothing to show that it's dead, other than…" He moved around the dais and signaled her to follow.

The angel's back was a scene of ruin. She hadn't known exactly what to expect, but as the word *wings* whispered across her mind, so she set eyes on where those objects of angelic legend should have been. The wounds glistened as if still fresh. Nubs of bone glimmered white in the artificial light, broken and splintered from the huge trauma perpetrated on this wondrous creature. The skin and flesh of its back was parted in several places, torn rather than cut, the exposed meat still appearing wet. A single white feather, the size of her little finger, was stuck in a splash of blood at the base of its spine, its ivory hue speckled red.

"I don't know anything about it," he said. "No history, no name. No clues about where it lived, or even when, nor what happened to it. It's like owning a billion-year-old fossil that you knew was once alive, but its life is so remote from you that it seems almost impossible."

"It looks like if you touched it, it might wake," she said, and she shivered.

"I've thought that." Meloy reached out and held his hand above the angel's head for a moment, looking Angela in the eye before resting his hand on its skin. Sadness painted his features. Tears formed, and his mouth screwed up, as if he was experiencing the greatest sorrow of his life. It shocked her to see him like this, and she wondered at a man like him letting down so many barriers.

"Try," he said.

Everything told her not to do it, but before she could question her actions she had reached out and placed her hand on the prone creature's bare arm.

Its skin was cold and as hard as marble.

An awful sadness filled her, and she felt her whole body slump as the weight of unbelievable grief pressed her down. She sobbed, and in those distorting tears she caught sight of Vince's face.

He was also crying.

Stepping back, banging into the wall, Angela struggled to compose herself. The feeling of deep melancholy evaporated as quickly as it had arrived, but like a dream it left dregs of itself behind.

I'll never get over that, she thought. But also like a dream—or like severe, crippling pain—she was already forgetting the details of what she had felt.

"Now can I leave?" she asked softly.

"A minute," Fat Frederick said. "You'll want another minute, just to look and wonder."

He was right.

10

Vince had never felt so exposed. So hunted. Everyone was looking at him.

Out on the streets he was the center of attention, even though the London hustle and bustle was as familiar as his lover's kiss. He walked with his head down, but not seeing gave him no comfort. They could creep up on him at any moment. So he lifted his head, watched where he was going, and met people's eyes, jigging aside to let them pass, glancing behind to make sure they didn't look back at him. Any one of them could have worked for Mary Rock. Any one of them might have a blade ready to slide in between his ribs, or a bullet for the back of his head once they dragged him into an alley, body destined to rot in a plastic bin until the garbage collectors came and found him.

Everyone he saw wanted to kill him, but Angela was in danger, and it was all his fault. He couldn't think of himself, only her. She was his focus. Everyone else could go to hell.

He never should have been lured by Mary Rock's promise of wealth. He should have remained working exclusively for Fat Frederick. He knew where he was with Meloy, at least, and he understood the big man's passion. Mary Rock… she was something else. He'd known that from the start. If only he'd listened to his inner voice before getting involved, he wouldn't be where he was now.

It only took him a few minutes to orient himself. He knew London like the back of his hand, and once he hit a main street his location was easy to pin down. Shoreditch. A way from home, but at least he knew where he had to go. His phone was lost or stolen, and anyway, he couldn't risk calling her. They might be listening and watching. They'd know that to find him they had to come through her.

He never believed it could have gone this bad so quickly.

The Tube would be fastest, but there was no way he was taking the Underground, not after what had happened. The flashbacks still surged, reddening the late afternoon light.

Someone bumped into him.

"Sorry, mate," the man said.

Vince looked at him and the man backed away. Vince hoped he saw only a scruffy, dirty figure, unwashed for a while, hungry and stinking and scared. Yet perhaps that look of sudden disquiet in the stranger's eyes was because of something deeper.

There was *always* something deeper.

When Angela emerged from The Slaughterhouse, it was into a whole new world.

She blinked at the bright sunlight, confused at what time of day it was, what time of year, and whether she was anywhere real at all. Mundane sights shocked her with their normalcy—a man tripping as he stepped onto a pavement and grabbing a lamp post for support; two young women walking side by side and chatting, eyes glued to their mobile phones; an old woman pushing a shopping trolley overflowing with tins of baked beans.

She crossed the street quickly and looked back at the door. Innocuous, innocent, it stood open a little way, and she could see Cliff's shadow inside. He was watching her and she let him, not caring. Maybe he wanted to see if her first reaction upon leaving was to reach for her phone, and if it had been, perhaps he would have been listening to her call. They must have a way. People like that would have a way to do anything.

A distant police siren sounded, and just along the busy road a man sang opera, voice merging with the tinkling of loose change and the growl of motors crawling along the street.

Angela stared back at the club's entrance until the door slowly closed.

Normal life continued, and that surprised her, considering all she had seen down in that basement. Surely people would know? Shouldn't the whole of London be stock-still with shock, amazement, and terror? She'd felt a similar disconnect several years ago when she'd had a health scare. That was pre-Vince, at a time when she was between relationships, and Lucy had been her angel.

"Angel," she whispered. She smiled at the irony, but the memory of that corpse thing quickly wiped the smile from her face. Its dead, staring eyes. Cool skin. The trauma of its back where wings had once been.

It had been a cancer scare, a lump in her breast that quickly started causing her concern and which her GP had recommended she get tested immediately. An MRI and a biopsy later and she had been pronounced clear, but for those few days, during which she had managed to convince herself that she had cancer, her whole outlook had changed.

Some of it had felt like jealousy. While she waited for a life-changing diagnosis, others continued with their normal lives, oblivious to how hers might change. In her darkest moments she had even resented Lucy.

You're born alone and you die alone. That was the saying she'd remembered, and for a while she had never felt more lonely. Then the all-clear, and she'd called home to tell her parents, and leaving that dark time behind had felt like being born again.

Just twenty feet below this street lay an angel. She closed her eyes and remembered Fat Frederick's final words to her, before they had emerged into the bar area again.

"Don't forget what I said. You can't tell anyone, and I'll know if you do. Find Vince for me. But all that aside… isn't it just amazing?"

Angela turned her back on The Slaughterhouse and started walking. She was confused and unnerved and seeking something familiar, and the sight of a Costa welcomed her in. She glanced around as she entered, suddenly certain that Claudette and Harry would be sitting waiting for her, knowing exactly where she'd be, and when. But the café was filled with people she didn't know. She ordered a coffee, took a seat at the back, and it was only as she went to sit down that she started to shake.

Biting her lip, trying not to collapse, she drew the chair in beneath her and dropped down into it, resting her head against the wall.

"Tough day, eh?" a voice asked.

Angela looked at the guy who'd spoken. Good-looking, a lot younger than her, sitting with an open MacBook on his lap and a coffee on the table beside him. He tried a smile and it faltered when she didn't smile back. Embarrassed, he looked down at his computer and took a swig of coffee.

"Yeah," she said. "Need my caffeine."

He smiled and nodded, but said no more. She guessed her expression was enough to tell him she didn't want company.

Everything she'd seen remained with her. It was as if she was still down there with Fat Frederick, looking at those things, not back in the real world where unicorns, angels, and people from Atlantis were figments of the imagination. It made her question her perception of reality, and whether everything around her was as real as she had always believed.

She brought out her phone and clicked it on, and even before placing it on the table it started pinging as several text messages came in. They were all from Lucy.

Where the fucking fuck? the last one read, and she guessed the earlier ones were similar. She smiled, and felt a rush of love for her friend. Lucy, who had always kept her grounded.

"Got your work cut out this time, honey," she muttered as she sent her friend a reply.

I'm fine. Still fancy that drink? Your place, 7pm? She sent it, drank some coffee, and moments later a response landed.

Affirmative.

Lucy must have been sitting with her phone in her hand.

Angela finished her coffee and tried to think around what had happened, what she had seen. But it was too large. Too unbelievable. Looking at her hand, remembering how it had touched the cold dead angel and what she had felt, she believed. Totally.

"Vince, you're going to owe me big time," she said. The young man glanced up, and this time Angela threw him a smile. She coveted his ignorance.

* * *

Stepping outside to the curb, waiting for a taxi, she felt someone's attention on her.

They weren't trying to hide. Harry was across the street standing outside a comic shop. Claudette emerged from a Chinese takeaway and handed him a carton of food. Neither of them looked her way.

Remembering Fat Frederick's indecipherable reaction when she'd mentioned these two, Angela jumped in a cab and told the driver to just drive, *fast*.

"Always wanted someone to say that to me," he said, but he must have looked in his rearview mirror and seen her face, because he shut up.

"So you still don't have a clue where the twat is?"

Angela shrugged, raised her eyebrows, and couldn't help admitting the truth. With everything she had seen and heard today, everything she'd discovered about Vince's secret life and the secret lives of London, she still had no idea where to look next.

They were sitting in Lucy and Max's dining room, at a table around which they'd spent many drunken evenings as a foursome, but now it was just the two of them and a bottle of rosé. Max would be home soon from his game of squash, but by then Angela would be gone. She couldn't face another barrage of questions.

Lucy stood and came to her, hugging Angela to her chest.

"He'll turn up. He's probably just... I dunno." There was nothing reassuring to be said, so Angela tried taking comfort from her friend's intent. It was difficult. There was so little she could tell her, and what she *could* convey didn't look very good. He worked freelance for one of London's most notorious crime bosses, rented a secret pad that was way above their means, and now he'd disappeared.

Beyond that...

The gangster was a little insane, driven by his desire to collect relics of mythological creatures which should have never existed but which, she was now certain, once had. Back in "The Time" angels and unicorns and cyclops had walked the land, and now they were withered dead things subject to a secret trade.

"It's all so weird," Angela said.

"That bastard doesn't deserve you."

"He's not a bastard," she said. "He might be in trouble."

"He'll be in fucking trouble next time I see him!"

"That I believe." Angela chuckled. *That I believe.* She wished she could tell, but Fat Frederick's promise hung heavy in her memory.

"Will you go to the police?" Lucy asked tentatively, her tone already providing the answer.

"And tell them my boyfriend's—?"

"A gangster."

"No, he's not that," she said, shaking her head.

"No?" Lucy asked. She took a drink. She knew so little.

"No," Angela said.

An idea was already forming.

"We need crisps," Lucy said with some gravitas. "And nuts." She started to stand and turn.

"And chocolate," Angela said. "Lots of your wonderful British chocolate."

Lucy froze and glanced back. "Fucking hell. It's more serious than I thought."

While she went into the kitchen to fetch their comfort supplies, Angela stood and looked into the big mirror hanging over the fireplace. Max had once told them they'd hung it there to make their small room look larger, but looking into it now, Angela saw a woman staring back whom she hadn't really seen before, and the reflection of a new world that she knew she must embrace.

Bigger than you thought, Max, she thought, smiling. There was no time to balance belief and disbelief. No time for doubt. An urgency bore down upon her—she had to accept everything she had seen, and open her mind to even stranger things she might yet see.

It was time to move forward.

"You look better," Lucy said when she returned. "Maybe the wine's working."

"Maybe," Angela said. "Let's have another."

As they drank more rosé together, and Lucy spoke inconsequentialities because she had no idea what to say, Angela quietly formulated a plan. She had always been told that she had a good brain—logical, ordered, and able to compartmentalise. She worked with that now. The outer her remained in the dining room, nodding and smiling and accepting her friend's well-intentioned spiel.

But inside she was filing away what she knew, separating it from speculation and guesswork, opening whole new folders waiting to be filled.

One of these she called *contacts*, and it was peopled with names and numbers she became more than eager to call.

Around nine o'clock, she made her excuses. She knew Max would be home imminently, and knew also that Lucy was trying to keep her there. Angela didn't want to face Max. She didn't want to face anyone, apart from her own reflection in the phone screen.

"Stay with us tonight," Lucy begged. "Really. I don't like the thought—"

"I feel much better already," Angela said. "Just from chatting with you, and there are a couple of people I've thought I can try. Maybe they'll know something about Vince."

"Who's that?"

"Work friends," she lied. She was disturbed to discover that she was a good liar.

"Then I'll walk you home. Or wait 'til Max gets here, and he can drop you off."

"He won't get out of second gear," Angela said, laughing. *I need to get out of here*, she thought.

"You shouldn't be on your own," Lucy said.

Angela smiled uncertainly, not knowing what to say.

"I mean…" her friend said. She shrugged. They hugged.

A few moments more and they were standing at the front door. By nine fifteen Angela was walking toward the junction at the end of the street, ten minutes from her own place, glancing back and waving at her friend's motionless shadow.

The Bear was exactly halfway between their homes. The streets around were mainly residential but usually quite busy, with shops, takeaways, pubs, parking areas, and a small police station interspersed with the rows of terraced housing. One street held more salubrious homes, mostly detached and some with front gardens large enough to park in—fancy for this part of London. As she walked along the pavement, Angela was already on the phone.

Professor Joslin was the lecturer assigned to oversee her doctorate, and he had quickly become a friend. Past retirement age, he looked ten years younger and had one of the sharpest minds she knew. He'd been in the police force until his mid-forties, after which he hit university to catch up on the education that he claimed had been denied him. He'd never told her who had done the denying, but Joslin had certainly made up for it, becoming one of the most highly respected criminology intellects in England. He was still in the same university, and as an old-age pensioner he delighted in telling her how university life agreed with him.

He was also a prolific boozer and consummate letch.

She rang him shortly before ten. "Angela, my darling, changed your mind?" It was the way he always greeted her, ever since he'd suggested they run away together. He treated it as a joke, but she wasn't sure what he'd actually say if she went with it.

"Of course," she said. "Any day, Tony, but right now I need your help."

"Right, well, it's…" He trailed off.

"I know it's late. And it's personal. It has to *stay* personal, and private, but I want… *need* to pick your brain."

"Of course," he said. She could hear him taking a drink, swallowing, clinking his glass against the phone.

"I need to know how to track down someone who's missing, and who doesn't want to be found. Who to call to trace debit and credit card withdrawals. Who to speak to about CCTV footage in certain areas, at certain times. Britain's the most watched country on the planet, and I need to be able to access that."

"Who's missing?"

"Friend of a friend."

"And the police are looking for them?"

"Just me." For a moment she thought he was going to decline, and she held her breath.

"I can text you some names," he said.

"No, no, just tell me. Hang on, I'll write them down."

She sat on a wall and dug one of Vince's notes from her back pocket. From her jacket she took the small pen she always carried.

A shadow drifted along the street, on the other side and a hundred yards away. She caught it from the corner of her eye and held her breath, watching, trying to spot where it had come to rest. She couldn't quite see. It was dusk, street lamps flickering on and warming up, and perhaps it had been a shape thrown by moving vehicle lights.

Getting twitchy, she thought. She wrote down two names and phone numbers, thanked Professor Joslin, and hung up.

At the end of the street she turned right, past a fast-food joint which always had a gang of kids hanging around outside. She dodged spatters of food speckling the pavement like bloody splashes and walked past the teens. There were fewer than usual, and they paid her no attention. Or if they did, it was silent, and directed at her as she walked away.

Angela glanced back. The kids were in their own world, bathed in the greasy light from the takeaway, laughing, joshing, and all was as it should be. No shadows slunk after her along the street.

The road was busy at this time of night and she was soon wending her way along the pavement, phone to her ear. She knew that this call was hit and miss, because the woman she was ringing might see her caller ID and not want to pick up. They hadn't spoken in years. The last time had been civil enough, but no one really needed to speak to their ex's new girlfriend.

"Hello." Maria's voice was flat and cool.

"Maria, hi, it's Angela Gough."

"Yeah, I see that. Never deleted your number. What's up? Is it Vince?"

"He's fine, fine," she lied. A group of young women approached, skimpily dressed and chirping like a flock of migrating birds. A couple of them carried bottles, and one was already staggering.

"So?" Maria asked. "It's... almost ten. Bit weird calling me after so long, and so late."

"Yeah, I know, but I wondered if I could ask you a couple of things."

"About what?"

"Well... his job. His *other* job, the one he never talks about."

"Oh, so you found out," Maria said, her voice lightening. "Took you long enough."

Angela stopped dead and leaned back against a wall. Beside her was the window of a bric-a-brac shop, and she stared at a display of brass ornaments, *Lord of the Rings* statuettes, and old kitchen implements.

"Found out what?" she asked, raising her voice as a lorry trundled past nearby. *Did she know? Did Maria know what he did, and it took me two years to find out, and what does that say about me and him?*

"Vince, and his secret life." Maria sounded doubtful now, and Angela could almost hear the awkwardness. She imagined Vince's old fiancée closing her eyes, silently cursing herself, biting her lip. There had never been any real antagonism between them, and on the few times they'd met they had actually shared a smile and got along well. Maria would have revealed any secrets long before now if she wished to do so out of spite, and perhaps she believed she'd let something slip she shouldn't have.

"It's only now and then," Maria said. "From what I understand. And he never told me much about it at all, not even who he worked for. Only that it wasn't exactly aboveboard, and the properties he sourced might be sold to people I wouldn't really want to meet."

"Yeah, that sounds about right," Angela said.

"How did you find out?"

Angela thought quickly. Maria thought she knew more than her, but in reality Vince's ex knew far, far less. Yet there was still information she might be able to provide.

"Hang on," Angela said. "Let me get off the street for a minute, it's really noisy and…"

She glanced back the way she'd come, and let her words trail off. Someone was standing there, on the other side. It wasn't Harry or Claudette, she was pretty certain of that, but she was also sure that the person's focus was entirely on her. Vehicles passed by, blurring her vision. The figure remained standing, watching.

"Hello?"

"Yeah, a minute," she muttered.

A bus passed, anonymous faces turned her way, bathed in stark light that made clones out of the passengers, downturned mouths and distant eyes. Angela hurried past the shop and paused outside a pub, and when the bus had passed and she looked again, the person had gone. A For Sale sign was stuck on a wooden stake in a house's small front yard, a lamp post rose above a parked truck, the vehicle's wing mirror protruding. Together, shadowed by the weak streetlight, perhaps they had given the image of a watcher.

"Angela?"

"I'm here. Sorry, just a bit distracted. Maria, I'm really sorry to call you, but it's shaken me a bit, that's all."

"That he didn't tell you, you mean?"

"Yeah, that."

"Shook me, too, but the extra lump of money he earned now and then always came in handy. And I was just relieved it wasn't what I thought it was."

"What was that?"

"Well, when he disappeared for a night sometimes, I got it in my head he was fucking Franca. I even tracked her down, scoped out her flat."

"His university friend?"

"Ridiculous, huh?"

"Where does she live?" Angela held her breath, worried that she'd asked too soon, blurted the question instead of being subtle about it. But after a pause, Maria replied.

"Down in Collier's Wood. I spent a couple of nights walking the street outside, until she asked me in for coffee." She laughed, and sounded sad.

"Franca's lovely," Angela said, thinking quickly, wondering how she could find the actual address of her flat. She'd never actually met her. "You *do* mean Franca White, right?"

"Franca Palmer."

"Oh yeah, yeah. She's cool, a really good friend. But with Vince, it's just… I don't know who he works for, and I'm worried it's someone unsavory."

"Unsavory, but not dangerous. That's what he told me."

"Right." Angela nodded to herself, thinking, *She knows nothing. I'm wasting my time.*

"So how are you two?" Maria asked. The phone line

crackled. Angela didn't know what Maria hoped to hear, but she could only give her honest answer.

"I really don't know."

"Well…" She paused, as if searching for words. "Say hi from me."

"Sure."

Maria hung up first.

Collier's Wood. Maybe, just maybe, but first I've got to—

The figure was there again. Across the street, standing beside a parked van, peering around the back and just visible as traffic splashed it with headlights. She blinked and it was gone.

It *had* been there. Hadn't it?

Angela started to run. She tried to appear calm, jogging rather than fleeing, but people still moved out of her way with raised eyebrows, holding an arm across a child's chest, or squeezing each other's hands and probably wondering, *What's her sad story?*

She passed The Bear without seeing if anyone she knew was outside, and by the time she entered the quieter street that led to home, she was breathless and angry. She paused on the pavement and turned to face the person following her. Fuck them. *Fuck* them! They had no right to scare her like this.

There was no one there.

When she turned again and headed along the street toward her house, she saw him.

Vince.

He was crouched behind a parked car, looking at her through its windows, and as soon as she saw him he dropped down out of sight.

In the distance, something screeched.

11

Of all the stupid things he'd done, this had to be the stupidest.

Vince had spent the last thirty minutes trying to persuade himself that he was safe. Coming home was *so* fucking stupid that, surely, no one would believe he'd ever do it.

Night had fallen, but it was never truly night on the streets of London. There were always streetlights, vehicle headlamps, the splashed neon of shop displays, illumination sweeping down from high-rise flats or display signs high above the city, and the glow of pubs, clubs, and restaurants that rarely slept. As well as the cloying exhaust fumes that settled into the city's streets during the busy days, light pollution also smeared its skies at night, less harmful but just as unavoidable.

But night wasn't only an absence of light, as he had grown to understand over the past few years working for Fat Frederick Meloy. Sometimes, night was when the normal went to sleep and the supernatural came awake.

Lately, night was a wilderness.

He'd seen Angela leaving Lucy's place, confidence and purpose in her step. His heart had jumped. It was only a little more than a day since he'd seen her, kissed her, and two days since they had last made love. In that time his world had changed more than he had believed possible, and he knew that hers had changed, too.

He had disappeared from her life. Or at least he should have. If everything he had seen, and all that Lilou had told him was true, he should never contact Angela again. The danger was too great.

Yet he could not keep away. He'd made a mess of things, but the one good thing in his life was Angela. He needed her now more than ever, and knowing that she was looking for him—knowing that she was hurting and uncertain—made him want to go back to her instantly.

That would be a stupid thing to do. He knew it. Death and danger stalked him still, and he had no wish to draw Angela in anymore than she already was.

Seeing her leaving Lucy's, Vince had known instantly that she was still searching for him. Of *course* she was. There was no way she would simply let him go. So he followed her. With every step, good sense told him to turn around and go back the way he had come. Love told him to call her name.

By now Lilou would know that he was gone, but he was also certain she would welcome him back into her protection. She'd understand his need to see Angela. She would acknowledge his confusion. He had enough to be confused about, and frankly he was amazed that he wasn't a gibbering, drooling mess.

That comes later, Vince thought, and a rush of memories assaulted him. Breathing heavily, he slipped into the shadows of a side alley while they played out. His palms were damp with sweat that felt like blood. He wished he could forget. Maybe he'd ask Lilou about that. She would know someone who could make him forget, he was sure.

Perhaps they could also wipe Angela from his mind.

The idea was shocking, and horrible, and he hurried to catch sight of her again. She was making her way along a busy street, glancing behind her now and then. His actions had caused her to become nervous, and he cursed himself for that, but it was too late for regrets.

Angela paused and stared back along the street, and Vince ducked into a shop doorway, peeking out. *I'll go to her*, he thought. *We'll face the danger together.*

Then he realised that she hadn't been looking at him. She stared across the street at a place a hundred meters ahead of him, where a truck was parked close to the curb. He squinted, shielding his eyes from the glare of the shop's illuminated display. He saw movement as a shadow shifted, but he couldn't make out who or what it was.

Lilou had warned him.

Vince moved quickly and quietly, trying to blend in with pedestrians, holding a pretend phone to his ear because no one would see him then, gazes would skim over him because to them, he was involved in another story that no one cared about. But however fast he moved, he couldn't find anyone else watching Angela. Sometimes he felt eyes on his back and turned to check, seeing only revelers and drinkers laughing their way along the street, or families keeping close together as they went from one unknown place to another. Never a watcher.

He took a shortcut down an alley and moved along a parallel street, running, finding true darkness in those back places where cats hunted and a fox screamed like a baby. It almost took him back to how things had been. But he knew that things could never, ever be the same again.

141

Emerging at the far end of their street he walked a little way, then leaned against a parked car. He knew he'd look suspicious if anyone saw him, but he had already made his mind up. He was going to wait until Angela reached home, then he'd go to her, quickly and quietly. Tell her of the dangers. Plead with her to come with him.

Lilou would protect them both.

Surprised to find tears blurring his vision, Vince wiped at his eyes and saw Angela staring right at him.

Her mouth fell open. He dropped down behind the car.

From further along the street, something screamed.

"Vince!" she shouted. She couldn't help it, couldn't hold back the terror and delight in her voice. If it *had* been him, though, he didn't show his face. As quickly as she saw him, he was gone.

The scream faded away, leaving behind it a heavy, loaded silence. She'd heard plenty of urban foxes, or cats, or other sounds in the night that she had never identified, and which the next morning had faded from memory. This one was already going the same way, replaced by a stillness back along the street from where she had come. Something waiting to happen, or pounce.

"Vince?" She looked back and forth between the car where the figure had been hiding, and the end of the street. No curtains fluttered, no windows opened, and at that moment there was no one else walking the pavements.

A car passed the street's end, lights flaring and fading again. Music from its stereo did the same. *Mumford & Sons*, she thought. *Great, that'll be in my head all night now, and I'll never—*

142

The scream came again, closer, followed by running footsteps. They sounded strange. Heavier than shoes, like something solid striking the pavement. A shape flitted through a pool of light far along the road, but it was too big to be a person, must have been a shadow.

Someone ran across the street from left to right, no more than thirty yards away. They were fast, feet barely touching the ground.

"Vince?" she said, quieter than before. She started backing away, watching as the shape melted into the shadows between a parked car and a white van. If it was Vince, he'd answer her. He would reveal his presence, not try to hide away and frighten her. She'd first seen him in the opposite direction, but then heard those footsteps as someone ran. Heavy shoes, *clop clop clop*, and maybe he'd been followed and was trying to shake them.

Angela pulled her keys from her pocket, and backed along the pavement.

Another scream. This one sounded different, more filled with anger and rage than anything else. Flowing with bloodlust.

She gasped and tripped over a broken paving slab, hitting the ground hard and clasping onto her keys. She quickly scampered to her feet, just in time to see the shape dart across the road again… and something else following it.

It was this second figure that screamed, and which was making those heavy footsteps, and Angela could see why. It was huge. The biggest man she had ever seen, incredibly fast for his size. She opened her mouth to shout something—a warning, a cry of shock, an expression of fear. As she did, the first figure tripped and fell against a parked car.

"Vince!" she cried again, because she was certain now

that the fallen shape was her love. And then, just as she stepped past a parked motorcycle and out into the road, the pursuing shape hit him.

It started kicking hard, then stamping. The sounds were awful, rapidly changing from dry crunching to something altogether wetter. Another cry rang out, from a different throat than before. It sang of hopelessness and untold agonies.

"No!" she screamed. She couldn't see clearly, but yellow streetlight glimmered on the spreading pool of black blood.

The attacking figure, tall and powerful and snorting with effort, lifted its head and looked at her.

Angela thought about backing away, but her feet would not move. She gripped her keys so hard that she felt the kiss of warm blood cooling as it dripped from her palm. Her heart hammered, so loud that she could hear little else but the buzzing, pulsing beat.

The goliath stared at her for a long moment. He tilted his head to one side, scratched at his bearded chin. Then he delivered one final, massive stamp on the fallen body. Angela heard a sickening crack, and saw blood and other matter splash across the side of the parked car.

A gasp escaped her. Her heart seemed to stop.

She took a step forward, and the big man dashed across to the opposite sidewalk. He flitted behind parked cars, seemingly dodging the splash of street lamps, and the shadows swallowed him far faster and more completely than they should have. Heavy footfalls faded quickly to nothing. Angela blinked and he was gone, almost as if he could have never been there at all.

"Vince…" she whispered, stepping toward the wet shape huddled down beside a car, splashed across its metalwork, pieces of crushed and torn meat sitting in wet puddles on the tarmac. "Help," she said, barely more than a breath. Then she was shouting. "Help me! *Please help.*" She looked at the rows of houses on both sides, amazed that no one had heard and come to her aid. Several curtains twitched and fell back into place, a door *snicked* closed, silence fell.

"Won't somebody help me?"

She couldn't force herself to move any closer. She didn't want to see. She could smell him—blood and warm meat and shit—and in the weak light she could see the inside parts of her lover that should never be seen, a terrible intimacy.

A car turned into the street ahead of her, drove for a few seconds, and paused. She blinked against the full-beam headlamps, then held up her hands as it crept along toward her.

Crime scene, she thought. *Murder. I've got to call the police now, because there's nothing else to do. No reason not to. No reason to go on.*

Angela sobbed, a shuddering cry that wracked her body and cramped the muscles in her shoulders. The car came on, pausing only when it was right next to the bloody ruin in the road. A door opened, vague behind the glaring lights.

"Please," Angela said.

"Oh, dear," a deep voice said.

And then the man chuckled softly.

Another door opened. "Come with us."

Claudette.

Angela took a step back, nudging against the parked motorcycle. She could run to her door and unlock it before they reached her, slam it behind her, through to the back garden and up the fire escape to her upstairs neighbours, bang on their door, get inside and call the police—

Then Claudette was standing in front of her, the woman's

slight form silhouetted against the car lights, and she held something in her hand.

"Come on, now. Quietly."

"But…"

Claudette glanced back at the car.

"Don't worry, Harry's on it."

Angela heard the scrape of metal against tarmac, then a sucking sound as something wet was scooped up. "Oh, fucking gross," she heard, then Harry chuckled again.

"No," Angela said.

"Yes," Claudette said. She reached out and touched a gun against Angela's stomach. "Yes."

Angela went with her and fell into the car's rear seat. There was someone else there, a much older man, who barely glanced at her. The car rocked as Harry opened the boot. Metal clanged, then a heavier thump as a bag or bucket was dropped in.

"Here," the old man said. He leaned across the back seat, and Angela felt a brief sting as something was pressed against the back of her hand.

Harry and Claudette got into the front of the car, moving in slow motion, slower, and then Angela's world sank away to nothing.

Some of the street lamps weren't working, and those that were cast weak glows, light filtering through decades of spider webs and dust coating the covers. Oases of comfort glowed behind curtains, some of which twitched and settled again as she walked by.

She wondered whether people had seen what had happened here, but could never ask.

Closer to the address Vince had given her she felt violence on the air. It wasn't a sensation that pleased her, like it did some of the others, because Lilou was built for love, not war. She couldn't understand how anyone might be attracted to such heavy, hot rot.

She had arrived just too late. The whole scene pulsed with the sense of having so recently ended, and when she moved carefully along the pavement, senses alert, sniffing the air for danger, she felt control slipping even further away.

The warm London air tasted of despair and the slick blackness of death, sounds traveled as if dampened by an atmosphere thickened by screams, and she smelled blood.

Not just the suggestion of spilled insides that manifested after any act of violence. Actual blood, and a lot of it.

She sought it out quickly and found the gruesome evidence on the road. Black in the night, there was still no doubting. She knelt and reached out her hand, touching her fingertips carefully, delicately, against the sticky mess.

Lilou stood and breathed in deeply, trying to rid her nostrils of the stink. She willed away the memory of violence and imagined distant places she had not seen for so long—wide open countryside with blossom-filled trees dancing to the breeze, sunlight dappling soft forest pools, flowers blooming with confidence and hope for the future. It was a trick Mallian had taught her. She didn't fully understand, because she was nowhere near as old as him, but for now it was all she could do.

Mind settled, she passed her fingertips beneath her nose and inhaled, and her heart sank as she fell to her knees. Tears burned. Her sight blurred.

In the distance a fox barked twice, and Lilou jumped to

her feet, head tilted. After a brief pause there came two more barks from further away. The fox was fleeing danger.

With a heaviness to her soul, so did she.

Mallian would need to know.

12

Vince asks her to marry him.

It's as she always imagined it, and although she used to regard herself as a modern woman, their relationship casual and beautiful and not needing anything to validate it or to make it more secure, a wedding has always been something she imagined in her future. She's tried to analyze why this is, and still isn't sure. Perhaps it's a scrap of traditionalism left over from her upbringing, but then her parents never pushed her toward marriage, employment, or two-point-four children.

Her father always told her to follow her dreams, and her mom said happiness is more about what you feel inside than what others expect of you. She's thought it through many times, occasionally chatting with Vince about it, though never in a serious way. He's been open to the idea, but it's never been a big thing between them. Not like having kids.

In the end, Angela has decided it's all about the fairy tale.

She was smitten with fairy tales as a child, as most children are for a certain period of time. Many grow out of it quickly, when reality starts to assert itself and all those stories of fantastic creatures and places become shadowy aspects of the imagination, instead of real things that can almost be touched. She held onto the dream a little while longer, and it was always the happy endings that set her imagination on fire.

And they all lived happily ever after. It was a magical phrase that she's tried to carry into adulthood. Something about standing in front of family and friends, confirming their love, exchanging rings, has always made her believe she could accept those words for herself.

They're walking through Hyde Park at dusk, having just been for a nice meal and a bottle of wine to celebrate their fourth anniversary. At least, she said it was their fourth, as it's the anniversary of their first real date. Vince protested, and said they should celebrate the day of their first kiss. That had been on their second date, three days later.

"So shall we get married?" he asks.

"Really?" she replies.

"I was hoping for a better response than that."

They stop, standing close to an enclosed pond where ducks, swans, and geese are settling as the sun smears itself down into the skyline. The air carries the smell of hot honey-roast nuts from a seller across the park, and elsewhere a group of people sing and dance, surprising choral perfection cutting through the more mundane sounds of the city.

"Of course," she says, delighted and surprised. It's already been a perfect evening. "I suppose you'll want sex now."

"Well, not *now*. Not with, you know…" He tilts his head to the side. "…the ducks watching."

They kiss, and when she pulls away something changes. The singing breaks in tone, becoming angry. A duck quacks, water splashes, violence erupts somewhere out of sight. Vince's smile fades away.

Without any change to his features, he becomes a stranger. She no longer knows him at all. He still holds her close and tight, and as she takes in a breath to scream in his face, he smiles.

"Old One-Eye is watching you," he says.

Angela closes her own eyes and screams.

A hand clamped down across her mouth. She opened her eyes and saw the inside of the car, and remembered immediately what had happened. The hand tasted old, dusty, as if it had been unused for some time.

"Shush, now," a man's voice said. "No use screaming. We're not going to hurt you." He moved the hand away.

"Vince," she said.

"Yeah, well..." Claudette said from the front seat. She didn't elaborate.

Angela shrugged herself upright. The back of her hand stung, her head swam. She felt sick, but she didn't think she had been out for long. Claudette was still driving, and the streets of London flitted by outside. She tried to make out where they were, but couldn't be sure. Familiar chain shops and restaurants meant she could be anywhere.

"What do you want with me?" she asked.

She remembered the big man stamping down on Vince, that final stomp that crushed and cracked whatever was left of his head.

And she remembered Harry scooping up his remains with a shovel.

Sickness rolled around her stomach and prickled sweat across the back of her neck. The old man beside her dropped an empty carrier bag in her lap, but she brushed it aside. If she was going to puke, she'd do her best to spray them all.

"Mary Rock wants to chat," Claudette said.

"Mary Rock?"

None of them replied. Angela stayed quiet. It was a name she had only come across once or twice, in her studies, and someone she'd quickly come to think of as a modern urban myth.

"You're shitting me," she said.

Harry turned around in his seat, looking at the old man and smiling.

"She thinks we're shitting her."

"You think we're shitting you?" the old man asked. Angela looked at him properly for the first time. He could have been anyone's grandfather, maybe seventy years old but carrying his age with grace and style. He looked fit and strong. His hair was shaved close to his scalp, and the small gray goatee he sported gave him a distinguished air.

"Yes, I do, Gramps," she said.

The old man's smile only slipped for an instant before returning. "My name's Kris, with a 'K'."

"You're a prick with a 'P'."

"Do you really need to be so foul?" Kris-with-a-K seemed genuinely offended, and Angela burst out laughing. It sounded manic, and quickly headed toward tears, so she turned away from him and looked through the window. She could see her own reflection, and the grief and terror in her eyes.

Vince was gone. He had come to find her, hidden away when she saw him, and then died out there in the street, in front of the place where they had grown to love each other. No one had come to help.

Reflected in the glass was herself without him. It was jarring and awful.

"What would Mary Rock want with me?" she asked.

"None of us presume to know what Mary wants," Kris said. At that, Claudette turned on the car stereo and started playing Metallica. Pounding drums and bass, thrashing guitar, and growled lyrics formed a theme to Angela's grief as they headed into wider streets with larger houses on both sides.

Her breath misted the window, faded, misted again. Her forehead bounced against the glass as it vibrated. Lucy wouldn't miss her until morning, her neighbours wouldn't notice her absence for days. For the rest of the night she might as well have never existed.

She was shaking with sick loss, and a desperate sense of unfairness at a world that could give her Vince, and then take him away again. She inhaled and smelled his breath. She blinked and saw his smile. Shock still numbed her, and she guessed that was good. To lose herself now would be to submit any control she had left.

Vince would want me to survive!

Examining her surroundings through the unmisted window, trying to keep track of where they were going, she slipped her left hand toward her jeans pocket. But her phone was gone. Of course it was. These people were professionals. When she'd mentioned Claudette and Harry to Fat Frederick, she'd seen a glimmer of something in his eyes that she realised now might have been fear. If a man like that feared Mary Rock...

Right then she couldn't find it in herself to be scared. She existed at a strange distance from the world, a chasm ringing with echoes of a cracking skull and a terrified scream, and memories of a dream that never was.

"So you're her goons," she said, not even bothering to raise her voice above the music. "That's what they call people like you, isn't it? Goons. You do her evil bidding. Execute competitors. Run the drug supply networks. Collect protection money." She glanced at the others in the car, and Kris was staring at her, frowning. Almost as if he'd heard. "Goon," Angela said, louder.

Kris looked away.

Angela searched her memory, tried to recall what she'd heard about Mary Rock, and it didn't take long. Where Fat Frederick Meloy perpetuated the myths surrounding him, Mary Rock was altogether a more obscure figure. More Keyser Soze than Al Capone, hers was a name uttered with a smile or a raised eyebrow, as if the speaker was never quite sure if they were subject of a joke. Rumour had it that she was an enabler for the obscenely rich, the wealthy criminals, and often a combination of the two. She made things possible. Illegal things, wrong things, yet she always remained several steps removed.

Angela found that she didn't give a shit whether Mary Rock was real or not.

The car turned left into another wide street, this one lined with mature trees and with very few cars parked on the roadway. The houses here were hidden behind tall walls or banks of shrubs and trees, the driveway entrances mostly guarded by stone pillars and metal or timber gates. A few of them stood open, most were closed. They drove toward an open driveway, Claudette taking them through without pause.

Darkness intensified as they left the streetlights behind. The gardens were heavily planted, mature growth sheltering deep shadows and huddles of shrubs that writhed and flexed as the car's lights washed over them. Wheels whispered over gravel, a smooth ride, and they soon slowed to a halt in front of a large house. Claudette had swung the car around so that the house was on Angela's side.

It was big, but not imposing. A two-story facade of London brick, door in the center, two windows to either side on both levels. Curved steps led up to the front door, and an attractive flower border separated the building from the stark driveway. Trellises adorned with climbing roses clung between windows, and low-level lighting illuminated the house, both from eaves-level and from down within the planting beds. Several security cameras were visible, small and subtle.

Angela made out a couple of outbuildings which might have been garages or workshops, but other than those the property seemed unremarkable. Somewhere she'd never hope to live, sure, but nothing that wasn't repeated across London five thousand times over. The place projected a restrained opulence, a shy, almost apologetic luxury.

"Come on," Claudette said. "Time to see the lady."

"Fuck you."

Claudette sighed. The atmosphere in the car changed. The three people looked at each other, each of them waiting for another to talk.

"Look, we're not going to hurt you," Kris said.

"After what you did to Vince?" She could barely talk. Once again, voicing what she had seen felt like acknowledging it, externalizing it, and making it real. She didn't feel ready for that. Not in front of these bastards.

"That wasn't us," Claudette said. She turned away from them all, stared out of her window into the dark gardens.

"Bullshit!" Angela shouted.

"It wasn't!" Harry said, like a kid accused of stealing a bike. "You were quick enough to… to scoop him up."

Harry smiled. "Would've been a waste otherwise."

She wanted to say more, scream some more, reach out and hurt every one of them, but her voice had stopped working, stolen by tears, and she could only use her arms to hug herself.

Kris got out and came around to her side, opened the door, and gently cupped her elbow.

"Come on, now," he said. She let him guide her from the car, and when her legs weakened he held her up. "We're really not going to hurt you."

Maybe it was his age lending gravitas, but she found herself believing him.

They waited at the bottom of the steps while Claudette opened the front door. She and Harry disappeared through it, and moments later Harry emerged and waved them forward. Kris guided her up the several stone steps and inside.

They stepped into a large hallway, with a wide staircase heading up on the right and doors leading off on either side. Most of them were open. Paintings hung on the walls. They looked original, and expensive. A corridor led past the staircase, and at its end another door opened onto a brightly lit kitchen. A shape passed the kitchen door and glanced out at them, uninterested. The man was wearing a chef's outfit, and the smells of cooking wafted out to them.

Angela hadn't eaten for a while, but she didn't feel even slightly hungry.

"Dining room?" Kris asked.

Claudette and Harry stood close to the staircase.

"Not today," Claudette said. "Take her through to the library." She nodded toward a door to the right, and Kris guided her that way—his hand on her arm gentle but insistent. As he did Angela looked left. The dining room door was open a crack, and she only caught a glimpse, but it looked like it was being prepared for a large formal feast.

They entered a living room that betrayed signs of a family in residence—spilled DVD cases next to the massive TV, dolls lined on the leather sofa as if to watch, several board games stacked on one of the wide alcove shelves. There were paintings and other works of art. The carpet was deep and lush. Angela thought they probably shouldn't be in here with their shoes on.

She barked a laugh, then looked down at Kris's feet.

"Mess up the carpet," she said.

He didn't respond.

Kris opened a door at the rear of the living room and they passed through into a library. It smelled shockingly familiar, with the must of books, dust, and the faint, warm scent of old leather-bound volumes. She'd been in many libraries before, public and private, and they always made her feel at home. Being surrounded by so many stories made her feel a part of things.

Here, now, she only felt alone.

She looked around for a phone, but there was nothing. Just several comfortable chairs, a couple of beanbags, and a large, low coffee table scattered with books and a few used mugs. In one corner was a child's section, a splash of garish colour amongst the browns and reds.

Another door on the other side of the library opened, and Claudette stuck her head in.

"She'll be here soon."

"Will she want me here?" Kris asked.

"Dunno." Claudette disappeared.

"Take a seat," Kris said to Angela.

"My boyfriend's dead."

"Just take a seat."

She didn't know how she was staying so composed. The distance that had fallen around her remained. She thought perhaps this strangeness, and everything that had happened since Vince failed to come home, was enforcing a calm. She should have been raging in grief, inconsolable, unable to think or walk straight, yet she felt remarkably composed. Guilt dug deep at that, but she was also eager to accept such composure. She'd need it.

Something more was happening here, and she wanted to know what. She had seen a murder—

Vince. I saw Vince kicked to death in the street.

—and when the time came, she wanted as much detail as possible to tell the police.

The door opened again and a small, gray-haired woman entered the room. She was black, wrinkled, old, yet she carried herself with such poise it was very hard to pin down her age. She walked directly toward Angela, looking her straight in the eye. As she did so, she smiled.

"Please, take a seat," she said. "Coffee?"

"Yes, please."

The woman nodded at Kris, who walked past her and out through the open door.

"You're Mary Rock?" Angela asked.

The woman's smile remained as she nodded her head from side to side.

"From time to time," she said. "It's a name that has its uses."

"So what do I call you?"

"Mary is fine. Please... sit." She spoke quietly, but with

a command in her voice that Angela felt compelled to obey. She reminded her of an old school principal. Although Mrs. King had been white, much younger, and large, her voice had held the same tone. Confidence, conviction, control.

Angela sat in one of the armchairs, and Mary Rock lowered herself into another.

"You've had a trying couple of days," Mary said.

Angela said nothing. She still didn't know why she was here. Somehow insulated from the shock of what she had seen, and the grief—like an observer viewing a recording of events rather than living them herself—she vowed to take advantage of that condition. She would gather all the information she could about these people, and end them. They had a part in what had happened, and blame must come home to roost.

Yet Mary's relaxed and confident demeanour wasn't the manner of a murderer.

"We have a lot to discuss," the old woman said. "Some of it might be a surprise to you, and most of it, I'm afraid, you're not going to like. Before we start the conversation, however, I want you to see something."

"And what's that?" Angela asked.

"My fairy." The woman's gaze did not falter. She did not betray Fat Frederick's childlike glee, but neither did she appear to be waiting for a reaction.

"Boring," Angela said. "Already saw an angel today."

"You saw a dead one," Mary Rock said. "Follow me. While we walk, I need to lay out some ground rules." She stood and turned her back on Angela, just as Kris opened the door and entered with a tray containing coffee cups and a cafetiere.

"Dead?" Angela asked as she stood.

"We'll have it when we return," Mary said to Kris.

"You're showing her?" he asked, looking aghast.

"Why not?" Mary said, glancing back at Angela. "We need her on our side, and she looks like a woman who cares."

"Dead?" Angela asked again. "As opposed to what?" But Mary was very much in charge of this conversation.

"Oh, and by the way," Mary Rock said, "that bastard Vince is still very much alive."

Angela expected to be taken down to a lower level, but Mary Rock led her through the busy kitchen into an annex, and then up a narrow staircase at the rear of the house. There was a small landing, then another twisting staircase that curved up into an attic area.

"Don't try to touch it," Mary said, and she wasn't even slightly out of breath. "It's protected by an electronic field, so you'll get electrocuted."

"What do you mean, Vince isn't dead?" Angela's thoughts were in turmoil. Her skin tingled, her insides buzzed as if from electricity. *Can I really afford to believe?* She wanted to sit down and gather herself, center her emotions, and try to pin down exactly what was happening here, but Mary would not stop. So Angela had no choice but to follow.

"Just what I said," she said, "but we'll talk more about *him* later." She said "him" as if spitting a vile taste from her mouth.

"If Vince isn't dead, then who—?"

"If you discuss with anyone what you're about to see, they'll never believe you. You'll be regarded as a fool. Mad. And you'll put yourself in terrible danger."

"From you?"

The attic was lit by a couple of bare bulbs, and there

were no nods to aesthetics. Not even carpet. Mary crossed the open space and paused by an innocuous wooden door. It looked old, warped in its frame, but Mary lifted a small timber hatch to reveal an electronic lock pad.

"Make no sudden movements," she said, fixing Angela with her gaze.

Angela smiled uncertainly, holding back a laugh. The smile slipped when Mary's stare did not alter.

"What have you got in there?" she asked softly.

"I told you." Mary tapped in a code. Angela tried to watch, but the woman shielded the pad with her body. The door hissed open. The timber was merely the facing to a modern metal door, with multiple locks and several small, purple lights that ran down its leading edge and must have been some form of alarm. She stepped through.

Angela followed her inside, and the door whispered shut behind them.

The room was lit by a subdued, bluish light, smoothing the bare walls and ceiling and washing across the lowered area that took up more than half the space. The two of them stood on a narrow walkway, and in a sunken pit below them—beyond a fence of narrow electrical wires on porcelain stems—was the fairy.

It was old, dusty and dead, just like the angel she had seen at Fat Frederick's place. Coming in here, Angela had held only a shred of doubt, and as she stood there and stared, everything she had so recently experienced winnowed that doubt down to nothing.

The fairy was the size of a toddler, probably no more than three feet tall. It was displayed curled in on itself as if asleep, its graceful hands folded beneath its head, athletic legs drawn up so that its knees almost touched its chest.

Even in death it retained an ethereal beauty, but there was also something troubling about the remains.

Lacerations, grazes, and impact wounds scarred its body.

Angela moved slightly to the side and crouched a little, looking closer at its face. The creature wore a frown, fossilised there forever and giving it an eternally sad visage. She wondered how it had died. She wondered who or what had killed it.

"It looks so sad," she said.

"It is," Mary Rock whispered.

Angela frowned, went to ask something more...

...when the fairy opened its eyes.

13

The safe place was close. It wasn't the only one in London, but this was the main one. Over the years the number of safe places had diminished. Some were discovered by those who searched for Lilou and her like, as moments of violence and upheaval were quickly followed by long periods of silence and stillness when they went to ground.

They were good at doing that. Hiding had become second nature to them. But more and more recently, they'd had to expose themselves and put themselves at risk.

As she moved, Lilou turned heads. She could not help it. Moving past a pub on the opposite side of the road, she saw several faces turning her way. Some were drinking on the street outside, but a couple of them watched her through the windows, glasses half raised and their thoughts no doubt tumbling, stuttering, losing themselves as they watched her enter and leave their lives again so quickly.

Deeper urges stirred, but she had learned long ago to master them.

She maintained caution, because the sticky blood was still on her fingers.

Avoiding illuminated areas as much as possible, wearing the darkness like clothing, Lilou made her way through the streets and back home. It took her longer than it had on the way out, because of what had happened. She was not really scared, but she was aware that danger might even now be stalking her. Senses alert for the stench of him, the sound of his heavy footsteps pounding in pursuit, the sight of his form breaking cover and coming at her, she counted as a blessing every second that passed.

She reached her destination at last, and it was then that she turned and ran back the way she had come. There were still no signs of pursuit. She circled the area, ducked into an alley and waited for half an hour, then moved again. At last, certain she was alone, she climbed a drainpipe, scampered across a roof, and dropped down on the other side.

Muscles singing from exertion, breathing labored but silent, she entered the building through a maintenance door and hid in a cleaner's cupboard to gather herself.

The sense of anger and grief was rich, but she would not let it possess her until she was completely safe.

At that thought she gave a silent, bitter laugh.

Safe? Where, when, and what is that?

Calmed down, listening intently, opening the door carefully, she left the cupboard. It was almost midnight, and the offices were empty. They took up all but three floors of the old tower block. A few low-level security lights remained on, and here and there dormant computer monitors cast a sterile blue glow over workstations scattered with family photos, files, and empty food wrappers. Spaces more used to bustle remained silent, and the whole atmosphere was one of a held breath.

She drifted through several reception areas as she went from one stairwell to another, using certain doors that were not alarmed, passing security cameras that were disabled.

Some of the corridors she traveled seemed unused, peeling paint resembling shed skin in the weak security lighting. Others were secured with locks that only a handful of keys opened. The safe route through this building was invisible, and known only to a few.

At last Lilou reached the upper floors. She used her own key to exit the staircase, and then she slumped against the wall, breathing deeply. Pent-up emotions threatened to flood through her, but she had to hold on. She wasn't the priority here. She wasn't the only one who would mourn.

She passed a couple of rooms where others like her slept, and one place where someone watched. The man knew who she was—if not, she'd have been dead already—but he was confused at the grief and turmoil she was exuding.

"What is it?" the man asked.

"Mallian has to know first."

She slipped into the large central room, cut off from the outside and the only place on this floor which benefited from utter darkness. Closing the widened, heightened door gently behind her, she muttered the words none of them ever wanted to hear, but which they heard too often.

"We've lost another."

Mallian stirred. She could smell him, the rich, spicy scent of age and strength. His presence was heavier than the darkness, thicker. He scared her then as much as he ever had before, but they all loved him without reservation.

"Was it Sandri May?"

"Yes," she said, voice breaking. The pain was biting in, now that she was here. She'd kept it at bay to make it home, but having arrived, all she wanted to do was grieve.

She heard Mallian's intake of breath, and then a gentle exhalation.

"I sent her to follow Vince's girlfriend. Make sure she was safe."

"The woman wasn't our concern." His voice was deeper, stronger. Lilou could feel the air move around her as he spoke, and a subtle vibration that traveled through the floor.

"She *was!*" Lilou protested. "After what he did for me, for *us*, it was the least we could do." She leaned back against the wall and slid down, drawing her knees up and hugging them. Closing her eyes made no difference in the darkness, nor in the terribleness of it all.

There weren't enough of them left. Every loss was a tragedy.

"Lights," Mallian whispered, and the room was slowly illuminated.

He sat on his bed, naked and magnificent. Ten feet tall, muscled, scarred and marked by conflict, he exuded age and strength. Yet Lilou knew that he had a more vulnerable side. She had once told him that he cared too much, and his reply had been, *"That is impossible."*

The last of the Nephilim had already begun to cry.

"I knew Sandri May for a long, long time," he said. "I first met her on the Persian Steppes, long before that place even had a name. Just a wild, untamed land of hunter and hunted, survivor and prey. There were mammoths in the land then, and even a few saber-toothed cats remained, here and there. It was a world that knew humanity, yet remained unchanged by their stain.

"She feigned indifference when she first saw me. She pretended not to be afraid. I liked that strength in her, and we became friends. We travelled east to west, slowly, spending centuries making the journey, and we saw humanity change on the way. For better or worse—we weren't sure at the time. Over the years, we came to know together. The Time was already long over by then, but it didn't seem so to us, not really. We parted company, sometimes for decades, but we always found each other again. We would have so many stories to tell."

He drifted a little, as if silently reliving some of those tales. Perhaps one day Lilou would ask him to share, but not today.

"She sometimes made me angry," he continued. "Other times, I loved her." His voice shifted from reflection to anger. "Was it *them*?"

"I don't think so, not this time. Sandri May was... shattered. Smashed to pieces. I think Ballus is back."

Mallian's eyes opened wider in surprise.

"I thought he was gone."

"We all did. Down deep, or crawled away somewhere to die."

"We should have never just assumed." Mallian narrowed his eyes into slivers of hate. "He might be one of us, but that bastard has to die."

"Fat Freddie is an idiot," Mary Rock said. She took a delicate sip of her coffee. By the time they'd returned to the library, the coffee Kris had brought was too old, so she'd sent him to bring more. After delivering it he had left the room without being told, and now there were just the two of them.

"He killed someone for calling him that."

"If so, that makes him doubly an idiot," she replied. "Mostly he's a fool because he can't understand the wonderful."

"He seemed pretty besotted with his dead angel," Angela said.

"He's a good actor. What gangster isn't? How do you think he got where he is?"

She wasn't sure Mary expected an answer, and she had none to give. She had no wish to discuss brutality and murder. She'd seen enough already.

"How many are there?"

"I don't know for sure," Mary said. "Their time has been and gone. Their numbers are fewer because of your boyfriend."

"Meloy told me Vince is his greatest relic hunter. He knows what's on the market, where to go, where to look."

"He knows how to kill them."

"Vince? Killing them?"

"That's where the real money is. He murders the rarest, most wonderful beings in order to sell their body parts to collectors, and others who use pieces of them in quack medicine. It's ivory poaching taken to the nth degree. A harvesting of the rarest things known to man, simply for profit. It doesn't even matter if they're fresh. It's usually better if they aren't. Meloy explains it away by telling his customers the parts don't putrefy."

"Incorruptible," Angela said.

"Like a saint's heart."

"Vince wouldn't do that. He wouldn't go out there and kill these things. If he even knew about them he'd be… amazed. He'd be in love with the idea of them." *As am I*, Angela thought, remembering the fairy opening its eyes and gazing at her, following her movements as she walked back and forth across the small platform. Such alien eyes, so knowing. She shivered even thinking about it. She wasn't sure she'd ever be able to sleep again.

"Then you don't know him as well as you think," Mary said.

"You're protecting the fairy?" Angela asked.

"Out there, in the streets, it'll be hunted and killed. It

doesn't like being here, but it's weak. It knows what I'm doing and appreciates it."

"*Why* are you doing it?"

Mary frowned at her as if it was the world's most stupid question. "Because they're beautiful, and they need protecting."

"So if it wasn't Vince, who *did* I see killed in my street?"

"I'm not sure. We think it was another one of them, perhaps a nymph or dryad of some sort, sent to keep watch on you. They know who Vince is now. His cover is blown, his identity out there, and they want him dead even more than I do."

"Who killed it?"

"Perhaps Vince, or those he associates with." Mary Rock shrugged.

Part of the play, Angela thought. *Giving me as much information as she wants, and not a bit more. But... I did see Vince there. Watching me, then hiding from me.* Mary knew a lot more than she was letting on.

"Why did your people scoop it up from the street? I saw them put bits of it in a bag. Harry and Claudette, they were so casual about it."

Mary looked away and sipped at her coffee. She seemed uncomfortable, and this time Angela wasn't sure it was feigned.

"Mary?"

"Something like that can't be just left around," she said at last. "The more secret their existence, the less they'll be persecuted. And... a fairy has to eat."

Angela couldn't respond to that. The thought was horrible, but she didn't feel in a position to judge. She wasn't sure *what* position she was in. Her world kept shifting, tilting, and every change took her further away from everything she knew. Safe and normal was now a long, long way away, and she didn't think she would ever know that place again.

Mythological creatures had once existed, and there was a trade in their remains.

Some of the creatures *still* existed, and they were hunted and killed for profit.

Vince was one of the hunters, and now they knew him. They, as well as Mary Rock, wanted him dead.

"I don't know where he is," she said. "I'm glad he's not dead, but I have no idea how to find him. I'm not sure I even know *who* he is anymore."

"He fooled you pretty well, eh?" Mary said. She chuckled and drank some more coffee.

"I don't understand you," Angela said. "I mean, you being involved in this. I don't get what your part is, or why your thugs brought me to you. What do you want of me? I've told you I don't know where he is, I have no idea, so why am I here?"

Will she even let me go? The sudden thought shocked Angela with its potential finality. Was she really that close to death? *A fairy has to eat.* Angela looked away from the older woman, around the library at the thousands of tomes. There were two doors, and she guessed that they'd both be guarded. One window, double-glazed and with mullions close together. If she had to run, it would have to be the door she'd entered through.

But if she ran, she might lose track of Vince completely.

"I've lived an interesting life," Mary said. "I'm not one for regrets, which is probably a good thing—otherwise I'd torture myself day and night. I dealt in ancient relics, just like Meloy, and he and I even did business a few times. I always found him crass, and too close to the cliché of what he really was. He always seemed one step away from being exposed, taken down either by the law or others with interest in taking control of his little empire. It's amazing to me that he's still there at all.

"When I discovered the truth, my life changed. I found... a cause. I think I realised then that, though I was very much in control of my life, I was also rudderless. I drifted from one place to another, building up wealth and respect, drawing people to me who I know I can trust with my life."

"Harry and Claudette?" Angela asked.

"Them, and others. Discovering the truth of these creatures opened up the world to me. I have a purpose now, something for which I can use my accumulated wealth."

"You're making yourself sound like some sort of saint," Angela said.

Mary Rock looked at her over the coffee mug. "Oh, far from it."

Angela had to look away. She managed to control a physical shiver, but a chill passed through her. She tipped her own cup against her lips, even though she knew it was empty. Glanced up and back at the door.

"Refill?" Mary asked.

"No. I'm ready to leave. If I hear from Vince, I'll let you know."

"Really?" the woman asked. She stood and came across to Angela, sitting on the arm of her chair and looking down at her, their faces so close that Angela could smell the coffee and age on her breath. "You'll go home, and if your murdering boyfriend contacts you, the first thing you'll do is let me know?"

Angela sank into the chair, struggling not to show her fear.

"Well, I'll make it easier for you," Mary Rock said. "If he contacts you and you don't let me know, I'll have you *both* killed." She smiled and finished her coffee, turning her head to the side so she could hold Angela's gaze.

"What choice is that?" Angela asked.

"No choice at all."

As if at a signal the door opened and Kris entered the room. He and Mary Rock exchanged a nod, and the old woman marched briskly to the doorway. She paused there and turned back.

"If I don't find him, they will," she said. "They're not entirely defenseless, you know. All they wish is to be left alone." Then she went, and Kris closed the door behind her.

"Here," he said. He handed Angela a slip of paper with a handwritten phone number on it.

She took the paper and stared at it. "Hers?"

"Mine. Which is as good as hers."

"Now what?"

"Now we take you home."

Helpless, hopeless, all Angela could do was to let them.

Every shadow might have been thrown by something she didn't know. Every movement across poorly lit streets, along darkened alleys, behind curtained windows, might have been the shifting of something extraordinary from here to there, a creature of legend using the night as its cape and the relative silence as its disguise.

Perhaps a few drunks leaning against walls, or homeless people sheltering wherever they could, caught sight of something from the corner of their eye, and dismissed it just as quickly. The drunks because they were used to seeing things that didn't exist. The homeless because they were scared.

With Kris next to her again, Angela sat in the back of the

car, trying to accept just how much her world had changed.

After the fairy had opened its eyes, she had backed toward the door, the creature's head turning slightly as it tracked her movements. Its body had flexed a little, and a low keening rose as it flinched in pain. Some of the wounds its body had displayed looked recent.

Harry drove, the passenger seat empty. Claudette hadn't come with them. The car felt strangely silent because of the woman's absence, as if hers was the personality that had filled it. Angela had no wish to break the silence. Though filled with countless questions, there was nothing she wanted to say to these men. One of them would probably be the person sent to kill her.

She had been threatened with death twice in a day, but Mary Rock's threat hung heavier than Frederick Meloy's. Perhaps because the woman had issued it so casually.

They passed a park, its boundary lined with street lamps which made its depths appear even darker and more impenetrable. Perhaps Vince was hiding in there. Or hunting.

Angela tried hard not to cry. She hated the sense of self-pity that had settled over her, and she missed the distance that she'd felt when she thought Vince had been killed. She was certain now, as much as she could be, that he was still alive, but the idea that he was a killer made her feel like a fool. Could she have lived with a murderer for two years, without suspecting something?

No. I don't believe it. I can't.

Yet much of what she couldn't believe was revealing itself as fact.

Even though they were taking her home, Angela felt lost.

14

A sickening stench made him queasy with every breath. Panic bit hard. If he vomited he'd choke, a wretched death, drowning in the puke that would never make it past the gag in his mouth.

His tongue was swollen and dry, and every time he unstuck it from the roof of his mouth it hurt more. He was blindfolded. However hard he strained his head and neck, or turned his eyes, he could see nothing but the vaguest hint of light. His wrists were tied behind him, arms in turn tied to a rigid metal chair. His arse and legs were numb, and a fire had been set in each shoulder. Every time he moved they flared more, spearing flames through his pressurised joints and stretched muscles.

Stay calm, stay calm, Vince told himself, because the more he struggled, the more it hurt. The more he panicked, the harder it was to draw the next breath.

Every sound echoed around him. At first he thought it was his hearing, distorted by the blood flow pulsing through his ears, but then he settled as much as he could, heart rate slowing, and scooted the chair to the left. The scrape had echoed, taking several seconds to fade away.

He was shut away in a large space.

Better than the cell Lilou had kept him in, at least.

He hadn't caught a good look at the man who'd taken him, but he had been big, immensely strong, and he'd stunk. Not just an aroma of sweat or dirt, but a true animal stench.

Nothing as bad as what he could smell now, though. At least his kidnapper's scent, powerful though it was, had been of something living.

All he wanted to know was that Angela was safe, but nothing of what he recalled could guarantee that. She'd looked his way, he had ducked down instinctively, and then the screaming and violence had begun. He should have gone to her and dragged her away, but even then his fear for her had been a confused, fractured concept—if he went closer, would he put her more at risk? If they were caught together, would they both be killed?

So he had turned to run, feeling guilty for having returned there at all. He should have remained in that little cell with Lilou tending him, making sure he was all right, and of course she would do that because he had saved her. Whoever she was, *what*ever she was, her gratitude was obvious, and her concern for him palpable.

He'd betrayed that.

In the darkness the man had tripped him, and punched him so hard that he saw stars. When he came to he saw cars, and buildings, and realised he was being carried. He'd tried to struggle. An elbow to the face, and he saw nothing else.

Now, helpless, constantly on the verge of drowning himself with his own vomit, Vince waited for whatever was to come next.

If they removed the mask and he saw that bitch Claudette's face, he'd know that whatever future he had left would be unbearably painful. He'd try to mock her, tell her how her brother had shit his pants as he'd fallen in front of the train. Maybe that would make her kill him quickly.

But I don't want to die. The thought brought back the panic, his breathing increased, and he drew in great gulps of the rancid stink that filled this place. Trying to calm himself again, willing his fear to subside, he heard footsteps.

Vince held his breath and tilted his head, attempting to hear more clearly. Metal-clad shoes, perhaps. Or heavy clogs of some kind. But the man who'd taken him had run quickly, and he couldn't imagine anyone maintaining any sort of speed with heavy, clopping shoes.

Then he could smell the man, past the stench of rot and ruin that he'd been trying to ignore. It was a damp, animal scent, like a wet dog that had rolled in shit, and though horrible it was also strangely comforting. Something alive, instead of the death that had assailed him since being tied here.

His blindfold was ripped away, causing a spike of pain. His gag was tugged free. Vince gasped and squinted in shock, but wherever he was, it was dim. As his eyesight slowly returned he saw only shadows and the hint of shapes.

The man paced behind him, just out of sight.

"Where are we?" Vince asked. His voice was barely a whisper, mouth dried, tongue swollen. His jaw ached, and he could feel the rough terrain of split lips and dried blood.

"Oh, if you're going to be that stupid, I might as well just throw you in with the rest." The voice was deep and strong, but tinged with the gravelly edge of age. Its owner remained out of sight.

His vision improved, or maybe the light filtering through the high-level windows was increasing, but it revealed the sad truth of Vince's surroundings. They were in an old swimming facility. It must have been closed for years. Once-white walls were smeared with moss and slime, lines of steel changing rooms were rusted stiff with doors half open or fallen off.

Higher up, the sloping ceiling had holes in it, some panels tumbled away, others grown black with decay. Two lines of windows ran lengthways high up, at the ridge. Many were smashed, and most of them sprouted weeds that grew in from the roof level outside. On the end wall was an old analog clock and scoreboard swathed in dust-filled webs hanging like children's forgotten shrieks. This would have been a fun place once, but now it was lost and fallen to ruin.

Vince was sitting in the pool itself, in the shallow end. Tiles were cracked and missing and black with moss. Ahead of him, in the deep end, a low level of water remained.

It was from here that the stink came. The water, black and stagnant, was not level. Things protruded.

"I can't swim," Vince said.

"Neither can they!" the voice said, abruptly hysterical. It was followed by a laugh, brief but high-pitched. It seemed to screech through the man's throat.

What are they? Vince wondered. He strained to see, but it was still too gloomy to make out any details. Maybe some of the shapes he saw there were limbs. The place certainly smelled like death.

"Did you kill them?" he asked.

"Ask me if I can dance."

Vince went to say something else, but thought better of it.

"Can you dance?"

"Maybe." Feet clopped and clapped, chipping slivers from broken ceramic tiles. "Maybe not."

"So can we talk face to face?" Vince asked.

"Oh, I'd like that very much indeed," the voice said, low and serious once more. The footsteps slowed and moved, and a shape circled around from Vince's left.

The man was close to seven feet tall. Exaggerated, almost simian features, a once-strong body now gone slack and covered with coarse, gray hair.

And the legs of a goat.

Vince's eyes went wide and he looked away, doubting what he was seeing. Even after what he had come to know, the truths that had been laid before him, he doubted.

"What's wrong?" the man-thing said. "Embarrassed?"

Vince glanced at him again. Scrappy fur covered his legs and formed a scruffy collar around his hooves. Between those legs hung a cock the likes of which Vince had only ever seen in porn films. It swung like a metronome as he swayed from foot to foot.

"Oh, useless thing!" the man-thing cried, that maniacal voice once again. He slapped at his cock and it swayed left, right, left again, before its weight hung it straight down. "Too old, too drunk, too angry, I don't know. But it's had its fun. It's had *more* than its share of fun."

"Who are you?" Vince asked, looking at the man's face. He might have been called ugly, with pronounced features and a bristly beard, but he could also imagine Angela calling him rugged. *A lived-in look*, she'd say he had. *There's a man who's lived a life.*

"I'm Ballus. Last of the satyrs." Ballus frowned, creasing that rugged face. "Think I'm the last, anyway. If not, soon will be. Very soon."

"What do you want with me?"

"I want… information." Ballus laughed. "You are number

six." He shrieked. High in the shadowy roof space, several birds shrilled and took flight, flapping invisibly in the grimy dawn.

"I am not a number," Vince said. He smiled, hoping to ingratiate himself with this man, this thing, but Ballus began pacing back and forth, skipping now and then in a half-dance. He mumbled to himself.

Vince strained at his bindings. His shoulders burned, and pins and needles bit into his arms and hands. His wrists felt cool and wet, air breathing on fresh blood.

"You won't get free," Ballus said, suddenly standing still and staring at his captive. He shifted from foot to foot—hoof to hoof—grinding broken tiles beneath. His cock swung. His face grew slack, jaw hanging slightly open. The gray bristles on his chin and around his mouth glimmering with moisture.

"Look, what do you want with me?" Vince said. "I'm helping you. I saved Lilou, and because of that—"

"Did you fuck her?"

"What?" Vince felt a rush of guilt, a heat in his face.

"Don't misjudge me, human," Ballus said. "Don't make the mistake of thinking we're all alike. Do you assume that a satyr thinks the same as a nymph bitch? You think *this* satyr—" he tapped his gray, hairy chest "—thinks the same as any *other* satyr? Don't paint me with the same brush. I'm unique. I'm Ballus. I'm the last of my kind."

He frowned and looked past Vince, eyes growing vague.

He's insane, Vince thought. *Fucking hell, I'm prisoner of a mad satyr with a twelve-inch schlong.*

"So where are they?" Ballus asked.

"Who?"

"Lilou. Mallian. The others."

"I don't know any Mallian."

Ballus snorted, bullish and furious, and stamped his hoof. A tile shattered.

"Maybe." The satyr frowned. "Okay. So where is Lilou?"

Vince shook his head. "Don't know." He couldn't tell him. If Ballus didn't know, there must be a reason for that. And if there was a reason, he had no wish to give away Lilou's hiding place. She had kept him safe, and he'd betrayed her by escaping and putting himself in danger. He wouldn't betray her again.

"Don't know?" Ballus asked. "Won't say?"

"Same thing," Vince said.

"Oh, no, not the same at all." Ballus came for him, and Vince flinched away in the chair, almost flipping it onto its back. If he did that he'd trap his hands and arms, might even break them if he fell hard enough. He held his breath and shifted his weight forward, tipping the chair onto four legs again.

Close up, Ballus was even more intimidating. He filled Vince's field of vision, a thing that should not be living and breathing, so close to him that he could taste its breath. It was stale and old, but strangely not as disgusting as he'd have thought. Like spilled ale the morning after.

"You don't know anything, really," Ballus said. He moved even closer, close enough to kiss. Vince felt the heat of him. "Your knowledge hardly breaks the surface. You're feeling dislocated from reality, probably. Me being here, talking to you, existing, alive, goes against everything you've ever known. Everything you've ever been taught. But learning never ends."

"I know you're real."

"I know you know. I'm in your space. Right now, I'm your whole world." Ballus's face dropped a little, and he indicated the bindings. "And I'm sorry about this, but it's more than necessary. You'll never know how *important* it really is. How urgent that you tell me what I need to know. It's a matter of life and death." He eased himself upright and stepped back, hooves clipping lightly on the broken tiles.

"Where are they?"

Vince frowned as if trying to think. He looked away from Ballus toward the edge of the empty pool, trying to ground himself in reality again—but this *was* reality. His hands really were tied and bleeding, his shoulders really were on fire. He had seen this beast murder someone brutally, in front of his own home. His and Angela's.

"I don't know," he said.

"Where are they?"

"I don't *know*."

Ballus moved again, striding across the pool and back, walking widths.

"*Where are they?*"

"How old are you?" Vince asked. He really was interested, but he also hoped that asking questions might distract his captor. He sensed a solid ego in this man-thing, something large that could be teased and stroked. He couldn't help looking at the satyr's flaccid, swinging dick. *Useless thing*, Ballus had said, and what was a satyr without his cock?

Ballus paused in his pacing and stared again.

"Where are they?"

"Look, honestly, I don't know where they are," Vince said. "I got away in the night, I was worried about Angela, and it was dark and—"

"You *should* be worried," Ballus said.

"Why?" A ripple of fear. "What do you mean?"

"Where are they?"

"Why should I be worried about Angela? They won't hurt

her, because they think she'll lead them to me." It was what he had banked on, and why he had drawn back when he saw her. Perhaps much later, if Mary Rock's people didn't catch up with him, then maybe they might see her as a target for revenge, but not yet. For now, he was still their prime focus. It was his blood they craved.

"Who do you work for?" Vince asked, and Ballus froze for a moment before releasing one of his high-pitched shrieks again. He skipped across the pool, fragmented tiles flipping up behind him and catching the growing light. Vince didn't think it would ever be fully light in here, because the windows were too overgrown and smeared with filth, and he was glad. He wasn't sure he wanted to make out this place in any detail.

Ballus stopped and stared at him again. "Where are they?"

Vince shook his head and looked down at his knees.

The satyr mumbled to himself, a sound like rocks rolled in a box. He turned his back on Vince and ran along the pool, down toward the deep end where stinking shadows still held out against the dawn. He splashed into the shallow waters there and, moments later, as if breaking the slick surface released it, a new wave of stink washed over Vince.

He struggled, took shallow breaths, bit his torn, bloodied lips, and then leaned forward and puked anyway. Not much came up. He was soon retching, and between each straining cry he heard Ballus's delighted shrieks.

Something hit the floor a few feet from him, landing with a wet thud.

Vince heaved again and spat, groaning as his restrained limbs pulsed with pain.

Another thud, this one closer, and something splashed across his bare feet.

Puke dribbling from his mouth and nose, he tried to focus on Ballus, twenty yards away in the deep end and leaning this way and that as he plucked objects from the rancid, watery stew. The satyr froze, then dashed to the left, as if he'd seen whatever he had been searching for.

"Here!" he said, plucking something from the water, turning, and holding it up triumphantly. "This!" He threw, and the object sailed through the air.

Vince cringed, trying to pull his head down and shoulders up. The thing struck his right cheek and shoulder. It was wet, heavy, slick, sticky, and when it tumbled to his lap and then to the floor, he smelled its unbelievable awfulness.

When he looked, he saw the wing. It was leathery, folded, its veins raised and solid. A slick film covered it, glimmering in the weak dawn light. Its leading edge was heavier and thicker, maybe as wide as a toddler's arm. The skin was riddled with holes, but where it remained whole there were dark, regular patterns. Tattoos. And at its end was a clawed hand.

Vince stared at the hand. It wore several golden rings.

"Her name was Bindi," Ballus said.

"Did you kill her?" Vince asked.

"Ask me if I can dance."

Vince did not look up. He stared at the hand, the accordioned wing, and did not look away even when he heard Ballus splashing in the rank waters, talking to himself and whooping in delight as he found something else.

Several other parts thumped and splatted down. None of them struck him. Ballus heaved something much heavier and it didn't even come halfway.

"I still don't know where they are," Vince said. The more Ballus tried to terrify him, the more certain he became that he could never reveal the location of Lilou's hideaway. He didn't know who or what Mallian was, but he remembered what Lilou had said that last time they spoke. *"Promise that you won't try to see who you're talking to."*

"Where are they?" Ballus was splashing his way from the horror-filled water and walking back toward the shallow end. His furred legs were dripping, and he kicked aside some of the body parts he had hauled out and thrown in Vince's direction.

He brought the stink with him.

Vince heaved again, and when he'd finished bringing up nothing, Ballus was standing before him. In his hand he carried a heavy, splintered bone.

"I'm going to ask you one more time," the satyr said.

15

Back in their apartment, with dawn smearing the streets and rush-hour traffic building, Angela listened to her neighbours making love and remembered Vince's gentle touch, his mischievous smile, his loving, and she could not believe that he was a killer.

She sat on their bed with her hands clenched between her knees and tried to make real everything she had seen and heard. In this place it all seemed so surreal, yet she had no doubts. She trusted her senses and memory. She believed in what she had witnessed and been told. She had to. There was no other way to move on.

On the floor in the corner lay Vince's underwear and tee shirt from the last time he had stripped off in this room, and she could not comprehend picking them up and dumping them in the washing basket. That was too mundane.

The bookshelves in the alcove needed dusting. So pointless. So banal.

Above her the couple cried and grunted together, and the frenetic creaking of bed springs ceased. Angela actually heard Vince say, *"And the judges go wild!"*

"Oh, Vince, what the hell have you done to me?" she whispered into the otherwise silent flat. Then she stood, marched into the kitchen, and switched on the kettle. She needed coffee. She hadn't slept and tiredness made things worse, but she didn't *feel* at all tired. She felt like someone who had to take control of things, not be controlled.

As the kettle boiled and the electric coffee grinder grumbled, she stared at the kitchen chalkboard. She and Vince would leave messages on there—funny, rude, loving. There was nothing on there now. Their future was a blank, and it was up to her how it would be written.

Mary Rock would be having her followed. That was a given. She reached into her pocket and took out the piece of paper that Kris had given her, then entered the number into her phone. She doubted that she'd ever call it. Being followed was a concern, but it was one she would address later. She found the card Claudette had given her, and tapped that number into her phone's memory, as well.

The kettle boiled and she let it settle for thirty seconds before pouring the water onto the coffee. The smell rose, familiar and calming, and she remembered the smell of the fairy's room, the scars across its body that might have been new or a thousand years old.

Angela knew she couldn't remain here for too long. Whatever the truth about Vince, finding him was her priority, and perhaps her first step back toward some kind of normality.

That was what she wanted. To wake next to Vince, drink tea in their small back garden, see him out to work and ready herself for a day's study.

Except his work was nothing to do with normal.

"Fuck it," she said. "Fuck, fuck, *fuck*…" She swore as she walked through to the front room, moved the blinds aside and looked out onto the street. Stretching, she could just see where she had witnessed the killing. So brutal, so horrible, Angela was certain the killer had not been Vince. The shape she had seen was too tall and broad, and besides, he didn't have such brutality in him. There was so much he had lied about, so many aspects of his life that she hadn't known and still barely understood, but that, at least, was something she believed.

Her lover was not a man of violence.

She tried to see whatever was left of the victim, but there were parked cars in the way. Maybe pedestrians would think the bloody smear on the road was the result of a cat or dog being run over, or an urban fox. Most people would simply avert their gaze and carry on with their day. The bigger the city, the more spilled blood became someone else's problem. Never more so than in London.

It was too late for her to call the police. Even if she did, what could she tell them? The truth would get her kicked out onto the street, or arrested for filing a false report. A *selection* of the truth would be harder to confer, and in her current state she had no confidence in her ability to spin a tale. Besides, it would gain her nothing. She didn't know who or what had been killed, by whom or by what.

The secret world she had entered danced to a different song.

She went back through to the kitchen, poured her coffee, took the mug into the back garden, sat down, and started drinking. Thinking. Planning.

Even before she'd finished the drink, she knew what had to happen first. Finding Vince was something she needed to do on her own. Everything and everyone else could fuck off. She had the names Professor Joslin had given her, but it suddenly seemed naive to believe she could track Vince in some covert way. It wasn't as if he'd vanished to avoid paying a fine.

First things first—she would have to lose her tail.

The landline rang as she prepared to leave. She waited, tempted to answer but knowing it would probably be Lucy. Her best friend, her confidante, the woman who had been there for her through good times and not so good. The draw of speaking to Lucy was almost too strong to bear.

The call switched over to the answerphone, and she listened to the message as it was being recorded.

"Hey, it's me. Just checking in. Any news from Vince? I've tried your mobile, too. Call me, yeah? Bit worried about you." There was a pause, as if Lucy was thinking of saying more.

Then she hung up.

Angela released a breath she hadn't been aware of holding, and went to the front door.

It was already warm outside. Someone shouted in a language she couldn't identify, a car horn sounded somewhere out of sight, and a siren wailed in from the distance. A typical London morning. She shrugged her bag higher onto one shoulder, closed the door, and walked along the street.

There were several crows pecking at the spot where she'd witnessed the killing. A dark stain marked the scene, but little else. Angela didn't pause to look too closely, though. She remembered the sickening sounds and the shocking animal brutality, and that was enough to speed up her pace. Soon she left her street, and five minutes later she was walking along the main shop-lined road toward the Tube.

She had no doubt that she was being followed. She suspected it was Claudette, as she hadn't been in the car when Harry and Kris brought her home early that morning. She made no attempt to try and spot who was keeping watch on her. Doing so would make them more alert, and she didn't want that. She wanted the opposite.

Angela had read so much about the minds and actions of criminals—books, papers, interviews, articles, research documents—but she had rarely incorporated any of it into her everyday life. Breaking into Vince's secret apartment in South Kensington had been scary and exciting, her knowledge of lock picking gleaned wholly from her studies. Now she would attempt something new.

Phone in hand, staring at the screen as she walked, she entered a grocer's store. She remained close to the front window so that she was visible from outside, selected a bag of crisps and a bottle of water, paid, nodded to the shop assistant, stood outside and dropped her purchases into her bag. Then she moved on, still staring at her phone. She'd brought up a news site and scanned the headlines for anything that might refer to what had happened the night before. There was nothing. No murder, no screams, nothing to remember the victim of violence. *Someone else's problem.*

The next door she ducked into was a health food shop. She browsed shelves close to the front window to begin with, then moved deeper in.

"Help you?" the shop clerk asked. She was a cheerful young woman with dreadlocks and an open smile.

"Just browsing, thanks."

"New York?"

"Boston."

She smiled. "Never was great with accents."

Angela returned the smile and picked up a basket, loading it slowly with dried apricots, quinoa, and some outrageously priced hot chocolate. She ambled to the counter and hovered there for a while, chatting with the clerk. A few other patrons milled about. She glanced at her phone a few times, reversing the camera view and holding it up so that she could look behind her. There was no one she recognised in the shop, and no sign of any observers out in the street.

"Don't walk into a lamp post," the woman said, handing Angela her change.

"Just waiting for an important message," she said. The woman wore a peace sigil earring, a "One Life—Live It" tee shirt, and they could have been friends. She seemed genuinely nice.

Angela felt a sudden rush of emotion, a flood of desperation at what was happening to her life. She wanted to ask this woman for a coffee, not caring if it was taken the wrong way. She wanted to sit and talk to a normal person about mundane things.

"Hope he's worth it," the young woman said before attending to another customer.

"Yeah, he is," Angela said as she turned away. She didn't think the woman heard.

Emerging into sunlight, she turned left and sauntered along the pavement, staring down at her phone and only glancing up every few seconds. She did her very best not to look behind. Passing a boarded-up shop that had once been a tanning salon, she spotted a spread of graffiti that would have meant nothing a couple of days ago. *One-Eyed Bastard*. Probably a nickname. Some weird gang thing, perhaps. It sent a chill through her veins.

Someone bumped into her and apologised, then said, "Get with the real world, love." Her heart leapt, but the man shook his head and walked on. He meant her phone, that was all. *Get your head out of the digital world, love. One life, live it, love.*

Angela felt her control slipping. Taking action was her aim today, not losing herself to the situation and letting it carry her along with its strange flow. She shrugged her bag higher on her shoulder and moved off, not looking around, trying not to appear paranoid. This was about putting whoever followed her at ease.

Two shops down…

The next one would be where she would take action.

She passed a Thai restaurant and smiled at a man cleaning the windows. She and Vince had eaten in there a couple of times, and she remembered that the toilets were downstairs. If it had a back door, she didn't know where it was. Besides, it would look strange ducking into a restaurant this early in the morning.

Clothes shop. It sold second-hand items and she'd bought a coat there last year, but she remembered the bags of stock piled behind the counter. Blocking the corridors back there, perhaps.

Horns blared. Car engines grumbled, brakes squealed, cyclists whizzed by. The impersonal city was home to millions of stories, and now it was time to become the narrator and change her own.

The Big Two Café would be perfect. Independent, a nice coffee shop that also served pretty decent food throughout the day, she had used it quite a few times as an afternoon retreat.

"Morning, Michelle," she said as she stepped through the open front doors.

"Miss Gough!" Michelle was short, wide, sporting a huge smile and a personality to match.

"Please, it's Angela." She rolled her eyes and looked around. A few people sat eating breakfast, most of them reading websites or messages on their phones. *Get with the real world*, she thought, laughing gently.

"Usual?" Michelle asked.

"No, large cappuccino today, and I'll have a bacon sandwich, too. I'm just…" She raised her eyebrows and pointed toward the back of the café.

"Sure, just drop your bag to save a seat, we're dead busy," Michelle said, making Angela's plan twice as strong when she added, "There, behind you! Window seat."

A man and woman were just leaving, gathering papers and pushing past her without catching her eye, and Angela shrugged off her empty bag and placed it on one of the chairs. She leaned it against the window, easily visible from outside.

Her internal stopwatch began ticking.

She strolled casually toward the rear of the café, heart hammering. A corridor led past a wall display of the café's famous patrons, a who's who of reality TV stars, a pop singer from the seventies, and a couple of sports people who lived locally. She paused as if examining the photos, then turned into the narrow corridor, slipping out of sight of anyone watching from the street.

The toilets were to the right. She went left, passing the open kitchen door and seeing the chef busy with an array of breakfasts. The smells were tempting, but so was freedom. As she approached the door marked "Private," she held her breath. If it was locked, she'd have to go back to her seat, finish breakfast, and make her move in the next shop.

The door opened. No alarms shrilled at her audacity. She entered a small, untidy office and closed the door behind her. Shrugged off her jacket and left it on the back of a chair. Rifled through the contents of a messy desk top scattered with old plates and half-empty mugs, found a rubber band, gathered her hair and tied it in a ponytail. There was another door across the office, and beside it a row of hooks. On one of them hung a loose, thin cardigan, on another a baseball cap. An unexpected opportunity. She took both, feeding her hair out above the cap's clasp, pulling on the cardigan as she opened the other door.

In a narrow corridor piled high with cardboard boxes, she turned left and headed for a fire escape door. It was difficult to reach past the boxes, but it was blocked open with a brick. She couldn't have asked for anything more perfect.

It was maybe a minute since she'd disappeared from view.

Her watcher—Claudette, Harry, or Kris—would hopefully give her a few more minutes in the bathroom before they started growing suspicious. Then another minute to enter the café, negotiate Michelle's loud welcome, find their way back to the toilet. If she was lucky, there'd be someone locked in there, so maybe that would be another minute before the watcher decided to knock on the door, or perhaps break it down.

Seven or eight minutes. *To be safe, bank on five.*

Outside the door, the alley entrance was to the right, and beyond it the main street bustled. She hunched down low and scanned from the shadows, not seeing anyone she recognised. The narrow view showed only people flitting by in both directions, and vehicles crawling past.

To her left, the alley went deeper. This was where it might all fall apart. If there was no other way out, she'd have to leave onto the main street, and then it was all down to chance. Would her follower recognise her instantly in the cap and cardigan? Probably. They'd know what they were doing. Maybe they'd done it a hundred times before.

This was her first.

The alley smelled of rotten food, shadows defied the morning, water dripped from somewhere high up on her left, and Angela thought she heard something rustling around in a pile of scattered refuse. She kicked an empty takeaway carton and the rustling ceased. Whatever it was listened, cautious and alert as she passed by. Something else that wanted to hide.

She already felt far removed from the street, even though it was only thirty feet behind her. The sounds were subdued, the sun on her skin a fading memory. She rarely saw places like this. They were back of house, functional parts of the shops and restaurants in the area she knew so well. Anyone or anything could be hiding here.

The alley wasn't wide enough for vehicles, but she passed several heavy plastic wheeled carts, a couple of them overflowing with black bags. Some were split, spilling packaging and cardboard to the ground. Others emitted smells she couldn't identify, from corrupted things she could not see.

At first she thought it was a dead end, but then the alley jigged left and opened onto a much wider area, a chaotic courtyard where two vans, several cars, and a motorbike were parked, wheeled refuse carts stood in disarray, and the rear facades of a dozen buildings rose damp and dilapidated. A few doors stood blocked open, and from one of them she heard the tinny hiss of music, clashing pans, and voices raised in busy dispute.

She scanned quickly, looking for the way out.

A fox stared at her from a shadowy doorway across the large courtyard.

She froze, neck prickling. Trying not to move, she looked

left and right for signs that anyone else was watching. She appeared to be alone. The whole courtyard felt out of time. Even the vehicles might have been abandoned here forever. It was a way station that people passed through but never really knew, and the fox was part of that hidden world.

The creature didn't seem afraid. Angela had seen urban foxes before, but this one looked healthier than most. Its coat was a familiar auburn, not grayed by the city. It seemed well-fed.

It turned and trotted away, glancing once over its shoulder.

"Nothing to lose," she muttered, and she started to follow. The creature was going the way she needed to go, away from the alley and along a canyon between buildings that led out onto another, quieter road.

Angela glanced at her watch. Five minutes had passed since she'd entered the Big Two Café. She started to jog. Her follower would likely be inside now, searching for her. She had to hurry.

Out on the road, she looked left and right. The fox had vanished. She smiled and shook her head. She was spooked, imagining things, seeing signs that weren't there. She turned left and walked quickly. At the end of the street the road joined a busier one, and she jogged across, dodging cars and raising a hand in apology when someone honked.

Seven minutes. They'd be knocking on the toilet door now, perhaps even trying to break it down. Or they'd be out into the alley, the courtyard, then following her if she didn't hustle.

Angela crossed another road and ducked into another alley, passing several motionless shapes sleeping beneath flattened cardboard boxes, their dogs growling at her. She emerged onto a canal towpath, followed it beneath a busy road bridge, left the path, crossed a small park, and only when she had successfully lost herself did she stop running, half an hour later and with very little idea of where she was and what she was going to do.

Reaching a small green set in a square of tall London townhouses, Angela sat to catch her breath. There was a prickle of excitement at what she'd done. She felt in control.

Something shifted to her left, caught by her peripheral vision. A fast shape, moving behind walls of foliage, startling chirping birds to the sky.

Angela stood. The small park felt empty, distant from the London sounds of motors, horns, and the plodding of feet taking everyone on a different journey. A moment ago the place had felt safe—but no more.

They can't have followed me, she thought. *It's impossible!*

Across a spread of untrimmed lawn, a fox emerged from behind a lush rhododendron bush. She couldn't tell whether it was the same creature that she'd seen behind the shops. It stared at her, then darted away.

She couldn't help thinking it had been watching her.

Gathering herself, breathing deeply, letting the anonymous sounds of the big city wash over her, she prepared to enact the next stage of her plan. She might have escaped Mary Rock's followers, but she was adrift in a city full of strangers and strangeness. She had to find something to grab hold of, a secure point to grasp before her search for Vince could really begin. There must be others who knew of these creatures.

She needed someone else with an awareness of this fantastical new world.

The easiest way to find the nearest cyber café would be to access an app on her iPhone, but she had no idea how far Mary Rock's reach extended, and she wanted to stay off the grid. She'd have to employ more basic search methods.

Pulling the cap down over her eyes, Angela left the park and started walking.

She found the café twenty minutes later, nestled in a narrow arcade between a laundromat and a Turkish food outlet. Inside it smelled of coffee and cleaning products.

She sat as far to the rear as she could, turning the screen so she could also face the door. Ordering coffee and carrot cake, she created an account using random numbers and letters and a made-up user name, then started searching the net. She used obscure terminology, worried that there might be filters set to scan for certain words used in tandem, such as "fairy in London" or "trade in relics."

The first few searches bore no fruit. She scanned many pages concerned with mythological creatures—storybooks, blogs, Wikipedia pages, school websites. There were dozens of photographs of blurry, hazed shapes that might have been anything. She even read accounts by apparently clear-headed witnesses of big cats on the moors and other creatures living in the shadows. But nothing she saw or read rang true.

She shifted her search to the science pages. Cryptozoology was at the periphery of serious science, but there were articles in respected journals that addressed this unusual branch of biology. Even they dealt with known creatures, such as leopards in the mountains, or crocodiles in the sewers.

Then she found a name. Dean Janowski. It appeared in several searches, always mentioned with a mocking lilt. He'd been a professor of palaeontology who seemed to have been derided and eventually shunned by his peers because of his outlandish studies and beliefs.

This had been a long time ago.

"Dean," she said, because the name jogged a memory. "Dean."

She sat up straight. Fat Frederick had mentioned a man called Dean. He'd called him a tramp and a fellow relic hunter.

Angela tapped in Dean Janowski's full name. By then, her coffee was cooling and the carrot cake sat forgotten, but she didn't care.

The website opened onto a brief, stark statement.

I'll always take you seriously.
No time wasters.

When she hovered over the message, there was a hyperlink. She entered, and on the new page there was a phone number. That shocked her, but then she realised it was a mask number, often used online to disguise someone's real number.

A set of headphones and a microphone hung on a hook beside the computer, already plugged in. Without giving herself time to think through what she was doing, she slipped on the headphones and dialed.

The phone rang several times, and she was just about to hang up when it was answered. She could hear someone listening. They said nothing, but she knew it was an active line.

"I saw a fairy," she said.

16

There were those among the Kin who believed the safest policy was to hide, and not long ago Lilou would have agreed with them. It was what they did best, after all, and their survival depended on it. It had been that way for centuries.

She was one of the few who could hide in plain sight, although her presence was often felt, sensed, unsettling to some. Those Kin not so human in appearance or outlook had no option but to always exist in the shadows, but with Ballus once again in their midst, everything had changed.

Mallian wanted to go out and find Ballus, and perhaps kill him, and Lilou could see the sense of that. They had to take action. Not only because Ballus was an ongoing danger—he'd already shown that in his brutal murder of Sandri May, and others over the years—but because he was an even greater danger to Vince. If Ballus captured him, he would do everything, *anything*, to find out what Vince knew about her and the rest of the survivors.

Unlike most of her kind, Lilou made occasional contact with the human world. She appeared human, mostly, and bore no gnarled horns or veined wings, no swathes of scales around her midriff or patchy fur across her back. She also maintained that it benefited them all if she kept her finger on the pulse of mankind.

Hidden away in the depths, or the shadows, or the narrow confines between spaces where humans rarely had the perception to see, it was easy to drift away from the reality of things, and to lose any connection with the world that had once been theirs.

Few alive today had existed during the Time, and fewer still could actually remember it. But survival necessitated thinking ahead and maintaining awareness.

She was a nymph, one of the Napaeae, a creature of glens and groves who now felt safer hiding in the concrete jungle. Intrinsically bonded to nature and yet forced through circumstance to live apart from it, she still occasionally went underground, seeking the sources of springs, following the rivers that flowed beneath London, those known by humans and some not. These were trips of fancy, brief sojourns rather than a return to her favored environment. They fulfilled a need.

However, she spent most of her life aboveground. She loved the sun and the air, the cool dead breeze of winter and the promise-laden sunrise of spring. She would walk in the parks in an attempt to forget herself, and in doing so remember herself fully. But such exposure was frowned upon. Mallian had reprimanded her more than once. A nymph drew attention, especially from men. Keen to walk among humans, loath to shut herself away, Lilou found it difficult to remain anonymous.

Dressing in shapeless clothing and drab colours, tucking her long hair up into a cap, she ventured once more into the streets, as she had many times before, determined to avoid being the focus of anyone's attention. She had become good at this over the years. Only occasionally did she let herself slip.

She worried for Vince. He didn't know what he had stumbled across, had no real idea about the reality of things, the tragedy and brutality. He had exposed himself to such dangers in order to help her, and now she needed to help him in return. There was something about him. Perhaps because she had seen a courage in him that she had never witnessed in a human before, or maybe it was because he had helped her in such a vulnerable situation. Whatever the reason, she had feelings for him.

That troubled her. None of the others would approve, and Mallian would be outraged. She had to keep such things to herself.

Moving through the streets of London, she passed Buckingham Palace, home to a woman who didn't quite rule over the whole of her domain. The Kin had no truck with royalty. Mallian was their de facto ruler, but in truth they existed under an assumption that all were equal. She walked along the Mall, hugging her gray shapeless coat tight and holding her secrets tighter. Entering the park at last, she sought the old man called Dean.

"Are you here to mock me again, girl?"

"When have I ever mocked you?"

He raised his eyes to the sky and pretended to count off occasions on his fingers. They were as grubby, old, and wrinkled as the rest of him. He didn't live on the streets, but he might as well have. They were where he seemed most at home.

"Well, I'm sure you have," he said, smiling. "I just can't remember, is all. That's what you get for being old." Still smiling, he looked at her in that curious way that always made her think, *He knows*.

"You're far from old, Dean," she said. Her voice almost a purr, and she saw his pupils dilate, his stance change. *Calm, Lilou*, she thought, silently admonishing herself. She knew she couldn't sweet-talk Dean or let him become besotted with her natural nymph's sensual charms. If she did, he really *would* know. For while his appearance might suggest otherwise, Dean was sharp—if not entirely sound—of mind, and she had given him plenty of opportunity over the years to feed his suspicion.

The truth was that she disliked being with him. Every moment felt like exposure, but Lilou also knew that their meetings served an important purpose. He was constantly close to discovering the truth he sought, and she was always there to steer him in the wrong direction.

Dean was a man who hid behind the perception of his madness. A bum, a wanderer, he pulled an old wheeled suitcase with him everywhere he went. It bulged with rolled and creased clothing, shirtsleeves protruding like uncoiling guts, stained jeans forcing themselves through the split zipper. But that wasn't all it carried. He'd once told her that he was a learned man, a former professor of palaeontology whose peers had driven him further away the more outlandish his studies became. That had been almost three decades ago. She didn't know the exact story of how he had become destitute, and she didn't need to know. His mind was still clear and rich and, much like her, he defied expectations.

Lilou had asked him to open his suitcase more than

once, and his willingness to do so for her formed the most fragile part of their relationship.

He wasn't quite sure what she was. To him, she might be a fellow searcher, or one of the things for which he was searching.

She could never be certain how much he knew.

Most people on the streets barely saw him. They paid him as much attention as they would a scraggly dog or an article of discarded furniture. He never begged, but he did follow his own regular route across the city, disappearing now and then for long periods but always returning, the suitcase a little fuller, his face bearing more wrinkles.

He was close to a truth that most people would never discern, or believe if they did. This gave him a certain value to creatures like Lilou. While maintaining a safe distance, she kept an eye on him because he kept an eye on them. If he drew too close to one or more of the Kin, she would let them know, and they would change their habits or move elsewhere. His was a life of disappointments, and Lilou was responsible for many of them.

"I haven't seen you for a long time," he said. "Where have you been?"

"Around," she responded. "How about you?" She knew where he had been. He'd spent several weeks prowling the Isle of Dogs, looking for evidence of a water ghost that several sports enthusiasts had reported seeing during nighttime canoeing excursions. She had spoken with Ghellia, the last of the ashrays, and she had floated closer to the center of the city, hiding herself deeper down.

"I've been exploring," he said. He tapped the suitcase that rested beside him on the park bench like an old friend. "Finding more stuffing for my library."

"More old shirts and underwear," Lilou said, and Dean smiled in return. They both knew better.

The city buzzed around them, leaving them alone. Hyde Park was always busy, but it was large enough to rarely appear so. Hundreds or thousands of people at a time might be using its paths, strolling across its lawns, or resting on its benches and bandstand seating, but it was generally possible to feel alone among such greenery. It was one of the lungs of the city, always breathing and maintaining its own rhythm. Lilou loved it here, yet it never took long before she felt exposed.

"Find anything new?" she asked.

"You're overdressed," he said, looking her up and down. Long trousers, jacket pulled tight, all to hide her figure and shield the world from what she was. But she knew it wasn't only about looks. She exuded grace and beauty.

"I feel the cold," she replied. "So?"

"Depends on what you mean by new. If you mean new as in older than anyone knows, then there's always evidence, if you know where to look."

"Where do *you* look?"

"You know where," Dean said. "You look there yourself. Or…"

"The hidden places," she said, knowing them so well.

"Yeah." He settled back on the bench and looked across the park, smiling. "I like the fact there can be so many secret places in a city filled with people. It gives me hope."

"Hope for what?"

Dean frowned, unsure. He searched for the words.

"For wonder," he said at last. "Mysteries. Mysteries are important, don't you think?"

"Definitely," she said. She sat next to him, not too close,

and he shifted slightly as if sensitive to the weight of her on the bench. She snorted and spat, trying to appear unattractive.

"There's a place close to here," he said, "just beside one of the north entrances to the park, hidden down alongside one of the stone columns that holds the gate." He leaned forward as if to pull something from the suitcase, then changed his mind. Maybe he thought she wouldn't need to see. "It's a metal cover to a hole in the ground, rusty and old. Set of broken steps leads down to a bare earth chamber, hacked out by tools a long time ago. I've been down there a few times, even slept down there once. Probably the start of an old maintenance tunnel for something that was never finished. Dunno what. Or maybe something to do with a building that might have stood there before. No one else seems to know about it. *No one.* The cover's hidden beneath shrubs and fallen leaves. You have to know it's there to even see it."

"How do *you* know it's there?"

"I look for these things." He glanced at her, smile dropping, as if expecting to see something in her eyes. Then he shrugged and continued. "You know that. So, this place exists a few feet from where thousands of people walk every day. A secret place. Anything could live down there."

"But nothing does, does it?"

"Not there, but there are other places like that."

"How about a satyr?" Lilou asked, deciding to take the leap. She heard Dean's sharp intake of breath, and wondered what he was thinking. That one question had moved their relationship onto new, uneven ground. She'd never asked about what he looked for, never requested information directly. Their conversations had always been obtuse.

"What *about* a satyr?" Dean asked.

"Have you ever heard about one?" she responded. "Could… something like a satyr live in a place like that?"

"Why do you ask?" It was a fair question, she supposed.

"Interested, that's all," she replied. "For my own research."

"And what research is that?"

She let her mask slip, just for a few seconds. She didn't need to loosen her jacket or shift from a shapeless slump into a graceful lean. All she had to do was let the face she wore amongst humans fall away, and his eyes widened when he glimpsed the alluring beauty beneath.

Only for a second.

"Come on, Dean," she said, her voice a song. "Knowing that would ruin our special relationship."

"Our relationship," he said. He looked away, leaning over his suitcase and checking the zippers, the clasps. "Our relationship is entirely to your benefit, I think."

Lilou frowned and drew herself in again, becoming as human as she could. She had no answer for that, because he was right. The fact that he'd perceived it, let alone stated it, was a surprise to her.

"I don't want anything but good for you," she whispered, meaning every word.

Dean was silent for a while, staring out across the park and the city within which he knew there were countless secrets.

"Come on," she said, trying to lighten the mood. "Open your case. Show me what you've got."

"Is it important?" he asked without looking at her.

Lilou thought about Vince, in Ballus's clutches, and the danger Angela was in. She thought of Sandri May, kicked and crushed to death in a city street by the satyr's brutal hooves, and all the other creatures she knew and loved, in danger from that beast. Herself included. She wasn't like some of the others. She wasn't a fighter, and if Ballus found her she would have no chance at all.

"Yes, it's important."

Dean nodded, pushed the suitcase onto its back, and unzipped the main compartment. He drew out several items of clothing, and the case's contents seemed to expand on contact with the sun. Soon there was a pile of tatty sweaters, jeans, and tee shirts around his feet, and the deeper contents of the suitcase were revealed.

Lilou had seen inside before, but the contents had grown. Sheaves of paper, cardboard files, photograph albums, folded maps, envelopes bulging with newspaper clippings, pen cases, and notebooks. Dean riffled confidently through the confusion.

"There's not much," he said at last, placing a file and a few other documents in his lap. He started going through them. "A sighting of a goat-man by Underground workers seventeen years ago. A photo of a severed leg, from an unknown goat-like species, that was found on a building site in Greenwich three years ago. A solitary tweet from more recently about the sound of ghostly hooves at an old indoor swimming pool."

"How recently?" Lilou asked.

Dean brought the wrinkled sheet of paper closer to his face, squinting. She forgot sometimes how old he was. He didn't have much time left, and perhaps he'd die without the proof he so desired. Face-to-face proof, hand in hand. She felt sad for him, but not sad enough to betray herself or the Kin.

"Couple of months ago," he said.

"Why did it make you think satyr?"

"It didn't at the time," he said, holding up the sheaf of papers in his hands. "Not 'til you mentioned it. Then I just pulled everything about hooves."

"And you didn't go on one of your expeditions to investigate?"

He took a deep breath, leaned back, smiling at her. "My girl, if I hurried about London chasing up every little whisper—"

"It's what you do, Dean."

"This tweet was from a mad old woman I know, thinks she's a medium, but she's a charlatan. I hold no truck with fakers. That's why I like you."

"Have you got an address?"

"Will you take me?"

"Dean..."

"I've been looking for so long," he said. "I've got a history you just don't know. A deep history. You might think you know my story, but you really don't at all. I'm haunted by things I've seen, but more haunted by those I haven't."

"It's all just a bit of fun," Lilou said, trying to inject humour into her voice.

She failed.

"I don't know what you are," he said, "but I know what you're not, and that's human." His expression was dead serious.

Just for a moment Lilou considered letting slip some more of the truth. Not all of it, not *nearly* all, but enough to secure his help. Yet Dean wasn't like Vince. She didn't think he could keep it all to himself.

...and there was his suitcase. It bulged with evidence he had been gathering for decades, and she was sure he wouldn't dare carry it all with him. What might happen to all this, if and when he died? It was something she had to address, though that was for another, calmer time.

So she laughed instead, tipping her head back so that he saw her profile against the morning sky and fell in love with her a little bit more.

A phone started ringing. Dean plucked it from his pocket, and Lilou sat upright in surprise. She'd never seen him use a phone before.

He glanced at the screen and connected without speaking. His eyes went wide.

"Where?" he asked. He glanced at her as if seeing her for the first time. "Okay, yes, I'll let you know." He disconnected, and then started packing his suitcase again.

Lilou knelt beside him and helped. She could smell him, the sickly sweetness of body odour, the scent of hopelessness that hung around him heavier and heavier each time she saw him. But he seemed excited now.

"Interesting call?" she asked.

"The swimming pool, it's in Tufnell Park." He knelt on the suitcase to close it, and Lilou helped by zipping it up.

"Thank you," she said. "It was nice to see you again."Dean froze.

"Did you know about this?" He held up the phone.

"Your phone?"

"The call! That call I just had."

"No," she said. She didn't have to feign her confusion.

"Tufnell Park," he said again.

Some children shouted from across the grassed area. A dog barked. Dean looked around as if seeing it all for the first time.

Then he stared at Lilou intently for a few seconds, trying to see past the facade and inside her, seeking the truth he seemed so sure hid just beneath the surface. He was right, but she made sure he didn't find it.

"See you around," Lilou said, and she turned and walked away.

All across the park men turned to watch her. Some were with their partners or wives, a couple were on their own. Absorbed in what Dean had told her, she let her defenses slip. For just a moment she became the center of attention, and every man loved her.

17

Vince's shoulders had gone from blazing with pain to uncomfortably numb. The chair pressed against his legs and back as if it was built from white-hot brands. He'd been beaten almost senseless by a satyr wielding the heavy thighbone of an unidentifiable creature.

A satyr.

Vince still had trouble believing that, but he was so wretched, so convinced he was soon to die, that such impossibilities didn't seem to matter. This did not feel like a dream. He didn't try to convince himself that he was imagining things.

Besides, it was all his fault. If he hadn't escaped Lilou's protection, Ballus wouldn't have caught him in the street. If he hadn't chosen to intervene and save Lilou's life from Mary Rock's thugs, he'd never have needed her protection in the first place, and he'd be back home with Angela even now.

If the lure of unimaginable money hadn't pulled him from his normal life, he'd have never even known about the relics. To him they had been old things, long gone. Fossils that he didn't try to understand, much less view as once having lived. He wasn't as imaginative as Angela, and such pragmatism had served him well in his dealings. His relic hunts.

Then, meeting Lilou—realizing that she wasn't human, and watching as Daley and Celine tried to take her—had changed his life.

Looking back, he realised he should have known. For a while he'd been hearing whispers, seeing things that hinted to him that the relics weren't just the old, dead things he'd come to believe. That some of them were perhaps still alive. He hadn't mentioned this to Fat Frederick, who still saw them all as ancient history, but then Mary Rock had approached him via one of her aides, courting his help in the hunt for "a very special object." He'd met her, agreed to her terms. Even then he'd suspected some far more intricate business was afoot.

He hadn't been prepared for the killing part.

That moment when he'd first seen Lilou in the shadows—seen her, and *known* that she wasn't human—had blown apart his sense of reality. It had gone from a wide open plain where everything was in view, to a land of mountains and hills, valleys and forests, where more was hidden than in sight. Acting to save her life had been purely instinctive.

Chin resting on his chest, head throbbing, blood dripping from some wounds, already drying on others, that moment swept past again and again. He couldn't imagine it ever having played out any differently, and as memory consumed him and became real—

Daley and Celine worked for Mary Rock, and they'd known what they were seeking. The *real* object of the hunt. They'd just never told him. Maybe they still didn't trust his reaction, and in that they were right.

They had chased the shape through hidden ways deep beneath the city, cornering it at last. Daley had shot the fleeting shadow with the dart gun. It had fallen, squirmed, then laid still. Celine laughed, swept her silver hair back over her shoulder like a flirty girl, then pulled the blades from her belt and advanced on the creature. The *girl*. Butchery was her intent.

Vince demanded to know what they were doing, and Celine gave him a withering glare.

"You really think this is all about relics?" she asked.

Vince struck Daley across the back of the knees with his carved oak stick, which he brought with him on every relic hunt. It had caved in rats' skulls, shoved aside floating isles of garbage in fetid sewers, felt the way into dark tunnels, and it was his friend. Now it broke, and Daley roared in rage as he fell. Vince used the sharp end to smack Celine across the throat.

Then he grabbed the shape. She was light, unconscious, and beautiful. As he slung her over his shoulder he fell in love with her, gasping at the foolishness of the thought. Fear was fucking with him.

Celine screamed after him into the darkness, through the tunnels, promising pain and death when she caught him.

The chase. He was the relic hunter, he knew these dark subterranean places well, but they pursued with the promise of blood on their lips. Celine had never liked him. Daley was muscle and hate on legs. If he was going to escape them he'd have to—

The woman woke and started thrashing.

He slipped and fell.

"No, I'm trying to help you," he said. "I don't know what you are but—"

She rolled away from him. There were cracked tiles beneath his hands, something roaring in the distance, no human voice. He'd found his way onto an old platform, long-since abandoned. He might have been here before. The signs said "British Museum," the station empty and falling apart for almost a century. Then he heard it.

A train.

Daley came first, bursting from the shadows and matching the approaching engine's roar. He charged into Vince and drove him onto his back, so that his head connected with the tiles in a blinding flash, the impact burning away shadows and giving him a white-hot clarity.

These were his last moments. What little light existed was swallowed by the knives in Daley's hands, making them shine. His head was full of fire.

Vince kicked up and out and his feet sank into the mountain of Daley.

Celine shouted a warning. Maybe her cry caused Daley's pause, which enabled Vince to piston his arms on the ground and push the huge man up and back. Or maybe he was already falling.

Daley, the brother of Claudette, Mary Rock's most brutal lieutenant, slipped from the platform and seemed to float there on solid shadows, taking forever to sink down onto the track even as the roar became a scream, warm air squirmed alive through the tunnel and across the unused platform, lights blossomed and blinded. Daley's scream seemed to become louder than the train's, even though that was impossible. It rose, swirled, higher than was likely from such a brute, and as the train swept him from the world the scream sounded so like—

* * *

A baby was crying.

It echoed around the old swimming pool, a pained call that grated against Vince's nerves and grasped his spine, squeezing. A horrible sound.

He jerked in the seat, bindings biting against him and pinching his skin even more. Blood dribbled. The bruises and ruptured skin all across his body sang out, begging him to remain motionless. But snapped out of his dreamlike memory, Vince had to see what came next.

Ballus had spent an hour battering and beating him with rotting body parts, prodding him with the splintered bone, breaking skin and allowing in infection, all the while demanding that he surrender what he knew. Yet somewhere, Vince had discovered a strength he never thought he had. The more he hurt, the less likely he was to tell. Lilou smiled in his mind's eye, and he couldn't find it in himself to betray her trust. He never would.

She and her kind could have killed him, after all.

The scream came again. Closer and louder, and Vince could tell that it wasn't actually human after all. He was glad for that, but also more terrified. If not human, then what?

He heard Ballus's pounding hooves before he saw him. The satyr ran into view at the far end of the hall, down by the deep end where dead things festered. Weak sunlight pierced the smashed high-level windows and slanted across the big space, some of it filtered green through the weeds that had taken root across the deserted building's roofline. Spears of light illuminated the big man-goat as he ran closer, making it difficult to discern the struggling shape he carried under one arm.

Ballus was laughing. His voice went high as a little girl's, then low as mud. He sang and grumbled, and as he drew closer, Vince could see the delight on his face.

He kicked aside the rotten limbs of impossible creatures, then stood just ten feet away, strong and upright as if waiting for praise from a proud parent. A fox thrashed and snapped beneath his right arm. Ballus barely seemed to notice.

"Dinner?" Vince asked.

"Now there's an idea," Ballus said. He flung the fox up with his right hand, caught it with both, and then squeezed. The animal yelped with that horribly human voice once again. Blood pattered across cracked floor tiles. Ballus grimaced, his muscles bulged, and he tugged hard.

With a cry that bit into Vince's heart, the fox was ripped in two. Fur stretched and tore, steaming insides drooped down, bleeding things splashing on tiles and flesh long-since rotten. The warm stench of death filled the air, but to Vince it was like a fresh breath. It overlaid the scent of decay.

"Huh!" Ballus grunted, dropping both parts of the ruined animal at his feet. He performed a grotesque jig, hooves stomping down and ripping more flesh, crushing more bone. Then he stood on the animal's back end, bent down, and tore off its tail.

"This is done, isn't it? This is one of your weird human customs."

He came toward Vince with the tail, once bushy, now heavy with gore and shit. Vince flinched back, but he had nowhere to go. Ballus slapped the tail back and forth across his face.

He tasted blood and faeces, smelled it, felt its warmth. It entered his eyes, turning his whole world red, but Vince did not gag. He grew angry, and that was something he was doing his best to grab hold of. Though terrified and disgusted, shocked and sickened, through all of this it was the anger that might save him.

"They're coming!" Ballus said. He was pacing now, kicking aside the dead things he had used to abuse and torture his prisoner. He seemed unconcerned with the question he had been asking again and again—*Where are they?*—and the anxiety was a hot ball in Vince's stomach.

"Who's coming?"

Ballus scooped up part of the dead fox and shook it close to Vince's face, laughing. "Them! Looking for *me*, looking for *you*, lambs to the *slaughter*." He paused, head tilted to one side as he mused, "It really couldn't have gone any better."

Vince spat blood from his mouth. His lips were split, burning, and he couldn't tell whose blood he was swallowing. He supposed it didn't really matter. Ballus would kill him soon, and he'd end up in that rancid water, rotting down into a mulch with creatures that should not be.

All these discoveries should have been wonderful, but right then nothing was.

Suddenly it stopped.

"Sorry to say, we've got to leave this place," Ballus announced.

"But I was just starting to like it here."

"You're joking with me?" The satyr leaned in close, his strange face chipped from harsh stone. Then he laughed out loud. Vince could only close his eyes and turn aside.

Ballus disappeared behind him and grabbed the back of the chair, tilting it backward and dragging it across the pool floor. The legs screeched against the tiles, jolting now and then when they hit a broken one.

Birds took flight up in the roof space, flitting from metal supports and then darting through smashed windows. Yet they must have heard much worse before, and Vince wondered why any of them had ever come back. He tilted his head and looked up at the back of Ballus's head. The satyr was mumbling to himself, words that Vince couldn't quite hear or understand. He found no hope of escape. Even if he could slip his bonds, the beast had just ripped a live animal apart with his bare hands.

"Why are you doing this?" he asked through swollen lips.

"It's complicated."

With a single heave, Ballus lifted Vince and the chair out of the pool and onto the poolside. Climbing to join him, he grabbed the chair and continued on his way. Moments later they passed out of the hall, along a darkened corridor, and into a lobby area.

Boarding had been placed across the wide front doors and windows, and Ballus passed them by. The floor was undamaged here. The chair slid almost noiselessly, and Vince actually relaxed back into the tilted seat, his wounds and bruises protesting but his tiredness embracing the opportunity to recline.

They entered a large room containing old, rusted pool machinery, then Ballus started descending a staircase. The chair thumped down onto the metal treads, each impact reminding Vince of every wound the satyr had given him. There were many. His clothes were wet with blood, and it was all he could do not to scream each time.

At the bottom of the stairs Ballus paused, kicked open a heavy metal door, and started down again. More thudding, creaking as the chair struggled beneath the impacts, and Vince closed his eyes. He remembered the many amazing things he had seen and accepted over the years, and the wonder he'd felt realizing that Lilou was one of them. A *living* one.

Ballus, too. Him and his pool of dead creatures that few people would understand, even if they were ever found.

"Why are you doing this?" he asked again. For a while Ballus did not reply. They descended into shadowy basements, then out through a door and along a corridor that appeared to be hacked into raw stone. The satyr grabbed a flashlight from somewhere, and then came a brick-lined tunnel, with a long slope heading steadily downward. Light danced, and Ballus's shadow bulged and stretched back the way they had come.

"Because I'm going to be the last of the Kin."

His voice was calmer than Vince had yet heard, though he sounded at his maddest.

"I'm going to be famous."

Angela hated the idea of telling anyone where she was. She'd made such an effort to lose any followers that to give away her location seemed like a backward step. But she also knew that she couldn't do any of this on her own. She was desperate to find Vince, but she had to face the sobering fact that she had to determine where to begin.

So in the end, she had to sit in the cyber café, drinking more coffee and eating a second slice of cake, until Dean called her back. Her phone was on silent, but there were already seven missed calls. It was the same number every time, not recognised. Having lost her, it seemed her followers were eager to regain contact.

Finally Dean's number showed up on the screen. Leaving the café, she stopped at a small shop to buy some new clothes, because wearing someone else's felt wrong. The light jacket fitted her better, the summer hat shadowed her features, and wearing a skirt for the first time in years felt strange, but good. She looked less like herself than she had in a long time.

Even so, she felt eyes upon her.

Years of research into the criminal mind had revealed some secrets of covert observation, and she knew just how dangerous electronic communications might be. Internet, email, texting, phone calls, online messenger, Skyping, and Internet calls—all of them were tied into a web that any skilled pursuer might be able to penetrate. When Dean told her his intended meeting place, she'd imagined Claudette and Harry sitting in a car somewhere, wearing small headphones and smiling as they closed a laptop and started the engine.

So she was especially careful as she approached the west entrance to the shopping mall. The streets were busy, a riot of colour and movement, with cars lining up, buses puffing diesel clouds, and pedestrians weaving singular routes through the chaos. Some of them chatted with friends, others walked on their own, focused and alone. A few stroked smartphone screens as they went, somehow managing to avoid colliding with others or being run over.

Angela watched them all from where she stood at a bus stop, and there was no sign of anyone she recognised. If Mary Rock's people had somehow found her again, they were keeping their pursuit well hidden.

She stepped away from the bus line, crossed the road with a group of people, then walked through the swinging doors into the mall. It was warm inside, and ringing with the sounds of shoppers going about their business. A street musician plucked Beatles numbers from his acoustic guitar, drawing a small crowd. A gang of teenagers slouched in seats outside an ice cream parlor, taking selfies and laughing, and she wondered why they weren't in school and why no one was asking them. Probably most people thought they were someone else's problem, and right then so did she.

Last thing she wanted was to draw attention to herself.

Two escalators rose to the second floor, and beside them was an electronic store locator. She tapped in "Gregg's" and studied the screen's map, then continued onward. The bakery was at the far end, and the man wanted to meet her there, but not inside.

"They won't want me in there," he'd said, and she was curious as to why. Perhaps he was even more cautious than her.

She left the mall through the eastern doors. Gregg's was busy, and shoppers spewed out into a large landscaped area with benches, fountains, several felt-smooth lawns and a few copses of trees offering precious shade. The day was growing warmer, and Angela hadn't had a drink in hours.

Standing outside the mall she felt a chill, a deep shiver that would usually make her comment to Vince, *"Someone just walked over my grave."* But not today. She didn't want to say that today. Coming to meet a stranger, with no one knowing where she was, was something she'd have never contemplated just a couple of days ago. How quickly a life could change.

"Fairy," a voice said, and when she turned around a man was sitting on a bench watching her. He was scruffy and old, with straggly gray hair and wrinkles deep enough to park a bike in. Although he appeared confused, she could perceive a deeper truth in his eyes. He wore his age as a disguise, and couldn't camouflage his simmering intelligence.

He glanced around and held out his hand.

Angela pulled a couple of pound coins from her pocket and gave them to him. He had a large wheeled suitcase, and she wondered what it contained. He wore a shabby old coat, and for a panicked moment she thought it might hide wings, or scales, or fur. Still, he looked so very human.

"You seem nervous," he said.

"Mary Rock's people are looking for me."

His eyes went wide. "That bitch?"

"You know her?" She'd spoken without thinking, and wondered whether she'd made a mistake. The woman's reach must go far, and she had no idea who it encompassed. Claudette, Harry, Vince… this man?

"I know something of her business." He almost spat the last word. He looked around, even shiftier and more cautious than before. "Come on, we can't talk out in the open. You're sure they're not still following you?"

No, she thought, but she nodded.

"Good. Come on then. Pretend you're buying me a meal." He rose, groaning and taking a while to stand. His joints clicked and creaked, and she saw just how old he was. "Actually, don't just pretend. A pasty would go down a treat right now."

Before they could move to the bakery, though, it all came pouring out.

"My boyfriend worked for her, and now he's vanished," Angela said. "She says he kills them. Butchers them for their parts. Like relics. And I think she wants to kill him for that, and she has a fairy she's protecting in her basement, and—"

"Protecting?" His surprise was evident, his voice edged with anger.

Angela frowned.

Someone grabbed her arm, tight, and started pulling her away from him.

Angela fisted her hand and swung around. She seemed to be watching and experiencing this moment from somewhere else. She felt the grip on her arm, saw the old man's surprise, and swung her whole body into the punch. She hadn't struck anyone in anger in over twenty years, since she'd had a fight in school back in Boston.

Her fist connected with the woman's shoulder, a glancing blow. Expecting to see Claudette or Harry there, she was surprised when the punch had little effect, and woman squeezed her arm harder. She was short and slight, with exotic features and piercing eyes. The sight gave Angela pause.

There's something about her.

"No more," the woman whispered. "I know Vince."

Angela looked around to see if anyone had seen the exchange. A mother urged her two toddlers away. A group of teenagers sitting on the marble wall around a fountain laughed and nudged each other.

"Angela!" the woman said loudly, and the faux delight in her voice elicited an unconscious smile. It couldn't be helped, not if they wanted to deflect attention. When the woman threw her arms around her, pulling her tight, she couldn't help but hug back.

"My name's Lilou," the woman whispered into her ear. "I'm a friend. I can keep you safe, and if you want to save him, you'll come with me."

A flush of emotions—fear, doubt, confusion—vied for supremacy within Angela, but it was grief that burst through. Feeling irrationally safe, she hugged Lilou even tighter.

"Not here. Not now." Lilou pried her arms away.

"You followed me?" the man asked.

"Dean, this isn't something for you," Lilou said.

"Of course it is!"

Lilou grasped Angela's hand and walked away, pulling her back toward the mall entrance.

"Wait!" Dean shouted. He came after them, towing his suitcase. It made a grinding noise as the wheels ground across the knobbled concrete paving at the entrance. "She knows something—you can't take her away, I've only just found her!"

"She found you," Lilou said quietly.

Angela went with her. The woman felt like control, while Dean, the old man, seemed chaotic. It was control that she craved. She'd had enough of chaos.

With Dean shouting and rushing to catch up, they arrived at the entrance. A big security guard who looked like a fatter and older Idris Elba stepped through the automatic doors, appraising the situation. He saw two attractive women approaching and an agitated old street guy hurrying after them.

"Is this gentleman bothering you ladies?" Idris said.

Angela glanced at Lilou. The woman said nothing. She only smiled.

Idris's eyes went wide, then he ushered the woman into the mall and stood across the doorway, almost blocking it.

"I'm afraid I can't let you in, sir," he said.

"What was that?" Angela asked. "What's happening? When you smiled something..." *Something happened*, she wanted to say, but she realised how odd that would sound.

"We've caused a stir," Lilou said. "We need to get away from here. It's far too open."

"Who are you? What's happening? Where's Vince?"

"Come on. I'll talk while we walk."

18

Whenever he closed his eyes, Vince saw Daley stumbling back from his kick, falling, consumed by the animal roar and blinding light of the Underground train. The big man's scream had combined with the train's and echoed along the tunnel, lasting far, far longer than the man himself. Vince had felt something splash his face. Later, he found blood caked there, but he wasn't sure it was Daley's.

It might have come from the second person he had murdered.

Because after Daley was pulped by the train, Celine had come for him, screaming like a banshee, silvery hair seeming to capture the weak light from Daley's dropped flashlight.

He hadn't even had a chance to stand. Still dizzied from the blow to the head, stunned by what had happened, Vince rolled and reached for the knife Daley had dropped.

He'd had only seconds. Nowhere near long enough to save himself—no chance at all. And yet in that subterranean darkness already smelling of blood and death, his splayed fingers had curled around the blade's handle as if fate itself was guiding his hand.

Celine had leapt at him, he'd rolled back with the knife held out before him, and she fell on it, unable to stop herself. A cold pain flared in his elbow. He felt the knife pop through her clothing and skin, a gush of warmth, her frantic writhing as she tried to lift herself away. It was horrible. He'd been able to smell her fear and pain. Her hair swept across his face and stung his eyes. He closed them, and then she butted him hard in the face.

A light flared, and then darkness.

The next thing he remembered was being in the room with Lilou, and the rescued had become the rescuer.

Vince opened his eyes to the dancing of shadows, and Ballus shrieked something incomprehensible. He was still in the chair, still being dragged, but now they were deeper. He felt the weight of the world around him, the heavy staleness of the air, the stink of old times and older shit.

He'd passed out, perhaps only for a few seconds. Maybe he'd lost too much blood. He hadn't drunk anything since Ballus had taken him. How long ago that was, he wasn't sure. Several hours? A day? Maybe more. His perception of time was stilted, confused by periods of sleep, waking, and unconsciousness brought on by the beatings to which he'd been subjected.

Perhaps he had broken bones.

He felt sick. Lost. Incredibly alone.

"Bastard," he croaked, dry throat rasping.

All movement ceased. The halt was so sudden, the stillness so intense, that Vince caught his breath and froze. He thought for a moment that he might have blacked out again, just long enough for Ballus to prop him here amongst the slime and shit.

Then he heard breathing, and a heavy shadow closed

over him as Ballus leaned down into view from behind the chair, his face upside down.

"I thought you were asleep," the satyr said, shattering the silence with another of his mad shrieks. It echoed through tunnels, breaking the darkness.

Vince bit his tongue to avoid crying out in shock and fear. He closed his eyes, making it only a little darker. The flashlight Ballus carried wasn't very powerful, and he dreaded the idea that its batteries might run out.

"I'll tell you where they are," Vince said. The words fell from his mouth unbidden, surprising him, and he had to question whether he really would tell. After holding out for so long, enduring such torture, it seemed as if his subconscious was ready to give up anything, just to escape this horror.

The chair tilted back again, feet dragging across the ground.

"Too late," Ballus said. "I don't need to know anymore."

"Let me go and I'll—"

"Have you met my new friends?" the satyr asked. "They know it all down here. They dance with me. Did I tell you I could dance? Did I show you?"

Vince said nothing, didn't want to encourage him, but Ballus was already whispering words he couldn't make out, a strange sing-song that might have been a poem in a lost language. Moments later, the first of the squealing and scampering began. The whisper of hundreds of claws on damp stone. The echoing tones of many small voices.

He tried to find sense in the sound, terrified that he would, and then the first shapes edged into the flashlight's weak influence. Dozens of them, following obediently, noses twitching, naked tails slipping across the ground behind them.

"You're friends with rats," Vince said, and he managed a laugh. "Why doesn't that surprise me?"

"Not only rats," Ballus said, and he continued that strange, unknown song.

Beyond the rats, larger shadows appeared. The flashlight beam seemed to veer away from them, unable to penetrate shape or form. There might have been doorways or hollows in the walls, home to a deeper darkness, but Vince knew they had passed none. The tunnel was old and relatively smooth. Vaulted brick ceilings echoed slithering, wet sounds.

Wet sounds that whispered eagerly of fresh meat.

"Meet my *true* friends," Ballus said. "I call them dregs."

Being in the shopping mall made Angela feel guilty. She was somewhere safe, protected, and so familiar that Vince's predicament seemed a world away. She was more and more certain that wherever he might be, he was in terrible danger. This strange woman, Lilou, had said as much.

Strange she was, for sure. Moving quietly together through the crowds felt natural, because such discussions couldn't occur in a place like this. Too many ears, too many eyes. Angela felt her attention drawn again and again to Lilou. In fact she could hardly look away, and several times she had to apologise as she bumped into other people when she didn't watch where she was going.

She could only think of how beautiful Lilou was. It wasn't a classical beauty, and it went far deeper than her appearance. She exuded magnetism in every movement, every look, the way she repeatedly flicked an errant strand of hair from her eyes, the arch of one eyebrow, her perky pointed nose and the glacial green of her eyes. She bore a natural grace.

She flows like nature, Angela thought, the idea odd and yet entirely apt.

As they passed through the mall's wide central area, she realised she wasn't the only person affected that way. Heads were turning, men mostly, but a few women, too. And with every moment that passed, Lilou was becoming more agitated.

"What is it?" Angela asked.

"Don't like places like this. Got to get out of here."

"What's wrong?"

"Too many humans."

Angela laughed, waiting for Lilou to look at her and smile, but the woman stared ahead. They took a wide corridor lined with small independent stores and leading away from the main shopping area. Lilou was breathing fast.

"Are you okay?" Angela asked, when a thousand other more impossible questions pressed at her.

"I will be," Lilou said. "There, that'll do." She headed for a door marked PRIVATE, pushed through, and Angela went with her. She expected alarms to sound and people to come running, but nothing happened.

Beyond was a narrow corridor, walls flaking with old paint, and several doors led to other rooms. Lilou ignored them all and marched along to a metal door at the corridor's end. It was bolted and padlocked, but the padlocks hung loose on their hooks. She drew back the bolts and hauled it open.

Once again, Angela stepped out into the secret back of things. The service area was large and well used. A dozen wheeled refuse carts stood lined against the shopping mall's wall, and across the yard a few more were fixed to the heavy metal fence. A set of gates stood open, and several small trucks were parked in delivery bays to their left. One had its engine still running, and a man and woman stood chatting beside the cab. They glanced across at Lilou and Angela but seemed disinterested.

"What's happening?" Angela asked. The question encompassed so much, and she felt a rush of desperation and panic at every possibility the answer might present.

"I'm getting control," Lilou said. She breathed deeply. In the light of day, she seemed not to glow quite so much.

"You said you know where Vince is," Angela said, stopping. "I need to know. I've lost him, and everything's gone so strange." That panic again, a building pressure and heat behind her eyes—but her anger was growing, too. It was time someone told her what the hell was going on.

"We need to keep walking," Lilou said. "Find somewhere quiet to talk. And I need to find a fox."

A fox? Angela thought. *I followed a fox. Didn't I?*

"Mary Rock's people might be following me," she said. "Not anymore."

"You're sure?"

Lilou glanced at her as if she was stupid. "Yes."

"A fox helped me lose them." It sounded ridiculous, and she waited for Lilou to mock her. But she merely grunted and led them from the yard.

They crossed a huge open-air parking lot, threading between cars and heading for a main road beyond. Once over a bridge spanning the road they came to a canal, and it was there that Lilou started to slow and relax. She paused and looked around, hands on her hips, as if searching for something or someone. Then she nodded and her shoulders slumped.

"What the fuck is going on?" Angela asked. "Where's Vince? How do *you* know him?" It came out like an accusation.

"Vince saved my life," Lilou said, then she pointed. "Over here. There's a bench, and she'll be here soon."

"Who?"

Lilou didn't reply. Angela felt like grabbing her, shaking the truth from her, but at the thought of doing so, she felt suddenly afraid. As if she didn't know what reaction such an act might cause.

They sat on a bench overlooking the canal. The bank was overgrown with brambles and wild flowers, empty cans were crushed and torn underfoot, smashed glass crunched beneath their shoes. Three used condoms were laid carefully over one of the bench's arms. The corpse of a shopping cart protruded from the water's scummed surface. Lilou seemed to see none of this.

"So tell me," Angela said.

"Vince saved my life," she said again. "He put himself in danger, and killed two people who were going to kill me."

"He… killed?" The idea was so alien that it wouldn't settle properly.

"Threw one in front of a train. Stabbed the other. He got stabbed in the arm and took a good wound to the head. It knocked him out, so I took him to the safe place and tended him until he was well again."

"Where was this? When?"

"Recently, but he escaped, probably because he was worried for you."

"I thought I saw him on my street, I'm sure it was him, but then I saw…"

"You saw Sandri May, murdered in cold blood."

"I saw *some*thing."

231

Suddenly Lilou started to cry. Her shoulders shook once, then she wiped angrily at her eyes.

"Are you…?" Angela asked, but she could not complete the sentence. *Human?* Even after what she had seen, what she had persuaded herself to believe, actually saying it seemed foolish.

"You're in danger," Lilou said. "I can protect you."

"You said Vince is in danger. I can look after myself."

Lilou actually smiled. "Yeah, you already lost them once."

"Claudette and Harry asked me where Vince was."

"It was Claudette's brother he killed. Daley. And Celine, the woman he stabbed, there are rumors she was Mary Rock's lover."

"Why were they trying to kill you?"

Lilou frowned, half smiling at the same time.

"I don't know how much you know."

"Assume I know everything."

The woman laughed, and it was as if she let something slip, a veil or shield that separated her from the world. Angela wanted to lean across and touch the curve of her throat, and she felt a strange tingling in her chest, like a yearning for something long-lost.

"No one knows everything," Lilou said, sighing sadly. "No one has a mind large enough." She glanced to their left, startled. Angela saw nothing, but Lilou seemed to be listening, their surroundings going silent with her, like holding a breath. Vehicle engines seemed farther away. Plane trails crossed the sky, engine sounds absent.

Vince has killed someone, she thought, and at that she accepted the fact without question. She hated it, it made her feel sick, but she didn't doubt. She did not believe that the woman with her would lie, and perhaps she *could* not lie. There was a purity to her that felt almost too large to understand.

My lover, my Vince, a killer.

"Why were they trying to kill you?" she asked again, and at that moment the answer was the most important thing in the world. Because though Vince was a killer, perhaps she could still love him. Maybe she could even love him more.

"They wanted to cut me up," Lilou said. "Slice me to pieces. Use me for all manner of things."

"He dealt in the relics of old dead things."

"To start with, yes, but then he learnt the truth—that some of us Kin still live—and Mary Rock got her claws into him."

Some of us kin, Angela thought. *There it is. There's the truth about her, and perhaps soon I'll ask what she is.* Instead she said, "But the people he killed were working for her?"

"The profit involved in fresh relics is unimaginable," Lilou said bitterly. "She uses our parts to make potions and medicines for various clients. There are rich people who like to collect certain parts... fingers, eyes, breasts, wings, or claws. Mary Rock's speciality is a dining club."

"A fairy has to eat," Angela said.

"Not that sort of—" Lilou said, then she froze and stared at Angela. For the first time the full impact of her stare, her presence, her *alienness* hit home, and Angela shoved herself back along the seat, her insides fluid and warm and as scared of this woman as she had ever been of anyone or anything.

"What did you say?" Lilou asked.

"A fairy has to eat. Mary Rock said it to me after she showed me."

"Showed you...?"

"Her fairy." Angela frowned, because little of what Mary Rock had told her now made sense. "The one she said she was protecting from people like Vince."

"She is still alive," Lilou said, eyes going wide. "She lives?"

"In a room. Locked away. Protected."

"Not protected. A prisoner. She's still alive." She stood and laughed. "She can't be killed. Of *course* she can't. She's still alive!"

"But... scarred. Wounded."

Lilou looked at her, blinking quickly, the smile still on her face.

"Look, I need to know where Vince is," Angela said. Lilou looked around, then crouched down and opened her arms wide, a welcoming gesture.

A streak of auburn flitted from the bushes, and a fox leapt into her arms.

"Lilou," Angela said. "Please. Lilou!"

But the woman was already talking to the fox.

Angela could only sit and watch. She heard Lilou's voice, low and quiet, and behind that were occasional strange growls and whimpers from the fox. It was a fascinating, disturbing scene, and she wondered what Lilou and the animal would do if someone came along and saw them.

Someone *else*. Because Angela was bearing witness, and neither of them seemed concerned. Perhaps some of the weird conversation was about her.

The strangest sound came from the animal. And then it seemed to cry, hunkered down at Lilou's feet where she crouched. She reached out and scratched the animal behind the ears.

Angela felt a vibration and checked her phone. A missed call from Lucy, but nothing else. She fingered the screen and brought up Dean's number, thumb hovering as she debated whether to call him again. She was growing impatient, and desperate, but Lilou seemed to have more answers. She was one of *them*, and she'd suggested that she knew where Vince was. He'd saved her life, so surely she owed him.

"Lilou," she said softly, and the woman stood and turned around, tears streaking her face, eyes wide, pupils dilated and irises a shimmering shade of yellow. She blinked a few times and they returned to pale green, and between blinks the fox darted away. Seconds later it was as if the animal had never been there at all. It might have been a dream.

Lilou came so close to Angela that she could smell her breath. It smelled wild.

"She is the only important thing now," Lilou said. "I'm sorry, Angela. The creature that has Vince knows we're searching for him. He's already killed one of the Seven, an old cousin of the fox I just conversed with." She looked down, as if the thought caused her pain.

"So what does that mean?"

"It means my priorities have changed. We all believed Her gone for many, many years. But now we have to get Her back."

"The fairy?"

"Yes. She's much older and more powerful than any of us." Lilou paused as if seeing a distant memory. "And as unknowable to us as we are to humans."

"Where has the fox gone?" Panic filled Angela now, simmering like acid in her gut.

"To tell the others." Distracted, Lilou stood and started walking along the canal path. Angela could only follow, jogging to keep up.

"But what about Vince?"

Lilou moved faster. Angela was almost sprinting now, even though the woman beside her wasn't even breathing hard. The canal curved, a tall wall to their left swathed in brambles, ivy, and colourful graffiti. She reached out and grabbed Lilou's arm, fingers digging in as she skidded to a halt.

Lilou spun around, eyes wide. She seemed excited and energised, and it took a second for her to focus again.

"He saved your life!" Angela said.

Lilou nodded.

"Where *is* he?" she demanded. "Please. I'm desperate here, and I have no idea what's going on, or who you are, or what's going to happen next. This isn't my world. I don't understand it, *any* of it. So you can't just run away and leave me now, can't just—"

"I'm not going to leave you," Lilou said. "I'll look after you. But we'll have to get Her back. We'll wait until dark."

"Why?"

"Some of the others don't look quite as human as me."

"I don't care!" Angela shouted. She looked around, hoping that she might cause a scene and force Lilou to take heed, but they were alone. The tall wall bounded one bank of the canal, and on the other side were the blank faces of old buildings, windows barred and smashed, stonework crumbling and damp. She was in the center of London, but she might as well have been nowhere. "Who's got him?"

"If you go alone, you'll die."

"So fucking help me!"

Lilou drifted away again, concentration focusing somewhere else. She started walking, and Angela matched her pace. As they walked she stroked her phone, fell back a few paces, and Dean picked up on the second ring.

"Where is he?" she asked without preamble. "Where's Vince?" She was whispering, watching Lilou a few paces ahead, but the strange woman seemed not to hear. She was too wrapped up in her own world. The world of fairies, and strange creatures slaughtered for fancies, exotic medicines, and dining clubs for the rich and grotesque.

A fairy's got to eat, Mary Rock had told her, and the wretched creature tracked her with sad, bottomless eyes as she walked from the room. *A cell*, Angela realised. *I'm a fool for not seeing that before, but everything was so—*

"She was asking about a satyr," Dean said. "Maybe that's got something to do with where your chap is. I told her about an old pool, a place where people have seen and heard things."

"Where?" she hissed. *A satyr!* She had an image of one from old movies, and as that vision played in her mind and she saw it stamping down its hooves, she heard the terrible crunching sound from her dark street, and the patches on the tarmac the next day.

"An old municipal pool, close to Tufnell Park. Been closed for decades. I'm on my way, maybe there's—"

Angela cut the connection. Her heart hammered. She was taking action, and now that she'd begun she would not stop. Lilou had come to her, after all.

"He's in Tufnell Park!" she shouted, and Lilou stopped and turned around. "I'm going to find him. Maybe I'll call the police, or…" Or. Another possibility was already presenting itself to her.

"You can't go," Lilou said.

"Watch me!"

"Ballus will kill you, and then he'll kill Vince. He's only holding him as bait, and when you turn up and he

237

realises none of us are coming—"

"He's *not* fucking *bait!*" Angela shouted. She saw movement past Lilou now, a man and woman jogging toward them along the towpath. "He's the man I love. I've been told so many lies about him, and by him, but I still love him, and I won't just abandon him when he's in danger."

Lilou looked torn. There was an excitement about her still, a wide-eyed wonder that would have looked more at home on a child's face. But she also bore a heavy sadness.

"Please," Angela said. "I'll help you rescue the fairy. I've seen her, I know where she is. I remember the room."

"Her scars," Lilou said. "How old?"

"Some of them looked fresh."

The couple jogged past them in a rush of lycra and sweat, and the man stumbled as he glanced back at Lilou. Then the woman. Her defenses were down. She was captivating, her beauty hypnotic, and Angela wondered about her and Vince. But there were only so many questions she could ask, and only so much pain she could endure.

Now was not the time.

"Mary Rock has been trying to kill Her," Lilou whispered. She turned to the wall, sliced her finger against her left canine, and started daubing blood amongst the graffiti. Angela watched for a moment, making no sense of the symbols and letters darkening into the stone.

"I'm going, with or without you," she said. "I'll get help. You can't stop me." Lilou appeared not to hear.

Watching an unknown creature leaving an arcane message in blood, Angela dialed The Slaughterhouse and asked to speak with Fat Frederick Meloy.

19

She's still alive.

More than that, She was still here! In the world, with them, a part of this damned existence that their lives had inexorably become.

Lilou could hardly believe it. She quizzed Angela more about the fairy, and there was no way this human woman could have made it up. She was speaking the truth. She had seen Her, and perhaps soon they could rescue Her from Mary Rock's clutches.

Once free, She could once again give Herself a name.

For so long She had been nameless, little more than a memory within the Kin. They'd believed that She had died decades before, during the latest of the great wars that humanity seemed so keen to fight amongst themselves. No one knew how She was supposed to have died, and songs had been sung about the possibilities. Sad songs that stopped birds in their flight and made streams flow uphill. Tales had been formed and told, edged with uncertainty but solid in their intent. She had been among the best of them, and to lose Her had been one more step along the long, terrifying path toward extinction.

Where had She been? Where had She remained hidden

for so long, and why?

How had Mary Rock managed to capture the fairy? These were important questions. The answers might inspire a dozen more songs, but right then the stark, wonderful fact of her survival was all that mattered.

Mallian would be so excited. Just fifteen minutes ago Ballus had been their focus, and Lilou's knowledge of where he might be would lead to conflict. Now that focus and emphasis had changed. Ballus had become an afterthought.

Still, Angela might cause them a problem.

"You can't tell them what I am," Lilou said.

"What *are* you?" Angela asked.

"A nymph," Lilou answered, then she added, "A sexual creature. Not the last of my kind, but there aren't many of us who remain."

She could see that the woman was bursting with questions, but everything about her was concentrated on getting her man back. Lilou could understand. Vince was a good person, with a solid heart. Angela was lucky.

A moment of uncertainty surprised her. She remembered the two of them in his cell, the flush of passion and desire, the animal lust she inspired in him. Yet a nymph had no truck with guilt, not for something that came as naturally as breathing. Lilou smiled inwardly and shook her head. Maybe she was spending too much time among humans.

"That's him," Angela said, pointing across the parking lot at the car that had just pulled up.

"I shouldn't be doing this," Lilou said.

"You promised. And he saved your life."

She sighed. In truth she was afraid, because she knew Ballus of old. He'd been a monster ever since she had known him, but back then at least he had still been one

240

of them. Brutal, angry, probably already mad, he'd still had the same aims and ambitions as most of the Kin. Survival and peace.

She wasn't sure when he had begun to change.

All she knew for certain was that it had not been gradual. His vicious murder of two of their kind, then his disappearance into the bowels of the city, had shaken everyone. Every rare life was precious, each death a tragedy, and the more of them who passed on, the more precious they became. There were so few left.

Lilou believed they had already passed the point of no return, and that they were railing against fate and time. Other Kin also accepted it, that their fate was to fade away. A few wanted to rage against the dying of the light, but they all sang a song of sadness, and even those prone to struggle were desperate and forlorn.

The Time when their ancestors had enjoyed dominion over the world was long gone. Their fate had been decided by history, and entropy, and the inevitability of moving on. Humanity would move on, too, and although as a civilisation it was still only young, they could all see the signs of its downfall and dissolution, blooming already.

She wasn't sure about Mallian. He bore an anger that blazed far hotter than good sense should allow. In a way he was the very opposite of Ballus. That mad satyr wanted to be the last of them. In Mallian's unguarded moments, when he and Lilou lay together in sweat and fleeting instants of love, he professed a desire for the Kin to rise again.

He even whispered a name, both title and intention.

"Ascent," he'd breathed into her ear, the word setting a seed of fear in her soul.

But it was fear of Ballus that troubled her now. A fear

that he would see her, kill her, and she would never see Mallian or the fairy again.

"What is it that changed you?" Angela said. "Why is she so important?"

"You couldn't understand," Lilou answered. Some of that was a lie, but she would never tell the human. There was too much at stake.

"What's her name?" Angela asked softly.

"Whatever She chooses to call Herself," Lilou said, "and that can change with every breath." She watched four men climb from the car and made certain that she was shielding herself from the world. They'd been waiting for fifteen minutes, so she'd had long enough to compose herself, draw inward, present only that part of her that it was sensible to show.

She had already arranged a place and a time to meet with Mallian, leaving news of the fairy's survival painted in blood-speak. The message would be carried by any of the remaining Seven who saw it, and would appear instantly at nineteen other locations around the city. Lost in graffiti, the messages her kin left were soon washed away by weather and time.

"I'm with you until this evening," Lilou said. "I'll help however I can. After that, you're on your own." Angela was wide-eyed but said nothing. She could see how serious the nymph was.

Lilou hoped it was not a decision she would live to regret.

Angela wasn't stupid. Academically she shone. She had a facility to absorb information and a power of recall that had always stood her in good stead. She was also as worldly wise as anyone like her could be. She hadn't travelled extensively, had only ever lived in the USA and Britain, but she read a lot about the wider world. Her parents were quite liberal, and had encouraged her to grow into her own beliefs, rather than imposing theirs on her.

She was nobody's fool.

Yet as Fat Frederick walked across the car park toward them, she wondered whether she was making the biggest mistake of her life.

"Don't worry," Lilou said, picking up on her concerns. "I've dealt with people like this before. Most of them are harmless."

"Not this one."

Fat Frederick was close now, looking from Angela to Lilou. His gaze lingered longer on Lilou. Cliff was close behind him, and the two other men remained leaning on the Mercedes. The open-air parking lot was busy with people going about their own business, blind to anyone or anything else. A small group meeting close to the exit drew no attention.

Fat Frederick grinned at her.

She suddenly regretted calling him.

"You said you might have something for me," he said, eyeing Lilou up and down. Cliff stared at the nymph as if she was the only person there, his tongue flicking nervously at his lips, but Meloy's expression hinted that he was sharper than she'd given him credit for.

"Not for you," Angela said. "I said I know where Vince is, and that's for me."

Fat Frederick shrugged. The smile slipped into a confused frown as he stared at Lilou.

"And who's this?"

"My name is Lilou. I'm Angela's friend."

"Right. An old friend?"

"Why?"

"What's her middle name?"

He already knows we're lying, Angela thought.

"None of your business," Lilou said, her voice dropping in tone, sultriness oozing through. Cliff blinked rapidly, but Fat Frederick seemed immune.

"We know where he's being kept," Angela said, "and it's dangerous. I couldn't think of anyone else who might be able to help."

"Or be willing to," Fat Frederick added.

"Yeah, that too."

"Who's holding him?" His gaze barely flickered from Lilou. He was appraising her, trying to see past her veneer. Meloy's passion was his relics. If he learned that Lilou and others like her still existed, Angela had no idea how he would react, or how far he might go.

As far as Mary Rock? Perhaps even further.

"Someone called Ballus."

"Eastern European?"

"Dunno," Angela said, "and I don't care. All I care about is Vince, and last time we met you seemed to care about him, too."

"Like I said, one of my best men."

"If we don't get to him soon, Mary Rock might."

Meloy didn't respond. He stared.

"I've found out why she wants him so much," Angela continued. "He killed two of her people. Ballus might sell him to Mary Rock. He's a sort of bounty hunter. Apparently." Still no reaction. Tales of death and murder might not be news for someone like Meloy.

244

He took a step forward, invading Lilou's personal space. He stared into her eyes. Sniffed at her mouth. It was strangely compelling, and disgusting. Perhaps it would intimidate anyone else, but Lilou seemed aloof.

"Hey! Back off, Fat Freddy!" Angela's heart hammered, but she felt curiously brave. *He won't hurt me*, she thought. Then the next second she realised her mistake. She'd let her own sense of what was right buffer her against truly believing what a man like this might do.

He blinked slowly and turned to stare at her. She'd never been stared at like that before. Cool shock pulsed through her body.

"Do you know what—?" he began, but then Lilou spoke. Her voice was low, the words barely even heard. Traffic noise, slamming doors, and the drone of a passenger jet trailing above the city strove to drown them out, but Fat Frederick heard, and that was all that mattered.

"Hurt her," she said, "and I'll hurt you."

He stepped back, confusion evident on his face as he and his bodyguard reeled.

"Who the hell are you?" Meloy managed to ask.

"Don't you mean *what* the hell am I?"

"Lilou, no, you don't know—"

"Enough of this," Lilou said. "I know your sort, Meloy. Help us and I'll help you, make you rich with more relics than you can dream of. Witches' tits, pixies' cocks. But if you choose not to help, then fuck off right now."

Cliff was looking left and right like a lost kid, but to Angela's surprise Fat Frederick gathered himself quickly. He grinned, staring at Angela properly for the first time since arriving.

"Feisty friend you've got here." Angela knew that his bravado hid a deeper uncertainty. "Okay, so let's say I do help you rescue Vince from this… Ballus. What's in it for me?"

"Don't you know yet?" Lilou asked.

All pretense fell away. Gangster, criminal, collector, and murderer, he was also a human, and Angela believed right then that anyone could become Lilou's plaything. He turned toward her.

"What are you?" he whispered.

"Just help us," Angela said. "Please. There's more to this than you can believe."

"And helping you will help me believe." It wasn't a question.

Angela nodded. Lilou sighed and turned away, appearing bored with the conversation.

Maybe he understood, maybe not. She thought he did, but the true implications would take a while to dawn. He wasn't a stupid man, but he was mean. The realisation that he had been wrong for so long might take time to sink through his hard exterior.

"Where and when?" he asked.

"Now," Lilou said. "I'll tell you where. Is that car big enough for six?" Without waiting for a reply she walked across the parking lot toward the gangster's idling Mercedes.

"Angela—" Fat Frederick began, but she pushed past him and shook her head.

"You'll see," she said. "Pretty soon, you'll understand."

I'm doing something so foolish… Lilou thought. She was scared of Ballus, and worried about Mary Rock and her followers. Yet she knew that this was right. Ballus might have already killed Vince, but if not, she should do everything she could to rescue him.

Mallian would be angry, but if she'd asked his opinion he would have talked her out of it. He had a gift like that. *"The fairy,"* he would have said, *"is more important than anything else."*

Yet he also had said of Ballus, *"That bastard has to die."*

Four of them were crushed into the back of the Mercedes. Meloy was in the front, his big bodyguard driving. Two men he'd introduced as Billy and Ming sat in the back. Billy was short, thin and covered in scars, Ming had a long pointed beard. Angela had insisted on sitting squashed in between Ming and Lilou, meaning Lilou was pressed against the door. That was best, she knew. She could rein herself in and keep everything calm.

Meloy was staring at her in the car's side mirror. He dealt in the relics of her dead kin. She didn't like people like him, but had encountered many through the years.

Lilou was not Time-born—few of the remaining Kin were—but she was still very old in human terms. She had known plenty of bad people.

A thousand years before, in a land to the north, soldiers had sacked and burned, raped and killed, all on the orders of a Frenchman who could not have his way. Lilou had been younger of mind and soul then, and she'd taken it upon herself to help a group of women and children fleeing one of the villages. She'd always had a weakness for humans, Mallian often said. She could hardly deny it.

Most soldiers had let them pass, but in a cold forest still gripped by snow they'd encountered one small group, drunk and fired up by blood already spilled. One of them had perceived something in Lilou that caught his eye, understood that she was different. Perhaps in that land of blood and conflict, her difference had shone bright. Whatever the reason, the soldier had dragged her from the small group she was helping, had thrown her to the ground, and pinned her through the shoulder with a pike.

Lilou's scream had brought help. Back then she and her Kin had a far deeper, wider feel for the land and the creatures that lived above, upon, and beneath it. In modern London they used the Seven, foxes that had been alive for a long time, making the city their own. A thousand years ago, it had been the wolves.

The pack arrived quickly. Four of them attacked the soldiers, while three others crouched down close to Lilou, keeping her warm and protecting her from further harm. She had welcomed the animal smell of them, the simplicity of their existence, and their loyalty.

Two soldiers went down with their throats torn out. Others fled. The man who had wounded Lilou remained, pressed against the tree by the alpha male.

"Bad man," Lilou had whispered, and with a twist of its head the wolf bit off the soldier's face.

She remembered the people screaming and crying, and the looks on their faces as the wolves left. She begged the women for help, but to them she was a monster, a witch, a demon, commanding wild animals to kill.

The people she had been trying to help ran away from her, and she never knew what happened to them.

Wounds healed, injuries faded away, and such long periods of time meant that even scars became little more than ghosts. But memories remained.

There had been many more bad men and women. Gertrude, the old woman with an unnatural appetite for children of the Kin. Before he went mad, Ballus had buried her alive in a peat bog in Wales. And there was Nicholas the Rat, a sword for hire whose men regarded him with terror and devotion. He had worked for a Middle Ages equivalent of Mary Rock, and his bloody group had taken a dozen Kin before they were trapped and killed by Mallian.

Such a long life, she mused. *The memories that fill it should be good ones.* But sitting in the back of that cramped vehicle, she remembered only the pain and darkness.

"Do you have weapons?" she asked. None of them replied, and she took that silence as assent. Meloy was still staring at her in his mirror. He exuded cockiness and arrogance, and a naive belief in his own strength.

Soon they'll meet Ballus.

Lilou laughed softly, silently, sending a shiver through the car.

20

"You lost her?"

Mary Rock never raised her voice, but the anger was evident. It could have reached through the phone line and ripped Claudette's brain through her ear.

"She gave us the slip. Knew we were following, left a café through—"

"Of course she knew you were following. She isn't stupid."

"We think she was helped."

"It doesn't matter." Mary Rock fell silent, but she was still there.

Harry tapped the steering wheel gently, humming a random tune. He knew the way the conversation was going. He knew pretty much everything Claudette knew, and that's why they made the perfect team.

But things had started falling apart. She'd felt herself starting to fracture from the moment she rushed down to the derelict British Museum Underground platform and found...

"Tell Harry he's a prick, too," Mary said.

"He knows."

Harry glanced across at Claudette, one corner of his mouth rising slightly. Contrite, embarrassed, angry at himself.

Not like her. Claudette's anger went way beyond anything he was feeling. She wanted to kill someone, and it should have been the girl. Probably would have been, by dusk that very day, if they hadn't lost her.

The world hurried past outside, back and forth along the pavement, as if Daley hadn't been killed beneath these streets. She wanted to shove the door open and scream at them all, pull her knife and get to work on one of the apathetic bastards. See red. Her heart fluttered as she thought of the violence she could wreak.

"We'll find her again," Claudette said. "We have eyes on the streets, they're looking, and as soon as—"

"There are several train parks and servicing depots on the tube line," Mary Rock said. Claudette imagined her sitting in the plush living room, coffee cup on the table, perhaps a plate of biscuits. In the dining room next door, arrangements would be continuing. There was going to be a feast.

"In one of these depots is a train that's been pulled off duty for a while. Some material was found on its wheels and undercarriage, and they have people cleaning it down. I doubt they're being too careful. Maybe they found scraps of clothing, perhaps even some hair, but nothing identifiable. Not after it continued running a day after Daley was pushed in front of it. So your brother's resting place is in the bins and drains of that train depot. They're washing him away, just as they wash down the remnants of squashed cats, dogs, and rats."

"I don't need to hear that," Claudette whispered.

"I think you do," Mary Rock replied, matter-of-fact. "I think you need to understand how much we have to find that fucker. And what of Celine?"

"Mary, *you* don't need to hear that."

"I don't?" Almost a laugh, but Claudette heard her boss's grief. "I see it every day, every night, even though it was you who found her. Tell me again."

"Really?"

"Tell me again."

"She was alone in the dark," Claudette said. Beside her Harry rolled his eyes, and she felt like punching him in the head. Her heart fluttered. Such violence.

"But she was dead when you found her."

"You know she was. I've told you before. The knife was still in her, she was cool. Her face... she didn't look in pain." She trailed off. Not only did she not wish to relive the rest, she had done her best to forget it.

"And the rats were eating her," Mary said.

"Yes," Claudette said, blinking and seeing that terrible sight again. Chewing into the wound on her stomach, opening it around the blade, making it larger so that they could reach the succulent parts inside.

"I think you stopped them just in time," Mary said. "I think she'll be all right."

Claudette said nothing. All the things she had seen, everything she knew, the incredible truths to which she had been exposed, none of them could make her believe.

"I'm sure she will."

Mary Rock kept her dead lover in a freezer in the basement. She was waiting to find the right magic to bring her back. They had heard that some of the Kin possessed such magic, and although it was perhaps a myth, Mary had become obsessed with the idea.

None of them had ever witnessed even the slightest hint that the magic existed.

"In the meantime, revenge," Mary said. "That's why you

have to find the woman again. While Vince is still alive, neither of us sleeps well."

"An added bonus would be the nymph," Claudette said. Mary was quiet for so long that she thought the connection had been broken, and she took the phone away from her ear. Mary's voice whispered in again.

"I don't want only her," she said. "I want them all."

21

From the moment they arrived at the old swimming pool building, Angela knew she should have gone to the police. This was way beyond her. She was here with people she did not trust, to do something she did not understand, and every instinct was telling her to run.

The front of the facility had been boarded up long ago, windows and doors closed with steel shutters screwed into the frames, and several large signs were added to state the obvious.

SWIMMING BATHS CLOSED
WARNING! DANGEROUS STRUCTURE

They sounded like invitations to any number of kids, junkies, and homeless people looking for a night's rest, yet it appeared as if the security shutters remained intact.

As they pulled around back, what they found there was different. Heavily overgrown with wild shrubs and brambles, the parking lot was a jumble of rusted machinery and refuse. Some of the machines were large, and she couldn't identify their use. Metal long exposed to the elements had rusted, sharp lines softened by rot.

The building itself looked like something out of a fairy tale. Which, she realised with a startled laugh, was quite apt. The whole rear facade was smothered in wild foliage that had crept up the walls and sprouted from the wide roof. The structure was built in sloping sections, allowing new growth from flat roof areas, providing a perfect footing for small trees and a wild spread of what Angela thought must be Japanese knotweed.

The uppermost peak was pitched with a glazed ridge, most of the glass smashed, plants reaching inward as if seeking entry.

"Nice place you have here," Fat Frederick said to Lilou. She ignored him and walked toward the building. Angela followed, weaving across the parking lot to find the easiest route through the rampant shrubbery. Where Lilou seemed to walk with ease, Angela forced past clutching branches, thorns catching her clothing and scratching her skin. Glass crunched underfoot.

"You're sure he's here?" she asked.

"Ballus, yes," Lilou said. "I've been certain since we arrived. Can't you smell it?"

"Smell what?"

"Death."

Angela paused and sniffed, turning her head aside from the gentle breeze. She inhaled again, a deeper breath. Nothing.

"What about Vince?"

"We'll know soon enough."

Know if he's here, or if he's dead? she wanted to ask, but the time for talking was over.

As they drew closer, Cliff drew a handgun, and Billy and Ming held knives. They also carried heavy flashlights.

"We go in there," Lilou said, pointing. Closer to the building, Angela could see that the shutter over one of the service access doors had been popped from its bolts.

She turned back to the four men still clumsily shoving their way through the undergrowth. Fat Frederick was in the lead, ignoring his supposed bodyguard. His eyes were wide and excited, like a kid's. She thought perhaps he was starting to understand.

His gaze remained fixed on Lilou.

"Meloy," Angela said. He blinked. "Stay alert. This is dangerous."

She'd expected mockery, but he nodded.

"Help me with this," Lilou said. Fat Frederick , pushed past Angela and joined the nymph at the broken steel shutter.

"Jesus, what's that stink?" he asked.

"Maybe they haven't drained the pool," Cliff said.

"Shit, I'd have brung my trunks," Ming said. It was the first time Angela had heard him speak, and his soft, high voice came as a surprise.

While Fat Frederick and Lilou strained at the shutter, Angela felt a rush of trepidation that caused her to take three steps back. Cliff grasped her arm gently, then stepped aside.

What the hell am I doing here? she thought. She remembered the darkness of her street, the feeling of being followed, the silence. Then sudden, shattering violence, the stamping and thudding. The crack of bones or skull breaking beneath hooved feet.

The mess she had seen Harry scooping up with a shovel.

The stain on the road the following morning.

"Keep your gun out," she whispered as the shutter

squealed open, revealing a triangle of darkness beyond.

Cliff held his weapon like something hot, and Angela realised without asking that he'd probably never shot anyone or anything.

Lilou disappeared inside, and Fat Frederick followed. Angela glanced around at the deserted lot, a wasteland in the middle of the city, unvisited, forgotten and abandoned. Then she followed.

As she stepped through the door the stench hit her, and she leaned over and puked. She felt a hand on her back and saw Lilou's feet beside her own, and she wiped her mouth, stood, squinted into the shadows.

"He's been murdering my kin," Lilou said, voice flat. "It smells like he's been saving them, too."

Plenty of relics here! Angela thought of saying that to Meloy, and manic laughter threatened. She was tempted to give in, let madness take her away from the awful, unbearable present. Then Lilou gripped her hand and squeezed hard, and for the first time she bent in close to betray something approaching hope.

"We *will* save him."

Angela squeezed back, then followed her along a narrow corridor.

Fat Frederick walked by her side, with Cliff and Billy behind them. Ming waited in the shadow of the broken shutter, guarding the entrance and the route of their escape.

I should have let Lucy know where I was going, she thought. *Should have called Mom. What if something happens to me, and they never...?* But "could have" and "should have" were too late now. She was in the thick of things, and this was all her own choice.

For Vince.

For the man she loved, who was in trouble because of his goodness, not because of what Mary Rock had said about him.

Billy took a flashlight from his pocket and shone it ahead. They followed a service corridor with doors leading off and pipes and wires running in trays at ceiling level. Many pipes had frozen and burst, and much of the copper wiring had been stripped and stolen. Every door had been smashed open, and the equipment rooms were home to bulky machinery and shifting shadows. The smell of rot was rich, but it did not originate from there.

"Up ahead," Lilou whispered, and Billy aimed the flashlight that way.

Double doors were propped open by a metal chair lying on its side. There was a sense of space beyond, deep shadows, a stillness swallowing any slight sound they made. The closer they got, the worse the stink became, a cloying, sickly-sweet aroma that coated the inside of Angela's nose and throat. Her stomach rolled, but this time she kept the vomit down.

She didn't want to make a noise.

They moved more quietly now, cautious without being told. Lilou took the lead with Fat Frederick close behind. Angela followed. Cliff and Billy were behind her, but they hardly made her feel safe.

Police. Lucy. Mom.

I should have told someone.

But it was too late.

Lilou stepped over the chair and through the double doors. As Angela and the others followed, she could already hear Lilou's gentle sobs. The stink was horrible, the air thick with rot, and she had never smelled anything that bad. It reminded her of a time when she was a kid, not even in her teens, exploring ruins in a forest with two of her friends. The place was widely reputed to be haunted, but when they finally plucked up the nerve to venture there they found little more than tumbled walls covered in vegetation. The old house must have been abandoned for decades, but Angela had been keen to explore, and after half an hour climbing over and around the remnants, they'd found an opening leading into a large, low-ceilinged cellar.

It was ridiculously dangerous, and only a child would have ventured below. Excitement and fascination drowned any sense of risk, and in the darkness they'd discovered an old chest freezer. Whatever was in there had been sealed inside for a long, long time.

She'd never forgotten that smell, and the memories rushed back rich and fresh.

"Oh, no," Lilou said. She walked slowly across cracked tiles to approach the old pool. Dragging her feet. Moving for the first time, Angela realised, like a human, graceless with shock and grief.

The baths were large, old, and had been abandoned for a long time. The high sloping ceiling was topped with a smashed glazed ridge, and it was from here that most of the illumination came. There was enough light to see things scattered across the shallow end of the pool. They were spread around an area from which two lines veered away, scratched into the dark moss and mold marring most of the surfaces.

The lines led to the side of the pool, then continued around the edge to a doorway on the opposite side.

Angela frowned, trying to make sense of what she saw.

Fat Frederick jumped into the shallow end and walked

around the dark, hunched things, trying to avoid their wetness. He bent and leaned in close, and Angela couldn't understand how he could stand to do it.

"Fucking stink," Cliff said. "I think I'm gonna puke."

"So puke," Angela said. She was watching Lilou, shocked at the change. Grief had drawn her down, hunching her over as she skirted the pool's edge and headed for the deep end.

It was there that the true horrors lay.

"Vince." It was little more than a whisper, but Angela's voice carried. Several birds took flight high above, their flapping wings startling her. They were out of sight, high in the shadowy roof space.

Recovering her balance, she followed Lilou. The nymph was standing directly over the deep end now, staring down into the black stew of sickness gathered there. It might have been water, once, but now it was more like oil, thick and heavy and sprouting shapes and shadows from its surface.

"That's a wing," Meloy said from the shallow end. "With a claw on it. A big one. I've never seen…"

Angela reached out and put a hand on her shoulder. Tentative at first, worrying what the woman might do. Then Lilou leaned in and she held her tight.

"What's got a leg like that?" Fat Frederick's voice went higher, all pretense stripped away. He knew what he was looking at by now. He had to. Maybe he was still having trouble believing. He'd spent his whole life dealing in old dead things. To suddenly discover that many of them still lived…

"Lilou," Angela began, but she didn't know what else to say. She was looking for something she recognised in the pool—clothing, hair, a face—and desperate not to see it.

"He's not there," Lilou said. "Not Vince. But…"

"I'm sorry," Angela said.

"An ear. A horn." Fat Frederick was crouched over something, reaching out and not quite making contact. He moved his hand back and forth above the slick, dark object, as if scared to touch.

"He's not here," Angela said, loud enough for them all to hear. She looked at those scratched lines again, where they disappeared through a doorway past the pool's rancid deep end.

"Yes, there," Lilou said. "Ballus has gone deeper. He must have a way out, a way down, to escape from this."

Try as she might, Angela couldn't estimate how many dead were down there. Probably not that many, but there were no whole bodies, only parts. Most of the parts were difficult to identify. For that she was glad.

"Why?" Angela asked.

"Because he's mad, and he wants to be the last of us," Lilou said. "There. I think that foot might have been Devalle's. She was a shapeshifter. I first met her in Persia. She was harrying a warlord and his warriors, teasing them, playing with them. She always liked to toy with the humans, but she was harmless. A lover, not a fighter. I'm not sure she ever hurt anyone. She's been missing for a while. Maybe others who have gone missing are down there, as well. In that." She pointed. "And over there. One of the Seven, ripped in two. He was a wise old fox." She smiled sadly at private memories.

"I'm sorry," Angela said.

"Follow me," Lilou said suddenly. "*All* of you."

Shocked and amazed as he was, even Meloy stood up straight, climbed out of the pool, and followed the nymph.

She strode toward the door at the deep end, and though small and slight, she looked formidable.

"Why didn't you tell me?" he said as he drew close to Angela. "When I showed you my angel, why didn't you say something?"

"I didn't know," she replied. "Not then."

"But Vince?"

"I think he only discovered the truth when he agreed to do a job for Mary Rock. He killed two of her people to stop them slaughtering her." She nodded toward Lilou. She was standing close to the doorway, staring through as she waited for the others to catch up.

"Who is she?" the gangster asked.

"A nymph."

"All my life, I've wondered."

Angela took a final look around the baths. It was a scene from hell.

"Welcome to the truth," she said.

"He's not far," Lilou said. "I can smell the murdering bastard." She disappeared through the door, and Angela was the first to follow.

There was a rat sitting on his knee. It was cleaning its whiskers, because it had been nibbling at a wound in his thigh, lapping at the blood that flowed freely after it chewed away the scab. His blood, on its whiskers. He shivered and shook from the pain, and from fury. The fear was mostly gone. Ballus had battered, beaten, and cut that away.

He would live or he would die, but all his rage was now directed at the mad thing that had done this to him.

Vince shook his leg again, jarring it against the tight

bindings, and the rat jumped away.

"A rat's got to eat," Ballus said from somewhere in the darkness.

Vince didn't reply. He did not want to give the satyr the satisfaction. Besides, he was too busy assessing his wounds, trying to figure out just how badly he'd been hurt. His body was one big agony now, and to narrow it down to individual wounds took concentration and focus.

His shoulders and arms were completely numb, wrists and forearms bound to the back of the chair. He tried to flex his fingers, but couldn't tell whether they even moved. He worried about lack of circulation and the potential for dead flesh. The front of his shoulders burned, and perhaps that was a good sign. His legs were partially numb, but he was able to move them and keep the circulation going.

He clenched and unclenched his toes, tensed his thighs, pressed his calves back against the chair legs. The pain was excruciating, but at least that meant his legs were still alive, and might even work.

His right eye was swollen almost shut. It pulsed with every heartbeat, feeling like it was going to pop. When he closed his left eye, he could still see a blurred, narrowed view through the right, so at least he still had *some* vision there. His nose was broken, lips mashed, and one of his lower front teeth was splintered, gritty beneath his tongue. The jaw around it had gone numb. His ears felt hot.

He tried counting the cuts and abrasions, but there were too many, and he was too worried about what had caused them—the old, fractured bones that Ballus had used to beat him. There was no saying how long they'd been rotting down there, nor what diseases they carried. If the injuries and blood loss didn't kill him, the infections probably would.

He wondered how long it took for blood poisoning to take hold, or gangrene, or hepatitis.

Still tied to the chair, waiting, Vince started to put every shred of his strength and effort into loosening his bonds. If the chance came to fight he would take it.

The satyr's flashlight cast a low gleam across the strange place where they'd come to rest. It seemed to have been carved from the earth and rock beneath London, hacked and hewn over time until the area was the size of a squash court. Walls were smeared with strange patterns and decorated with handprints that weren't human. The designs extended outward and upward in all directions, beyond where the beam gave way to shadows. There were several tunnels leading off from the subterranean room. All of them were dark and silent.

The floor was home to a carpet of rats. Sometimes a few would stir and scuttle into one of the tunnels, or a group would appear from another tunnel and join their cousins. The stench of piss was almost overwhelming.

In the corners, where light barely reached, were the dregs.

Vince had tried to make them out, but looking at them was too disturbing. It felt like trying to see an unknown colour. To begin with he'd believed they were Kin of a kind he could not place, but now he thought not. Ballus used these things, and he had either created them, or drawn them from somewhere no living thing should be. They were like holes in the world.

After what seemed like hours in the room, Ballus had barely moved. He sat against the wall, sometimes snoring, sometimes muttering or singing to himself. On several occasions he shrieked, a mad laugh or cry that almost scared Vince to death. The echoes lasted for some time. Vince wished he could follow the echoes and flee.

He thought he would probably die down here, and he so wished he had said goodbye to Angela. She might never know what had become of him. Perhaps that would not be a bad thing.

But he hated the idea that she was in danger from Mary Rock.

A shadow moved, a breeze whispered through the cave, the rats shifted and parted as a dreg drifted in from one of the tunnels. It hunkered down close to Ballus and the satyr leaned to the side, head tilted as if listening.

Vince heard nothing, but whatever the creature said infuriated the satyr. He stood and roared, stomping on rats, bursting them beneath his hooves. Others quickly dashed in to eat the dead.

"No!" he raged. "They should *all* be coming! Mallian's a weak, frightened fool." He stormed over and pressed his face so close that Vince couldn't focus on him. "But all's not lost," he said. "There's one with them, at least, and she's bringing fresh meat."

Ballus turned away, whistled and whispered, and the rats and dregs flowed quickly from the room. He and Vince were left alone, and the satyr paced the perimeter, hooves clopping on bare rock. He scooped up the flashlight, causing shadows to dance.

"Who's coming?" Vince asked.

"Friend of yours," Ballus said, distracted. "And an old friend of mine."

Angela, Vince thought, fear eclipsing the pain. He closed his eyes and wished her away. She had no idea what she would find.

"Don't need you anymore," Ballus said. He skipped across

the room, his sudden activity alarming. "But I'll let you live 'til they're all dead. Then maybe I'll leave you down here. In the dark."

The flashlight flicked off, and Vince had never experienced such darkness. Eyes open or closed, it enveloped him completely. Somewhere in that darkness he heard the soft, low grumble of Ballus's breathing.

He focused on tensing and relaxing his muscles where he could, working against his bindings. His right hand might have been coming loose. It gave him a spark of hope in the blackness.

From far along one of the tunnels, someone or something screamed.

22

The rats came first. A river of them, flowing along the corridor and washing against their feet. Billy and Cliff carried heavy flashlights and wielded them like clubs, sweeping them back and forth and throwing rats against the walls. They stamped. They jumped. They cursed. Shadows danced and deformed, giving the whole scene a sense of constant movement.

Angela watched Lilou, because now they were in her domain, her world of shadows and strangeness. Fat Frederick and his men were surprised and shocked by the rats, but Angela knew there would be much worse to come.

Lilou simply walked forward. If a rat jumped at her she swatted it aside, but otherwise she waded ahead as if through water, and they parted around her boots. Angela did the same, kicking out, keeping calm, moving in her wake.

"Follow us!" the nymph said to the men, raising her voice above the squeaks and the sounds of horror and disgust. Fat Frederick seemed unconcerned, but Cliff was on the verge of hysteria. He aimed his gun here and there, but did not fire. He knew it wouldn't do any good.

They followed. Meloy caught Angela's arm and walked with her, and Angela realised that he thought he was protecting her. It was a ridiculous gesture, but she said nothing.

The flow of rats paused for a moment, the animals suddenly growing still. The only sound remaining in the corridor came from Billy and Cliff, muttering in disgust.

"There," Lilou said. She pointed at a shadow ahead, an uneven hole in the corridor's block wall. As if responding to a signal, the rats reversed their direction of travel and rushed back that way, pouring through the hole as if part of a wriggling sheet that was being withdrawn.

"What is it?" Fat Frederick asked. He still sounded like an excited child.

"That's where Ballus is. They'll tell him we're coming."

"They?" Cliff asked.

"The rats, stupid," Fat Frederick said.

Angela looked at Lilou for confirmation, but the nymph was staring at the hole, frowning.

"We need weapons," she said. She glanced back at the men. "Metal bars. Clubs. Blades."

"Guys, find what you can," Fat Frederick said.

Angela shoved a jammed door open and peered inside a small room, using her phone as a light. It was a bathroom. There was a towel rail on one wall, an end rusted free of its fixings. A good tug tore it away, and then she was outside again, standing with Lilou where she stared at the hole in the wall. The metal bar felt good and solid in her hands.

"He's gone deeper," Lilou said. "There's a whole world beneath London. He might be miles away by now. Except…"

"Except he isn't."

"No. He's probably waiting for us."

"Why?"

"He intended to lure the Kin after him. He wants to be the last one."

"That's why he's killing them?"

Lilou nodded.

"That's... sick," Angela said.

"That's Ballus," she replied. "Come on."

The hole had been punched through a solid concrete block wall. Beyond was a narrow space, and to the left a tunnel led gently downward. It was old, lined with slimy bricks, and the floor was a sunken water channel, dry now but showing signs of decades of abrasion.

"One of you, with the flashlights," Lilou said. Billy moved to the front, crouched down to avoid the ceiling, aiming his light directly ahead. He moved slowly. Several rats skittered from view, and Angela thought, *lookouts.* It was a weird, unsettling idea, but no stranger than anything else that had happened since Vince vanished.

They moved forward and down, and Angela used the light on her phone to examine the rough floor. Two uneven lines were scratched into the slime, the same distance apart as the ones in the swimming pool. Something had been dragged down here recently.

"Junction," Billy said. He paused, and Lilou grabbed his flashlight and moved ahead. Angela went with her.

Before long they reached a chamber that was small and dry. Three other tunnels led off from it.

"That way," Angela said. The scratched lines disappeared along the tunnel to their right.

"You go first," Fat Frederick said to Billy. The frightened man grabbed his torch and took the lead, and the nymph did not object.

They moved forward cautiously for twenty minutes. The tunnels changed from brick-lined to hacked into rock, and back again. Angela thought some of them were old sewers, but other routes they followed looked diffcrent, their purpose purely for hidden movement. She wondered how old they were and who had made them.

The rats were always there, sometimes fleeting shadows, more often revealing themselves brazenly to the questing torches before scampering away. Angela felt like they were being drawn on and down rather than making their own way. She went to mention this to Lilou several times, but the nymph surely knew what she was doing.

Lilou grew even quieter and more serious. Try as she did, Angela couldn't hear her making a single footfall, a single breath. She was hardly there at all.

Just ahead of her, Billy still led the way. He became more confident, moving faster and kicking out at any rats that waited too long to move. He never quite touched them. Fat Frederick followed behind Angela, and Cliff brought up the rear. She heard Cliff mumbling a few times, and Meloy's whispered, urgent replies. They were nervous. She could hardly blame them.

When the shadows came alive, it was Billy they struck first.

Everything changed so quickly. Angela had believed herself ready and alert, but she stood in shock as she watched the shapes manifest before them, swirling around Billy's head, swallowing the torchlight and then driving him to the ground.

He screamed.

Lilou grabbed her arm and pulled her back and down.

Fat Frederick and Cliff began shouting, edging ahead toward their fallen friend. Meloy swung a length of wood he'd picked up somewhere, shouting when his arm jarred with the impact. Something hissed, but the shadow remained curled around Billy's throat.

"What is it?" Angela shouted.

"Dregs," Lilou said. "Don't worry."

"*Don't worry?*"

"They can't last for long. They're just trying to scare us."

"Shit, it's working!"

Billy was thrashing on the ground, splashing through puddles and releasing the stink of them, striking his head on the wall.

"Keep still," Lilou called, but not too loud.

Cliff stepped forward and Angela saw what was about to happen. Her stomach lurched, and she only managed to shout as the gunshot flashed and echoed along the tunnel.

"Oh, fuck," she said. Because everything stopped.

The shadows melted away. The remnants were gone, but Billy kept moving. He was writhing now, squirming like a toy winding down. Cliff stood several feet from him, stooped to prevent his head from touching the ceiling.

"I'm sorry," Cliff said. Billy said nothing.

Angela dashed to the fallen man. He had dropped his torch and it lay propped against the tunnel wall, casting its light up and out. It splayed shadows across his face, but they didn't hide his pain.

"I'm *sorry*," Cliff said again.

"You shot Billy," Fat Frederick said.

"I'm sorry, boss."

"Give me the gun."

As Angela knelt by the wounded man, she was dimly aware of the two others standing a few feet away, swapping words and a gun while their friend lay wounded in the muck.

No, not wounded. Dying. She saw that even as she felt slick water seeping through to her knees. Blood was pulsing from the side of his head and across his neck. The water touching her knees wasn't as cold as it should have been.

He stopped moving. Stopped breathing.

She had never seen someone die before.

"How is he?" Fat Frederick asked.

"Gone," Lilou said, stepping past Angela and the now motionless Billy.

Fat Frederick shook his head, muttering. Angela caught his eye. This wasn't *his* first dead body.

"Oh fuck," Cliff said. "Oh shit. Billy. Billy? Billy." He moved from foot to foot. To her surprise, Fat Frederick embraced him.

"We need to hurry," Lilou said. "He knows we're here. We can collect the body later."

"Collect?" Cliff asked.

Angela stood and turned her back on the corpse. She couldn't shake the stomach-deadening shock. She felt watched. The sounds of grief formed a gentle echo in voice and breath, like a secret sea washing against the day's shores.

"We shouldn't have come," she said, and Lilou turned on her. The nymph drew close quickly, silently, and Angela had never seen her this angry before.

"We're here because of Vince," she hissed. "This is all for *him*."

"Please, don't make me feel—"

"Guilty?" Lilou glanced at the dead man and turned away again, snatching up his torch and stalking along the tunnel. "Follow me, quickly. Before he goes even deeper."

After only a moment of hesitation, Angela followed. Behind her she heard hesitant footsteps, and when she looked back she saw the two men following. Fat Frederick stared at her, his expression unchanging. His world had been torn apart, and she had no idea how it might be reconstructed, or even if it could.

Billy was a shadow behind them, and soon he was swallowed by the darkness.

Lilou led the way. Rats scampered ahead of them, or disappeared into cracks in the walls. They passed two junctions where the tunnel split, and she barely hesitated before choosing a route. They stepped into filthy water that came up to their ankles, and the scrape lines were no longer visible on the floor. Angela could only trust and follow.

At the second junction the surroundings changed. The tunnel was now carved into the rock of the land, rather than brick lined.

A few minutes later Lilou stopped. There had been no rats for a while, and something about the silence hung heavy, as if it was part of the darkness. The torch batteries were running low. Or perhaps darkness held weight, and the deeper they went the heavier it became.

"Close," Lilou whispered. She walked toward an opening in the tunnel wall and Angela went with her, hefting the broken towel rail in her right hand. The two men stood either side of her, both of them aiming torches, and Fat Frederick wielding the gun.

The darkness beyond the opening shifted as the torches found it. Then the small cavern beyond was illuminated.

And she saw Vince.

Her heart dropped, she gasped, and he squinted against the sudden light.

"Vince!" she called. She couldn't help herself.

"Angela," he said. He sounded reduced, distant. He struggled in the metal chair, crying out as he squirmed against his bindings, and she could see that terrible things had been done to him. She was shocked at how real this felt. Last time she'd seen him, he had been leaving their home for work, just as he had countless mornings before. The world had been on an even keel. Nothing prowled the darkness beneath the city, no creatures from make-believe hid from hunters seeking to butcher them for crank medicines, or cook them for ultra-rich clients.

Yet this was her world now, and this bloodied, tortured version of Vince was the one she most recognised.

She took one step forward.

"Ballus," Lilou gasped. Her voice was rough with hate.

"Watch out," Vince breathed.

A shape moved across the opening, and then through it into the tunnel. A flurry of movement, a high, piercing shriek, and someone shoved her aside. Not yet to the chamber, Angela hit the wall hard. Winded, shocked, she slid to the ground.

A gunshot deafened her for a few seconds, the sounds—shouts, screams, and a maniacal laugh—fading back in with a low, steady whistle. In the weak light made frantic by movement, she tried to understand what was happening.

Cliff backed away, then surged forward again, bringing a heavy length of wood down on top of the thing that was attacking Fat Frederick and Lilou. Angela heard the *stomp-stomp* of hooves and saw what might have been sparks.

Another gunshot blasted.

Ballus, the beast that had taken Vince, leapt away from where Fat Frederick lay atop Lilou. The gangster's left hand held her down, his right was aiming the gun. She struggled beneath him, desperate to escape. His face was bleeding. He fired again.

The satyr leapt back into the cavern, and for a second

or two Angela had her first good look at him. She wished she had not, but at the same time she accepted what she saw, because there was no other choice.

"Vince!" she shouted, dashing after the monster. She could smell it now, a wet-dog smell mingled with the stench of filth and rot. She found herself strangely shocked that he would smell more animal than man.

Before she could reach the chamber the tunnel darkened. A flow of shadows poured out at them. They were the things that had come at them earlier, and Angela skidded to a halt, hands held out as if she could ward them off.

One of the shadows expanded in her vision and then closed around her, like slow-motion water sweeping across her skin, drowning her senses and taking her away from the world. She slapped her hands at the thing, waved the bar, hacking at nothing. Trying to breathe, she sucked it in. It was as heavy as the heaviest fog, tasting of time like a library locked up for a thousand years. She felt as if she hadn't taken breath for a month. She screamed and gasped, clawing at the shadow where it hung around her head.

Something grabbed her hands and squeezed, and she turned her head slowly, expecting to see the monster before her, ready to tug her through the hole and into his lair where she and Vince would be tortured together forever.

Instead she saw Lilou. The nymph's mouth moved slowly, but the words sounded and made sense.

"It's *nothing.*"

Angela sucked in a shuddering breath at last. The tunnel grew lighter, and the thing flitted away.

"A dreg," Lilou said. "Less than a memory. Don't let it scare you, because if you stay calm, it can't do you any harm."

Even before the remnants of the dreg had faded away, Angela shoved forward again toward the opening, and Vince.

Lilou held her back. "He's drawing us through."

"He's running," Angela said. She could still see Vince in the chair, slumped forward now, barely illuminated by torchlight. "Wounded!"

Lilou shook her head, and then Angela's view of her beloved was snatched away again as Ballus appeared in the opening. He reached out for Lilou, grasping, and for a second Angela saw only his face. It was a nightmare etched with inhumanity, hunger, and madness, and she knew that she would dream of him forever.

His hands closed around Lilou's shoulders. Angela swung the metal bar and brought it down onto the monster's arm, just above his wrist. He roared, and Lilou twisted her way free, falling to the left and shoving Angela aside as she did so. As Angela stumbled back into someone, Lilou fell and rolled, kicking out with her left boot as she came to a crouch.

Ballus was overbalanced and fell half through the opening onto his hands. Lilou's boot caught him across the cheek with a heavy thud. Something cracked.

He laughed.

Angela stood and lashed out again, the bar ringing from his skull with a dull *clang!* The impact vibrated up her arm, hurting her shoulder and jarring her neck. She looked past this beast she could hardly believe existed at the man she knew so well, and Vince was struggling in his chair, squirming and writhing as he tried to free himself.

She raised the bar again.

"I'm gone!" a voice shouted from behind Angela. "I'm outta here!" Cliff ran back the way they'd come, dropping the length of wood and quickly disappearing into the darkness.

Fat Frederick pushed past Angela. She staggered and dropped the bar, losing it in the shadows. He stepped closer to Ballus, aimed the gun at the back of his head, and fired.

The bullet ricocheted from the satyr's skull and along the tunnel, sparking where it struck.

Angela couldn't quite see what had happened. It was as if the scene had stuttered, a film with a few missing frames. Ballus was no longer on the ground, but rearing up beside the opening, a monstrous, impossible shape.

These are things that should not be. It was a surprisingly calm thought, and she was filled with a brief, intense certainty that she was about to wake up. She looked through at Vince and he was smiling at her, that lopsided grin she was so used to, and so loved. She'd wake next to him and tell him her dream, and he'd grasp onto the satyr concept and try to prove that she need not imagine one.

Lilou was frozen, standing with both arms twisted back over one shoulder. Something glimmered there. The metal bar that Angela had dropped. Her eyes flickered to Angela, and that single movement made the awful present more real than ever.

Ballus slammed both hands together on either side of Fat Frederick's head. The gangster raised his arms to deflect them, preventing the creature from crushing his skull, yet he couldn't stop the impact altogether. The slapping sound was almost gentle. The man crumpled, dropping the gun as his knees gave way and he slumped into the muck.

The satyr laughed, a shrieking sound that drew fingernails across the blackboard of her mind. The gun bounced toward her, and she winced, expecting it to discharge.

As the creature reared over the fallen man, lifting one hooved, hairy leg ready to bring it down on his head, Lilou struck. She had been waiting, Angela realised. Using Fat Frederick as a distraction.

The metal bar whistled through the air as she brought it around with all her strength, connecting with the back of the satyr's head.

Ballus staggered three steps forward, striking the tunnel wall opposite the opening. The dregs swarmed around him like puppies attending a wounded parent. He whined and grabbed the back of his head. Angela saw his eyes actually swivelling in their sockets, but as Lilou stepped forward again his expression hardened.

He growled.

Another shape appeared in the opening, pale and bloodied.

Vince, she tried to say, but her voice failed to register. He had been so battered and abused that she hardly recognised him. One eye was swollen shut, his mouth leaking blood. More dried blood clotted his hair, his shirt was tattered and torn to reveal the damage done to his torso beneath. His jeans were dark and ripped. His hands were swollen and startlingly white, and around his wrists were bracelets of pouting wounds.

Yet his smile for her remained, and in that she recognised everything she loved. She was ashamed of ever doubting him. The idea of losing him again now, after all that had happened, made her heart grow cold.

Ballus leapt forward, Lilou swung the bar, and they met in a violent impact.

Vince half leapt, half fell, and he had both hands outstretched. A rope or cord trailed from one hand. He landed on Ballus's back and threw the cord around his neck, pressing close to reach for its other end.

"Lilou, down!" Angela shouted, and the nymph must have understood the urgency in her voice. She slipped from Ballus's grasp and rolled away, metal bar clang-*clang*ing against the rock.

Vince's flailing free hand grasped the cord and he swirled it three times, then a fourth, wrapping it around his forearm and then shoving backward, knee pressed hard into Ballus's back. He screamed. She had never heard such a sound, and never imagined Vince capable of so much rage. It must have scorched his throat. The dregs flowed and twisted around his head, but his scream seemed to drive them away to nothing.

His smile was gone now, his face so set in fury that Angela couldn't imagine it ever having been there at all.

Ballus tried to reach for him, but he was leaning too far back, all his weight pulling the cord into the satyr's throat.

Angela glanced at Fat Frederick. He was motionless, and she was surprised at the pity she felt. He might well be a monster himself, but he had an innocent streak, and a passion behind his facade.

She picked up the gun. It was heavier than she'd imagined, and colder.

Lilou stood beside her, wielding the metal bar again.

"Lilou, we've got to—"

"Let go!" Lilou shouted. "Vince, jump off!"

Ballus staggered left, then right, hands flailing behind him but not reaching, eyes bulging. It looked to Angela as if Vince had the upper hand, but she also had to place her trust in the strange woman. This was her world, after all.

She pointed the gun.

"Vince!" she shouted.

Ballus crouched low, and she heard the twin shots of his massive goatish knees clicking. In that moment she saw what was about to happen, and she shouted her lover's name one more time.

Vince let go one end of the cord and slumped to the ground, just as Ballus launched himself upward. He crashed against the tunnel's ceiling. Dust and grit pattered down, and the satyr was instantly back on his feet. One hand pulled the cord from where it had buried itself in the fur and folds of his neck. The other held his huge, flaccid cock, waving it, and he grinned at Angela.

She pulled the trigger but nothing happened.

Ballus lifted one leg, pivoted backward, and slammed his hoof down. Vince rolled aside, and the hoof struck an inch from his head. Sparks and shards flew.

Angela squeezed the trigger again. Not even a *click*. She knew nothing about guns.

Vince crawled away from Ballus. Lilou stood with the metal bar raised again, shifting from foot to foot like a dancer. Fat Frederick hadn't stirred, and Angela thought perhaps he was dead.

"Move again and I'll shoot!" she shouted. Ballus laughed and stepped toward her. She tugged at the trigger one more time.

Vince could not understand how he was still moving. The ghosts of his hands reached out, slapped down, and pulled. His left arm still had the cord wrapped around his wrist, sunken *into* it. His right hand was pale like a landed, gutted fish. The pain was so intense, so prevalent across his body that it was almost numbing. His heart pummeled in rage, the fury seeming to have opened his wounds again, pulsing, bleeding into this hellish underworld.

I saw Angela, he thought, but already that felt like a dream. Maybe those dregs were smothering him again, edging him toward a nightmare-laden unconsciousness where he *might* remember some good times he had once lived. *I saw Angela.*

He wasn't sure where he was anymore. Perhaps still in the chair and imagining all of this. Or on the ground, soaking up the cool dampness of this deep place. Lights danced around him, or they might have been in his head, pulsars of pain.

Ahead of him was only darkness, and it was from here that he sensed something coming.

Something huge.

It drove a breeze before it, a scent-laden wind that reminded him of the pulse of a tube tunnel. The darkness intensified, and whatever came bore a startling gravity.

He ceased crawling, because whatever was behind him, or in front, could not be escaped.

"I saw Angela," he managed to croak, and he tried to turn to catch one last glimpse of the woman he loved.

She saw him. Her eyes were wide and frightened as she stared, because she felt it, too. Beside her was Lilou, that sweet, bewitching thing he had rescued, but that was part of a life before Ballus, the beast.

The beast was also staring. Not at Vince, but past him, at whatever was coming.

Vince smiled at Angela, and the smile she gave him in return melted the cold anger and agony around his heart. She had come to find him, and fight for him, and he hated himself for every mistake he had made that put her in such danger.

The thing was close. He could smell its forbidden scents, taste its mystery on the air it pushed before it.

Ballus backed up. Lilou reached for him but he kicked her aside, his foot connecting squarely with her chest and powering her back along the tunnel. Then the satyr was through the opening once more, disappearing into the cavern where Vince had been so certain he would die.

The shape passed him by. It might have stepped over him, or might have flowed. Its shadow was warm. He felt the overwhelming desire to reach up and touch whatever this was, but his hands would not obey such commands. It was huge, filling the tunnel and his mind, and he caught Angela's eye again. She was staring at him, only at him, because to look at this other thing might bring madness.

Vince was already mad, and he looked.

As the creature pushed through the opening after Ballus, crumbling rock as it forced its way, Vince saw how tall it was, how huge. It disappeared as quickly as it had come, and a sound came that pierced him with horrible memories— Ballus laughed, high and wild.

Then screaming, impacts, falling rocks. Rats poured from the room, fleeing the thing that had appeared among them. Many of them rolled and thrashed, dying from shock or fear on the tunnel floor. Ballus's screech came again, rising into a high-pitched roar.

Whatever the other beast was, it fought in silence.

Angela was by his side, holding him. He tried to speak. All the pain flooded in once more, and he groaned. Darkness pressed in, even though she wielded a torch and tried to light their world. Lilou was there, too, one hand pressed against her chest. But the look on her face was confusing. She looked... guilty.

"We have to go," she said, and she was strangely calm.

"Oh Vince, oh baby," Angela said, leaning over to protect him with her body. She held him and it hurt, but he never wanted her to let him go.

"We have to leave," Lilou said again. Beyond her, Vince saw movement. The man sprawled on the tunnel floor was up on his hands and knees, swaying slowly back and forth and dripping blood.

Angela glanced back and saw, but did not react.

"It's over," Lilou said. "We need to leave!"

It didn't sound over. The screaming continued, the heavy impacts, groans and grunts and shouts. There came a pause, followed by the sound of something huge being crushed, and then the cracking of bones and the spilling of something wet.

"*Now!*" Lilou said.

"I... can't move," Vince said. Even in pain he could remember the smoothness of Lilou's skin, warm porcelain beneath his fingertips. A rush of shame overwhelmed him, and then a warm flush of love for Angela that he knew he would never lose, no matter what.

"It's too late," Lilou whispered, lowering her head. Beyond her, beyond Angela, past where the man in the tunnel was spitting blood, a huge shape was pulling itself out through the opening and back into the tunnel.

By the light of a discarded torch, Vince saw a limb smeared with gore.

23

Dean made sure he remained hidden as he spied on the man behind the swimming pool building. He'd seen thugs like this before. Brash, hard, they were bullies who made London their playground. He knew well enough not to confront him, and because the man was there, Dean also knew that he had come to the right place.

He had to get inside. Lilou was in there with the others, including the woman who had lost her boyfriend. Something was happening. Maybe at last Lilou would reveal herself, show him who or what she really was. She had been teasing him for long enough. Playing him. Now it was time to call her hand.

He should have been more afraid, but excitement overruled that. Perhaps Dean was too old to be truly scared. He had been searching for so long. A long while ago it had been about finding proof of the creatures' existence so that he could reveal them to the world, find fame and fortune. Be someone who other people looked up to, and admired. Then, as his old life had receded into a dim haze of disgrace and mockery, the search for proof transformed into a personal quest, and an intimate need. An obsession, some might have said, and he would not have argued.

"I always knew there was something, Lilou," he whispered. "I always knew you were something. A fairy? An elf?" Old he might be, but he recognised her unnatural beauty and allure, more so for the fact that she attempted to hide it. "We'll find out."

He took a last look at the bearded man leaning against the building's rear wall, then ducked down the alley running alongside the dilapidated structure. He had no wish to meet a man like that, and he wouldn't have to. For this was Dean's world. In years of searching, stalking, and sleeping in forgotten rooms, he knew that there was always more than one way in or out.

It took some climbing to find it. He was getting on in years, but fit, and his constant meanderings through the city kept his muscles supple and his bones strong. He shimmied up an old metal drainpipe, crossed a gently sloping roof, then climbed a rusted roof ladder toward a higher ridge. This had a raised structure that had once been glazed, but most of the glass was smashed away now, and plants had taken hold in muck collected across the roof over the decades of abandonment and neglect.

A stink rose from inside. He was used to the stench of hidden places—piss, shit, refuse and rats, things dead and dying—but this was an amalgamation of reeks, rich and heavy in his throat.

The drop down to the old pool below was long, so he edged along to the opposite end of the roof ridge. Where the roof ended, an access ladder was bolted to the gable's outer face, ending on a small flat roof below. It was difficult to see from this high angle, but he thought there might be a maintenance door down there.

He climbed down, smiling when he found the door. Its

old metal was painted green, rusted in great swathes like lichen on rock. It creaked open just wide enough for him to slip through.

The room inside was dark, but Dean always carried a torch.

It might once have been an office, but many of the trappings of business and bureaucracy had been torn and smashed up, then used for a fire in the corner. Though it had been contained well enough, there were great blackened scars where two walls met. The smell of damp ashes hung in the air, and among the cinders were the remnants of old beer cans. That was one thing Dean had never been drawn to. He might be a man of the streets, but he needed his mind clear and sharp.

An interior door had been smashed from its hinges to add fuel to the fire, and on the other side he headed down a curving staircase to what might have once been the reception area. Now it was dark and empty, with fading posters on the damp walls casting echoes of older times. The air stank—the same sickly scent he'd caught up on the roof. Something had died and rotted in here, perhaps a few things. Dean had encountered human corpses before, and others.

Never what he sought, though.

He paused at the center of this larger space and listened, breathing softly through his mouth. He was just about to head through one of the changing rooms and into the main swimming hall when he heard a noise.

A scraping. Metal on concrete, perhaps. It didn't repeat, so it wasn't likely a loose flap of metal blown in a breeze. He moved quickly into the shadows at the far edge of the lobby, and behind a door he heard another noise.

A voice.

Dean held his breath. It had been a man's voice, words indecipherable. He'd expected Lilou and the other woman, but they had recruited help.

Of course they had. If Lilou sought a satyr, they'd need all the help they could get.

He had to temper his excitement. He checked the small camera he always carried, made sure his phone's charge was decent, then felt in his coat pocket for the comforting weight of his gardening knife.

He had attempted to follow Lilou before, but she had always lost him. Not today. She had more urgent things on her mind.

Camera in hand, he shoved the door. It opened onto a long, narrow corridor, and just as he peered through he saw a flicker of torchlight disappearing halfway along. He followed, slow and cautious to begin with, then speeding up. He didn't want to lose them. This moment felt loaded with possibilities.

The movement led him into an old sewer. In the past it might have been the flushing point for the pool, but now it was clear, and relatively clean. Dean kept his torch turned off, and eventually the others came into view. In a deeper, longer tunnel, he saw them. There were three men with Lilou and the woman, probably compatriots of the man left guarding the entrance. Danger came off them in waves, but they put themselves in a pool of light, deepening the darkness around him.

He fixed his camera to a headband he had adapted, and started filming.

Moments later came the shouting, screaming, a flashing of lights. Dean ducked down, trying to make out what was happening. Someone fell. Their lights were lessened somehow, as if smothered in fog.

As the shouting and panic faded a little, a gunshot blasted along the tunnel.

Dean gasped and dropped, pressing himself to the junction of floor and wall, remaining there even when a flood of rats swept past and over him. Some of them jumped onto his head and skittered along his body. He was used to rats. He didn't like them, but his attention was focused ahead.

There was more shouting, and then a quieter voice. Lilou. She was stern but calming. Torches were picked up and the group moved on.

Dean followed, and found the body.

It was a shock. Not the death itself—he had seen bodies before, and witnessed death several times—but the casual way the others had left the fallen man behind. Dean checked that he really was dead, and a selfish part of him hoped he'd find no pulse. If he did, he'd have to get help. He might lose their trail.

No pulse. The man was dead.

The vague light from the torches receded ahead of him, and he hurried on before he was left behind. Passing junctions in the old tunnel, he found himself in a passageway hewn from rock. Dean had been in places like this before. There were warrens beneath London, networks known and used, and many more long-forgotten. He possessed maps and accounts of certain areas, but none of them were complete or accurate. Their edges and extents were always uncertain. Tunnels continued on into mystery. He often wished he were a younger man, stronger and more capable of the endurance required to explore properly.

But there were people who had disappeared down here.

At last they stopped again, and Dean was glad for the rest. He sank down into the tunnel and watched, motionless and silent. The four of them stood close, aiming their torches at an opening that seemed to swallow light. He smelled something strange, different from the stench he'd detected up in the main hall. This was the musk of an animal. It wasn't a rat smell, either. It was like the warm aroma of a wet dog, mixed with a lifetime of filth.

He lifted his head and inhaled again, trying to concentrate and sense past the familiar smell of the underground.

And then violence erupted, fast and furious.

It startled him, but he hunkered down.

Stay low, keep quiet, pretend you're not really there. Make yourself invisible.

The torches swung and danced, throwing staccato shadows back in his direction. They flitted across ceiling and walls, elongated and inhuman, and Dean drank in the sights, searching for some indication that he had been right. He had followed them all the way down here, certain they were coming for something unknown. One of the Kin.

If this was just gangland activity…

The gun fired again. More shouting. A loud, exuberant shriek that set his balls tingling and hairs standing up across his body. He hoped his camera was picking this up. He didn't want to miss anything.

There came the sounds of close fighting. Grunts, shouts, the dull impacts of something heavy hitting flesh. There were voices in there, too, confused and lost amid the chaos. That awful shriek came again, and he realised that it was laughter.

Another gunshot, and then he saw a shadow growing wider in the tunnel as someone or something ran toward him.

He kept low and still. A weak torch jumped left and

right, and then he saw a tall man approaching at speed.

He'll see me! Dean thought, but there was nothing to do.

If the man did see him, he paid no heed. Dean caught only a glimpse of his face, cast in a rictus of terror.

His feet slapped along the tunnel and away, seeking the relative safety of daylight, but Dean wasn't sure there was anything like safety up there, in that old pool building. The stench of death hung about the place. Whatever had caused it might now be down here.

He crawled along the tunnel floor, keeping low, edging forward slowly. He had long suspected that the Kin hid behind a veil of fear, whether they were dangerous or not. Hiding in London made sense, because the larger the concentration of people, the more they kept to themselves. Anything out of the ordinary was invariably someone else's business, and a sense of danger would ensure that the Kin were left alone by all but the most determined of hunters.

People like him.

There seemed to be a pause in the violence, but it was loaded.

"Move again and I'll shoot!" the woman shouted. Then that awful laughter.

Nothing human, Dean thought, and his skin crawled. "That's nothing human," he said softly so that the camera's microphone could pick up his voice. His excitement rose. He imagined a million people viewing this footage, then ten million, and then the scientists and naturalists, all clamoring to quiz him about amazing discoveries.

Yet fame felt distant and hollow.

He craved the truth for *himself*, to disprove that niggling yet insistent voice that constantly whispered in the darkest hours, *You're just old and mad.*

As he prepared to stand and run toward the altercation, he felt something approach from behind.

It was a sensation unlike anything he had experienced before. Dean believed in the idea of a sixth sense—of knowing when someone was watching you or creeping close—but he had never been so hideously aware of it as he was now. It exerted a terrible gravity on his consciousness. It drove a warm breeze before it, something rare in such places but common in tube tunnels. This air carried no diesel, however, no burnt tang of electronics. It was the aroma of something that should never be known.

Dean felt himself melting, flowing lower into the ground in his attempt to hide. He wished he could close his eyes and not see, hold his ears and never hear. *I don't want to know*, he thought, and years of curiosity suddenly felt ignorant and immature.

There were some things best left unknown.

As he heard the impossible footsteps, he craved the innocent comfort of the small bedsit that he called home.

It drew close... and then stopped.

Dean feared his heart would fail. The awful presence demanded something in complete silence. Nothing was said, no invitation made, but the sudden stillness felt like the instant before a lightning strike.

There was very little light, but even that was too much.

The figure was hunched over in the tunnel, too tall, yet still full of grace. It regarded Dean, eyes filled with humour or delight. Its head was too large, body too tall, limbs too long, and Dean's only reaction was to think, *I'm far too small.*

"You see me," the creature whispered. It moved on without saying more. Dean knew that those words would stay with him forever, an echo that would never fade.

"You see me."

He watched it go, terrified and enraptured. He feared that he would never again be able to move, speak, or function as a human being. Finally grabbing the camera on his head strap, he unclipped it and checked that it had been filming. He paused, skipped back, then froze the image on that huge, amazing face. Proof, recorded and beyond doubt. An inhuman shape projecting human features, yet like nothing he had ever seen or known before.

Huge, naked, unbelievable, and unknown.

Yet as this long-sought moment arrived, the delight he had always expected was tempered with fear. His blood ran cold. If a creature such as this did not mind being seen, what did that mean?

As it swept along the tunnel with the promise of more violence, Dean fled that terrible place.

24

It wasn't Ballus emerging from the subterranean room. It was that other beast, huge and spattered with the satyr's blood.

That didn't make Angela feel any safer, but she had Vince back with her now. Though her world had gone insane, she could ride out the storm of change if she was with her love.

Deep down, she had always known that he was a good man.

Sometimes bad things happened to good people.

She supported him, helped him walk as Lilou and the other thing—

—*angel? Demon?*—

—followed behind them, whispering unknown words and drawing shadows in their wake. She felt the weight of the creature behind her. Behind them all. Only once did she try to glance back, but none of the torchlight dared touch him. Even so, unseen and barely there, he remained the center of attention.

Angela still remembered the darkness that had enveloped her, the dreg, and how it had pushed everything around her into a vague distance. Although it had disgusted her, she still felt pangs at its passing, like a junkie craving a fix.

Fat Frederick lurched ahead of them. He hadn't spoken a word since the burst of shattering violence. His ears were bleeding, and she wondered whether his eardrums had been ruptured by Ballus's assault. When they reached Billy's corpse, he stopped and hefted it over one shoulder, staggering beneath the dead weight.

Finally they emerged into the pool's main hall.

"Not here," Vince said, groaning and leaning even heavier against her. "Anywhere but here."

"Okay, okay," she said. She steered them toward a doorway and they passed through into a lobby area. It was dark, windows and doors boarded over. Fat Frederick followed them, slumping to the floor and easing Billy down beside him.

Angela helped Vince sit down against a wall. Then she held him. She could smell him, a rich odour of sweat and blood and fear, and she liked that. It proved to her that he was real.

"I thought I'd lost you forever," he said. "I thought Ballus was going to kill me."

"He was," Lilou said. "Mallian saved you. He saved us all." She stood in the doorway looking at the humans, and Angela could tell from her stance what was happening. She was leaving them, here in this place of death and rot and torture. Behind the nymph, still in the main hall, a deeper shadow moved in the gloom.

"Don't go," Angela said.

A sound rose, a voice like the rocks of the earth grinding together. The nymph tilted her head without looking back, then nodded almost imperceptibly.

"What?" Angela asked. She was afraid again. After all that had occurred, would the thing that had come to save his Kin dare to leave witnesses?

"You should get away from here," Lilou said. "It's a sick place. Haunted."

"But Ballus is dead," Vince said.

"Mallian took him to pieces, as Ballus did to others of our kind, yet what he did here will scar."

The voice again, throaty and deep, its words mysterious. Angela frowned, trying to make sense. It didn't sound like a different language—more like an arcane use of words she should have known. Meaning tickled at her ears, but eluded her.

"I'm coming," Lilou said, again without looking back. She stared at Vince for a moment, and Angela wasn't sure whether something passed between them. Or perhaps what she sensed was a connection between them giving way.

"Don't go," Vince whispered through split lips.

"Thank you, Vince," Lilou said.

"Are you just going to abandon—?" Angela began.

"Of course not!" Lilou snapped. "But Mallian can't be seen. He can't be noticed."

From the cavernous baths behind her, heavy with the stink of rotting Kin, the creature

said something more.

It sounded like, "Not yet."

"Go with him," Lilou said, nodding toward Fat Frederick. "Accept his protection. I have to tend my own, and give the dead a proper resting place. But I'll be in touch again later."

"Home?" Angela said, a one-word question. Vince squeezed her hand as she spoke.

Lilou did not even reply. She glanced around the lobby one more time, then backed through the door and let it drift shut.

Angela heard the clomp of impossible feet. They reminded

her of Ballus's terrible hooves, but while these were softer, the impacts were far greater.

What did I see? she wondered. *What the hell is Mallian?* Then she let it go. Only one thing really mattered.

Kneeling, she took Vince into her arms and hugged him tight. He groaned where she hurt him, but it felt good, and she would never let him go again. Over his shoulder she saw Fat Frederick sitting on the floor, staring at her. Billy was sprawled beside him, dead. Then she realised that Meloy wasn't looking *at* her, he was looking *through* her, at the doorway that had just closed.

He shifted slightly, rocking back and forth. His hands lay clenched in his lap. His ears were swollen, and blood slicked from the right one and down his neck.

He opened his mouth and it moved, but no sound emerged.

"Are you all right?" Angela asked, forming the words carefully.

He blinked a few times as his eyes refocused.

"An angel," he said. "An angel saved us?"

"We need to do what Lilou said," Vince said. "Get out of here. Get back to The Slaughterhouse."

"But I want to go home," Angela said. She felt like crying, and hated the weakness that might portray. She didn't feel weak. She had helped fight a monster, and helped save her lover.

"Babe," Vince said. He groaned again, stiffening and then shivering as pain cut in.

"How bad are you?" she asked. She leaned back and looked him over, shocked again by how much the man she loved had changed. He was smeared with filth, his face bruised and swollen, one eye puffed shut. His clothing was torn, and through several rips she could see deeper wounds clotted with black, dried blood.

There was a deeper change, too. Last time she had laid eyes on Vince, her world had been calm and normal. Peaceful, even. Her lover had been a good man, perhaps unremarkable, but loving and funny. Now he was someone else. Still her lover, still her man, but one who had seen amazing things, and someone who had killed. Since before she had known him he had been involved in this, and it had always been a separate part of his life.

She wasn't sure whether she loved him more or less. She was equally uncertain whether she would ever know.

"I'm alive," he said, "and you came to find me."

"Of course I did."

"And you found Lilou."

"She found me, really." That ghost of suspicion made itself known again, but in truth it barely seemed to matter. Not right then. Later it might, but by then a lot would be different.

"I'm sorry you had to see…"

"Why didn't you tell me?" she whispered.

Vince looked away, wincing as pain bit in again.

"We need to leave," he said. "Boss, we need to get to your place."

He'd called Fat Frederick "boss." That sent a chill through her, but when she looked at Meloy she also felt something like pity. He was still shivering, pressing at his left ear, tilting his head as if he'd been swimming and needed to clear out the water.

"Boss?" Vince repeated, but the man didn't reply.

"Vince, I want to go home," Angela said again. "You can take a bath, I'll see to your wounds, go to hospital if we need to, and tell them you were mugged. I want us to be there together again. Share a bottle of wine on a Wednesday, a pizza on a Friday. Watch cooking programs in bed on Saturday morning. Take bets on who'll come first upstairs. I want…"

She wanted her old life back.

Even thinking those words felt naive.

"Babe, we can't do that," Vince said. "Not after what I've done. After what we've both seen."

"I won't say anything," she protested, sobbing at the unfairness of things. She hadn't asked for any of this.

"It's not about that," he said. "The world's got bigger for both of us. Things can never be the same again."

Still holding his hand, Angela looked at the new man before her, and knew that he told the truth.

"Boss," Vince said again, louder. "We need to get away from here."

"You didn't tell me about them," Fat Frederick said. He spoke loudly, the words slurred.

"I only just found out myself."

"When you did a job for Mary Rock."

"Yeah. Sorry." Vince sounded apologetic. "It wasn't the money, boss. She said she needed my help to find something amazing, and I just… you know."

"I know," Meloy said. "It's never about the money." He looked at the dead man lying beside him. Then up at the doorway leading into the main hall.

Vince struggled to his feet. Angela helped him, neither of them willing to relinquish contact.

"Has the angel gone?" Fat Frederick asked.

"Yeah," Vince said. "Whatever it was, I think so."

"Will it come back?"

"Dunno, boss."

"You've got a good woman there, Vince." Fat Frederick was looking at the dead man again, his friend, one hand resting on his back.

"So what the fuck do we do now?" Angela said softly. "People are dead. *Things* are dead."

"We do what Lilou says," Vince said. "We're in their world now."

"We shouldn't have left them," Lilou said.

"We have to plan, find a way to rescue Her," Mallian replied. "Besides, they don't matter."

"He saved my life!"

Mallian laughed softly. "You think he'd do so again?"

"Of course he would!"

"Of course he would. He's probably in love with you already."

They were down in the tunnels again. A different junction, an alternate route, Mallian was sniffing his way. Above, outside, it was almost dusk. Where they walked, the darkness was absolute.

"We can't let anyone else see you," Lilou had said. Mallian had seemed unconcerned, smiling at her worry.

"We can't hide forever," he'd replied. It was a familiar refrain.

This was their world. The underside, the hidden depths. They moved via shadows and made them into friends. Sometimes they threw shadows, casting vague deceptions to avert attention so that they could slip past. It wasn't magic. Once upon a time it had been, but that was long, long ago. Very few of them held magic anymore.

Lilou had never witnessed it in its truest form. With the fairy still alive, perhaps she would.

"Thank you for following," she said.

"The word is out to the Kin that the fairy's still alive. Some are coming to help, others I fear are beyond our reach. But you knew I'd come for Ballus first, didn't you?"

She smiled to herself. Guilty and pleased.

"You know me so well."

"I know you *too* well, Mallian. That's why I'm glad we're leaving this way." She could feel the Nephilim's heat, his mass.

"You know I'm not stupid," he said. "I'd never reveal myself like this. Not coated in the gore of a dead Kin. Besides, we *all* have to be ready for Ascent. We have to be stronger."

"Even if we don't all agree?"

He snorted, harsh and angry. "Only fools sit on the fence."

"Then *I'm* a fool." Her words echoed away to silence. She thought perhaps a dreg had followed them, but it could do no harm. Now that its familiar was dead, it would soon melt away into the darkness, become less than nothing. She almost felt sorry for the wretched thing.

"A fool is the last thing you are," he said.

They hurried on in silence. Mallian paused now and then to assess their route. He seemed unfamiliar with their surroundings, and Lilou wondered which way he had come. Surely he hadn't moved across London in the daylight?

"We have to clear the pool," she said. "It's good that Ballus is dead, but now that he's no longer using that place, the curious will find their way in. If they discover…"

"Our dead friends," Mallian said. His voice was heavy with grief. Lilou wished they could see each other and share comfort, but a touch sufficed. A squeezed arm, a hand on her shoulder.

"At least he's gone now."

"Yet he did so much damage," Mallian said. "He killed our friends, but it didn't feel good to kill him."

"We have to take them all away, put them at peace. They can't be found."

"If they are, they are. Besides, I was seen. A man was down there."

"What man?"

"Older. Scared, but he knew what he was seeing. He had a camera."

Dean, Lilou thought, her eyes widening. *I was stupid. He was bound to follow.*

Mallian smiled. "The human world changes quickly, and it is difficult to keep up, but even I know that those images may be everywhere by now. Perhaps it's for the best."

"You can't believe that!" Lilou caught her breath, waiting for the thunderous voice of an angry Nephilim. Few ever questioned Mallian, not like this. He had been their leader for so long, and his immense age carried a weight of experience and wisdom. He was one of the few remaining Time-born, and that engendered respect.

Sandri May had been another. Ballus was very old, but not of the Time. Even Lilou herself, born more than three thousand years ago, had never known an era of true freedom and expression. Still she had spent her childhood wandering forest glades and bathing in woodland pools.

The Kin were hunted even then, though more out of fear than greed, and there had been enough of them to offer protection. She had witnessed and lived through their decline. For her, humans had always been the dominant species.

Mallian came from a Time when he was a king.

"Your feelings will change when you see Her once more," he said. "Now hurry. We need to move quickly, reach the safe place, and plan the rescue. She's been gone far too long."

"Angela could help. She's been there. Mary Rock showed her."

"Perhaps," Mallian said, but Lilou knew he was far too proud to accept aid from a human.

"There's something I have to do," she said. "You go and prepare the Kin. I'll meet you there."

"Where are you going?"

"To see a man about a camera."

"Lilou—"

"Mallian, please. Whether I agree with you or not, about Ascent, this would not be the way to do it."

He sighed heavily.

In the darkness, Lilou and the fallen angel parted ways.

By the time they made it out of the building, Angela's phone had reception again. She was about to contact Lucy to let her know she was safe, when notifications began to chime.

There were three missed calls from her friend, and another from a number she didn't recognise. Vince leaned against a wall as she tapped her phone's screen.

"Not now," Fat Frederick said. They met Ming at the rear door, and when he saw the body, the man was on the verge of weeping. As he cradled the dead Billy in his arms, Meloy gathered himself, but he seemed quieter, weakened and confused by his injuries. He was also wide-eyed, looking around as if everything he witnessed was new. In a way it was. Angela knew how he felt.

"My friend will be—" Angela began.

"The Slaughterhouse," he said. "We have to get Billy back there. I'm not just leaving him."

"Of course not," she said. She glanced at Vince, trying to gauge what he was thinking. Had he seen this sort of thing before? Was it commonplace in Meloy's world? Ming's reaction indicated not, but the big man seemed sad, rather than shocked.

"Ming, you seen Cliff?"

"No, boss."

"He ran."

"Cliff? Why?"

"Scared."

"Cliff isn't scared of anything."

A brief silence fell, and looks were exchanged. Ming had no idea what had happened down there, and no amount of explanation could come even close to the truth.

"He'll find his own way back," Angela said. "Meloy, Vince needs a doctor. You must have access to one."

"What, for all my gangland injuries?" he asked, trying to smile. Angela didn't know whether he was attempting humour or a threat, but she didn't reply.

"I'll bring the car closer," Ming said, still staring down at Billy. "Who shot him, boss?"

"Cliff."

"What?"

Fat Frederick looked around, never focusing on anyone or anything for more than a second. Searching for reality, perhaps.

"It was an accident," Meloy said. "Get the car, Ming. Quick."

The man jogged off, and at last Fat Frederick's gaze settled on the building's back door. Angela knew that he was thinking about everything the building contained. All those body parts. All those unimaginable relics.

"Meloy," she said. "They're not for the taking."

For a moment he looked so cold, so distant, that she thought he was going to lash out. But she stood up to him, chin out, trying to exude strength and defiance. If he was any sort of man, he'd leave those wretched things behind for the Kin.

The big man sighed heavily, slumped a little, and looked down at his dead friend.

"Everything's changed," he said.

"It's still changing," Angela said. "Mary Rock has one of them, alive. A fairy. The Kin want it back."

Before the mobster could process that, Ming arrived with the car. He and his boss lifted Billy into the boot. Ming closed the lid gently, as if worried about waking him. Angela and Vince climbed into the back, and as soon as the door closed she dialed Lucy.

Vince slumped against her. He stank, and seeing his wounds she could almost feel the pain herself. But however strange things had become, and however frightening their situation was, it felt good to be with him once more. For a while he had become a stranger, but now he was back.

Lucy didn't pick up. It was almost 7:00 P.M. She'd be home from work by now. Angela tried to remember what day it was. Thursday? Friday? Lucy did something most evenings, whether it was squash, swimming, or running with the local club. Still, she was rarely more than ten feet from her phone.

The voicemail kicked in, but Angela hung up.

She sighed and leaned back. Ming started the car and drove them out from the debris-strewn service area at the pool building's rear. As they slipped onto a side street and accelerated away, the phone rang in her lap.

Lucy's face smiled up at her from the screen. Angela grinned, and put the phone to her ear. Through all that had happened, she still had good news to relay. The *best* news. People, and things, had died, but she had Vince back.

It wasn't Lucy on the end of the line.

"Have you found him?" the voice said, and she instantly recognised Claudette.

"No."

"That better not be the case. You'd better have found him. Lucy wants you to find him."

Angela held her breath as the situation sorted itself in her shocked mind. Claudette was speaking on Lucy's phone.

"Lucy *needs* you to find him. Don't you, Lucy?" In the background Angela heard someone struggling to shout, but the sound was muffled.

"What have you—?"

"That's your friend, Lucy. Harry's got her tied up and gagged, but she's still fighting. Plucky little fucker."

"Leave her alone," Angela said. Fat Frederick turned in his seat and stared back at her, hearing something in her voice. Vince stirred and sat up straight.

"I'll leave her alone when we have Vince. That's the deal. That's the trade. The bastard boyfriend who lied to you, and who kills those beautiful things for profit, in exchange for your best friend's life."

He doesn't kill them, he saves them! But that would be revealing too much of her knowledge. She pressed her finger to her lips, making sure the three men in the car all saw.

"I have no idea where he is," she said. "I've been looking. I'm still looking, and I'm no closer."

"We were following you and you lost us. Now, why would you do that?"

"I don't know what you're on about. I didn't know you were following."

"Liar." In the background, Lucy squealed loud against her gag. It was an expression of pain, rather than frustration and anger.

"What are you doing?" Angela shouted.

"Every lie hurts her more. Every hour that passes without us having Vince hurts her more. How much hurt can one woman bear? Is she strong?"

"Threatening me can't help you, not if I don't know where he's gone."

"Doesn't matter. It's just another avenue we're exploring."

"I'm doing my best," Angela said.

"Do better. I'll call again at eight o'clock."

"Let me speak to Lucy."

The line went dead and she was left in a silent car, expectant faces turned her way.

"Claudette and Harry have Lucy," she said.

Vince groaned. Fat Frederick raised an eyebrow and the corner of his mouth, a facial shrug that said, *Oh well, she's dead then*.

"She had nothing to do with this!" she shouted, slamming her hand against the back of his seat.

"They don't care," he said. "Not about anything."

"They cared about Daley and Celine," Vince said.

"And?"

"I killed them both protecting Lilou."

"You killed Claudette's brother and Mary Rock's pussy. Holy shit, Vince, no wonder they've got a hard-on for you." He shook his head and looked in front again.

"We have an hour," Angela said. "Then they'll start hurting her more. We have to go to the police."

"You fucking crazy, woman?" Fat Frederick turned again to give her the full weight of his stare.

"They have Lucy," she said. "Meloy, you might think you're a big shot. You might have killed people and seen others die, but you're like a kid in all this, wide-eyed as if you've just seen Father Christmas."

"Don't talk to me like that."

"What're you going to do, fucking skin me?" she shouted. Vince squeezed her leg but she shook him off and leaned forward between the seats. "You saw what happened down there, you *saw* those things, and I know you're feeling the same sick wonder I am, Meloy. It's written on your face. So don't retreat into your fucking hard-man image. I don't give a shit about your organisation or who you are. I just give a shit about the people I love. One of them is here, and the other one..." She clammed up, unable to finish.

"No police," Fat Frederick said. "We've got a body in our boot, girl. I'm holding the gun that killed him."

"No police, babe," Vince agreed. "Mary Rock's powerful. So much more powerful than Meloy."

"Yeah, thanks Vince."

"Just the truth, boss. I only saw a shadow of what she can do, and it scared the crap out of me. She has reach. Call the police, she finds out, and Lucy will disappear."

Angela slumped back in her seat, more lost than ever before.

"Then what can we do?" she asked.

"We help those things," Fat Frederick said, his voice growing dreamy again. "And they help us."

"Lilou, maybe," Vince said. "But that other thing... the one she called Mallian..."

"I don't think helping us is on his radar," Angela said.

"We'll see," Fat Frederick said, pulling out his phone. "Now a bit of quiet. I've got some stuff to arrange."

"What stuff?" Angela asked.

"Doctor for Vince. Find Cliff. Resting place for Billy."

Vince and Angela leaned together, their warmth and pain merging. Angela closed her eyes and wished herself back home.

25

Dean sat on the bench. It wasn't his own special bench like some people had, because he preferred to move around different parks. He didn't want to become comfortable in these places. He had no wish to encourage routine, because he believed that might trap his mind in a closed loop.

He needed to let his thoughts wander free and fly high.

But now... now, his world had changed. Everything he had dreamed of for so long had happened. And it was terrible.

He shivered, even though the early evening was warm and kind, with no breeze and the scents of roasting nuts and coffee drifting from a pavilion to his left. Without his case on wheels, his history, he felt naked and incomplete. But if that contained his past, his future might rest with the camera in his lap.

The past was over two decades of searching. It began with ridicule from fellow scientists when he'd started talking to them about the creatures he believed still existed. He'd even shown them scraps of evidence he had acquired—a tooth, some pelt, footprints cast in plaster. Their mockery had been harsh. Combined with the breakdown of his marriage, his growing obsession had been easily labeled a madness. In truth, through those turbulent months it was the only thing that kept him sane.

He became the "crypto-man," the nutjob his former colleagues talked about at parties and crossed the street to avoid. His fall from grace begun, he quickly slipped out of society, parting ways with normality and finding himself surfing the undercurrents of London. He started to learn about the real city—the true streets beside those lined with chain stores and restaurants; the rivers that flowed beneath, both known and unknown; the byways and waterways that worked as its nerves and arteries.

Never quite a bum, still he spent so much of his time on the streets that he was considered one. This suited his needs, as anyone in need of help, money, or food became invisible.

In a way, he was trying to lose himself just as much as the creatures he sought.

Now he had found them.

Dean looked around the park at the metropolis he had always called home. He could see the tall buildings and hear traffic, but he felt disassociated from it all.

They know nothing, he thought. *They have no idea what lives among them.*

And what did? He didn't know. He had yet to rewatch the footage. Since fleeing those tunnels, escaping back through the old pool building the same way he had entered, he had grasped the camera in his right hand, clutching it like a talisman. Nevertheless, the prospect of watching that footage again terrified him.

You see me, the giant had said, its voice filled with glee. As if seeing him, her, it, did not matter. As if the proof contained in the camera meant nothing.

"Maybe they'll come to kill me," he whispered. Pigeons pecking the ground around his feet looked up, heads jerking.

They acted almost as if he wasn't there.

"You look cold," a voice said, and Dean closed his eyes. He supposed he had loved her for a while. Perhaps because he could not help but love her. He had long suspected that she was something other than human.

"Not cold," he said. "Petrified."

"Can I sit?"

"Could I stop you?"

Lilou sat on the bench, close to him but not quite touching. He glanced at her, heart tripping at her perfect profile.

"You've beguiled me for years," he said. "I've been a toy to you. You've played me just as you needed to, giving a little but never too much."

"No, Dean," she said.

"Really?"

"Well… maybe just a little, but all for a good cause."

"What cause is that?"

"Self-preservation." She looked right at him when she said that, and he saw something that might have been fear in her eyes. That, or vulnerability. Either one was strange, coming from her.

"I saw it all," he said. "I know for sure, now, and it's not as wonderful as I've always hoped."

"It can be… sometimes," she said. "It once was, a very long time ago, but these are changing times. Danger stalks us."

"That thing I saw…" he said.

"A friend of mine."

"Who? What?"

Lilou sighed. She stretched out her legs and crossed her ankles, relaxing back into the bench. She pressed a hand between her breasts and groaned, face twisting in pain.

"Lilou?" Dean asked.

"I have to ask you to destroy that," she said, ignoring his concern and nodding at the camera in his lap.

He stared down at it. The metal and plastic were warm from his grip, the screen misted with condensation from his sweat. It held the memory of the thing he had seen. A giant, much larger than any man, and possessed of a dreadful presence.

"I don't know," he said.

"Dean, if the Kin are exposed we'll be hunted down. There are those who seek to kill us now. Including, sometimes, our own kind, but more often a human or humans who see us as… fair game. They will be relentless."

"I've never understood who would want to do such a thing."

"Mary Rock's one, and I think you know of her. To her, relics of the dead are simply currency for the wet remains of the living. But if we were exposed, made public, the pressure would grow. It would become intense. People like her would call a hunting season on us. Scientists would pursue us, security services, anyone. *Everyone*. There's no way any of us could survive. Would you want that on your head?"

"No," he said. "No." She sounded sad, tired. Sometimes when he'd met Lilou he'd felt hypnotised by her, entranced by her beauty and aura, and he'd guessed that she had some means to produce that effect. He did not feel that now. She was speaking honestly with him, stripped of everything but truth and reason. He wasn't being steered or coerced. They were together on this bench as equals.

"I'm asking you as a friend," she said. Whether or not a threat might come next, Dean didn't wait to find out.

"Simply knowing is enough," he said. "I always hoped it would be." He turned on the camera and went through the deletion process so that Lilou could see. When it prompted him, ARE YOU SURE? he did not even hesitate.

ALL IMAGES DELETED.

He sighed, but felt as if a weight had been lifted. The choice of whether to view that haunting footage again was no longer available to him.

"Thank you, Dean," Lilou said.

"You're going to leave me now."

"Yes. Things are afoot, and I'm needed elsewhere. These are dangerous times."

"So you said." He looked at her. "Will I see you again?" Such a question sounded strange, directed by an old man to an attractive younger woman, but Lilou only leaned across toward him, smiling. She planted a soft kiss on his cheek. *I might never wash again*, he thought, chuckling. It was like being a teenager.

"Some of the Kin don't like humans, but I do, and I like having a human friend. So I'm sure we'll see each other, from time to time. You probably know more about us than any human alive."

"Should that worry me?"

Lilou stood. "Not at all. That's not the way we are." She smiled. "Live your life, Dean. You know you were right, even if others never will. You were *always* right. Make that enough."

She turned and walked away. Dean watched her crossing the park, visible for five or six minutes, until she was completely out of sight, swallowed by the shadows beneath distant trees.

"Live my life," he muttered. "Right. What's left of it."

Human existence continued around him, ignorant of the truth.

* * *

It was growing dark by the time they reached The Slaughterhouse. Ming parked around the back of the building and they entered through a rear door, descending two narrow staircases into the basement club. Angela helped Vince walk. He was almost unconscious on his feet, stumbling and barely coherent. Some of his wounds had opened again, and she smelled the rich tang of fresh blood.

Cliff was there. He was sitting in Fat Frederick's office, slouched on the end of the sofa and nursing a half-empty bottle of vodka. It looked as if he'd been crying. Reputation was everything to people like this, Angela knew. The man was broken.

Meloy showed them along the corridor to an adjoining room. It was a small messy office, but it had a sofa and was warm and private.

"Doc will be here soon," he said.

"You okay?" Angela asked, surprised that she meant it.

"Head hurts. I hear ringing. I think he might have fractured my skull." He pointed down at Vince where he'd collapsed onto the sofa and was snoring softly. "Look after him. Good guy."

"Yeah, I know," Angela said, "but I can't stay here for long. I have to find Lilou, get their help, then we've got to rescue Lucy."

"Phone." He held out his hand.

"No way."

Fat Frederick sighed and lowered his hand. "You'll call the law. Or a friend. Or your mom and pop in the land of the free and home of the brave. Any mention of what happened will bring attention down on us, and that can't happen."

"Because of your 'legitimate' enterprises?" she asked.

"No. Because of my collection, and what else we've

discovered. It's bad enough Mary Rock being after them, for fuck knows what. What if *everyone* knew about them?"

Neither of them had to say it, though. The implications were clear enough.

"They must have been hiding for..." he continued, frowning into the distance.

"Forever," Angela said.

"Mary Rock," Vince whispered. He shifted on the sofa, gasping as different pains kicked in. "She's an evil bitch, boss. She cuts them up. Kills them. Medicines, body parts, she makes a fortune. I even heard whispers she holds dining parties."

"Dining?" Fat Frederick echoed.

"Daley told me about it," Vince said. "That guy was big as a mountain, but as thick as shit. He never said anything directly, but he hinted that she had influential people around for dinner parties. Local politicians, businessmen, law, couple of military guys, Brits and foreigners. Intelligence agencies. Corporate fat cats. He said she feeds them the good stuff. I can only imagine that means..." He shrugged, then flinched at the pain.

"Them," Fat Frederick said, finishing his sentence. "She catches and kills them to feed them to rich fucks."

"Shit," Angela said as it all clicked. "When I was there they were preparing a dining room for a feast." She thought of Lilou, Mallian, and that fairy she had seen, supposedly under Mary Rock's protection. But she wasn't protecting it. She was looking for ways to kill it.

As she'd walked from that room it had watched her with such sad, pathetic eyes.

"Phone," Fat Frederick said again.

"No," Angela said. "I don't want to hurt them, either. I

won't put them at risk, but I *will* go to find Lilou again, as soon as I can."

He paused for a moment, then offered a sad smile. It was a strange moment, a silence that stretched from before to after.

"They're amazing," he said.

Angela nodded.

Vince said, "Yeah."

Fat Frederick pointed toward a closed door in the room's far wall. "Little bathroom through there, shower, you can get cleaned up. Vince, I'll get Ming to bring you some clothes."

"Yours? They'll be like a tent on me."

"I'm not so fat anymore." He turned and closed the door, and Angela and Vince were left alone.

"Come on," she said. "Clothes off."

"Babe, I'm too sore. You'll have to sort yourself out."

She slapped his arm. He winced and laughed. She still knew him. Even though her knowledge of him had changed so much, she still knew who he was.

The bathroom was barely big enough for the two of them, but she was worried about him slipping or collapsing when the hot water hit his wounds. As she helped him strip, she was shocked by the state of his body. Aside from the cuts and abrasions she had seen, there was heavy bruising around his ribs and chest and across his back. His limbs still shook from the long periods they had been restrained, and he'd lost several fingernails.

But in his eyes she saw that he was back.

The constant flicker of humour she'd fallen in love with was still there, and the cheeky smile. He leaned against the shower wall as she washed him, using a new sponge and shower gel. She was as careful as she could be, but his gasps and hisses matched the steady swirls of dirty, bloodied water shushing down the drain.

Even beyond the pain, his arousal soon became obvious.

"Bloody hell, you can't be serious?"

"Guess not," Vince said. "Ballus put me to shame in that department."

"At least yours isn't attached to a goat."

She helped him dry, and heard someone in the office. Making sure he wasn't about to fall, she wrapped herself in a towel and stepped through the door. It was Ming, and he had brought some clothes. There was also a tray of food and drinks on the desk, and Angela suddenly realised how famished she was.

"He okay?" Ming asked.

She nodded. "How's Cliff?"

Ming tapped his head. "Whatever happened to you down there, it's got him scared. And Cliff's not someone who scares easily."

He left. Angela returned to the bathroom and helped Vince dress in the fresh clothes, which seemed to fit him quite well. They stepped back into the office, she got him settled on the sofa, but then she found that she couldn't eat or drink. She paced the room, five steps one way, five the other, clasping her phone.

They were right, she knew, that the police wouldn't be the answer to this. Yet every instinct urged her to call them.

"There was so much you didn't tell me," she said. "Meloy. What you did for him. That apartment in South Kensington."

"You know about that?"

"I went there. Picked the lock."

He smiled and looked impressed. "It's not mine. Meloy lets me use it, that's all. Sort of a base for…"

"Expeditions."

"Yeah, sometimes."

"Where did you go?"

"Here and there." He shrugged. "Sometimes deep down beneath London. There are places down there you won't believe. Tunnels, sewers, abandoned tube stations, caverns, catacombs visited by one person every decade or century, and surely some still never visited at all. Sometimes I just went to places that no one really knows or cares about anymore. London's a big city with a deep history, and it has its echoes. It's filled with lost places hidden in plain sight."

"How come you're so good at it?"

"That's always been a part of me. I was the first kid to find fossils on a fossil hunt at school. I knew where to look when our pet dog went missing a couple of times when I was a teenager. I just had a nose for it, and that never went away. When I found out about the relics ten, twelve years ago, they became a fascination. It went dangerous when I met Fat Frederick. I never meant to drag you into it."

"Well, that worked out well." He looked wretched, but she smiled to show she didn't mean it. Then she glanced at her watch. It was edging toward nine o'clock in the evening, and she didn't have a fucking clue what to do next.

"Vince, do you know where they are?"

He blinked at her like a rabbit in headlights.

"That's what he was asking me."

"And you never told him, but now I'm asking, and you know why."

He looked away from her, down into his lap. His hands twisted there.

"Vince, Mary Rock's people have Lucy!" Her voice rose with every word. "Unless we do something they might—"

The phone vibrated in her hand, and she almost dropped it. Lucy's smiling face appeared on the screen, and Angela hated herself for unwillingly involving her friend in this.

She accepted the call.

"I think I might know," she said without thinking.

"Where?" Claudette asked.

Angela frowned, thinking quickly. "Not sure, but—"

"You said you might know."

"What I mean is I might know someone who knows where he is."

"Who?"

"I…"

Lucy screamed. They'd taken off her gag, allowing her to give full vent to her agony. Whatever they were doing to her hurt a lot.

"You bitch," Angela hissed.

"Yeah, yeah. Fuck you. So, this person who might know…"

"Give me two hours and I'll tell you."

"You're in no position—"

Angela disconnected, switched the phone to silent and slipped it into her pocket.

Vince stared at her, eyes wide. He nodded slowly.

"So we have two hours," he said. "Maybe. If they don't just kill her."

"They won't. They want you, not her. She's just to encourage me to find you."

"I'm sorry," Vince said.

"Not your fault. They're the bastards." She turned away from him and opened the door, leaning out into the corridor. She heard music from upstairs in the Slaughterhouse bar, and she envied those people up there drinking, beginning their night out and with only drink and food, laughter and friendship to look forward to.

There was something altogether different in her future.

"Vince, you have to tell me—"

"Angela." Fat Frederick appeared along the corridor, a man she didn't recognise behind him.

"That the doctor?" she asked.

"Yeah, this is Doctor Khan, but there's no time," he said. "We have visitors." He seemed suddenly excited, like a kid waking on Christmas morning.

"Who? Where?"

"Down in my basement. They came in the back way."

"Lilou," she said, breathing a sigh of relief.

"Not just her," Fat Frederick said. "Come on. They want to talk."

Even holding the hand of the woman he loved, Vince felt that familiar thrill when he set eyes on Lilou once again. She was beauty in motion, the origin of grace, and the whole room seemed to revolve around her. For him she remained the center of things.

She saw him, smiled, then glanced at Angela before looking away again. He squeezed Angela's hand as if to say, *It's all fine, there's nothing between us*, but the memories of his lust seemed as fresh as his last breath. He had to close his eyes for a moment to gather himself.

"I am Mallian, and I speak for the Kin," a deep voice said. He crouched at the back of the large, low room. A door behind him stood open, its top hinge deformed, door hanging off and frame splintered. He must have broken it, pushing through. Even hunched down he was huge, a heavy presence that seemed eager to repel Vince's gaze rather than attract it.

Only one light was working, and Mallian sat in shadows. Though so obviously *other*, Vince was surprised at how very human he appeared. His face was strong and handsome, hair long and hanging in several thick braids, cheeks and chin heavily stubbled. His unclothed torso was knotted with muscle, shoulders wide and hunched to afford him space. There were charcoal trails across his shoulders and chest that might have been tattoos, or were perhaps a map-work of old scars. His nakedness did not appear to trouble him.

Mallian looked more out of place here than he ever had down in the tunnels. Here he was hunched, crouched, compacted down to fit into the human world. Vince couldn't help thinking that it should be the other way around—the human world trying to fit in with Mallian.

Angela squeezed his hand again. He'd dragged her into trouble, and she had embraced it. Come through to find and rescue him. Her presence pinned him to the world, and she was glad for it.

"These days, it's unusual for the paths of Kin and human to cross, and for both to remain alive," Mallian said, and Vince couldn't tell if it was a threat. "Much of that is due to Mary Rock. After what you've revealed about her—what she does, and what she is holding prisoner—we need to return her violence, and…" He trailed off, his deep voice hanging heavy in the echoless room.

"We've come to ask for your help," Lilou said.

Accompanying her and Mallian were three other Kin. They shifted uncomfortably at Lilou's words. Vince saw pride in them, and perhaps fear, as well. Or maybe he was unqualified to guess at the state of mind of myths and legends.

One was a young man, as human in appearance as Lilou, yet half her size. He seemed to possess no attributes of a dwarf or midget. He wore simple clothing and his long hair was a flaming red. He returned Vince's stare with blazing, vicious eyes. *Pixie*, Vince thought, and he closed his eyes and looked away.

He had no wish to become pixie-led.

"Thorn has been Her friend for a long time, and long believed Her dead," Lilou said, following his gaze.

"It's those keeping Her prisoner who'll be dead," the small man declared. His voice was surprisingly deep and loud. His stature didn't detract from the violence that simmered within him.

Just outside the broken doorway stood a very old woman. She might have been a statue, but for the breath misting from her mouth, even though the room was warm. She had a full head of wild, gray hair, so unkempt that it appeared sharp. Her face was severe. Her eyes were black, her skin the deepest shade of blue, and her hands were hidden beneath loose clothing. She wore a necklace of bones Vince couldn't identify, and she was pierced liberally through ears and nose. The jewelry was as dark as her eyes and reflected no light.

"This is Jilaria Bran," Lilou said, gesturing at the old woman. Jilaria Bran said nothing. Her hands moved beneath her cloak. Vince imagined her crossing fingers and casting glamours, but perhaps he was misled and she wasn't a witch at all.

"And who is...?" Fat Frederick asked, pointing at the fifth Kin in the large room. It was nowhere near human.

Six feet tall, scaled skin, heavy lower limbs, and the head of a snake, the thing breathed quickly and deeply. As with Jilaria, steam or smoke wafted from its wide nostrils. Its yellow reptilian eyes watched them, and they were filled with a cool intelligence. Its arms were short but muscled, tattooed with strange designs and tipped with three clawed talons. Hunched over, its back was lumpy and broad, bearing smoothed humps that might have been folded wings. It wore leather bands around its torso and upper legs, and a selection of knives and shaped blades hung from loops and slings.

Vince had no idea what it was, but it frightened him more than any of the rest. Even Mallian. At least he had human features, and could speak his mind.

The creature opened its mouth and a long, wet, forked tongue lapped at the air.

"Her name is Mhoumar," Lilou said. "Sometimes she's with us, sometimes not. When she heard about the fairy being held prisoner, she was the first to come."

"So, what can you all do?" Fat Frederick asked.

"Do?" Lilou asked, tilting her head.

"Yeah, I mean… fire breather?" He pointed at Mhoumar. "I'm guessing Jilaria casts spells. And what about Thorn?"

"Boss, they're not the Avengers," Vince muttered.

"Show respect!" Mallian said. His voice was like an earthquake, shaking the room and all those within. Vince thought that if he truly shouted, the world might break in two.

"I do respect," Fat Frederick said. His voice sounded small, yet he managed to keep it firm. "I do, with every piece of myself. You're… I don't know how to express what…"

"What we are, what we do, is our business," Lilou said. "We're here to rescue one of our kind, with your help. In return we'll rescue Angela's friend."

"We'll help," Vince said. "We'll help each other. Right?" He looked at Mallian, shaking and feeling his skin crawl, balls tingle, but he willed himself to hold the big creature's stare. He even thought he caught the glimmer of a smile in those strange, golden eyes.

"Of course," Mallian said.

Before Ballus, the only Kin Vince had ever seen alive was Lilou, and he had been sent to capture and kill her. After he'd rescued her, and she had saved him, he'd caught sight of others in the safe place she'd taken him, but those had been fleeting glimpses, less than shadows. Then Ballus had taken him, and his worldview had opened wider.

Now, faced with more of the Kin, his previously uneasy world was teetering on the brink of collapse. Looking at them was like staring into the clear night sky and trying to comprehend the depth of distance and time presented there. A humbling endeavor, almost impossible to conceive. His understanding of things was wrong, and so much he believed as fact had been shown to be a lie. Whole histories—complex interactions between Kin and the world—were missing from his understanding of reality. It was as if the world had been living a secret life all along.

He had always been prone to flights of fancy. Holding a relic, he had often lost himself, constructing stories about its history, imagining the life it might have led and the things it had done. Now, he longed to speak to these things, and know them.

To Vince's left, Angela was cool and still. To his right, Fat Frederick shifted slowly from foot to foot. Vince could not pretend to truly know the big man, and he had never tried. He'd heard the sickening stories, but he'd also seen the wonder in his eyes, the flame of imagination ignited. Meloy was an enigma, probably to himself as much as anyone else.

"You've both been to Mary Rock's house," Lilou said, nodding at Vince and Angela.

"I worked with her and her people, briefly," Vince said, "but

I only ever met her once, and I didn't see much of the house."

"I did," Angela said. "I spoke with her. She showed me things, including the fairy."

The whole room seemed to draw in a sharp breath. The Kin… *shimmered*. A wave of emotion passed through them, making them more real than anyone or anything else. More *there*.

"Why would she show you *Her*?" Mallian asked.

"She never meant for Angela to live," Lilou said.

"Mary Rock spun lies about Vince, then showed me the fairy and told me more lies," Angela said. "I think Lilou's right. She expected me to be dead by now, and she expected to have Vince."

"She'll be scared," Fat Frederick said. "She'll move the fairy, leave the country."

"I don't think so," Vince said. "I don't think she's scared of anything."

"How can you know?" Mallian asked.

"You must believe it, too. Otherwise why come and ask for our help?"

"Because interacting in your world is something we never do," Lilou said. "Our Time ended so long ago, and since then we've been creatures of shadows. We're tales told around campfires, legends passed down through the generations. We're whispers and glimpses. You'll find us in storybooks and make-believe films, but through it all we're in hiding.

"If we're fiction, we're left alone," she continued. "If we're fact, we're hunted. We *never* expose ourselves to the human world—not like we're about to, because that puts every one of us at risk. So we're asking for your help because this is *your* world we're venturing into now."

"Maybe you won't have to," Angela said. "I've got an idea."

26

"Did you fuck?"

"Fuck?"

"You and Vince."

"After everything that's happened and is still happening, you're really worried about a moment of love?"

"Love?"

"All sex is love." Lilou almost purred. It was unsettling.

"I asked, didn't I?"

"You asked, but do you really want to know?"

"I want to know."

"Has he said anything about me?"

Angela continued emptying bottles down the sink. The beer foamed and swilled. She did not reply, and the silence grew heavy.

"Angela, there's something you need to understand," Lilou said. She put down the bottle she was emptying and sat on the bar. Fat Frederick had closed The Slaughterhouse to customers, and now the humans and Kin were preparing. Vince was being tended by Dr. Khan in another room. Angela hated the idea that they would soon be parted again. She was also starting to regret asking Lilou the question that had been burning ever since they had met.

"That doesn't sound like a 'no'," she said.

"No, I didn't fuck Vince. And no, he didn't fuck me. We were together, I was treating the knife wound in his arm and watching him. He was concussed. He was conscious but confused, and I'd been closer to death that day than I had in a very long time. I was confused, too, and I let my guard down. Usually around humans I throw up a veil. It hides the real me, and that goes against a lot of what I do and what I am. But I know the dangers of being seen for real, and I fight every day to hide what I really am." She grew quiet, contemplative. "Shit, I really fight."

For a long moment the nymph was silent.

"So?" Angela prompted.

"So he saw and sensed the true me, and no human can resist that. He wanted me. I wanted him, because that's simply my nature. I want the love of a man in the same way a fish wants water, or a bird wants the weight of air beneath its wings. He was as hard as rock, but when I touched him there he flinched back." She frowned. "That rarely happens. I think it was because of you."

"Me?"

"I was open to him, and in that moment I was the most beautiful, sensuous thing he had ever seen, smelled. Tasted."

Angela closed her eyes, fury and upset boiling her emotions.

"He was so conflicted. His body wanted me, and most of his mind, too. But his real self, the real Vince that exists within and around his raw instincts, held him back. I think if I'd stayed a moment longer he might have broken, but… I respected that will in him. That love for you. Because he's only the second human who has ever saved my life, and I care for him."

"Is that supposed to make it all okay?" Angela asked.

"I'm not human, Angela. I've seduced kings and sorcerers, outlaws and monks, and a thousand men have died with me on their minds. That's my nature, and the way nature made me. Whatever Vince wanted of me, he didn't betray you. He's only human."

Angela popped the top from another bottle and emptied the beer down the sink. She wished she could let her jealousies flow away with it.

"What happened to the first human who saved your life?"

"His name was Zahid. He died badly."

Fluid glugged and bubbled, glass tinked, and Angela heard muted conversation from elsewhere.

"There are more important things," Lilou said.

Angela emptied another bottle and handed it to Lilou. The nymph filled it with fuel from a metal can, tore a strip from a bar towel, stuffed it inside. She moved like a human, looked like one, yet she was something else entirely.

"He *really* loves you," Lilou said, laughing gently.

"Good fucking job," Angela said. She laughed as well. Whether it was fear or madness, hysteria threatened, but the thought of where Lucy was and what she might be experiencing leveled her, because she had to maintain her strength.

A few minutes later they'd filled a dozen bottles with fuel. Fat Frederick and Vince entered the bar and joined them. Meloy had instructed Ming and Cliff to remain in The Slaughterhouse, because he didn't believe either of them would be able to help. Cliff was still shaking with terror. Ming was quiet, distant, refusing to believe.

"We're ready," Fat Frederick said.

"We're nowhere near ready," Vince said. "I feel like shit. I want to sleep for a hundred years."

When Angela glanced up he was looking at her, not Lilou. She smiled, he smiled back, and she thought, *It doesn't matter.*

27

"You're early," Claudette said. "You better have some news for me."

"I know where he is," Angela said. "Fat Frederick has him. He's had him for days, maybe from the beginning, and I don't know why, I don't know what to do and—"

"Calm down," Claudette said.

Angela quieted. She glanced around the car at the others, hating being the center of attention, but this call was essential to set up their plan. She had to make Claudette believe.

"How do you know?" Claudette asked.

"I went back to The Slaughterhouse," Angela said. "I was going to ask Fat Frederick for…"

"For help. Against us."

"I don't know," she said. She forced a sob, finding that it barely needed forcing at all. "But I saw him being dragged outside and put into a car boot! That's all I know, and I've told you everything. So what about Lucy?"

"Lucy will be safe with us until we have Vince." Claudette hung up. Angela blinked at the sudden silence. She'd expected to hear Lucy again, or for Claudette to issue more instructions.

"She took it?" Fat Frederick asked.

"I think so," Angela said.

"Get out, then."

She leaned forward between the front seats and pulled Vince to her. He was in the driver's seat and he had to twist around, eliciting a gasp of pain. Their lips met and she held him tight, relishing his familiar taste and scent. She heard Meloy sigh but ignored him. For that moment she ignored them all.

It was Vince who broke away.

"I'll see you soon," he said. "It's a good plan. It'll throw them, and that'll give us an edge."

"It's Mallian and the others who give us an edge," Angela said. "Just don't get yourself killed." It should have sounded melodramatic, but the words hung heavy in the car as she and Lilou jumped from the back seat. She glanced back in at Fat Frederick. "Look after him."

"Sure."

In the back, Thorn's small shadow shifted slightly. He looked like a child in the big car, but light from a street lamp slanted across his face. He had old, leathery skin, a fixed expression, and scars.

Angela watched the car move away. Lilou grabbed her arm.

"Come on," the nymph said. "Mallian and the others will be waiting."

They hurried into the night, searching for things that should not be.

"Still suffering."

The voice was surprisingly low and deep. For a moment Vince thought that Fat Frederick had spoken, but the big man sat silent in the passenger seat. He'd turned the rearview mirror so that he could look at the creature in the back seat.

"Still pained. Still wondering why."

"Every part of me hurts," Vince said. "The longer I sit here, the more worried I am that when we stop—"

"Think about the pain," Thorn said. The pixie barely whispered yet his voice filled the car, as if vibrating from the heavy door speakers and sub-woofer in the boot. "Focus. Dwell."

It took little prompting for Vince to consider the pain of Ballus's tortures, and as he did so something remarkable happened. The agonies started to recede. Thorn continued speaking, but his words quickly lost meaning and context. Instead they became warm, comfortable sensation, enveloping him in a soft hug that stroked away discomfort.

Vince gasped. He eased his foot off the gas, but he was still in complete control of the car. Glaring lights filled it as vehicles passed in the other direction, and for the first time in a while the night no longer seemed filled with dread.

"He's healing you!" Fat Frederick said, his voice little more than a whisper.

"It's all fading away," Vince said. With one hand he touched some of the dressings Dr. Khan had applied, pushing on them and feeling no pain from the wounds beneath.

"Only glamour," Thorn said. "Distraction. Pain will come again, worse."

"Well, that's something to look forward to," Vince said.

"Thanks would be good," Thorn muttered.

"Sorry. Thanks."

"Welcome."

Vince glanced across at Fat Frederick. The gangster was

still staring in the mirror, mouth slack. Vince smiled. Maybe the Kin had more of a sense of humour than he'd given them credit for.

"So what other glamours can you cast?" he asked.

"Plenty. Some light. More dark. You'll see soon."

They continued the journey in silence. Vince thought he might have trouble remembering the way to Mary Rock's house, but that single visit he had paid her months before was imprinted on his mind. He parked the car along the street and switched off the engine. It ticked and cooled. He had to glance around to make sure Thorn was still with them, the pixie had become so quiet.

"I'm afraid," he said. "Maybe they'll just shoot me the moment they see me."

"I doubt that," Fat Frederick said.

"Why?"

"If I was Mary Rock or Claudette, I'd have some pretty gross tortures waiting for you."

"Good. Great. Nice to know." Vince glanced at the car's digital clock. It was almost 11:00 P.M. Ming had been told to call Mary Rock's assistant Kris twenty minutes ago and inform him that Fat Frederick was about to deliver Vince to her. From that moment the lie was set, the plan in motion, and now they were governed by time.

"They'd better be ready," Vince said.

"Mallian is ready." Thorn's voice was heavy and full again, and so certain that it invited no doubt.

"You're sure you can..." Vince began, but when he turned around, Thorn was already gone. One rear door was open a crack. There hadn't been a sound.

"Oh, I think he can," Fat Frederick said. "You ready?"

"No."

"We'll be fine." Meloy surprised Vince by tapping his knee. "We've got wonders on our side."

"One of those wonders gored me with a dead thing's splintered thighbone."

"Nobody's perfect." He reached for the door handle. "Come on."

They left the car. Vince went first, with Fat Frederick behind him, grasping his arm with one hand and pressing a gun into his back. Vince glanced around, looking for Thorn, but there was no sign at all of the pixie. The Kin's glamour had settled across his body, shielding the pain and making him feel stronger, more filled with energy, than he had since he'd killed Daley and Celine.

The memory of that time on the abandoned Underground platform was a dull, emotionless dream. He had no regrets, and he found that troubling, but now wasn't the time to question his feelings.

Mary Rock's front gates stood open, and there were several vehicles parked in her wide driveway. Each of them was worth six figures. The unassuming house had a few curtained windows lit from within, and five exterior lights at high level.

"She's got visitors," Vince muttered.

"Shut it!" Fat Frederick said, shoving him along the graveled driveway. Maybe it was part of the act, maybe not, but it reminded Vince that they were in the enemy's domain now, and he couldn't afford to slip up. He began to worry about their plan, his heart started sprinting, and he wanted to turn and flee, regroup to scheme some more.

But it wasn't only his life on the line.

Somewhere to his right a bush rustled, and he resisted the temptation to turn that way. He didn't remember Mary

Rock having guard dogs. It was probably Thorn.

Fat Frederick squeezed his arm tighter and pressed the gun barrel uncomfortably into his spine. Vince wanted to object, but then he saw movement at the window beside the front door. A curtain twitched aside. A pale face appeared, too far away to make out.

"Forward," Fat Frederick said. He sounded excited, and Vince's doubts multiplied even more. Could he really be trusted? Had they thought this through properly? Fat Frederick professed disgust at what Mary Rock was doing, but he also stood to gain quite a lot if he surrendered Vince to her. Mary Rock had excluded him from her true calling, but it was possible that she might consider taking him under her wing. Especially now that he had seen things, *met* things.

"Meloy, look, you know that—"

The front door opened and Kris appeared in the doorway. At the same time Fat Frederick shoved Vince forward, so hard that he lost his footing and sprawled in the gravel. The impact caused flares of pain in some of his wounds.

"Not here!" Kris said, stepping outside. "Mary's entertaining! Around to the side entrance." Just as Kris reached to close the door behind him, Vince saw a shadow flit from the undergrowth and disappear inside. Thorn, quieter and quicker than he'd thought possible. "Hurry!" Kris said. He marched across the front of the house and around the corner, glancing back to ensure they were following. Then the darkness swallowed him.

Fat Frederick scooped Vince off the ground and dropped him on his feet, as easily as a child picking up a kitten, then shoved him in the back with the gun once again.

Already the plan had changed—they were supposed to

enter through the front door—and they would be forced to adapt to circumstances.

"Here," Kris said from somewhere ahead. He opened a side door and a splash of weak light barely touched him, but Vince saw enough to make out the cold smile. "Someone's very much looking forward to seeing you again. Fucker."

We should go, abort, get the fuck out of—

As if reading his mind, Meloy nudged the gun into the small of his back, urging him forward.

"Wise of you to give him up, Freddie," Kris said. "Mary's very pleased."

Fat Frederick's fingers squeezed Vince's arm so tight that he gasped and bit his lip to prevent himself crying out.

It's all right, Vince thought. *He's mad at being called Freddie. He's still here with me, not with them.*

Then as Kris gestured for him to climb three stone steps up to the side doorway, and Vince saw who was waiting for them, he knew that everything was not in the slightest bit all right.

In her right hand, Claudette nursed a meat cleaver.

Angela shouldn't have been surprised at how easily the Kin melted into the shadows. Lilou stood beside her like a normal woman, but somewhere out of sight to their left was Jilaria Bran, and to their right Mallian's shadowy bulk was swallowed beneath a tree. The gardens were large, enclosed, and had access lanes between them. At this time of night they were also deserted.

They waited in the lane behind Mary Rock's house. There was an eight-foot wall bordering the garden, but the dark outline of the large house was clearly visible above it. When the time came they would have to climb the wall. On her own, that would have worried Angela, but in present company she had no concerns.

She watched the house, her gaze drawn to the pitched roof with its several rooflights. Beneath those windows, the fairy was prisoner. Somewhere in there, too, was her friend Lucy. At least, that's what she hoped.

What if they've got her someplace else, she thought, then she shut it down. It didn't bear thinking about.

Fear constricted her throat, making it hard to swallow. Events felt so out of her control. She and her loved ones were at the mercy of unknown creatures and brutal criminals, and she had already seen too much pain and death. She couldn't bear the thought of more, perhaps greater loss.

"Thorn is in." Coming from their left. Jilaria's whispered accent was strange, a weird amalgamation of Irish and French but, Angela suspected, not related to those places at all.

"Mhoumar passes over us," Mallian said.

Angela looked up. The night was overcast, and London's glow made the clouds a uniform, pale gray. Against that background she caught sight of a fleeting object, like a buzzard flying so low she could almost feel its downdraft. She thought she heard the gentle chink of bottles, but it might have been her imagination.

Mhoumar settled on the roof ridge close to the large chimney, and in stillness she became invisible.

Nobody moved or spoke.

Angela felt a pressure building, the threat of action, and the silence seemed so loaded. She suspected that the three Kin were communicating somehow, though she didn't know how.

"Thorn has disabled the security," the witch said.

"Let's go." Lilou touched Angela's shoulder and shoved her forward gently, and together they dashed across the lane to the house's boundary wall.

Once there,

Angela looked up. She couldn't even touch the top if she jumped, and the brickwork was smooth, no handholds or footholds, especially in the dark. The whole point of them going in this way was to avoid gates or any easily seen access, so they had to—

"Hurry," Jilaria Bran said. She was on top of the wall, sitting astride it and leaning down to present a low silhouette. Even as Angela glanced at her, the witch dropped down the other side with little more than a rustle of clothing.

Angela felt herself lifted. The arms that closed around her were surprisingly warm and so, so strong. She smelled Mallian's breath close behind her, sweet and mysterious, and she had a sudden urge to turn around and stare into his face.

Then she was on top of the wall, holding on as the arm let go.

Mallian pulled himself up and over, so graceful and silent for such a large creature. He had lifted Lilou with his other arm, and she smiled at Angela as she dropped into the garden.

Angela lowered her legs, and then let go.

The garden was heavily planted, and the four of them moved quickly through shrubs and low trees toward the rear of the house. They reached an exposed lawn and Angela paused, but Mallian did not. He strode out, and even in the poor light he would have been obvious to anyone looking from any of the rear windows. Imposing, striking, terrifying, he crossed the lawn in ten long steps.

Downstairs, several windows were lit, and there was movement inside.

No voices called out. No warnings were shouted.

They followed Mallian, and as he reached the house and pressed himself against the wall, his voice rumbled out one single word.

"Mhoumar."

If anyone heard, they might have mistaken it for an animal calling in the night. From around the front of the large detached building came the faint echo of smashing glass.

Then, smeared across the deep undergrowth and trees bounding the garden, the suggestion of firelight.

"Time to go inside," Mallian said.

Angela saw his teeth glistening as he grinned.

"I'm going to make this slow."

"Yeah, right," Vince said. "Because a meat cleaver is great for killing someone slowly."

Fat Frederick still had the gun pressed into his back. The door behind them remained open, and in the small hallway Kris turned on the light, dazzling them.

Vince tensed as his eyes grew accustomed to the bright glare. Claudette still stood several feet away, blade twitching in one hand. She didn't look very happy. He'd pushed her brother in front of a tube train, so he guessed that was understandable.

So when does this all change? he wondered. They were inside, Meloy had a gun, but still the situation felt uncertain.

"Mary Rock would like to extend her thanks," Kris said to Fat Frederick. "Unfortunately she can't be here to greet you in person, as she's entertaining this evening. It's not a very convenient time, I'm afraid." He smiled. It would have sent children and small pets fleeing in terror.

"No worries," Fat Frederick said. "So long as I get what's due."

"Of course," Kris said. "I've been instructed to offer you a sit-down with Mary, and an ongoing involvement in her enterprises."

"A partnership," Meloy said.

"It'll be what Mary wants it to be."

"What about the woman you're holding? His girlfriend's friend?"

Kris shrugged as if Lucy was of no consequence, and Vince had the sudden certainty that she was dead already.

"So what's on the menu this evening?" Vince asked.

Kris stiffened. Claudette took a step forward, holding the cleaver across her stomach. She was boiling, and he wagered it was only Kris's presence that kept her restrained.

"Not here, Claudette," the older man said. "Mary wants it done quietly, and out of sight. Mr. Meloy, if you'd be kind enough to follow my associate downstairs, there's a room in the basement where—"

From outside came the smashing of glass and a *whoomp* as splashed fuel ignited. Another smash, another eruption of flame, and Vince knew that it was time. Now was when he'd discover whether Fat Frederick really was on their side, and the side of the Kin, or whether pure greed and power were his true driving forces.

Kris's eyes went wide at the gun that suddenly appeared over Vince's shoulder.

Claudette crouched, heaving the cleaver underarm as she did so.

The gun fired, so close to Vince's ear that it was akin to

a punch in the side of his head. He winced and fell, right hand clasping his ear, left held out to break his fall.

The cleaver swished past his elbow and struck Fat Frederick in the stomach. He looked down, apparently uninjured, but momentarily distracted.

Kris stepped backward through a doorway and slammed it shut. Claudette glared at Vince, furious, undecided, then darted through another door, leaving them alone in the hallway.

Fat Frederick shouted something at him, his voice distorted as Vince's hearing began to return, whining, humming.

"We can't stay here!" he shouted again. He picked up the cleaver and shoved it against Vince's chest, then tried the door Kris had backed through. It was locked. The only other door in the small hallway was where Claudette had gone, and Vince got to it first.

Meloy shouted something else behind him, but Vince's concentration was on what lay ahead. He hefted the cleaver in one hand and turned the door handle with the other.

It opened onto a short corridor. It was empty but for a shoe rack and a few coats hanging on hooks. The door at the far end stood ajar. From beyond came bustling sounds, metallic clanks, and the mouth-watering scents of cooking.

Vince moved. He heard Fat Frederick behind him, and was comforted by his presence. Even so, when he reached the door he paused and pressed himself to the wall, trying to peer through the crack without putting himself in danger.

The kitchen was large and messy with the chaos of cooking. He caught the flicker of white clothing as someone fled from the room, and he was left staring at a bubbling pan on the hob, a large board of chopped vegetables, and a set of square plates laid out on a serving island at the center of the room.

If Claudette was waiting inside the door with a knife—

Fat Frederick pushed past him and kicked the door open. It slammed back into the wall and rebounded, bouncing off Meloy as he stormed into the room, gun held out and aiming left and right. The lighting was bright, glaring. No one sprang from hiding.

Vince didn't understand. Claudette had been so close to him she could have smelled the stale blood of his wounds, and her vengeance was at hand. Surely she wouldn't have fled at the first sign of trouble? She'd be waiting, hiding… wouldn't she? The face of her dead brother would have allowed nothing else.

The plan had been daring from the start. Angela had wanted to carry out the rescues of both Lucy and the captive fairy with as little violence as possible, and with no one else getting killed. When Fat Frederick approached with Vince, she'd hoped it would lull Mary Rock and her people into a false sense of security. But it was also risky, because no one knew if Claudette or Mary Rock would want to kill Vince on sight.

Angela had gambled that they wouldn't. She had met the older woman, seen composure and calmness there, as well as a hidden coldness that she hoped would crave more than a simple, quick revenge.

As it was, Mhoumar had launched their distraction right on time, and if the plan was working, Thorn would already have disabled the house's security systems. Angela and the others would be making their secret, silent way into the house.

"She's still here somewhere," Vince warned, but Meloy

didn't seem to hear. His attention had been stolen, and when Vince saw what he saw, he felt his own alertness dissipate, as well.

On a chopping block beside the tall built-in oven was a chunk of meat, steaming and bleeding juices across the worktop. It was resting, waiting to be carved. As Vince realised what it was, the heady scent of cooked meat went from appetizing to sickening.

The skin on the small, limbless torso had been slashed and seasoned so that it crisped in the oven, but the exotic tattoos were still plain to see.

"Oh, Jesus," Vince said. He felt bile surging in his throat and swallowed it down, its staleness burning his gullet.

"The sick… fucking… bastards!" Fat Frederick said. That was when Vince became certain of the big man's allegiance. He saw the disgust in his eyes, the disbelief, and the tears that streamed down his cheeks seemingly without him realizing.

"Meloy, we can't help that one, but we can help the others," Vince said. "The fairy, and whatever else they might have here. Meloy!"

Fat Frederick's head snapped around, and it took a second for his expression to settle. It was replaced by a cool, calm rage, and Vince was so glad he wasn't on the receiving end.

"We can't let this happen," Meloy said.

"No," Vince said, and his thoughts were for all of the Kin. Those he had met, and those he had not—such amazing, beautiful creatures. They were fighting against fate and time, doing their best to weather the dying of their light in dignity and peace.

There was nothing about dignity here.

"Stay close to me," Fat Frederick said.

They skirted around the island unit and headed across the kitchen. Eight plates, Vince noticed. He'd counted eight big cars in the driveway, including a Bentley and a Maserati. One or more of them was on fire now, and he couldn't help feeling a grim satisfaction at that.

Yet such people, such monsters, couldn't be hurt by material damage. If these exclusive diners knew what they were eating—and Vince was certain they did—they were sick to their souls.

As Fat Frederick eased a door open with his foot, a shotgun blasted. He fell back and to the side, dragging Vince with him. The first shot had gone wide, shattering crockery behind them and ricocheting against pots, pans, and the kitchen's tiled walls.

Through the door Vince saw a flurry of confused movement. A shadowy figure stood close, but beyond, in a wider area lit by a brighter light, Claudette and another woman dashed toward a staircase. Claudette glanced back at the doorway.

The other woman was Mary Rock.

A split-second later a second shot erupted. Fat Frederick grunted, and Vince felt his jacket and left sleeve plucked as if by a curious child. He saw the blood but felt nothing more than pinched skin. He did not look again.

Time for wounds later, he thought, and Fat Frederick fired his gun three times.

Someone dropped beyond the door, and as it drifted shut Vince saw them scrambling away.

"You got them!" he said.

"No, they fell. Backed away."

Then from beyond the door came a strange, high song. It sounded like a small child singing an unknown nursery rhyme, and the hairs prickled on the back of Vince's neck. The volume rose and fell, as if the singer was far away and then closer, far away and closer. The song was calm and bewitching, and so out of place following the sudden violence.

Fat Frederick stood slowly, gun aimed at the door, left hand held awkwardly by his side. Vince saw blood dripping from his splayed fingertips. As the gangster walked forward, Vince reached for his shoulder to hold him back. But too late.

The door opened. Beyond, Kris was leaning back against the wall, shotgun dangling from one hand. Thorn stood before him, barely as tall as a toddler yet filling the large lobby with his song.

Vince checked out the hallway. His one visit to the house had also been at night, entering through a back door, and he'd not seen this place. There were several other doors, some open, some closed, and to the left a staircase led upward. There was no sign of anyone else.

"Claudette and Mary Rock have gone for the fairy," Vince said. Meloy did not reply.

Thorn glanced at them and raised an eyebrow, one corner of his mouth twitching up into what Vince could only describe as a cheeky smile.

Of course it's cheeky. He's a pixie.

Kris barely seemed to notice their presence. His mouth hung open, his eyes were hooded, and his head turned slightly, back and forth, his eyes fixed on the singer. Whatever the words and rhythms conveyed, they were meant for Kris alone, though Vince still felt some fallout effects on his own senses.

Fat Frederick stepped forward, crouched, and pressed his gun against Kris's stomach.

"Meloy!" Vince said. He whispered, loath to disturb the song. "Meloy, no!"

"No need," Thorn said. The words were spoken very calmly, but the song did not cease. It was as if the air was alive with the glamour, and echoing with its wonder.

Next moment, the house echoed to another gunshot.

Even as he slid down to his right, Kris was still gazing at the pixie's face with something approaching adoration.

"What the fuck?" Vince said.

"This song's ended," Thorn said, and a moment later he was gone. Vince didn't even see where he went. It was as if he'd blinked too slowly, and when he opened his eyes again everything had changed. Fat Frederick stood over a crying, dying man, and past the staircase another door opened.

28

Angela heard the shooting, but Lilou pressed a hand to her mouth and shook her head. They couldn't give themselves away. Vince and Meloy were always going to be the bait, and she had to accept that. She had to hope that Meloy really could look after himself.

The door was locked. Mallian was about to smash it down, but Lilou stopped him. Their entry had to be silent, maintaining the surprise. So Angela picked the lock. As the tumblers clicked, she heard what might have been a snort of respect from the huge man.

Inside, they found themselves in a large utility room with laundry goods, a big chest freezer, and a walk-in closet. There was also a low, narrow staircase leading up, dog-legged after just seven steps, and Angela guessed it might once have been a servants' access to the upper floors.

Ideal for three of them, but not Mallian. He was too big.

"See you in the attic," he said, and there was a defiant, gleeful look in his eyes.

"Keep hidden," Lilou murmured as the Nephilim squeezed back through the door to the outside. His scarred, knotted back was plainly visible in the harsh artificial light. Angela had no idea how someone could survive such wounds, but had to remind herself that he wasn't someone. He was some*thing*.

"How can he fly if…"

"Mallian doesn't fly." Lilou glared at Angela. Then she whispered something in Jilaria's ear, turned, and said, "We need to—"

"Where's Lucy?" Angela asked. She faced Jilaria, not Lilou. Speaking directly to her felt somehow unclean, unallowed. The witch turned to her slowly, sneering.

"*She* is all that matters."

"Where?" Angela demanded. Even raising her voice to this woman scared her. She felt like a young kid talking to a stern, unapproachable school principal, but she had to reach past her own discomfort and fear. For her friend.

Jilaria Bran, she realised, was equally unused to dealing with humans. In the witch's downward glance she saw nervousness… and a giveaway.

"Basement," Angela said.

"*She* is all that matters!" Jilaria hissed again.

"You save your friend, and I'll save mine."

The witch nodded.

"Angela—" Lilou began, but Angela shrugged a hand from her shoulder and backed away.

"You might be right, but Mary Rock hasn't been able to kill your fairy, and if she tries again now, with all this going on, she'll fail again. But if they try to kill Lucy…" Her voice caught in her throat, because such words inspired a terrible image—Lucy tied to a chair, Harry grabbing her hair and tilting her head back, Claudette sawing into her neck.

The gush of blood as her friend died.

Not even knowing why.

"I'm to blame for her being here," Angela said. "Please

help me." She hadn't meant to plead, but she felt barely in control of her emotions, an innocent bobbing in violent seas that hid horrors in their depths.

"The plan," Jilaria said.

"It was hardly a plan at all." Lilou looked aside, thinking. Then she nodded once. "Mallian will match anything they have waiting in the attic. We could use your help, Jilaria."

The old woman hissed and shook her head, pacing back and forth. Then she nodded.

"She's still alive."

"How do you know?" Angela asked. From nearby, another gunshot made her jump.

"I can hear her heart. Now follow."

Fat Frederick walked calmly across the lobby, gun held in front of him, and Vince had to follow. For a second he'd considered taking the shotgun from Kris, but he'd never fired a gun before. He had no idea how to use it, and he had no desire to touch the dying man.

As they skirted around the foot of the staircase he glanced nervously up. No movement. The windows on either side of the large front doors flickered with reflected firelight coming from outside. Another set of double doors, closed now, must have led to the dining room.

Where are they now, what are they doing? he wondered. It was doubtful that Mary Rock would leave her guests unguarded, but Vince couldn't really claim to know her. For all he knew, she might have slit their throats at the first signs of trouble.

A door slowly opened.

Lilou stepped out.

Even recognizing her, Fat Frederick was still tensed, gun shaking ever so slightly in his hand. After a moment he slowly lowered the weapon.

"What's happened?" Angela asked, pushing past the nymph, staring at Vince, then at the downed man. Kris was squirming against the side of the staircase, but his movements were lessening, the pool of blood around him growing.

"We don't have much time," Vince said. The exploding Molotov cocktails, the flames, the gunfire—even though the detached house stood in large grounds, such events in a salubrious neighbourhood would attract plenty of attention. The police and fire brigade would be on their way. They might have only minutes.

"Lucy is in the basement."

"Then let's go."

"But the fairy—" Fat Frederick began, before Jilaria Bran cut in.

"You." She turned on Angela. "You have responsibilities, knowledge. Now that we're together, you come with us. You've been to the attic. You know where She is being held against Her will. Lilou and the others can rescue your friend, but..." She reached out and clasped her fat, pale hand around Angela's wrist. "You're coming with me."

Angela glanced despairingly at Vince.

He smiled and nodded.

"Meloy and I have got Lucy. Right, boss?"

"Damn right," Fat Frederick said. He was staring at Lilou. He'd gone quiet since shooting Kris, but in a way he seemed more in control, exuding calm.

The nymph smiled and nodded. "I'm with you."

Vince went to Angela and took her in his arms, squeezing hard and moving her back so that Jilaria had to let go. He pressed his face to hers and whispered in her ear.

"It's all going to be fine."

She nodded, her cheek rubbing against his.

"But we don't have much time," he added.

"Okay. Yes. Please, Lucy…"

"We're going now." He pulled away, nodded at the others, then headed back toward the kitchen. Fat Frederick and Lilou followed. Glancing back he saw Angela and Jilaria starting up the staircase, and he felt a moment of shattering, gut-dropping dread. *I might never see her again!* But now wasn't the time to let doubt or fear weaken him. They were in the midst of things, and none of them could hesitate.

Kris was still. Stepping over his sprawled legs, Fat Frederick snatched up the sawed-off shotgun. It was a single pump action, and he pulled his belt out and slid the weapon underneath.

"Hurry," Vince said. "We haven't seen Harry yet."

"Then he's down there with her," Meloy said.

No more killing, Vince wanted to say, but no one could guarantee that, and he was nowhere near in charge. His wounds were flaring again, and across his left forearm were blazing pinches where the shotgun pellets had stung.

Fat Frederick still bled. He seemed not to notice.

"Basement this way," Vince said.

"What about those car owners?" Fat Frederick asked.

"Thorn is entertaining them," Lilou said. "Hopefully he got to them before they pulled out their phones."

"One way or another, this place will be crawling with police soon." Hesitating only slightly, Vince pulled open the narrow door set in the side of the staircase. He was the first inside, heading down toward the basement. The light was on, but the stairwell jigged to the right at the bottom, roughly plastered walls on either side. There was no way of telling who or what awaited them, but he didn't pause.

Lucy depended on him, and Angela had put her trust in him. He'd already betrayed that trust once too often.

He reached the basement with Fat Frederick and Lilou following close behind. It was a small room, poorly lit, the only contents a floor-to-ceiling wine rack against one wall, and a chair on its side at its center. There were dark, wet patches on the floor around the chair. There was also a doorway in the far wall, door removed and light spilling out. Shadows shifted beyond.

Vince dashed forward, and Fat Frederick was beside him now, wounded arm held across his stomach and gun pointed forward. A thought struck Vince—

I wonder how many people he's really killed.

—and then they reached the doorway together.

This room was smaller still, and lined with an array of cardboard and wooden boxes, some open and spilling polystyrene packaging. At its center stood Lucy, ankles bound, wrists tied in front of her, gagged and terrified. Harry was behind her. He held her long hair in one hand, and the other nursed a knife against her throat.

His eyes flickered left and right from Vince to Meloy, then back again. They settled on Meloy. He knew where the main threat came from.

"Mary told me to slit her throat," he said. "Soon as we heard the first shot, the first fire from outside. Sent me down to kill her… but I didn't."

"Because you want to live," Fat Frederick said.

"Partly that. Partly because I just don't want to kill. Defenseless girl, all tied up. Claudette would have done it, sure. And Daley, he'd have done it with a smile and a hard-on. But not me. I'm not like that."

"Bullshit," Vince said. He was looking at Lucy, trying to calm her with a smile, but she was terrified. Traumatised. Her clothing was filthy and fouled, hands pale, wrists bleeding.

"So, what now?" Fat Frederick asked. He edged into the room. Harry stiffened and pressed the knife harder beneath Lucy's throat, forcing her to stand up straighter on tiptoes.

"I didn't say I *wouldn't* kill her," Harry said. "Just that I don't want to."

"Harry, let her go," Vince said. "If you do anything, Meloy will shoot you. Hurt her anymore and you die. You're not in charge here anymore."

"I'm going out that door," Harry said, gesturing behind him with a nod of his head. "Neither of you can stop me, and…" He drifted off, eyes going wide as he stared past Vince. Even without looking Vince knew that Lilou must have let her guard down, and memories flashed at him, images of pure beauty and lust untainted by guilt.

"Let her go, Harry," Lilou said. Her voice was the sweetest song.

Harry took a step back and lowered the knife. He still held Lucy's hair. She was frozen, eyes turning left and right, breath held, not knowing what was to come.

Fat Frederick moved inside the room and shifted right to get a clear shot.

"You lie," Lilou said, and now her voice was tinged with anger. "You're trying to save your own skin. Using her as currency. You've killed plenty of times, haven't you? Just not humans."

Harry opened his mouth but could not speak. He could not tear his gaze away.

Vince feinted to the left, then darted forward in a crouch

in the hope that he could reach Harry before this all went bad. But his efforts were in vain.

Fat Frederick fired.

Harry hit the floor, his brains hit the wall, and Lucy swayed where she stood, eyes wide and a scream struggling to escape her gag. Snot poured from her nose, her whole body shook, and Vince stepped in close just in time to catch her. She leaned into him, then slumped against him, and he closed his arms around her, hating the way she shook and sobbed, hating the way she stank. Hating himself.

With a *snick!* Fat Frederick appeared beside him and slashed her bindings with a flick-knife. Lucy reared back, holding onto Vince's collar with her left hand, and punched him in the face.

Meloy sniggered. Vince's eyes watered with pain.

Then she tugged her gag aside, leaned into him again.

"Get me away from here," she demanded.

"You're safe," he said. Her shaking continued, betraying the knowledge that he was lying.

"Now that we have her," Lilou said, "you help us."

"Of course," Fat Frederick said. "Yes. Anything."

Lilou turned without another word, headed back across the basement, and the rest of them followed.

"What can She do?" Angela asked as they ran upstairs.

"Anything."

"Anything except free herself?"

Jilaria Bran scowled at her, but said nothing.

Angela led the way, remembering this journey from the last time she'd made it. Then, everything had been different. Vince was still missing, and though she had believed her life upside down, it had merely been slightly askew. Now, she would have done anything to be able to switch back to that moment. She knew things that she could never unknow, had seen things she could not unsee, and she dreaded what might await them all.

Every time she blinked she saw Kris lying dead. Bad as he was, seeing his corpse had still been a shock. Any doubts about Fat Frederick's allegiances had been blown away. Any thoughts that, perhaps, some of those stories about him were exaggerated, and he was simply a hard-core businessman, were similarly expunged. Such brutality drove home how much peril she and her loved ones were in.

She hoped that Vince had found Lucy. Alive.

They reached a landing, and Angela recognised the narrow staircase that led up toward the attic. She went first.

Three steps up she was stopped by several loud impacts smashing down from above. Cracking, crunching, shattering, they shook the entire house like a series of detonations.

"Mallian is entering," Jilaria said. "Hurry. I don't want to miss what happens next."

The staircase curved around into the attic space, and it was here that they found the Kin leader. He had come through the roof, smashing slates, snapping rafters, and forming a hole through which the night poured. His entrance had broken one of the weak lights, and the other bulb swung on a loose wire, throwing his majestic shadow around the empty space.

"Where?" he demanded as Angela topped the staircase. His attention switched to Jilaria Bran and again he asked, "Where?"

"Through there," Jilaria said, pointing at the simple wooden door in the far wall. "I *hear* her."

"It's reinforced," Angela said. "Metal with an electronic lock."

Mallian was breathing quickly. His dark skin glimmered in the night, speckled with a thousand droplets that might have been sweat, or moisture from the outside air. He stank, too, exuding an odour of excitement and exertion. Though naked, there was nothing at all vulnerable about him. He was terrifying.

"Are there other ways in?" Jilaria asked, and Angela felt the power of the Kin's withering attention. She closed her eyes and tried to recall the last time she'd passed through this door.

"I don't think so," she said. "Inside, there's a pit for the fairy, a platform…"

Someone approached them up the staircase. The footsteps were rapid but gentle, and Angela backed away, pressing herself against the wall beside where Mallian crouched. She felt the cool night air flooding through the hole smashed in the roof, and smelled burning from outside.

Where are the sirens? she wondered. *Where's the help?*

Lilou appeared at the head of the staircase.

"Lucy?" Angela asked.

"Safe. Shaken. She's downstairs, waiting." Behind Lilou came Fat Frederick, groaning in pain with each breath, yet hanging on her every word. He held his gun by his side in his right hand. His left dripped blood. Vince was there, too. He caught Angela's eye and nodded once.

That was good enough for now.

"I feel attention on the house," Jilaria Bran said, shivering, though with fear or delight, it was difficult to tell. "Several sets of eyes, from a distance."

"The police will be coming," Angela said. "We need to hurry."

"Mhoumar," Mallian said. A shadow moved across the jagged opening in the roof, and the indistinct face of the winged Kin appeared. Mallian whispered something, then looked back at the others. "Wait here. Get ready." Then he hauled himself back up through the hole, kicked his legs and was gone.

There was long enough for Angela and Vince to smile at each other before the banging began. The impacts were huge, shaking the whole attic, plaster and dust falling from the sloping ceiling and floorboards jumping.

"What's through there?" Fat Frederick shouted, pointing at the door. Vince said something to him and the big man nodded, crouching down and aiming his gun.

Lilou came close and pressed her mouth to Angela's ear. "We have to talk about what comes next."

"What do you mean?"

"Mallian is tired of hiding," Lilou said. "Jilaria is with him. The others... I'm not so sure, but when we rescue Her, we need to melt away. This house is the center of attention now, people will be coming, lots of people, and we need to avoid them."

Angela nodded. The police and fire brigade would arrive, finding bodies downstairs, discovering those diners still present and what they had been prepared to dine upon. Lilou might pass for human, but Jilaria Bran was so obviously something else, and Thorn, and Mallian himself.

"Does he want to reveal you all?" she asked.

"He wants Ascent," Lilou replied. "Humans ousted, Kin superior. Violently, if necessary, and I'm afraid that She might help."

"But there are so few of you," Angela said, pulling away to look at Lilou.

The nymph's expression said, *If only you knew.*

Then there was shouting, a *whoomph* and a flash of fire from beyond the hole in the roof, and a heavy thud as something dropped into the room beyond.

Immediately the wooden door burst, pushed outward by the metal door beneath. It slammed into the wall, plaster and wood exploding all around.

The fire from the other room was sucked through with the pressurised air, and Angela and Lilou dropped together. Angela covered her eyes and curled into a ball, feeling the heat wash over her and her skin tightening, smelling singed hair and spilled fuel, drawing in a scared breath and instantly terrified that it would scorch her lungs.

A gun fired. Someone shouted.

Another voice screamed.

Angela rolled against the wall and risked a look.

She glimpsed a shape leaping for the narrow staircase, taking advantage of their shock and surprise. Vince was close by, reaching for the fleeing figure, just failing to clasp the trailing jacket. It might have been Claudette, but Angela wasn't sure.

There was a grunt and Fat Frederick was on his back, both hands clasped to his chest.

Vince went to follow the retreating figure, but Jilaria blocked his way. He flinched back, careful not to touch her. She didn't even need to speak.

She stared past Vince toward the burning room.

Flames danced and roared inside, but there was something curious about them that took Angela a couple of seconds to understand. Lilou held her arm and helped her up, staring only toward the doorway. The fire was reflected in her eyes.

The flames flowed and rose like waxy balls in a lava

lamp, breaking against the ceiling and rolling across it, missing the hole smashed through the roof and washing up against the walls. Once there it dropped and formed across the floor once more, boiling and pulsing yet apparently under complete control.

Angela shuffled sideways to Vince, and together they looked through the open doorway at what was happening beyond. They held hands. She thought perhaps she might have gone mad without that simple, human contact.

Mallian knelt among the flames, seemingly untouched where they broke against his body,

parting and disintegrating into a thousand separate fires. He held Mary Rock with one hand, squeezing her throat so tightly that her eyes bulged, and her tongue, and blood flowed from her ears. She might have already been dead, but Mallian's attention was fixed not on her, but on the creature in the pit.

In his other hand he held a nest of wires that spat sparks of electricity. He tugged on the wires and they broke through from inside the wall, chunks of plaster pattering down among the slow-moving, globular flames.

Angela stepped into the smashed doorway so that she could see better, and Vince went with her.

The fairy was climbing slowly from the pit, her electrical bindings broken. She looked like a child, terribly pale and malnourished, naked and vulnerable. Their eyes met, and Angela had never in her life sensed such power in a living thing. Her gaze was pained, but held total assurance, complete confidence in herself and her old, old soul.

The fairy lifted a hand and the flames curled around it like puppies drawn to their mother.

Mallian hefted Mary Rock high.

"No!" Angela breathed. "Killing her won't be justice."

He paused, staring right at her. "*My* justice," he said, and he heaved her over the barrier, down into the pit where she had imprisoned the fairy for so long.

"She lives!" Jilaria whispered from somewhere behind Angela. To her left Lilou said, "Beautiful… beautiful."

Angela wasn't so sure. There was beauty in the fairy, in every movement and moment, but also something that scared her more than anything she'd seen or experienced over the past couple of days. It was like staring into the depths of a nuclear reactor, and realizing that thing was alive.

Mallian knelt before the fairy. She approached him and put her small arms around his big neck. For a moment Angela thought he would lift her, like a parent holding a sick child, but there came a pause. Even the fire curling around the fairy's hand and body drew back and hung in the air like glaring mist. She whispered something to Mallian, and he smiled.

Then the fairy let go and turned around. Looked into the pit. Pointed.

"No!" Mary Rock croaked through her damaged throat. Her first word, and her last. The fire returned to its normal, natural state and flowed into the pit, consuming the woman and cauterizing her first awful scream into little more than an echo.

Angela turned away. Fat Frederick was on the floor behind them, watching through the pain. Both hands were holding the blade Claudette had slammed into his chest as she made her escape.

That was meant for Vince, Angela thought.

He caught her eye, and she saw the flames reflected there. He blinked slowly, and Angela wished she could extinguish the sights from her memory so easily.

The stink of burning flesh tainted the air.

"She's gone," Vince said. "The fairy's gone, up through the roof."

"It's over," Angela said. "We need to go. We have to—"

"Mallian, no," Lilou said. Mallian squeezed through the open doorway, slapping at his shoulder where the now-normal fire had taken hold. His skin was red. He seemed unconcerned. He came for them, and Angela knew that she and Vince could do nothing, not a thing, to stop him from cutting them down.

After all this, she thought, but the Nephilim was not coming for them. He shoved them aside, planted one foot either side of the fallen Meloy, and reached for the hole in the attic roof.

"Mallian!" Lilou shouted.

Mallian glanced down at the nymph, smiling, then hauled himself through.

"What's happening?" Angela asked.

"Exactly what I feared," Lilou said. "They want to leave their mark."

29

They gathered in the ground-floor hallway with fire crackling high in the house above them and smoke heavy on the air. Outside, several vehicles were burning. Inside, Kris's corpse lay in a puddle of blood. Lucy was slumped beside the closed front door, hugging her knees, shivering, crying.

Angela was shocked by the sight of her friend. She held her left arm out from her body, nails ripped away. Her hair had been hacked. Harsh lines were cut across her right cheek, close together so that they could not be stitched. She was covered in blood, stark and fresh, and dried dark. When Angela walked over she looked up, then lowered her head again without speaking.

"You're safe," Angela whispered, but she couldn't really promise that it was the case. In fact, she was far less certain now than she had ever been before. They had been inside the building for ten minutes, and with the explosions and fires, the police would be here soon.

Mallian had climbed down the building's exterior and entered the sumptuous dining room. There he stood, blocking their view of what had him frozen to the spot. Gently touching his scarred back, Lilou squeezed in past him. Jilaria Bran went next. Thorn was still in there, singing his song to bewitch the late Mary Rock's guests.

Behind where she and Vince stood in the large hallway, Angela heard Fat Frederick making his cautious descent of the staircase, gasping with every step. She should have been amazed that he could walk with a knife in his chest, but nothing amazed her now. Maybe he'd been lucky and Claudette's knife had missed everything vital. Or maybe he was a dead man walking.

There was no sign of the fairy. She might have been outside in the cool darkness, hiding with Mhoumar.

"Mallian, we have to leave," Lilou said from inside the dining room. "This doesn't matter."

"Doesn't matter," the Nephilim echoed. He was so tall that Angela couldn't see his head.

"You know what I mean. Mallian, I've been with you for so long, followed you, schemed with you about how best to survive. You *know* no one will believe them. They'll be found in a burning house with dead people inside, and even if they try to tell what they were doing here, they'll be ridiculed. We'll take away the evidence and—"

"*Evidence!*" the fallen angel roared. Angela felt her guts sink, her skin tingle with a rush of ice-cold blood through her veins. She had never heard such a voice, and she truly believed she was never meant to. Behind her, Lucy began to cry with deep, throbbing gasps. When the echoes of Mallian's shout died away, Thorn had fallen silent.

No one spoke. There was no answer to such an exhalation of rage.

Vince moved forward, toward the doors. Angela snagged his jacket with one hand, but she didn't hold him back. Instead she went with him, because his fascination had become her own. They'd come this far, and to not see now would be to deny themselves the full truth.

As they reached the wide double doorway Mallian moved forward into the room. He skirted around the large, long dining table and stood by a curtained window, the reflections of flames from outside casting his huge shadow across the beginnings of the feast.

Around the table sat five men and three women. They were dressed in evening wear, and they all looked confused, glancing around as if suddenly waking in a strange place. Also present was the chef, and he looked terrified.

Thorn stood on the chair at the far end of the table. His mischievous glint had vanished, and his face was pale and grim.

Angela remembered the awful sights that had greeted them in the kitchen, but nothing could have prepared her for this.

The large table was set for a grand feast with crystal glasses, silver cutlery, and antique candelabras. Candles burned, oily smoke curling ceiling-ward. The lighting in the dining room was low, but complemented by the candlelight and the flames from outside, it was more than enough to illuminate the table's central feature.

A cooking pit had been built there, lined with gas flares on low, an automatic spit slowly turning above it. On the spit was a man. He must have been cooking for some time, because his body was hairless, skin a rich, crispy red. His legs were fixed straight along the spit by wires, his hands similarly wired behind his back. The spit entered between his legs and emerged through his mouth. His lower jaw swung low as the spit turned, connective tendons burned away. Angela saw long, clawed fingers on his hands, and his toes were the same. His legs had an extra knee, and his nose and mouth formed a protruding snout.

She knew it was a man because his genitals had been pinched together with a tight garrotte. They were crisped and blackened, no doubt intended as a delicacy for one of those attending.

The one who bid the most, perhaps.

"Chenoweth," Lilou said. "They took him. All this time I thought he'd gone deep beneath London. He did that sometimes, relished the time away on his own. As many of us do. But…"

"What is he?" Vince asked, leaning into Angela so he could whisper.

"Don't know," she said.

"Chenoweth the goblin," Jilaria Bran said. "The last of them that came with the Vikings."

"Not the last," Mallian said.

"Oh?" Jilaria asked.

The eight diners and the chef remained seated around the table. They had been enraptured by Thorn's glamourous song, but now it was Mallian's fury that kept them pinned to their seats. Rage simmered from the Nephilim, hotter than the cooking flames, more all-consuming than the fires beyond the window or high above in the attic. Most of them looked terrified, but even so there were expressions of superiority, defiance.

Angela recognised a couple of faces. One man might have been a politician, another she'd seen on American TV, though she couldn't place the woman who sat with him. Perhaps an actor, or someone famous for becoming famous. Sometimes such rich people didn't accept that they could be wrong, and even through their fear they retained a stubborn belief in their rights to do what they wanted.

"Not the last!" he roared. "*None* of us are the last!" Mallian stepped behind the nearest chair. A tall, old Chinese man sat there, knuckles whitening around the seat's arms as he continued staring down at his plate, dwarfed by the Nephilim.

Mallian placed his hands either side of the man's head.

Look away! Angela thought.

The muscles on the Nephilim's arms rippled and flexed.

Close your eyes!

But sick fascination meant that she had to see.

"We are the *first!*" Mallian shouted, and with a grunt he shoved his hands together. The man's mouth fell open, his eyes opened wide, and with a grotesque crunch his head was crushed. Its remains splashed onto his plate and spilled down his brilliant white shirt.

Vince's hand sought hers and squeezed.

Behind them, Lucy gasped, breathless, winded by shock.

"Mallian..." Lilou said, voice filled with despair. Jilaria Bran giggled. Thorn jumped onto the table and stalked around the goblin's cooked body, staring at the diners and singing again. Even through their terror they turned his way.

Mallian moved to the next diner and twisted her head around. Her neck snapped. He twisted again, again, until it came off in his hands.

"They'll see us," he growled, throwing the head against the wall. A crystal wine glass shattered at the sound of his voice. The next man was shaking and crying, struggling to tear his attention from the hypnotic pixie song. He was fat. Mallian pushed him down into his seat, head almost disappearing into his bloated neck. With a crack the chair legs gave way, and so did the man's spine.

"They'll know us again."

"Not like this," Angela said, despair evident in her voice. "Why like this? What good can come of murder?"

Mallian turned his gaze upon her. His eyes were wide and mad, his skin slick with sweat and blood, gore dripping from his hands and splashed up his arms.

"Just another human," he growled.

"Mallian, the Time is long passed," Lilou said, drawing his attention. "And we have to go!"

The Nephilim glared at her.

"This is a new Time." He tore out a throat with his clawed fingers. Smashed ribs and ripped out a heart. Slammed a face onto the table so hard that plates shattered, wood splintered. Blood splashed and flowed. Tears were cut off, pathetic whining fading into Thorn's continuing, hypnotic song.

Mallian killed, and when he reached the last one left alive—the chef—he paused.

Angela felt sick. Yet Vince's expression displayed that other emotion she was struggling to deny. The sick, bloody fascination which was perhaps distinctly human.

"Please..." the chef said. Thorn stopped singing and crouched on the table. The pixie was splashed with blood.

"Please?" Mallian said.

"It's my first... I didn't know... Didn't mean..."

But there was no pleading with the Nephilim, and no begging. He stood behind the chef and rested his heavy, gore-slimed hands on his shoulders.

"May all of your dreams be red," he said to Angela, to Vince, to everyone, before he took in a deep breath and tore the man apart.

Angela backed toward the door. Vince went with her. Mallian glanced their way, then snorted.

"Lilou," Angela whispered. Lilou was leaning against the wall next to a window, head lowered. When she looked up she looked defeated.

"You'd better run," the nymph said.

Stunned, numbed by such violence and brutality, yet with senses sharpened by gore, they bolted through the doors. Angela grabbed Lucy, and Vince was on her other side, holding her up.

"We have to go. Now." Angela said this into her friend's face, and Lucy's tears, her softness, almost made her cry.

"Me..." Fat Frederick said behind her. "Don't forget..." The blade protruded from his upper chest just below his right clavicle. He kept glancing down at it.

"Follow us," Angela said. The gangster was pale, but still mobile, and she couldn't leave him behind. She wasn't sure who was good or who was bad. She wasn't certain there was any such thing.

They made their way back through the kitchen where another sick course of food awaited, never to be eaten. The door through which they had entered stood open. As they ran outside, the gardens were illuminated by the burning cars, and the high roof wore a halo of flames. Angela looked around for the fairy but saw nothing moving in the flickering firelight.

Fifty meters along the driveway they found Claudette. She was slumped against a tree with her head ripped off, blood blackening the ground around her. Mhoumar roosted in the branches above, the head clasped to her mouth, taking her fill.

Angela looked to the sky, glowing with the light of this great, terrible city. Cool air washed against her face, chilling the tears beading down her cheeks.

Sirens sang to the night.

30

They can never be revealed.

This was their vow after they left the grounds of Mary Rock's burning home. Fat Frederick was still with them then, moving at their speed even with the blade in his chest. He echoed the words. Angela believed him. Whatever else she thought of Meloy, she knew that the Kin were even more wonderful to him than they were to her. As well as their beauty and uniqueness, she had seen their brutal side and been repulsed by it.

Fat Frederick was not repulsed by brutality.

He pulled out a phone and arranged for his man Cliff to collect them from several streets away. Waiting for him to arrive, the four of them hid in the shadow of a row of garages, listening to the concerto of sirens and roaring engines that descended on the big, burning house. None of them spoke. Maybe because there was too much to be said, or perhaps because there was nothing.

Lucy was silent and withdrawn, shivering in shock, almost not there. She shrugged off any attempts by Angela to touch or hold her. She wouldn't catch her eye.

Meloy leaned against an ivy-clad wall and hummed softly. Angela couldn't place the tune. The blade protruding from his chest glimmered in the moonlight.

Once in the car and with Cliff driving, the gangster insisted that he take them home first.

"No, really, it's fine," he said as if this were a lift from a party, and Angela found herself giggling. It was that, or allow in the terror and madness that stalked her mind.

The last she saw of Fat Frederick was as Cliff drove away along Lucy's street. He was in the car's passenger seat staring from the window, one hand nursing the knife in his chest without actually touching it. Anyone watching might have believed he was looking at her, Vince, and Lucy. But Angela thought not.

Lucy turned her back on them and slammed her door. Angela had wanted to take her to the hospital but her friend had responded with the only word she'd spoken since being rescued.

"Home."

After she shut them out, they rang the bell, but there was no reaction. No response to phone calls or texts. Vince thought she would come around, but Angela feared that she'd lost her friend forever.

At least she's alive.

Afterwards, she traced his wounds, tending them as best she could. She told him that he should really go to the hospital, but Vince shook his head, sitting naked on the edge of the bed and wincing as Angela cleaned his battered and cut body. She bathed his swollen eye, then ushered him into the shower. She joined him there. Water flowed red down the plughole. They held each other until the water ran cold and clear, then went to bed.

"Everything's changed, but we have each other."

She and Vince breathed these words into each other's mouths that night, warm and afraid in their bed, making love, together again at last.

As darkness gave way to dawn, the world seemed so naive in its ignorance. Their neighbours woke them as usual, coming together to usher in a perfect day. The postman brought an electricity bill and a charity appeal from WaterAid.

Angela stood staring at her desk, frowning and trying to understand how she had ever been able to sit and work. The reality of what she knew made the everyday more mundane than ever. Yet she craved mundanity. Vince bore the wounds and scars, her friend had nearly died, she had witnessed murders more brutal than she could ever have imagined.

She wished that she could forget.

The massacre at Mary Rock's house was all over the news. The dead included a disgraced former MP from Devon, an American football player fallen from grace, and several prominent business figures from home and abroad. It was also rumored that the house's owner was among the dead, and the press were digging deep. It seemed that Mary Rock had a shady past and had been the subject of police interest for years. In a time when scandal traveled at the speed of a keyboard click, there was already talk of a sinister club for the mega-rich, peddling drugs and other forbidden offerings.

Their discussion was brief. They were both in agreement. Their involvement at Mary Rock's house haunted them, and every time they saw or heard a police car they jumped. Getting away from everything—the shadow of Mary Rock, memories of the awful massacre, and the Kin—became a necessity.

Neither of them put a duration on their trip. Angela had been promising to introduce Vince to her parents for more than a year, and the timing felt ideal.

By mid-morning, Angela and Vince had packed their bags and were heading for Heathrow. She tried calling Lucy one more time, but had to make do with leaving a voicemail message.

"Hey, Lucy. You know I love you. I hope you'll talk to me sometime about what happened and what we saw. You're my best friend. So much has changed, I'm so adrift, that… I just can't bear to lose you, too."

At Heathrow, she kept her phone switched on until the last moment, but there were no calls.

They took separate flights. Vince didn't want to, but she insisted, especially after he revealed that he owned a false identity to travel under. He'd used it a couple of times, flitting to Europe to sell relics to rich continental collectors. Angela felt a weight closing in on them, and while she wanted nothing more than to be with him, she knew that they each would be safer alone.

They would meet up in a hotel in Boston. They even arranged a time, less than twenty hours in the future.

"Not even a day," she told him as they kissed goodbye outside a bustling Costa in Heathrow. Then Angela sat alone in the coffee shop for an hour, reflecting on what had happened and what was to come.

A little more than ten hours later she landed in Boston. The police were waiting for her at the terminal.

Angela had no idea how she had been traced or caught, who had seen her, or how anyone knew she had been at Mary Rock's house. To begin with, she didn't even know whether or not Vince had been arrested. Maybe Lucy had given them away, still angry, or unable to think quickly enough to lie after visiting hospital to treat her wounds. Or it could have been Fat Frederick, furious that Vince had run instead of coming into the fold once again.

It didn't really matter. Her boot treads had been identified from the scene, cast in dried blood. Her fingerprints had been found on smashed bottles around the burnt-out cars. Once caught, there was no use in denial.

Angela began to understand what the fairy must have felt. Shut away in a cell, kept from the real world outside. But really, she could *never* understand. She and Vince had been offered a brief glimpse into a wider, deeper, more wondrous and terrifying existence, and it had been their choice to try and remove themselves from it once again.

At least he might find freedom, and peace.

She felt so alone.

A day after her arrest, Detective Inspector Volk and his team arrived in Boston from Scotland Yard. The questioning began.

Sleeping in the cell was difficult. She had been assigned a lawyer, but he told her that being moved to somewhere more comfortable was unlikely. Not that she'd asked. The sleeplessness had nothing to do with her surroundings, or the fact that their escape to her home country had been short-lived.

It was because all of her dreams were red.

EPILOGUE

"Angela." It's Inspector Volk again. She pretends to be asleep, but he can see through her. She is afraid that he will eventually see all the way inside. "Angela. Wake up."

She opens her eyes and sits up. Volk stands in the open doorway, a big cop behind him. With his scruffy shirt and cheap supermarket trousers, the detective inspector seems a throwback to simpler times.

She sighs and leans back against the wall.

"You get my coffee right this morning?" She's lost the taste for tea. It reminds her too much of London, the place she's come to think of as home.

"I found a Dunkin' Donuts three blocks down. Got you breakfast, too."

"Pastries for breakfast. That's why you really came here, huh, Volk?"

"Can we chat?"

"Are you allowed to interview me in my cell?"

Volk smiles. He is being her friend, but she's withholding information about thirteen brutal slayings, and a lot more besides. At the moment it's just the good cop, but the bad will have to make an appearance soon. Maybe when they take her back to the UK. Deportation papers are already filed, and her lawyer has told her there's been a special intervention that will speed up the process.

Even thinking about going back to London makes her heart beat faster. *They* are there. Under the ground, hidden away, living their own precarious lives. Lilou, the beauty who can entrance any man. Mallian and his plans for Ascent. Mhoumar, Jilaria Bran, Thorn, and others she has not seen or met. The fairy is with them now, too, and Angela sensed a power in Her that goes way beyond anything she can understand. Wonderful beings, beautiful creatures. Yet they scare her almost to death.

She's quickly come to realise that is part of the reason she will never betray the Kin. It isn't only because she believes they deserve the peace and anonymity they have drawn around themselves. She's also terrified of how they might react if exposure is forced upon them. Everything will change.

Such change always comes at a price.

"They found something in the house," Volk says. "It's troubling me."

"More than all the murdered people?"

Volk ignores her. She's neither denied the murders, nor claimed that she carried them out, but she knows that Volk knows she isn't guilty. Of *that*, at least, though there is plenty more she's hiding from him. He's been a cop for a long time, and she can see how this case vexes him. Very high profile, it should have been a gift for an ambitious detective inspector.

But every question Volk believes he's answered presents him with three more.

It's a jigsaw where the edges do not fit, a puzzle without an end. Angela almost feels sorry for him.

"One of the corpses in the dining room had something

in her pocket. A tooth. Looked odd, so we sent it for analysis, and the results came in a couple of hours ago."

Angela feigns indifference.

One of them was stealing, she thinks. The Kin must have cleared away their dead and cooked brethren before fleeing, whether Mallian wanted to or not. She's still confused about that, but in their haste they neglected to check the murdered diners for anything they might have hidden away.

"Not human," Volk says. "It looked like an incisor, though a little bigger, but our specialists couldn't identify it. Not human, canine, feline. No species they could recognise. It had been well-worn, so it definitely belonged to an adult. But other than that... nothing."

Try goblin, Angela thinks. She shrugs, sips at her coffee.

"Is this part of what you're afraid I'll believe if you tell me?" he asks.

"Where's my donut?"

"You get your fucking donut when you tell me something!"

Angela glances up, startled. It's the first time Volk has raised his voice, his first loss of control, and it brings a small, shocked chuckle from her. But when she sees him she feels suddenly sorry and sad, because he's a man used to making loose ends fit together. He hates this. He wants to fly back home with the solution, but every hour that passes makes things more inexplicable. It's as if mystery was planted that night at Mary Rock's house, seeded in flame and blood, and now it's blooming.

"I don't know what they had in their pockets," she says softly. "I don't know anything that'd make any sort of sense to you, Volk. I'm doing you a favor."

He snorts and turns away. The American cop blocks the doorway, expressionless. Angela has no doubt that he'll shoot her down if she makes any threatening moves. She and Vince have become notorious, and the public and press love the juice of the story. They have little time for all the factors that don't make sense. It's too meaty a tale to ignore.

"You're driving me mad," he says, turning back, sitting on her bed. "You weren't the only one there. There was Vince, too, and we'll find him soon enough."

"Vince is dead."

"Yeah. Right. So you keep saying, but we have other footprints in the blood." He trails off, frowning down at his hands, and Angela knows these footprints are as confusing to him as the strange tooth found in a corpse's pocket. There are other mysterious traces, too. Solidified fat in the kitchen ovens, hair and fur found in the corners of rooms, the holding pen in the burnt-out attic, holes smashed through the roof with no signs of tools or explosives, bullets in two corpses with no guns found. There are lists of things that don't make any sense.

"We'll be flying home in a few days," he says. He sounds tired, and she wonders how he's sleeping. He wears no wedding ring, though he's definitely struck her as someone in a relationship. She guesses he's missing whoever he left behind.

As she's missing Vince. At least Volk has a reunion to look forward to. She has nothing.

"I don't want to go," she says.

"Don't care." Volk sighs and stands. "You have to talk eventually."

"No, I don't," Angela says. Lilou told her of Ascent, and Mallian's desire for the Kin to rise once again and present themselves to humanity, and she thinks that was why he slaughtered those rich scumbags. To leave them as a sign, a calling card. But with every day that passes—without stunned news items or social media footage of fantastical creatures—she realises that something has changed.

Maybe Lilou has persuaded him that now isn't the time.

Or perhaps he and the fairy are waiting until they are stronger.

"Who are you protecting? Who are you afraid of? We can keep you safe, you know."

Angela smiles. Then laughs. As soon as Volk leaves the room and her cell door slams closed again, the smile drops from her face.

"Lilou sends her thanks."

The voice startles her from red dreams, and she sits up quickly and wipes the sweat from her face. Faint light comes in under the cell door, but otherwise it's dark. She tries to calm herself, shed the memories of what she has been reliving while asleep, but those terrible images will always be with her. It's at these times, alone in the dark with her dreams still bleeding, that she feels most wretched.

"She sent me to help."

Angela gasps and shuffles back along the bed, hugging her knees and pressing herself into the corner.

"Who are you? Where are you?" She thought she'd left them behind, in London. She believed them to be focused there, but maybe she's been wrong all along.

"I'm in here with you," the voice says. "Don't be afraid. I'm at home in the night, and I can tell you that you're safe."

"From your kind?"

"Perhaps. The Kin owe you both a tremendous debt. It's the first time I remember this happening, but we have sworn to protect you both."

"Both?"

"Vince, too. I've been to him. He's close."

Angela smiles in the darkness. "What are you?"

"A wisp of shadows. I'm not strong, Angela, but I can carry messages and perhaps, if your own desire is strong enough, I can help you get out of here. You have to want it as much as you can. You have to crave release."

Angela scans the shadows but sees no movement, and neither can she sense anything in the cell with her. That doesn't make her doubt, but her heart sinks at the wisp's words, because since their arrest she has let hopelessness settle within her. She's lost so much that she can't imagine what is worth escaping for.

"There's *plenty!*" the wisp says, anticipating her response, or perhaps reading her mind.

"Like what? A life on the run?"

"So much beauty and wonder you haven't seen. So much hope and potential. So many Kin you can't even imagine."

"So many? I thought you were so few, and only in London."

"Who said we live only in one city? And what we lack in numbers, we make up in other ways."

"But Mallian. Ascent."

The wisp sighs, a breath in the shadows.

"A dream. The Nephilim thinks strength means fighting. There are other ways to be strong. And the fairy was mad. Not the thing he thought She would be. She vanished as soon as you freed Her that night, and no one has seen Her since. Many believe She's gone away from the world forever."

"To where?"

"Other places," the wisp says.

It settles close to her then, its movement sending a cool shiver across her exposed arm, a hardening of shadows beside her bed. Shapeless, formless, still Angela feels its presence.

"There's schism within the Kin, with Mallian at its fore. Everyone has been stirred up, but Lilou is working to mend the rift. Mallian is… temperamental. She wants your help."

"Mine?"

"And Vince."

"What can we do? We're just normal people."

"In my world, there's no such thing. Neither of you can function in society anymore," the wisp says, harshly perhaps, but it tells the truth. "Prison awaits, or the asylum if you attempt to tell the truth. Which Lilou knows you never will."

"So how can we help?"

"In countless ways. The human and Kin worlds often touch, sometimes even interact. On those occasions you could help us maintain our secrecy."

"But I'm being deported back to Britain, a trial, jail. They don't really know what happened, but they have a trail of corpses and a suspect who isn't denying the murders." Angela actually chuckles into the darkness, feeling a strange reciprocation from the wisp. "I'll be famous."

"You already are, amongst the Kin." The wisp comes even closer, a shadow growing heavier around her, and its next comment comes from so close to her ear that Angela feels the touch of its breath. "Rest, and be ready for tomorrow."

"And what's tomorrow?"

"The first day of the rest of your life."

Angela doesn't believe she can rest, but sleep takes her again. For the first time since Mary Rock's house, she does not remember her dreams.

When she wakes it is light. Her cell door is open, and Vince is standing there. He grins. She sits up.

"Vince?"

Everything is quiet. The station beyond the cell is still and silent.

"Hey, babe," he says. "Welcome back to America, eh?"

"Where's Volk? Where are the cops?"

"They're... sleeping."

"What's happening?"

"It's time to go. The thing that came, the wisp, is helping me get you out, and there are others waiting for us."

"Others?" Angela stands, breathing in a rush of fresh air that carries a hint of unknown places. "What others?"

"It'll be easier if you see for yourself." Vince holds out his hand, eyes wide with excitement. "Come with me. You're never going to believe this."